Praise for *Buffalo Trail*

"Outstanding . . . Guinn never loses focus. . . . This is an engaging read that's hard to put down."
—*Roundup*

"An excellent account of just one of the clashes between settlers and Indians. . . . Well-written and thoroughly engrossing."
—San Antonio *Examiner*

"[A] gripping, plot-driven [tale] of aggression and survival . . . Stirring . . . One of the many fascinations of *Buffalo Trail* lies in Guinn's blunt descriptions of the barbarities Plains Indians and white frontiersmen practiced on one another."
—*Four Corners Free Press*

"Guinn does an effective job of pulling together a dramatic and compelling fictional story from the collision of the actual characters and events of the late-19th century West. . . . You can't help rooting for Cash to make it through the battle of Adobe Walls and back to Gabrielle. This is the second novel from a writer worth watching."
—*Big Sky Journal*

"Well-written, eye-opening . . . Guinn is an accomplished writer. . . . History-based Old West fiction at its finest."
—*The Dallas Morning News*

"An action packed historical novel . . . The era come[s] alive. . . . Puts readers right into the battle and on the western frontier. It brings to life the era and the western legends that have fascinated people. . . . Riveting and filled with action."
—*Crimespree Magazine*

"The Old West has never felt more alive."
—*East Valley Tribune*

"Guinn expertly weaves the drama of Western history into his narrative. His adept, empathetic ability to bring voice to historical men and women of the West side-by-side with his fictional characters places the Texas author in a rarified group of authors including Jeff Shaara, Larry McMurtry, Loren Estleman and Lucia St. Clair Robson. . . . Guinn's gritty ride through the Southern Plains from Dodge City to Adobe Walls . . . will keep readers turning the pages and eagerly awaiting the next volume in the series." —*True West* magazine

"The author has provided a well-written novel of early western Americana." —*Historical Novels Review*

"A riveting and extremely even-handed account . . . Guinn does a wonderful job of combining real-world historical characters to provide a historically accurate work of fiction that makes one appreciate what has gone before and what may lay ahead." —Bookreporter.com

"Western historical fiction has rarely been as entertaining and satisfying, as well as smart and human." —*Lone Star Literary Life*

"A masterful Western adventure." —*Garden & Gun*

"A grand effort, and Quanah and his bogus medicine man, Isatai, are an entertaining pair." —*Booklist*

"Full of historical notable figures from the Old West, this second volume in Guinn's trilogy not only provides a buoyant narrative but also several lessons in Western history. This title is so well constructed that it could stand alone (for readers new to the trilogy). Guinn skillfully ties his carefully constructed prolog outlining the Massacre at Sand Creek (1864) to a lone female warrior he imagines at the Second Battle at Adobe Walls." —*Library Journal*

"Guinn makes lively characters of historical buffalo hunters, and his imaginative take booms like a Sharps .50 as cultures collide across the Cimarron River. . . . Guinn's research brings to life the daily lives of the Comanche. . . . Few Westerns reach the level of *Lonesome Dove*, but Guinn's latest is a better, more rambunctious tale than the trilogy's opener." —*Kirkus Reviews*

Praise for *Glorious*

"Since he's already written about Wyatt Earp, Bonnie and Clyde, and Charles Manson (*Manson*), Jeff Guinn might as well create his own attractive bad boy. He's done so in this first-in-a-trilogy Western. . . . There's an interesting contemporary feel to this Western. City boy McLendon doesn't know how to ride or shoot or bust heads; what he knows how to do is observe, spy and think on his feet." —*Tucson Weekly*

"An affable . . . bit of frontier mythmaking. . . . Readers may find by the end that, like Cash McLendon, they've become inexplicably fond of Glorious and its colorful denizens." —*The Washington Post*

"[Guinn] knows how to dig into the past . . . an absorbing, informative and entertaining tale of life, love, hope and ambition in the American West." —*The Dallas Morning News*

"A worthy addition to the western genre . . . Catnip for *Lonesome Dove* fans." —*The Seattle Times*

"Delightful . . . Wonderfully appealing. *Glorious* is an old-fashioned western with likable characters who, because Guinn projects a trilogy, will return shortly." —*Booklist*

"This first installment in a trilogy will delight historical fiction fans longing for the return of classic Westerns. This entertaining outing is sure to keep the saloon doors swinging for more entries in the genre." —*Library Journal*

"The Wild West comes alive in this novel of prospectors, desolate cavalry posts, rotgut saloons and Apache raiders. . . . The plot is classic. . . . Good fun."
—*Kirkus Reviews*

"A trip to Glorious, Arizona, in Jeff Guinn's new western novel is like a cool draft beer after a long, hot day on a dusty trail. *Glorious* is old-fashioned in the very best way: It's good-hearted, optimistic, compelling, comfortable, and extremely well told. It's wonderful when an author clearly has affection for his characters, and readers will feel the same way."
— C. J. Box, *New York Times*–bestselling author of
The Highway and *Stone Cold*

"If like me you've been waiting for the next Louis L'Amour or Zane Grey, the good news is his name is Jeff Guinn. His newest novel, *Glorious,* has all the elements of a fabulous western: compelling characters, breath-taking scenery, and something more—an unblinking take on the western frontier."
—Craig Johnson, *New York Times*–bestselling author of the Walt Longmire mysteries, the basis of A&E's hit series *Longmire*

"I've long admired Jeff Guinn's straight and unfiltered histories of American icons such as Bonnie and Clyde and the Earps. I was thrilled to know he'd be turning that eye for detail and incredible research to revive the Western. *Glorious* is a blazing return of the American art form, bold, realistic, and a hell of a lot of fun."
—Ace Atkins, *New York Times*–bestselling author of
Robert B. Parker's Cheap Shot and *The Forsaken*

BUFFALO TRAIL

JEFF GUINN

G. P. Putnam's Sons

New York

G. P. Putnam's Sons
Publishers Since 1838
An imprint of Penguin Random House LLC
375 Hudson Street
New York, New York 10014

The Library of Congress has catalogued the G. P. Putnam's Sons
hardcover edition of this book as follows:

Guinn, Jeff.
Buffalo trail : a novel of the American West / Jeff Guinn.
p.   cm.
ISBN 9780425282410
I. Title.
PS3557.U375B84   2015   2015007432
813'.54—dc23

First G. P. Putnam's Sons hardcover edition / October 2015
First G. P. Putnam's Sons trade paperback edition / September 2016
G. P. Putnam's Sons trade paperback ISBN: 9780425282410

Book design by Meighan Cavanaugh
Cover design by Richard Hasselberger

147468846

For all of my friends at Putnam,

past and present

QUANAH PARKER

BILLY DIXON

PROLOGUE:

NOVEMBER 29, 1864

The icy dawn wind brought tears to the eyes of the men on horseback and they had to squint hard to see. There were almost six hundred of them, and besides the wind, many had their visions blurred by terrific hangovers. In camp the night before, they'd pulled bottles of whiskey from their saddlebags and gotten drunk in anticipation of a great victory the next day. It was against U.S. Army regulations to drink on duty, but they didn't care. Most of them were "100 daysers," members of an Army-affiliated civilian militia who'd enlisted for the express purpose of fighting Indians after a long summer of deprivations. Marauding Cheyenne and Arapaho had been bloodily active throughout Colorado Territory, and some of these militiamen had lost loved ones. All of them knew someone slaughtered by the savages. For the better part of three months, they'd scoured the countryside without finding any marauding Indians to kill in reprisal. Now, with their enlistments almost up, they were about to have their revenge.

The village of Cheyenne chief Black Kettle's people abutted the scaly shores of Sand Creek in eastern Colorado Territory. It was a desolate place, far from shade trees, abundant grass, and decent hunting, but when Black Kettle made peace with the white men, this was the place he'd been ordered to go. He did so willingly, telling his tribesmen that if they demonstrated *good faith, the whites would realize that they could be trusted, and then they could move to a better location. To reinforce his point, Black Kettle flew two flags over his tipi—one the Stars and Stripes, the other plain white in the universal signal of nonviolence.*

Two militiamen, sent ahead as scouts, cautiously crept to the crest of a nearby hill. Looking down, blinking against the wind, they saw the flags and dismissed them as a ruse. Indians weren't to be trusted. They pretended to be tame and then attacked any fools who believed them. The ones in this camp by the creek were going to meet white men who knew better.

The scouts inched back down the hill, mounted their horses, and rode a half mile to where the main body of troops waited. Their commander, burly, bearded Colonel John Chivington, said, "Well? Are they there?"

"They are," one of the scouts said. "A lot of them, all unaware."

Chivington, a battle-tested veteran, mistrusted such optimism. "You're certain? We're not riding into a trap?"

"No danger of that," the second scout said. "Why, I hardly saw a warrior, just some women and children and old people. The men must still be asleep in the tipis."

"Well, then," Chivington said. He turned to his officers, who stood nearby. "Have the men mount, but keep it quiet. Those red devils have good ears."

One of the officers objected. "There's a treaty, sir. It's well known that this camp is at peace."

"Captain Soule, the savages have not honored the treaty," Chivington snapped. "Just ask some of the men here, maybe the ones who knew the Hungate family." Back in June, Nathan and Ellen Hungate and their toddlers, Laura and Florence, had been butchered by Indians. They were far from the only whites to die recently at the hands of hostiles, but the outrage over their murders was widespread after their mutilated bodies were taken by relatives to Denver and displayed for a day before burial. There'd been

unstinting public demand for retaliation ever since. This put great pressure on the Army. The War Between the States was finally winding down; the last thing the Union needed was for the people of Colorado Territory to decide the Lincoln administration couldn't defend them from the Indians. They might then turn to the Confederates for protection, giving the rebels' morale a much-needed boost. To forestall that possibility, Chivington had volunteered to organize and lead a civilian force dedicated solely to reprisal. He felt it was his patriotic duty. They had repeatedly failed to catch savages in the act of raiding. Now, as winter set in and his militiamen's enlistment periods were up, Chivington decided to attack any Indians he could find. In its isolated location, and with its very existence infuriating most white territorial settlers, the Sand Creek camp was an easy choice.

"It's believed Arapaho killed the Hungates, sir. This is a camp of Cheyenne." Captain Soule wouldn't back down.

"Indians are all the same," Chivington said. "Cheyenne, Arapaho, Comanche or Kiowa or whatever. The ones down there deserve to die for what they've done."

"Sir, not all Indians are hostile," Soule said. "We have no proof any of them in that camp have killed any white people."

Chivington had no patience with softhearted fools. "Count on it—there are warriors with white blood on their hands skulking in some of those tipis." Before Soule could protest, he added, "Even if not, we're sending a message here. It's time for the Indians to know what it feels like, having noncombatants taken down. Lord knows, they've done it enough to us. Maybe they'll think twice next time, before attacking innocent families like the Hungates. We're going to do a thorough job of this. Yes, in some ways it's distasteful, but it's in service of an honorable cause." He looked past Soule and said to the other officers, "Above all, no quarter. The savages never show mercy, so they'll get none from us. Our purpose is to exterminate every one."

Soule pleaded, "Surely not women and children."

Chivington glared at him. "Captain Soule, you're insubordinate. All of you have your orders. Kill everyone in the village, and have your men do as they will with the corpses. We must demonstrate to the people back home that the Indians were repaid on their own hateful terms. None are to be spared, big or little. Females can always produce more nits, and nits grow into lice." The officers saluted, Soule reluctantly, and then came the creak of leather and muted jangle of spurs and bridles as men mounted. They eased their horses forward. The sound of hooves on the hard winter ground was smothered by the howling wind.

IN THE VILLAGE, *a few hundred people ate breakfast—not much, just soup warmed by tiny fires inside the tipis. Boys ate quickly; they had to go out and tend to the horses tethered nearby. Women nursed babies or else fell to the endless chores that were their daily lot—sewing, mending, things that could be done inside, close to the fires and out of the cold. Later, whether the wind abated or not, they would have to go out and chop wood so that the fires could keep burning, and also forage for anything remotely edible. Some old men sat in the tipis, too, but they had no obligations beyond smoking their pipes and reminiscing about better days, before there were so many white men and so few Cheyenne. Except for a dozen men recovering from wounds or illness, there were no warriors present. Black Kettle had sent them all away on a hunt. Because the camp was in such a bad place, the men had to travel a long way to find any deer or winter buffalo. They'd left only two days before, and weren't expected back for another week. A few of the men grumbled about leaving the camp defenseless, but Black Kettle convinced them that it was all right to go. The chief himself stayed behind; Black Kettle felt that he must be available should anyone from the white government come calling. A modest cache of pemmican was always kept on hand in his tipi, so that such important visitors could be treated to a meal. Even if the villagers were hungry, none of them, including Black Kettle, could touch that food.*

Black Kettle had just decided to leave his tipi and walk among his people, comforting them as best he could against the cold and their mostly empty bellies, when he heard the first shouting and screams.

CHIVINGTON LED *the charge down the hill, brandishing his saber and roaring, "For your loved ones! For America!" A few of the men behind him began shooting, but most used their sabers. The thick column of riders smashed into the center of the village, where screaming Indians milled frantically. Chivington experienced a moment of surprise—there was no return fire from the savages; why?—and then he was in their midst, swinging his sword, feeling its keen edge carve through flesh and bone, a marvelous thing to be delivering justice. All around, his fine men doing the same— God's work, it was. Before joining the Union Army, Chivington had pastored a Methodist church, and he felt the presence of God with him this morning. The Almighty approved.*

Now a few warriors emerged from tipis, but they all seemed slow— something was wrong with them—and Chivington's troops cut them down almost effortlessly. They'd ridden all the way through the village now, the first portion of the attack was over, so they doubled back to focus on individual targets, women and children mostly and also a few stumbling old men, all trying to get to the creek, the fools. It was shallow and no trouble at all for the soldiers and militia on horseback to splash in after them and swing their sabers. The water soon turned red.

Amid the confusion came moments of clarity. Chivington saw one Indian, a man of middle years, emerge from a tipi holding some kind of skin pouch in one hand while he pointed to fluttering flags at the top of the tipi with his other, a white flag and an American flag—sacrilege for Old Glory to fly above the dwelling of a heathen. Chivington meant to cut down this miscreant himself but someone else beat him to it, slicing into the Cheyenne's shoulder with his sword. The Indian shrieked, dropped his pouch, and fled toward the creek. Chivington lost sight of him then because his own gaze fell on a smallish Cheyenne fleeing not toward the creek but up the hill. This one ran very fast and looked to be getting away, and the colonel spurred his mount in pursuit. He was almost on his quarry when the Indian turned and stood at bay. It was then he realized that it was a girl, a very young one, maybe ten or so, Chivington always had trouble estimating the age of children. She looked straight at him, afraid but brave, fists clenched at her sides. The colonel felt a spark of admiration but ignored it because she was a savage and even the nits among them must die. "Close your eyes!" he shouted, thinking she might understand English. Instead, she arched her back and spit at him. Chivington swung his saber to strike her head from her body, but as he did his horse bucked and the blade bit into but not through the girl's neck. She fell and Chivington prepared to dismount and finish her, but before he could he heard someone back in the village shouting, "Stop! That's enough!" Captain Soule was trying to call off the attack. Chivington rode back down the hill and, in full view of everyone, ripped the captain's insignia off the shoulders of his uniform. "I'll deal with you when we're home," he said coldly. Then, to the rest of the men, he shouted, "Finish the job!" and they knew what he meant. Chivington rode back to the hill to kill the girl he'd wounded, but when he got there she was gone. There was blood all over the grass and he decided she'd crawled off to die; good riddance. He returned to the village, sat on his horse, and watched his men as they went about their holy work. They scalped the bodies and cut off fingers and ears and genitalia. Chivington hadn't realized you could do such things with women's private parts, but some of the men were particularly inventive with their knives. They threaded leather thongs *through their trophies and draped them from their saddle horns like garlands on Christmas trees. Chivington imagined a grand parade of his victorious troops down the streets of Denver, the impressive souvenirs of their fine morning's work dangling proudly on display. The cheers would be deafening. It would be the kind of approbation that might get a commanding officer called to high office once his military duty was behind him. Territorial governors enjoyed both prestige and opportunities for personal wealth. If elected by a grateful public, John Chivington would humbly serve.*

On the ground nearby, Chivington saw the pouch dropped by the Indian who'd come from the flag-flying tipi. He picked it up and found strips of dried meat inside. The colonel felt peckish. All he'd had since the night before was coffee.

Chivington withdrew one of the meat strips, sniffed it suspiciously, then took a cautious bite. It was venison seasoned with plums, and tasted very good.

PART ONE

Winter 1873-74

ONE

As a man who loved his tribe and understood its ways very well, Quanah was worried.

Winters were always hard, with the buffalo gone and most other game skittish and hard to track. But this year when the cold months came, the People began observing many strange signs. Rocks resembled faces of long-lost loved ones. A crow spoke to some hunters and told them where to find a bear who should have been hibernating but wasn't. Someone saw a six-legged buffalo, but its two extra limbs allowed it to run away so fast that it was lost to sight before the rest of the village could be alerted. At night, huddling around fires, trying to ignore the hunger pangs that wracked them, everyone discussed these things, pondering what they might mean. Though they believed in spirits and omens, the People had no formal religion, and unlike the Kiowa and Cheyenne, did not designate official medicine men to explain signs. Among the People, anyone was free to interpret and prophesize, and everyone else could either agree or not, as they chose.

Though he accepted the possibility of spirits, Quanah did not believe in omens at all. In his twenty-eighth year and a full warrior since his fourteenth, he thought people saw signs when they wanted to. A profusion of omen sighting was inevitable whenever there was wide-spread desperation, and this bleak season was the most desperate time in memory for the tribe called Comanche by outsiders, white and Indian alike. Those on the reservation who depended on the white man's char-ity were starving, because the promised cattle and corn were not sup-plied in sufficient quantities to feed even small children, let alone hungry adults. The People who still roamed free were hungry, too. Traditionally there were winter stores of pemmican—dried turkey, venison, or buffalo meat pounded into strips during the bountiful hunting months and fla-vored during drying with honey, piñon nuts, and wild plums. Though pemmican was not as delicious as fresh meat, it was nourishing and could tide everyone over until the cold broke and the game returned. But now there was very little pemmican, either, because white hunters encroaching on Indian land in the warm season thinned game that be-came even scarcer in the winter. In particular there were far fewer buf-falo; the whites who killed them took only the hides, leaving to rot the meat that the People required to survive the winter.

So as the snow and ice storms loomed, there were meager food stores and little hope of replenishment for some time to come. In their present straits, the very old men and women and weak babies would soon begin to die. They could start eating their horses, but among the People no possession was as prized as a man's horse herd. Instead of acting as su-perior beings should, arming themselves and going out to take what they needed, most of the warriors seemed resigned to endlessly discussing reported signs and accepting a diet of horsemeat or the rumblings of their families' empty bellies. This made Quanah furious; he railed at his fellow Quahadi, "Antelopes" in the People's language, urging them to put aside their obsessions with omens and mount a large-scale expedi-tion instead of sporadic raids against the white men. When his own camp wasn't sufficiently responsive, Quanah rode to several others, as the

People lived in scattered bands that formed a loose confederation. He imagined all the fighting men from each band combining in a massive war party, perhaps one augmented by warriors from among the Cheyenne, Kiowa, and Arapaho. Together, they would present such an invincible force that the whites would either be driven or choose to withdraw from Indian Territory, and the hunting would be good again.

Everywhere Quanah went among the People, he was greeted with respect. In recent years he'd earned a deserved reputation as a great fighter. But there was little enthusiasm when he described his grand plan. Those willing to go out and fight preferred doing so in the traditional way: in small parties that attacked swiftly and just as quickly threw off pursuit in the foreboding reaches of their vast territory. These raiders made up in ferocity what they lacked in numbers. Collaboration was not the People's tradition, and what Quanah wanted to do would require considerable cooperation. Besides, as much as he was renowned as a warrior, he was also somewhat suspect as a half-breed, the child of a Comanche warrior and a white woman rescued as a girl from her lesser race and eventually given the privilege of living as an equal among the People. One of the many reasons Quanah hated whites was that some years later they stole his mother back, also taking his baby sister and killing his father, a renowned warrior named Peta Nocona, in the same attack. Quanah had his father's battle skills, mahogany skin, and thick black hair, but also his mother's gray eyes and a white man's height. He towered over the other braves. Many of the People were of mixed blood, Mexican and black as well as white, but Quanah's appearance made it particularly obvious. In battle they trusted him, but in counsel had their doubts. When the Quahadi scoffed at Quanah's suggestion of a unified war party, he mounted one of his best ponies and took his plan in turn to several other Comanche bands. Try as he might, none were persuaded.

After several frustrating weeks, Quanah gave up and began the long ride back to the main village of the Quahadi, which that winter was north of all the other People's camps. It was a dismal journey and he brooded along the way. When he arrived home at the Quahadi camp it was possible, even likely, that many there would mock him—he'd failed to convince outsiders to join in his scheme, just as his own Quahadis had rejected it. In better times that failure might have been overlooked, but with everyone edgy from hunger, Quanah felt certain that ridicule awaited him. His immense pride made him highly sensitive to even the mildest slights. He understood that this was a great personal flaw, but Quanah couldn't help it. The stigma of being a particularly obvious half-breed among the People left him insecure in a way that no battlefield triumphs could entirely ease.

Quanah was imagining the jeers he would surely hear in his village when he first sensed rather than saw movement in a shallow valley to his right. He hopped down off his horse to diminish his own silhouette against the sky and led his mount behind a small grove of trees. Then, looking down, he spied a small band of white men riding south. There were four on horseback, plus another on the bench of a wagon pulled by a two-horse team. Typical of white buffalo hunters, these men all had long hair hanging to their shoulders. Watching them, Quanah initially felt a spark of hope. If he could take them by surprise, cut down two or three while the others ran away in panic, then he could return to the Quahadi laden with dripping scalps and something to brag about. That might deflect any comments on other, less positive aspects of his excursion. The odds of five to one didn't bother him. Most white men were bad fighters, and cowards besides.

But as he studied his potential prey, Quanah hesitated. They were well armed with powerful rifles, and clearly wary. They crossed the valley slowly, taking care to watch on all sides. Regretfully, Quanah decided not to attack. He still thought he could kill one or two and get away, but the other whites would prevent him from taking scalps and so he would have nothing to show off to his village. Feeling thwarted and even more miserable, he watched the five men as they rode. One was the obvious leader, even though he was younger than the rest. He rode in front, studying the ground and occasionally calling back to the others. A red dog romped alongside his horse. As Quanah looked on, this young leader pulled up, dismounted, and shouted to his companions. They hurried over and dismounted, too, exclaiming about a wide swath of months-old tracks cut deeply into the packed dirt. Quanah had seen the tracks as well. Sometime earlier a big herd of buffalo, escaping their widespread slaughter in the white man's territory to the north, had moved across several rivers into this region, supposedly reserved for Indian hunting by the white government. These intruders were breaking the treaty, but Quanah knew why they had come. Just like the People, they were looking for better hunting, though of course whites already had all the food they needed without coming here and taking what belonged to the Indians. The interlopers in the valley beneath him just wanted the buffalo for their hides. For now, the herd would have migrated so far south that neither the whites nor the People could hunt them; but when the weather warmed, the buffalo would return here, and so would these white men, who now knew where to come in Indian land to find them. This proved again why Quanah's plan was necessary. When the warm season was back and the white men returned, the People needed to be ready to kill or drive all of them off, no matter how many came.

As the hunters crossed the valley and disappeared down a ravine just beyond, Quanah took a corn cake from his pouch and moodily ate it. He gagged on some dry bits—corn being almost as scarce as meat that winter, his wife had to mix in ground husks to bind the patty together before cooking it—and wished the next water hole was closer than an-other half day's ride. After choking down the food he pissed against a tree, remounted, and began riding north again.

Almost immediately he saw more movement, this time above the en-trance to the valley. He nudged his horse along, making certain to keep its unshod hooves from clopping on the hard rock, and after a few mo-ments saw there was another white man coming south. At first Quanah thought the white man must belong to the others, and was lagging be-hind to guard their rear. But then Quanah realized that this one was alone, and stupid besides. Though it was not unusual to come upon white hunters in Indian lands during the winter, it was rare to find one crazy enough to venture there alone. That this fool had done so, let alone was about to pass by Quanah right on the heels of a smarter, well-prepared group of whites, was clearly tremendous luck. Now Quanah would have a trophy to bring home to his village.

Almost without thinking, Quanah began to stalk him. He tethered his horse to a raggedy bush, running his hand over the animal's nostrils as a reminder for it to keep silent. Then Quanah checked his bowstring to ensure it was properly taut. He left his rifle back with his horse, be-cause the sound of a shot might reach the five other hunters who'd just crossed the valley. He could get away if they returned on the gallop, but then he wouldn't have time to do anything other than kill his victim—which, to him, was only part of the thrill.

The lone white man now entering the valley was on horseback, and his mount picked its way carefully around sharp rocks. Its rider peered intently at the ground ahead of him, oblivious to Quanah, who swiftly and noiselessly rushed in behind him, closing ground fast. He had an arrow nocked on his bowstring and could have shot the man out of his saddle at almost any time, but there was no sport in that. Instead, he came up a few paces behind the rider and deliberately kicked a fist-sized rock into another larger one. At the sound of the loud *clack* the white man turned in his saddle and saw Quanah there, his bow now drawn and ready. The white man squealed, a high womanish sound, and scrabbled for the rifle hanging in a scabbard by the side of his saddle. Quanah waited and let the man's fingers curl around the stock before he loosed his arrow, which tore into the fellow's shoulder and knocked him off his horse. The white man hit the ground hard; the breath whooshed out of him, and he gasped for air as he writhed there. Quanah hooked his bow over the quiver on his back, drew his knife, and moved forward. The white man tried to scream but still didn't have enough breath. Quanah grabbed him by the hair and yanked him into seated position. He pressed his knife just below the man's hairline and began to cut. The wounded man pounded at him with his left arm; his right one dangled uselessly. The point of Quanah's arrow protruded several inches in front of that shoulder. Quanah ignored the blows and sawed away. He got a lot of blood on his hands and arms, but the warm wetness felt good in the cold winter air. Just as the scalp came loose the white man finally had enough air in his lungs to scream. Because the other five white men might still be close enough to hear, Quanah regretfully leaned down and cut his victim's throat. He would have enjoyed playing with him some more. The People knew many ways to mutilate enemies without quite killing them on the spot, and Quanah was a master of them all. He dumped the white man's body and examined the gory scalp in his hand. It was a fine one. The hair was thick and dark brown, almost black. Quanah had cut it away from the skull so well that there were few unsightly flaps of skin dangling from the edges. He trimmed these away with his knife. The white man's horse had stopped a short distance away; Quanah draped the scalp on the corpse and wiped off as much of the gore on his hands on the dead man's shirt so the sharp smell of blood wouldn't panic the horse and cause it to bolt. He caught the horse's bridle and muttered soft words to it. The animal's tail twitched nervously as Quanah went through its saddlebags. He found a few bright, shiny cans whose contents sloshed when Quanah shook them. He tossed these away and took the dead man's rifle from its scabbard. It was a Winchester, a good gun, and so Quanah kept it. He was disappointed to find only a handful of shells in one saddlebag. There was a little tobacco, too, always good to have, and a canteen of water. Quanah took a hearty drink. Then he led the captured horse back through the valley to where he'd tethered his own mount. As he passed the body of the man he'd killed, he leaned down and grabbed the fine scalp. That, along with the Winchester and the horse, might deflect criticism when he got home.

As a prominent warrior who'd been gone on a well-known if controversial mission, Quanah expected to attract considerable notice when he rode into the Quahadi village. Just before he did, he prominently placed the scalp on the neck of his horse where everyone would see it. But when he arrived, leading the captured horse and brandishing his victim's Winchester, no one paid attention. They were all gathered around a man proclaiming loudly that he'd just received a message from the spirit world beyond, the place above the clouds. The identity of the speaker and the villagers' willingness to listen raptly to his words astonished Quanah. Previously, most of the camp considered Isatai something of a buffoon. Moon-faced and stout even in times of hunger, with a neck so short and thick that it seemed his head sprang directly from between his shoulders, Isatai was a liability in battle, lumbering clumsily about and getting in the way of more skillful fighters. The People generally had no regard for a grown man like Isatai who couldn't fight well. In the summer just past, he was relegated to helping hold horses away from the fighting, a lowly chore usually reserved for young boys on their first raids. Despite his obvious failings as a warrior, no one bragged more after battle than Isatai, who always described some heroic action on his part that had been completely overlooked by everyone else. Even his name was derogatory. The People assigned adult names based on physical traits, personal history, or perceptions of character. Quanah's name meant "smell"—women thought he exuded a particularly pleasant body odor. His younger brother, who'd died of a fever many seasons ago, had been called Peanuts because he was a runt. Isatai's name meant "Wolf Cunt," a blatant insult to his manhood. He either misunderstood or ignored the slur, decorating his breechclout with bits of wolf fur and claiming the animal as his special totem. He was mocked for this, but now, to Quanah's astonishment, everyone hung on his words.

"Two days past, I rose straight up in the air," Isatai boasted. "Maybe some of you saw me." His audience mumbled among themselves, with a few agreeing that, yes, they thought that perhaps they had. Quanah steered his horse past the crowd, snorting loudly to indicate derision. No one paid him any attention. Their eyes were locked on Isatai, who began jerking his jiggly body to mimic passage to the spirit plane. "The spirits live high above us, and when I glanced down, the village seemed very small."

"What do the spirits look like?" a woman inquired. "What did they say to you?"

"The spirits are more of a feeling than a sight," Isatai replied. "If you are chosen to rise up among them, one or more will blow into your heart and then you understand their messages without any words spoken." There were nods and murmurs of assent. After Isatai explained it, the villagers realized that of course this was the way spirits communicated with someone chosen from among the living.

Quanah dismounted in front of his tipi. He was gratified that his wife Wickeah was there, instead of among those surrounding Isatai. He handed her the reins to his horse, and also those of the captured one. She seemed not to notice he'd returned with an extra mount, and if she was aware of the fine thick scalp she failed to mention it. Irked, Quanah demanded, "What is this foolishness?"

"Isatai has been away two nights," Wickeah said. "When he returned just now, he started talking about spirit messages. Can we go listen?"

"Take care of these horses, then make me something to eat," Quanah said sharply. "I've just won a hard battle with a fierce enemy, a white hunter, and I'm very hungry."

"There isn't much," Wickeah said, looking past Quanah at Isatai. "You've been out talking again instead of hunting."

"I've been out fighting as well as talking," Quanah said. "Care for the horses and then get me whatever food there is. You need to work instead of wasting time paying attention to that fool." Wickeah obediently led the horses away. The comeliest woman among the Quahadi, she could have married any man in the village, but chose Quanah because he was the best fighter. When Wickeah's father refused to let him have her, she and Quanah ran away together. They only rejoined the camp when Quanah gave her father some fine horses and he relented. This was another reason why many of the other warriors, especially the older full-bloods, harbored some resentment toward him. Wickeah was a once-in-a-generation beauty, and all of them had badly wanted her.

While she was gone, Quanah hung the scalp by the outside flap of his tipi and leaned the Winchester beside it. That way, everyone in the village would be reminded that Quanah was a great warrior. Then, despite himself, he sidled over and joined the crowd. Having described his ascension, Isatai was now regaling his audience with the messages passed on to him by the spirits.

"There are five deer a short ride to the east," he said. "As soon as I'm finished talking, some of you should ride in that direction and kill them.

But as you ride, be sure to believe that they will be there. If any of those who go don't truly believe—if they have any doubts at all—then the spirits will make the deer disappear."

Quanah stood beside Crippled Foot, an older warrior, and asked, "Why is everyone listening? He's making this up to get attention."

Crippled Foot hushed him. "There's something about Isatai that's different. I think the spirits really did speak to him. They can choose anyone they like."

"Think about it. Why *him*?"

"That's for the spirits to know."

"About the six-legged buffalo," Isatai continued. "It was a very important sign."

Quanah couldn't help himself. "A sign of what?" he called out sarcastically. "A sign that there are buffalo all over our land right now, and all we have to do is ride out and kill them? But if we don't believe you, they'll disappear?"

Some in the crowd shouted for Quanah to be quiet, to go away if he didn't want to listen. But Isatai calmly said that it was a good question.

"This sign is about more than what we can hunt and eat right now," he said. "It's a signal to prepare."

"Prepare for what?" Quanah demanded.

Isatai looked stern. "The spirits want us to know that when the buffalo disappear, we will disappear too. The fate of the buffalo will be the fate of the People. We must preserve them for our own use. Very soon we will have to make some great thing happen to save the buffalo, and ourselves. It will probably be a very hard thing and daring, but the spirits command us to do it and so we must."

"The spirits told you this?" Quanah asked incredulously.

"They did. And when they had, they lowered me to earth, and as instructed I came back to my village to tell you all about it."

Quanah looked around at everyone listening raptly to Isatai's words. "The spirits told you that we must do something daring," he said.

"They did, though they didn't say what. That will be revealed to me sometime soon. And now I'm tired from my trip to see the spirits and must rest. Some of you go kill those deer to the east, and be certain to believe."

A half-dozen warriors rushed to their ponies. Later they returned empty-handed and ashamed. They agreed that someone among them must not have believed, but no one would admit that it was him. Somehow their failure seemed like more proof that Isatai was indeed singled out by the spirits. Everyone wanted him to visit them again and learn more about what the People had to do.

Quanah still believed Isatai was making everything up, but that didn't matter. At least the attention Isatai called to himself meant no one gave any further thought to Quanah's failed embassies to the other tribes.

That night Quanah woke with a start. Somehow, a plan had come to him in his sleep. Fat liar that he was, Isatai might be very useful.

TWO

The four grazing buffalo were a scraggly lot. Three were bulls so old that their thick winter fur only sprouted in irregular tufts. The fourth was a younger cow limping badly on a damaged back leg. They were the dregs of their species, decrepit enough to fall far behind as the main herd migrated south. Backs turned to the biting north wind, they cropped listlessly at yellow winter grass.

Sixty yards away, partially obscured from the buffalo by scrub brush, Cash McLendon lay on his belly and tried to keep a heavy Sharps rifle trained on the cow. He'd pulled back the first of the double triggers to cock the gun and prepare the second hair trigger to fire. Because he was downwind of the animal, the frigid air blew directly into his face, and his eyes watered.

Bat Masterson, squatting just behind McLendon, whispered, "Remember, shoot right behind the shoulder blade. You want to get her through the lungs. Imagine a target about the size of a hat."

"I know," McLendon growled. "Quit talking. I'm trying to concentrate." Telling Bat to stop talking was, he knew, a waste of time. The outgoing twenty-year-old never shut up.

"I got my rifle ready too. If you take her down with a single shot, I can probably get one of the old bulls before they know what's happening."

"Will you shut up and let me shoot?"

"Well, shoot, then," Masterson urged. "We got to keep moving if we're going to be in Dodge by dark. Sure would be better to get back with hides to sell instead of another load of bones."

"I know. I'm just waiting for this cow to turn her side more toward me."

"Piss on a buffalo that won't cooperate with its own demise," Masterson muttered sarcastically. "Pull the damn trigger and get us a hide."

McLendon waited another moment, trying to steady his rifle. Oblivious to danger, the cow buffalo continued cropping grass, her thick body mostly turned away from McLendon so that her tail more than her side was toward him. Behind him, he heard rustling and then a brief click as Masterson impatiently raised and cocked his own Sharps. If McLendon hesitated any longer, Bat would shoot the buffalo himself, and then rag on about it for the whole six-mile trip back to town. So McLendon fired, the crisp *crack* making his ears ring. The butt of the Sharps recoiled hard against his shoulder; for a moment he stumbled back and wasn't able to see the result of his shot. Behind him, Masterson fired too. The cow bellowed and stumbled awkwardly after the three old bulls as they began to trot away.

"You plinked her goddamn ass, but I think I caught her solid," Masterson shouted. "Quick, get on your feet! Shoot again!" McLendon scrambled up, and though his shoulder was still aching from the first shot, he slammed another cartridge into the breech of his rifle, raised the Sharps, and fired again, trying to aim between the lurching cow's shoulder blades. She was eighty or ninety yards away now; even wounded as well as crippled, she presented a moving target, and McLendon had trouble hitting tin cans during target practice. He thought his second shot might have hit the cow somewhere, and then Masterson fired again. The side of the fleeing animal's head exploded and she dropped to the ground.

"*That's* the way we do it," Bat exulted. "Come on, C.M., let's go get us a hide." Lugging the heavy rifles, each weighing about ten pounds, the two men hurried to the fallen buffalo. Masterson drew his handgun to finish off the animal if necessary, but when they reached the cow she was obviously dead. McLendon massaged his aching shoulder while his companion squatted down to examine their kill. "Hellfire," Masterson muttered.

"What's the matter?"

"Ah, we'll never be able to sell this hide. Look—your first shot ripped a patch off its rear, and then it deflected and tore some more hide at the shoulder. The first one from me went in here, low on the neck; that's another hole. Your second shot gashed up her side. My finish shot to the head didn't mar anything, but it was already too late. That's why we all keep telling you, you got to get one clean shot in behind the shoulder blade, a kill shot. There's too many tears and perforations here. Charlie Rath back in Dodge wouldn't pay us five cents for this one. It ain't worth skinning her. Leave her where she lays, and let's go pick up more bones so this trip ain't entirely wasted."

"Maybe we should take the hide anyway," McLendon suggested, though he didn't feel or sound enthusiastic. After nearly four months in Dodge, occasionally working as hired help to various hunters, he still hated the bloody, smelly business of skinning dead buffalo and staking their hides out to dry. "Whatever Charlie would give for it is more than we've got now."

"We need to put together something closer to five hundred dollars than five cents if we want to partner up with Billy Dixon on his hunts next spring. We need our own guns, ammunition, camp supplies, the works—though I believe Billy won't spurn us if we're not completely outfitted. When he likes you, he's a true friend, and he likes us a lot, or at least me. I'm accurate enough with my shots not to ruin the hairy merchandise. You, Billy may not want to tolerate. He's a businessman, after all."

"I'm aware of my shortcomings as a marksman," McLendon said. The whistling wind stung his ears and made him feel depressed. He was a slender man of average height, and the cold cut through him. His thin, dark beard afforded no protection to his face. That was the problem with the West Kansas plains in the winter. There were no high trees, let alone mountains or even many hills, to block the freezing air blasting in from the north. "Bat, quit wasting your time working with me. Go out with somebody better and build up your stake. I'm just holding you back."

"Oh, don't talk like that," Masterson said. "Like I been saying, C.M., it just takes time to learn how to shoot. When Daddy moved our family down here from Canada a few years back, neither me nor my brothers knew the barrel of a rifle from the stock. You're getting better. Hell, at least you hit the damn buffalo with your first shot, and you didn't miss completely with the second. We'll keep at it, and by summer you'll be rivaling Billy as the best shot among the hide men of Dodge City."

"I very much doubt it. Even the veteran hide men can't compete with Billy, and him just a kid not much older than you. I'll never be a good shot, or even a fair one. It's just a fact."

Bat pulled his coat tighter around his body and grinned. It was a wonderful grin. When he smiled, his thick mustache crinkled and his eyes came close to disappearing in folds of glowing skin. Bat was a stocky youngster, several inches shorter than McLendon. He had a natural swagger in his walk and a generally jolly nature, though if provoked Bat was capable of striking hard and fast. He'd quickly become a favorite among Dodge's grouchy buffalo hunters. They were mostly frontier veterans with limited senses of humor and dogged determination to kill and skin as many buffalo as they possibly could. After almost two prime years of hunting in the area when almost everybody made a fine living— as much as a hundred dollars a day for the best shots like Billy Dixon— late summer and fall of 1873 had brought ominous signs. North of the Arkansas River, it suddenly appeared possible that the buffalo were getting hunted out. It took many more miles of riding and days of shooting to bring down enough to make excursions even remotely profitable. Word was, the main herd was now to the south, into that hard, wild land known as Comancheria in recognition of the bloodthirsty tribe lurking there. By treaty, whites were forbidden to trespass, but the buffalo hunters were contemptuous of arbitrary boundaries. Even as McLendon and Masterson perforated the crippled buffalo cow, Billy Dixon and some of his veteran crew—a backup shooter, two skinners, and a cook—were scouting beyond the Oklahoma panhandle and down into Texas, looking for sign of the migrating herd and risking their lives with the Indians in the process. Anything below the Arkansas River was forbidden by treaty; nobody, white or Indian, honored it. A bit farther south, the Cimarron was the real line of demarcation. The land practically crawled with hostiles after that. Farther still was the mighty Canadian River, where it was strongly suspected in Dodge that the only remaining great buffalo herd would be found. There was some gossip about Billy planning to go down and hunt near the Canadian in the summer, the treaty and the Indians be damned. If he could buy enough rifles, ammunition, and other necessities, Masterson meant to go along if Dixon said that he could. McLendon was less certain: Billy would probably want only seasoned hunters along on such a dangerous expedition, and besides, McLendon was leery of the risk to his own life if he went along. He wasn't a competent hunter or fighter, and he knew it. Bat wanted adventure and riches. McLendon just wanted to make enough money to get out of Dodge City, which he loathed, at minimal risk to himself.

"I'll tolerate no more moping," Masterson declared. "Let's fetch the wagon and get back on bone detail. There's enough daylight left to gather a few dollars' worth before we have to return to town." He and McLendon shouldered their rifles and trudged back to where they'd left a team of ground-hitched horses and a wagon. The weapons, as well as the wagon and horses, had been lent to them by Billy Dixon, since the two had insufficient funds to buy their own. During the winter many of the seasoned hide men drifted off to spend some months in balmier climes. Those who stayed around Dodge had enough money to tide themselves over. Penniless novices like McLendon and Masterson were reduced to gathering up the bones from buffalo carcasses and selling them for seven dollars a ton to town merchants, who in turn shipped the bones back by rail to Eastern companies that used them in the manu-facture of china and fertilizer. It took about a hundred sets of buffalo bones to make up a ton. The bones were plentiful—dead buffalo were scattered all over around Dodge, since the hide men took the skins and left everything else to rot. No one in town wanted the meat. There was already too much buffalo in their diets, and they were sick of it.

Gathering the bones was a tedious business. Some of the buffalo skel-etons were pristine, picked clean by buzzards and easy to gather and toss in a wagon. But most were still in various stages of decay; remaining organ and muscle tissue had to be stripped from the bones with a knife or by hand, and even in winter the stink was fearsome. When Masterson and McLendon worked at it all day, they could collect three wagonloads, each totaling about half a ton. At best, that meant they had about ten dollars to split between them at the end of a working day, enough to live on with a few dollars to spare. Bat was saving for hunting gear and the chance to partner up with Billy Dixon. Despite Masterson's certainty that he shared the same ambition, what McLendon really wanted was a few hundred dollars for train fare to California and a stake to live on for a while once he arrived there. Bone picking was a slow, hard way to make the money they needed. Since Charlie Rath and the other Dodge City hide dealers paid as much as three dollars apiece for prime, sparsely perforated skins, McLendon and Masterson jumped at any opportunity to shoot living buffalo. Since their odds of gaining a saleable hide were much better when Masterson did the shooting, McLendon realized how generous it was on Bat's part to let him have an occasional turn. McLendon met Masterson in a saloon on Cash's first night in Dodge, when the younger man came over and struck up a conversation. Soon afterward, Bat invited McLendon to "partner up" in the buffalo bone business, which provided income the Dodge newcomer badly needed. Masterson also introduced McLendon to his friends among the buffalo hunters, Billy Dixon especially, and tutored him in marksmanship, skinning, and other skills necessary to make more money in the buffalo trade. McLendon had previously found few real friends in life, which made him appreciate Bat all the more.

"That was a nice shot of yours, the last one that took that buffalo cow in the head," he told Masterson as their wagon rocked slowly along the flat ground. "If Billy does decide on that southern hunting expedition in the spring, he's certain to ask you along. You'll be an asset to his operation. I'll bet you end up like J. W. Mooar, knocking down eighty or a hundred buffalo every day."

Bat belched. The onion sandwiches they'd eaten for lunch were repeating on him. "Josiah goddamn Mooar is one of those Yankee tale-tellers who's lied so much that he don't realize he's doing it anymore. No man kills a hundred buffs in a day—your rifle barrel would melt. Billy says he occasionally gets fifty or sixty. I'd be happy with thirty. At two or three dollars a hide, even with paying my share for skinners and a camp cook, that would still provide a nice, fat living. And it's easier than you realize, C.M., because you've never seen one of the great herds. They say that just a few years back, a herd of buffs three miles wide and ten miles long blocked the railroad track near here for ever so long a time while they wandered on across. You come on a bunch like that, hell, even you could set up, start shooting, and hit something every time. You wait—maybe they're hunted out around here, but Billy's gonna find that kind of herd down in Comanche country. Come late spring, you and me'll be right down there with him, killing so many buffalo that we become rich men damn near overnight."

"It seems like everybody I've met out in the West expects to get rich quick," McLendon said. "Strange how so few actually do."

"Well, we're going to be among them." Bat swung his head around, looking for carcasses. He was twisted almost completely around when he barked, "C.M., behind us—look!"

McLendon turned on the wagon bench. About a quarter mile away, two figures crouched over the carcass of the buffalo they'd just killed and abandoned. He squinted against the wind. "Who are they? What are they doing?"

Bat hauled his Sharps out of the wagon bed. "Indians, that's who. Stalking us, for sure. Get your damn gun so we can set about defending ourselves."

McLendon's heart lurched. Indians terrified him. He fumbled for his own rifle and had trouble grasping it. His hands were suddenly sweaty despite the cold. "How many?" he asked. His voice trembled.

"I just see the two, so we may be in some luck. Stop this wagon, I need to take aim."

McLendon awkwardly yanked on the reins with one hand while try-ing not to drop the bulky Sharps with his other. The wagon jerked to a halt. Bat jumped down and raised the Sharps to his shoulder. "Damn if they're not just staying out there, doing something with the buffalo," he muttered, and pulled the trigger. The rifle thundered, and a high spray of dirt kicked up a few feet to the right of the buffalo. "Pulled the goddamn shot," Bat said. "C.M., you shoot while I reload."

McLendon, still sitting on the wagon bench, contorted so he could fire. As he stared down the barrel he said, "Bat, they're not trying to find cover. They're—what?—I think they're cutting at the buffalo or something." He lowered the Sharps. "Hell, they're not even adults; they look like boys."

"Indians of any vintage can kill you," Bat said. He shoved a cartridge home and raised his rifle again. "Shoot 'em." Bat fired again and the buffalo carcass jerked. The Indian boys finally bolted away. The land all around them was flat, but somehow they almost instantly disappeared from sight. "Come on," Bat said. "Let's go back and see what's what. Be alert, now. They may be trying to gull us."

Cautiously, McLendon turned the wagon around. Bat, rifle at the ready, walked just ahead. When they reached the dead buffalo there was no sign of the Indians. While Masterson poked around nearby clumps of weed, McLendon got down and examined the animal's body. "Look at this, Bat," he said. "There are some chunks of meat cut right out of it. I'll bet those kids were starving."

Bat examined the bloody fist-sized craters in the carcass. "Maybe so."

"Do you suppose they're somewhere out of sight and eating that meat raw?"

"I suspect that they are. They daren't risk a fire. We ought to find 'em and cure their hunger for good."

McLendon was relieved not to be fighting for his life. "What the hell, Bat. They're just boys. Hungry ones."

"I suppose," Masterson said, sounding doubtful. "Well, keep a sharp eye out. Once their bellies are full, they might feel like a fight. And when we get back to Dodge, don't you dare tell a soul that we spared them. You don't kill Indians when you have the chance, many folks won't forgive you."

"We probably wouldn't have been able to catch them, anyway. They moved pretty fast."

"Speak for yourself—I'm personally quite swift of foot."

FOR THE NEXT THREE HOURS Bat and McLendon picked up, cleaned, and loaded buffalo bones in the wagon, stopping every so often to rest and drink water from canteens. They remained remain alert for Indians. Though the two starving native boys apparently posed little threat, this far above the treaty line there were occasional attacks by raiding parties of adult hostiles, even in winter. Mostly McLendon and Masterson picked up bones, often groaning as they bent and then straightened up. Individually the bones weren't too heavy, even the skulls and spines, but they found over forty skeletons, which meant lots of trips back and forth to the wagon. As the afternoon wore on, the wind turned even colder. Both men had mufflers wrapped around their necks, and their hats mostly kept their heads warm. But they had to use their bare hands to pick the bones clean, and their fingers grew very cold and sore. When the last bones were finally piled in the wagon, Masterson jumped up on the bench and jammed his hands in his pockets.

"You take the reins on the way home, C.M.," he said. "Damned if my fingers don't feel like they're about to fall off. If I don't warm my hands enough for circulation to return, I won't be able to thrill the girls at Tom Sherman's dance hall tonight."

"I don't know why you spend so much time in that particular place," McLendon grumbled. His hands hurt too. As soon as they'd finished cleaning and loading the bones, he pulled on gloves, but as he took up the reins he felt bits of buffalo offal stuck under his nails. It always took considerable scrubbing to get clean after a collecting day. "Tom Sherman's prone to fighting or even shooting his customers if the mood strikes him. If you're set on getting drunk and whoring, Jim Hanrahan's saloon is safer. At least if you get hit or shot at there, it won't be by the proprietor."

"That's so, but Sherman takes care to hire only the prettiest young ladies, and the Hanrahan whores tend toward the well-worn side. I'm saving most every cent in hopes of joining Billy's expedition, so I can't afford to do any actual dallying. But I do enjoy at least the sight of pretty girls as I sip my hard-earned beer. Tonight you ought to come with me for a change, C.M. Drinks and conversation with some attractive females would help lift you from your present sour mood."

"After such a long day I prefer a quiet evening," McLendon said. It was getting dark and it took concentration to keep the horses going in the direction of Dodge. "You might try it on occasion."

Bat scrunched his shoulders against the cold. "C.M., certain aspects of your demeanor continue to puzzle me. To begin with, there's your habit of letting your mind wander as you set up to shoot. You can't aim straight if your mind's miles away."

"Maybe I'm just trying to be watchful for Indians."

"Hardly. Those two boys earlier could have walked right up and lifted your hair. No, you daydream about that woman back in Arizona Territory."

McLendon shook his head. "You're wrong, Bat. She seldom crosses my mind." It was an egregious lie. There were some days McLendon found himself thinking every spare minute about Gabrielle, the woman he'd loved and foolishly spurned back east, and then found again in the dusty Arizona mining town of Glorious. They'd parted there for the

second time under dire circumstances that left him constantly aching
with a soul-deep sense of loss.

"Well, maybe you've forgot her, but surely not her angry husband, the
one you think may still be on your trail. I see the way you peer down
alleys and behind buildings when we're in town. You always assume he's
about to jump out and get you." McLendon had never mentioned anything about a lost love's husband. Bat assumed that himself. It was safer
to let him believe it than to tell the truth.

"I'm not the only one with mysteries," McLendon said, trying to
change the subject. "What about you with that notebook you always
scribble in? You won't tell me what it is you're writing."

"My writing is of no concern for you, because it don't put your life at
risk. Your wandering thoughts are my business because they might im-
peril me."

"Fine, whatever you say," McLendon agreed. "Now, how about we
get back to town, sell these bones, and get out of the wind? My very
bones are chilled and I want a quiet evening."

"I can suggest ways to warm up your bones as well as other body
parts. Not that you'll listen. The problem with you is, you've forgotten
the difference between quiet and boring. You'll lay on your bed reading
a newspaper or that same old book—"

"*The Last of the Mohicans*, a classic."

"So you say. And while you're wasting your time that way, I'll have
myself a few beers and dances and get myself warm, then go to bed and
dream about killing a thousand or so buffalo down in Comanche country. And that's a dream that'll come true."

"What if, instead of you killing buffalo, the Comanche kill you?"

"Goddamn, McLendon. It's a low fellow who tries to spoil his friend's
dream." Bat drew his hand from his coat pocket long enough to punch
McLendon on the shoulder that was already sore from the recoil of the

Sharps rifle, and chuckled when McLendon grunted with pain. They passed the rest of the ride back to Dodge in companionable silence. Masterson thought about the buffalo he'd hunt with Billy Dixon down in Comanche country, and McLendon pondered where he should go once he finally saved up the train fare to get out of Dodge City. Where would he be hardest to find for the killer on his trail?

THREE

In the time immediately following his revelations from the spirits, the rest of the camp treated Isatai with new respect; some gave him small presents, like twists of tobacco, but it was obvious that they still didn't like him. None of the other warriors invited him to share a smoke or a bowl of mostly meatless stew. What everyone wanted from him was additional spirit-inspired revelations, not friendship.

Quanah was different. For a few days he came by the ragged buffalo hide tipi Isatai shared with two ugly wives—no beauty like Wickeah for him—and casually visited with the fat man, who was initially suspicious when Quanah told some jokes and speculated on when the first hard winter storms would come. Previously, Quanah had been more contemptuous of him than anyone else in the village. It was at his suggestion that Isatai was demoted from full battle participant to horse-holder. But now the great gray-eyed fighter was treating him as an equal. Isatai thought at first that Quanah, like the rest of the Quahadi villagers, was just awed by the messages from the spirits and wanted more, but all Quanah did was chat about ordinary things, and despite himself Isatai was charmed.

After a week of daily small talk, Quanah came by Isatai's tent one morning carrying his rifle, bow, and quiver. Quanah had a fine rifle, a fifteen-shot repeater that the whites called a Henry. He'd taken the gun from a white settler he killed far to the south, along with a claw hammer that he used as a war club.

"Get your weapons and let's go hunting," he suggested to Isatai. "We'll ride north a little, see if there's anything to find."

"Maybe I won't come," Isatai said. He wanted to, but he was ashamed by the contrast between his weapons and Quanah's. His only rifle was a battered old muzzle-loader; battle trophies from the whites were largely picked over by the other warriors before bumbling Isatai got a turn. His arrows were inferior too. Isatai had trouble attaching the feather fletchings and so his arrows rarely flew straight. Quanah's arrows were perfect, as was his aim with a bow.

"Ah, I'd enjoy the company," Quanah said. "And if you don't mind, let's take two of my horses. I have a pair that are restless and need some exercise." It was a suggestion that allowed Isatai to avoid additional embarrassment. His few horses were dull-coated and stringy, and none would have matched up well with even the least of Quanah's many sleek steeds. When Isatai hesitated, Quanah added, "If we bring back fresh meat, our wives will reward us in our blankets tonight."

The ribald comment won Isatai over. It was the kind of joke Quahadi men shared with their friends.

"I'll get my things," he said, and briefly disappeared into his tipi.

They cut two fine horses from Quanah's herd, a paint for Isatai and a gray for Quanah. Then they rode north out of the village. It was cold, but at least there wasn't much wind. They had their rifles ready, but only for any unexpected encounters with enemies, not game. Ammunition was too precious and needed to be reserved for battle. Because of that, most warriors among the People and other Indian tribes were terrible shots with guns. They couldn't spare cartridges for target practice. When they encountered deer or turkey or, really, almost anything edible, they used their bows instead. Isatai doubted that he could hit anything with his arrows, even at close range, but it was traditional for hunters to share whatever they got, no matter who made the killing shot. Quanah's skill with a bow might provide Isatai and his wives with a rare, satisfying winter evening meal.

For a while they didn't talk, concentrating instead on scanning the horizon and studying the ground. A few times they saw faint marks in the dirt that they hoped might indicate the nearness of prey, but try as they might they didn't encounter anything they could shoot. Isatai had just resigned himself to a long, empty-bellied hunt, when Quanah gestured toward a low hill and said, "Let's rest there out of the wind. I have a little pemmican." They ground-tied their horses and crouched on the bank of the hill. Quanah reached into his pouch and produced four thick strips of buffalo meat pemmican. Dark dots indicated to Isatai that it was flavored with wild plums. He took two of the strips, thanked Quanah, and tore into the food, trying not to take huge, mouth-stuffing bites.

Quanah ate more sedately. He chewed calmly for several minutes after Isatai was finished. Then Quanah produced a canteen filled with water, the one he'd taken from the white hunter he killed on his ride back to the Quahadi village, and they each took a good drink. Though food was scarce among the people in winter, water never was. With intimate knowledge of their wild region, they always could find freshwater in streams and wallows.

"You know what I think of on these winter hunts?" Quanah asked. "I think about seeing small herds of buffalo, the kind we used to find even in the cold season. We'd kill a few and summon the rest of the village and there would be great happiness. The women would get the hides to make into warm robes and also cut up the meat, and we'd take that back to camp along with the dung to make fires and the bones for needles and other tools. Nothing would be left. Don't you remember?"

"I do," Isatai concurred, wondering if there might be more pemmican in Quanah's pouch and whether, if they kept sitting and talking instead of riding and hunting, his new friend might get it out to share. "It wasn't that long ago."

"How we'd eat afterward," Quanah continued. "The livers dipped in gall right on the spot—that warm goodness—and then later in camp the tongues and huge roasts and ribs dripping with juice. All we could eat until our bellies hurt and we had to sleep. The next day, more eating."

Isatai's mouth filled with water at the memory. "Good days."

"They were, and we have to make them come again. The white hunters—if we can get rid of them, all the buffalo will be ours again, in cold seasons as well as in warm ones. Don't you agree?"

"I do," Isatai said.

Quanah sighed and sat quietly for a moment, staring off into the distance. Then he said, "Well, let's go find something to kill and bring back to camp," and jumped briskly back on his horse. Isatai mounted more slowly, hauling his thick leg up and over his mount's back. He had to kick the horse into a trot to catch up with Quanah, who now rode harder and apparently with more purpose.

After a bit Quanah pulled up. "I think I see turkey tracks," he announced, pointing down at the ground. Isatai looked and didn't see anything, but he wasn't about to contradict his new friend. So he agreed again, and they rode on. After a few minutes Quanah said he thought they were getting close and ought to dismount—the sound and vibration of hooves striking hard winter ground would alert their prey. So the two men got down and tethered their horses to a low shrub. There was a thatch of thick brush a few hundred yards ahead and Quanah hissed that this was probably where the turkeys were.

"Let's use our bows," he whispered, and Isatai felt a little hurt that Quanah felt it necessary to remind him of such a basic thing. But he pulled one of his unimpressive arrows from his quiver and nocked it on the gut string of his bow.

The two Quahadis crept toward the brush. Isatai didn't think there were really any turkeys there—Quanah was indulging in wishful thinking. But then there was a sudden rustle and several birds burst out, moving in a speedy waddle. The lone male had bronze and green feathers, and the females' were dull brown.

"Now!" exclaimed Quanah. He loosed his arrow and one of the females dropped. Isatai, unsettled as usual in moments of action, fluttered a shot at the male, who veered back toward the brush. Isatai tried to nock another arrow; by the time he did and was ready to release it, the male was heading into the thicket. Isatai shot at him anyway; his arrow disappeared into the brush at the same time as the turkey.

Quanah released three more arrows before Isatai shot his second, and brought down another turkey hen. Several other turkeys flew frantically away.

"Good shooting," Isatai said, feeling simultaneously elated and glum. Quanah would probably give him one of the hens, so Isatai and his wife would eat that night. But he'd been reminded all the same of his inferiority. If he'd been hunting alone, he would have returned to camp empty-handed as usual.

"Well," Quanah said, "our wives will be happy. Why don't you go for the horses, and I'll get the turkeys and retrieve our arrows." That was traditional too. Arrows were hard to make. Whenever possible, after battles as well as hunting, the People tried to retrieve them for future use.

The horses had been left several hundred yards away. Quanah went over to the first hen he'd shot and pulled out his arrow. Then, as soon as Isatai was out of sight, he picked up the first arrow his companion had fired and darted into the brush. The brilliantly feathered male lay dead a few yards into the thicket with one of Quanah's arrows through its neck. Quanah yanked out his arrow and jammed in Isatai's. Then he let out a loud whoop, which Isatai heard as he untied the horses. Puzzled, he led the ponies back by their buffalo-hair hackamores and asked Quanah why he'd shouted.

"You made a great shot! This turkey was all the way into the brush and your arrow still found him. You're better with a bow than I realized, Isatai. I'm sorry for ever saying otherwise. I only got two slow hens with ordinary feathers, but you got the real prize."

Isatai was stunned. He'd never made even a fair shot before. But still, there was the gorgeous male with Isatai's arrow in him, and Quanah was a witness to what had happened.

"A lucky shot," Isatai said.

"Not luck. Skill," Quanah pronounced, and Isatai had to believe him, because Quanah after all was the greatest among the Quahadi warriors and knew about such things. Isatai didn't ask what had become of his second arrow. His already-fat chest expanded farther with pride and he took the turkey that Quanah held out to him. It was very heavy; there would be feasting in Isatai's tipi that night.

"Your shots were fine too," he assured Quanah.

"Ah, my targets were practically roosting. Let's take these turkeys home so our wives can pluck and cook them. I can't wait to tell everyone about your shot. It was a fine thing."

On the ride back, with the turkeys slung on their horses in front of them, Quanah was chatty. He confided to Isatai that he was ready to take a second wife, but Wickeah was already jealous.

"Women are so difficult. I tell her that with a second wife she won't have to do so much work, but she says that all I want is a different woman in my blankets, I don't want her anymore. You've got two wives. Advise me in this, I need your counsel. How do you keep your women under control?"

The great warrior Quanah wanted his advice—Isatai's joy compounded. He forgot that his pair of wives were both starving widows desperate to marry any man in the village willing to have them. Isatai, always rebuffed by more desirable women, was the only one who would.

"I make it clear that I am the master of my tipi and that I will be obeyed. Women need firmness. Just tell your wife that you're taking a second one, and no complaining or you'll beat her. She'll stop objecting—you'll see."

"Master of my tipi." Quanah nodded. "I'll do as you suggest."

They rode some more in silence, Isatai already imagining how he'd describe his great shot to his wives, and then Quanah said, "I think maybe it was Buffalo Hump."

Isatai was startled from his reverie. "Who was Buffalo Hump?"

"The spirit that called you up into the sky and gave you the message about the People having to do a great thing. You were the one chosen, so what do you think?"

It hadn't occurred to Isatai that he might be called on to identify a specific spirit. He knew, of course, who Buffalo Hump was, the great chief who many seasons earlier led a great band of fighters down into Texas and fulfilled his vision of driving white people into the sea. The People had no written language, but they honored their past with descriptive oral history.

"Buffalo Hump," Isatai mused, stalling for time.

"I ask because his feat was one of the finest acts ever, a true great thing. So his spirit might decide that now is the time for another one—a great attack against the whites, maybe. And so he caught you up into the air."

"It could have been Buffalo Hump." Isatai tried frantically to figure out how the dead leader might fit into his current prophecies. "I need time to think on this."

"We know that Buffalo Hump demanded the best of the People. It may be he wants you to realize quickly that it's his spirit who has called you, and if you don't, he'll move on to someone else." Quanah looked and sounded very concerned. "If it was, indeed, the spirit of Buffalo Hump. I might be wrong. You understand these things much better than I."

"Yes, I do," Isatai said. "But I thank you for your words. I'll consider them tonight." He tried to think of something to add, something impressive to reaffirm his spiritual authority over Quanah.

"I'm grateful to you. All of us are. We need to understand what the spirits want from you—from us. And at least you'll think on Buffalo Hump tonight with a full stomach after eating as much turkey as you can hold. And look over there—a skunk! A few more bites, and a small, thick pelt besides."

Quanah nocked an arrow in his bow, but Isatai raised a hand and stopped him. "Don't shoot that skunk. I forget to say when I first returned from the sky that the spirits are fond of skunks and don't want them killed. If you shoot that one, I might never be raised up again and we'll never know what we're supposed to do."

Quanah lowered his bow. "All right, your wisdom must guide us. We'll tell everyone not to hunt skunks. But first I'll tell them about your great shot that killed the turkey in the brush, if that's agreeable to you."

"You can talk about whatever you want. And when the spirits next call to me, I'll tell them that Quanah honors them too."

"Thank you," Quanah said, trying hard to sound abashed.

When they reached the Quahadi village Quanah told everyone about Isatai's magnificent shot, announced that it was the will of the spirits as revealed to Isatai that no one should kill skunks anymore, and insisted that one of the two hen turkeys be cooked in a communal stew so that everyone could have at least a small taste of Isatai's bounty. He neglected to say that he was the one who had killed the hens, and was so eloquent that Isatai felt no need to speak for himself. He stood to the side, nodding gravely as Quanah spoke. Those who remembered that Isatai was a wretched shot with a bow told themselves that the spirits had guided the arrow for him. It was further proof that he was their chosen spokesman.

Quanah and Wickeah ate the second hen, sharing with some others in adjacent tipis, and the fine male turkey was entirely reserved for Isatai and his wives, who gorged themselves. Afterward Isatai tried to use the bird's colorful feathers to fletch arrows, but he still couldn't do it well and most of the feathers stuck crookedly to the shafts. When Quanah noticed, he asked to take the feathers and fletch Isatai's arrows for him, since a man favored by spirits shouldn't waste his time on such small tasks. Isatai was pleased to oblige him, and considered it a generous thing for his friend to do. He went back inside his tipi to smoke and to decide what it was that the spirit of Buffalo Hump might have to say to him soon, since an edict not to kill skunks wasn't grand enough.

It dawned on Isatai that he was, in fact, a human conduit for the spirits. At first he had believed that the words were his own, spoken to end the mocking he had endured; but the more he thought about it, the more it seemed possible, even likely, that he was speaking on behalf of the spirits after all. They summoned and then blew into him just as he'd said, maybe when he was dreaming, and the words that later came from his mouth were theirs and not something he was making up. And with that in mind, he decided to nap, giving any of the spirits—Buffalo Hump, maybe?—an opportunity to commune with him again. It was time. The villagers were impatient to hear more from the spirit world, and Isatai did not intend to disappoint them, his good friend Quanah especially.

FOUR

In late 1873, Dodge City was unsightly and dangerous. Established just fifteen months earlier, when the railroad came through the area and offered a convenient means to ship buffalo hides east, the town was populated by merchants, railroad depot employees, cardsharps, and whores, with as many as two thousand hunters drifting in and out, depending on the season. The hunters preferred to be called hide men because it made them sound like the entrepreneurs that they considered themselves to be. With the Arkansas River and the Atchison, Topeka, & Santa Fe railroad tracks serving as anchors to the southern boundary of the settlement, and the old Santa Fe Trail just to the north, Dodge City's permanent residences consisted of sod huts and wooden shacks. Its businesses were located in long, low board buildings behind high false fronts. In between were rough streets of hard-packed dirt. The hide men slept in tents or under wagons on the outskirts of town. Thick coats of prairie dust were permanently plastered over everything. But nobody cared what the place looked like; aesthetics were secondary to commerce. The population wasn't particularly clean, either. There weren't many wells and bathwater was at a premium. Nobody bathed in or drank from the Arkansas River; like all the other rivers in the region, it was tainted with gypsum, a powerful natural laxative. In Dodge City, a glass of potable water was often hard to come by.

Yet, despite its unattractive appearance, it was possible to buy every necessity and many luxuries in Dodge. The railroad freighted in whatever commodities town merchants ordered, and in 1872 and most of 1873 the buffalo herds were so extensive, and the hunting was so good, that everyone except the most sodden drunks had at least some money to spend. Besides its ubiquitous saloons, dance halls, and bawdy houses, Dodge boasted several dry goods stores, a gunsmith, a saddlery and harness shop, billiard parlors, a drugstore, several restaurants, a bottle shop selling fine wines and liquors, a blacksmith, a barbershop, stables, and even a fine hotel, the Dodge House. Rath & Company bought most of the buffalo hides, paying two or three dollars apiece for the best ones and shipping them off to sell to Eastern manufacturers at a substantial profit. New methods of turning the hides into leather belts for manufacturing equipment created a constant demand for buffalo pelts. In its earliest days, the Dodge City economy boomed.

So, constantly, did guns, in as well as outside of town. There was no law to speak of in Dodge. The town remained unincorporated, so there was no Dodge City marshal or court system. The hide men were a rugged bunch prone to constant quarrels, many of which quickly disintegrated into drunken brawling and gunplay. Most of the town businessmen, especially the saloon owners, were just as violent. An attempt to form a citizen's vigilante committee failed miserably when the vigilantes launched their own spree of indiscriminate killing. Dodge was part of Ford County, and after elections in June 1873 the county had a sheriff, Charlie Bassett, who was tough and honest. But Bassett couldn't be in Dodge all of the time, and even when he was, it was impossible for one man to completely suppress the violence. Killings continued, and Dodge needed a place to bury its numerous dead. Boot Hill, the place chosen, was a barren bluff near the Arkansas River, not far removed from Front Street and Second Avenue, where most of the main businesses were located. Town wits gave the spot its name because most of those buried there expired in street fights rather than in bed, dying "with their boots on."

Fort Dodge, an Army station, was several miles east of town. But its commander and troops had all that they could do trying to defend against the roving Indian bands that plagued the area. By treaty, the Cheyenne and Arapaho were confined to their agency below the Cimarron, with the Kiowa and Comanche on a reservation even farther south. The wild Indians who refused to live on agency lands and under agency rules rampaged farther off to the west and south. White men had the exclusive right to hunt above the Arkansas River, and the red men had the same rights below it, but both sides resented the restriction and neither abided by it, try as the Army might to enforce the boundary. There were plenty of Indian raids, in Kansas and Texas and the Oklahoma panhandle, wherever white hunters and settlers could be isolated in small groups and attacked. Dodge City was no exception. There were periodic ambushes outside of town, and corpses were left scalped and mutilated in ways that nauseated even the most hardened frontiersmen. The Indians especially loathed the hide men, and the hatred was mutual.

Dodge City and its rough-and-tumble residents were unpopular with virtually everyone. Newspapers in other Kansas towns like Topeka and Wichita denigrated the town on a regular basis, deriding its constant violence, its lack of social sophistication, and particularly its horrific stink. Especially during the hot summer months, when hunting was at its peak, stacks of buffalo hides—many of them dozens of feet high—towered along the railroad lines south of town. Every day they were loaded onto freight cars and shipped east, only to be instantly replaced by new piles that smelled of blood and animal funk. There was usually a brisk wind, and if it blew in from the south, people in Dodge were obliged to hold handkerchiefs over their noses when they ventured outside. Everyone put up with it because the stench represented an influx of money. But by late 1873 the smell was becoming less of a nuisance because there weren't as many hides brought into town and piled up for shipment. What would have seemed impossible just a year earlier became too obvious to ignore: the hide men had been too efficient in their slaughter. The buffalo, at least in the vicinity of Dodge City, were almost wiped out. Those that survived shifted south of the river, down into the forbidden territory where the Indians held sway. For the first time, the town economy was in jeopardy.

WILLIAM AND HANNAH OLDS operated a boardinghouse in Dodge City. A few blocks removed from the saloons and dance halls, it wasn't much, just a square plank structure with living quarters for the owners in back and a half-dozen tiny cubicles in front. Cash McLendon and Bat Masterson shared one of the cubicles, which had just enough space for two rickety cots and a battered dresser with a washbasin, a pitcher, and a kerosene lamp on top. They paid a dollar a day to live there, fifty cents apiece. The walls were thin and they could clearly hear every snore, belch, or fart from those occupying adjacent cubicles. There was also a cramped kitchen for Mrs. Olds and a dining room where boarders could join their hosts for dinner if they had twenty-five cents to pay for the meal. McLendon usually didn't, preferring to dine in his cubicle on a few pennies' worth of crackers and cheese. He wanted to save every cent he could for train fare to the West Coast. His goal was to lose himself in one of the main cities there—San Francisco, maybe, or San Diego—where he might have a decent chance to make something of himself. Crowded Eastern cities offered anonymity but little opportunity. Mrs. Olds some-

times took pity on McLendon and let him eat for free if he looked particularly tired and hungry. Whenever McLendon joined his landlords
for a meal, William Olds ate silently, belching softly after every swallow.
He was rumored to have some sort of stomach disease that sapped him
of most of his strength. In contrast, Hannah Olds chattered constantly,
leaving her food untouched while she took advantage of the opportunity
for conversation. McLendon felt sorry for them both.

Most evenings when he and McLendon returned to town from a long
day's bone collecting, Bat Masterson headed directly to the Sherman
dance hall or, less frequently, to some other Dodge saloon. McLendon
would use the washbasin in their cubicle to clean up, buy his dinner
from one of Dodge's several general stores, and then lie on his cot, reading and thinking. Almost two years after fleeing the civilized streets of
St. Louis for the stringent life on the frontier, he still hadn't completely
adjusted to long days of grueling physical labor, and his lean body always
hurt, his back and knee joints especially. His cot was uncomfortable.
The tick mattress was lumpy and the blankets—there were no sheets—
were threadbare and unevenly patched. But he stretched out on it anyway, because he badly needed to be off his feet and there was no chair
to sit on. He and Bat had been roommates for almost four months, and
as much as he enjoyed his friend's company, McLendon longed for the
day when he would leave Dodge City and the boardinghouse behind.
By his calculations, train fare to California and a grubstake would require a minimal $350, and to date he had accumulated a little over $80
in the poke sack that Jim Hanrahan let him store in the office safe of
his billiard hall and saloon. Bone picking provided minimal income during winter; after paying for food, lodging, and the occasional beer,
McLendon was lucky to save three dollars a week. But when spring came
and the hide men resumed shooting, he thought that things would pick
up. Then McLendon had hopes of finding indoor employment, maybe

helping out at Rath & Company or Hanrahan's, working behind the counter in an establishment where the hide men liked to trade, and where the money he earned might be better. McLendon hoped to escape Dodge City by sometime in midsummer. He heard a lot of talk about how the buffalo had moved south and the town economy might collapse, but he tried not to dwell on it. Nobody wanted the buffalo back in great numbers more than him.

ON THE NOVEMBER NIGHT after they'd encountered the starving Indian boys, Bat disappeared in the direction of the dance halls and McLendon wearily plodded back to the Olds boardinghouse. They'd only gotten two dollars for their load of buffalo bones. To compensate, McLendon decided to skip dinner entirely. He was so tired that he thought he would tumble on to his cot, reread a few pages of *The Last of the Mohicans*, and try to fall asleep—he suffered from chronic insomnia. But it was apparently to be a night of frustration, too, because when McLendon tried to light the lamp in his cubicle it was out of kerosene. Sighing, he carried it back into the kitchen, where Hannah Olds was working at the stove.

"I need some kerosene, Mrs. Olds," McLendon said. "I know you're too busy just now to get the can and spout. So if you don't mind I'll fetch them from the cupboard and fill this lamp myself."

Hannah Olds, a nervous woman in her mid-forties, wiped her hand across her sweaty brow. It was cold outside but stifling in the kitchen. The woodstove was throwing out tremendous heat. "Help yourself, Mr. McLendon," she said. "I know how you like to read at night. A drummer who moved out today left behind some newspapers from Wichita, if you'd like to have those. Give me a moment to get this stew stirred and I'll find them for you."

The stew smelled good. "Beef?" McLendon asked as he filled his lamp.

"No, buffalo. Mr. Mitchell at the grocery had expected a few cattle brought in from Wichita, but there was apparently some delay. You seem tired. Would you like to share supper with Mr. Olds and me? No charge."

Like everyone else in town, McLendon was sick of eating buffalo. The thought of its strong taste repulsed him, and he decided that if Mrs. Olds was cooking buffalo stew rather than beef, he'd rather skip supper as planned rather than choke down any more of the gamy meat. "Thank you anyway. I think I'll just stretch out on my bed and read."

"Well, if you change your mind, there'll be plenty. Here's that newspaper."

Back in the cubicle, McLendon lit the oil lamp, pulled off his boots, and glanced at the Wichita paper. Like most frontier publications, it combined local gossip with months-old national news. Its front-page feature was a story about a woman assassin who the reporter claimed was known as the Witch of the West. Operating mostly in California and Arizona Territory, she allegedly hunted down victims on behalf of her clients and, according to the reporter, killed them in ingenious feminine ways—a knitting needle through the ear, a strangler's noose fashioned from corset strings . . . No one seemed able to describe her, and, despite the writer's feverish insistence, there was no concrete evidence to link any one of the nine murders cited to another. Several of the killings— a shotgun blast from ambush, two knifings—seemed completely unrelated in terms of the Witch's supposedly preferred methods. Frontier newspapers like the *Wichita Gazette*, trying to build a base of steady subscribers, often resorted to exaggeration or outright falsehoods to attract notice with sensational stories. McLendon suspected that the Witch of the West fell into this category. He smiled ruefully; unlike the fantasy figure in the *Gazette*, the assassin on McLendon's trail was far too real.

Patrick Brautigan, nicknamed Killer Boots for his habit of kicking victims to death with his steel-toed footwear, had been hunting McLendon since February 1872. Prior to that, both men worked for Rupert Douglass, an unscrupulous St. Louis businessman willing to murder competitors who wouldn't agree to let him buy them out. It was glib Cash McLendon's job to persuade reluctant rivals to take his boss's money and leave town. If he failed, Brautigan became involved.

McLendon, who grew up as a homeless, illiterate orphan on the St. Louis docks, earned Rupert Douglass's favor by working first as an informant, then as Douglass's right-hand man. In his off-duty hours McLendon courted Gabrielle Tirrito, the daughter of a small-time Italian merchant who stubbornly refused to sell his shop to Douglass. Gabrielle taught McLendon how to read and gave him *The Last of the Mohicans*, the first book he'd ever owned. But in spring 1870 he put the kindhearted, high-spirited young woman aside to marry Douglass's only child, Ellen, taking his place as heir apparent to the burgeoning family empire. Gabrielle, hurt and furious, left St. Louis with her father for Arizona Territory.

Because he believed McLendon wasn't tough-minded enough, Douglass brought in Patrick Brautigan from Boston, where the hulking Irishman had gained a considerable reputation for violent union-busting. McLendon was repulsed by Brautigan's bloody acts on their employer's behalf, and shaken to learn immediately following his marriage that Ellen was mentally ill and prone to violence against herself. In early 1872, when his carelessness resulted in Ellen's suicide, McLendon took $2,000 from Douglass's safe and fled St. Louis, assuming correctly that his grieving, vengeful father-in-law would set Killer Boots on his trail.

McLendon planned to lose himself in San Francisco or some other California city. On the way, he detoured to the small mining community of Glorious in Arizona Territory, where Gabrielle and her father now operated a dry goods store. He hoped to persuade Gabrielle to come to California with him—they would start a new life there. But Gabrielle had put her St. Louis heartbreak behind her by starting a new romance with Joe Saint, the sheriff of tiny Glorious. Reluctantly staying in town while he tried to win her back, McLendon was drawn into a conflict between the townspeople and powerful rancher Collin MacPherson, who, like Rupert Douglass in St. Louis, wanted the owners of Glorious's few small businesses to sell out to him and move along. When they refused, he employed his own thugs to force them out. Thinking of others instead of himself for one of the few times in his life, McLendon helped the townspeople thwart MacPherson's plans. But in the process he was betrayed to Douglass by someone he trusted, and had to flee again when Killer Boots unexpectedly appeared at the end of a frantic night gun battle between the townspeople and MacPherson's Mexican vaqueros. He thought that leaving Gabrielle behind to marry Joe Saint—she probably had a baby by now—was the worst thing that could ever happen.

Then, through a combination of his own stupidity and bad luck, he found himself in Dodge City, and realized that he was wrong.

WHEN MCLENDON ESCAPED Killer Boots in Arizona Territory in the late summer of 1872, he traveled south and east, reasoning that his pursuer would expect him to continue west. He was certain that he would be running for the rest of his life. Killer Boots would never abandon pursuit until his boss ordered him to, and Rupert Douglass was not a man to ever give up. McLendon did his best to throw off pursuit. He sometimes used the pseudonym H. F. Sills, the name of a railroad man he'd known back in St. Louis. The constant fear of turning a corner to find Killer Boots waiting, combined with his terrible sense of guilt for Ellen's death and his anguish at losing Gabrielle, haunted McLendon whenever he closed his eyes at night. The more he tried not to think about any of it, the more he obsessed. He rarely slept more than two or three hours a night. He believed that his nerves would never mend, and, remembering his accidental complicity in Ellen's death, thought he deserved it.

There was one advantage. For the present and at least for the short term, money was no problem for McLendon—he still had nearly seven hundred dollars of the money he'd taken from Rupert Douglass's safe in St. Louis. He thought he'd disappear into Texas for a few months to throw Killer Boots off the scent, then resume his flight to California. San Francisco sounded like the kind of city where a smart, ambitious young man could avoid much notice while still making a good living.

Traveling mostly by stage, McLendon lingered awhile in Austin and San Antonio, enjoying the latter so much, with its constant *fiesta* atmosphere, that he considered staying there. He started using his real name again—surely Killer Boots would never look for him in such a far-flung place. Gradually, he felt a little safer. So long as he avoided attracting attention and remained far away from the remorseless thug's home base of St. Louis, he would probably be all right. But in the end the town didn't seem quite sophisticated enough. McLendon had enjoyed enough of the fine life in St. Louis to want it again, so in May 1873 he set out once more, intending to reach San Francisco sometime in the summer. Rather than ride the main stage from San Antonio to Houston and then turn west, he decided to take a series of smaller stage lines, just in case Killer Boots had spies watching major city depots. That was how, in early June, he found himself in Fort Griffin, a desolate Army post and adjacent town in West Texas. It was a crossroads of sorts for drummers and gamblers, and McLendon was stuck there for three days while a broken axle on his stage was repaired. He checked into a bug-infested hotel and tried to catch up on his sleep, but as usual he was haunted by

regrets and lay awake most of the night. By the end of his second day
there, he decided to distract himself by seeking out whatever entertainment Fort Griffin had to offer.

A poker game was in progress in a town saloon; sipping beer, Mc-
Lendon watched as the hands were played and relatively small stakes
were won and lost. The four players consisted of two off-duty Army
sergeants, a fat drummer who'd come to town on the same stage as Mc-
Lendon, and a wraithlike, coughing fellow with fierce eyes who took
most of the pots.

"Goddamn, it's your lucky night, Doc," one of the sergeants complained. "I might as well hand over what's left of my pay and save myself
additional trouble."

"Suit yourself," the emaciated fellow grunted. He was wracked by a
coughing spasm. Another onlooker whispered to McLendon that the
man's name was John Henry Holliday. He was called Doc because of
his dental practice in Dallas, where he'd just won the grand prize at the
Dallas County Fair for crafting the best set of false teeth.

"Doc's got consumption something awful and prefers poker to pulling teeth," the fellow told McLendon. "He comes this way every other
month or so, cleans out whoever he plays with, and goes back home."

"Does he, now?" McLendon said. "Is he that skilled a player?"

"We all think he's benefiting from marked decks or other tricks, but
we dassn't make the accusation. Doc's got a bad temper, and is quick to
go for his gun."

McLendon watched the game a while longer, trying to discern how
Doc was cheating. The dentist always agreed whenever any of his playing partners asked for a fresh deck of cards. When it was his turn to
deal, his short cuffs rode high up on his forearms—no cards were con-
cealed there. As he studied Doc, McLendon switched from beer to whiskey. The bite of the hard liquor relaxed him. He had two glasses and

called for a third. By the time he'd drained that one, he found himself thinking that maybe Doc wasn't cheating. Maybe he was just good at poker. McLendon hadn't played cards much, but he'd always suspected he would be an excellent gambler, since he was adept at reading expressions and guessing what others were thinking.

Just then the drummer lost his last few dollars and quit the game. Doc glanced around at the onlookers and said in a syrupy Southern drawl, "We're down a man. Who's the next huckleberry?"

McLendon said impulsively, "That would be me." He got another drink before he went over to the table, carefully setting the glass down so the liquor wouldn't spill. He and the two sergeants shook hands and introduced themselves, but when he held out his hand to Holliday, Doc asked sharply, "Can you pay off if you lose? I want to see your money."

"By all means," McLendon said. Feeling reckless, he pulled a wad of bills from his boot, his remaining stake of about five hundred dollars. He was pleased to hear a collective sharp intake of breath from the onlookers, and even Doc Holliday nodded approvingly.

"You can afford to participate," he said. "Now let's see if you can play."

The first hand was exhilarating for McLendon. The two sergeants soon folded their hands, and McLendon found himself gazing at Doc Holliday over a pot of nearly twenty dollars.

"How many cards will you have?" the dentist asked courteously. He was dealing. McLendon, who had a pair of jacks, asked for three cards, and one was a third jack. Doc took two cards. Trying hard not to look too confident, McLendon chewed on his lower lip a moment before raising the pot by five dollars.

"The rich stranger isn't afraid to push," Holliday announced to the crowd. "I believe I'll just test his mettle." He matched McLendon's five dollars and raised him another five. McLendon made a show of trying to decide what to do, then called Doc's raise. The dentist slapped down a hand with three tens and reached for the money in the middle of the table.

"Not so fast," McLendon said, and showed his jacks. Holliday, obviously impressed by such coolheaded calculation, grinned ruefully and tipped his hat.

McLendon's luck held. He won several more pots, once bluffing his way to victory with only a pair of treys. After a while the two sergeants were cleaned out, and McLendon was up by almost ninety dollars. Instead of calling for new players, Doc suggested that he and McLendon play a two-man game "so the best player can be determined." Fortified by several more drinks, McLendon agreed. He was having fun, and for the first time in quite a while wasn't obsessing about Ellen's death, Killer Boots on his trail, or Gabrielle and Joe Saint being in each other's arms back in Arizona Territory. It was a fine thing to have a little recreation. The last months had been hard going, and he'd earned a chance to enjoy himself.

Doc and McLendon dueled at the card table for several more hours. McLendon still won more hands than he lost, but the pots Doc took were usually bigger. They both drank hard while they played. Doc didn't show any effects from the liquor and McLendon didn't think he did, either, though it seemed to him that the stakes must have been gradually raised because suddenly every hand involved a hundred dollars or more. McLendon studied the dentist's face closely, but there was nothing to read in his eyes but a certain belligerent gleam.

Sometime around four in the morning, when he'd lost count of the drinks he'd consumed and the number of hands that had been played, McLendon suddenly found most of his money on the table, matched by a high pile of Doc's. How did that happen? He wasn't sure.

"How many cards?" Doc asked impatiently, punctuating his words with coughs. The dentist dabbed at his lips with a handkerchief and McLendon thought he saw a red smear on the linen.

"What?"

"How many cards?"

McLendon studied his hand—two nines, two sevens, a deuce. "One, I suppose."

Doc shot a card in his direction. Cash picked it up—a six.

"Dealer takes three. What's your bet?"

McLendon tried to cut through the alcohol haze enveloping his brain. Most of his stake was already on the table. If he won the hand, he could travel to San Francisco in style with enough left over to live on for months. He had two pair, and Doc had just drawn three cards. The odds were very much in McLendon's favor, and for a moment he thought a hesitant expression flickered across the dentist's face. McLendon pushed his last hundred dollars across the table and announced, "I'm putting it all in."

"Well, now," Doc said. He studied his own hand. "What the hell. Can't let you just walk away with it. I call."

McLendon tossed out his nines and sevens. "Two pair."

"Impressive." Doc spread out his cards. "Three fours, two fives. Full house." He had to use both hands to rake the massive pot over to his side of the table.

"Full house? When you drew three? Why, that's— You—"

Doc pulled back his coat and rested his palm on the butt of a handgun. "What are you saying?" he asked quietly, and everyone in the saloon shut up.

McLendon looked at Holliday's face and sobered up enough to see the eagerness for violence there. "Nothing. I'm not saying anything."

"All right." Doc stuffed the money into his pockets and walked out.

Afterward McLendon slumped on the plank sidewalk in front of the saloon, his battered valise at his feet. All he had packed in it were a rumpled suit, two shirts, a change of underdrawers, *The Last of the Mohicans*, and the Navy Colt .36 that he'd only fired on a single occasion, the climactic shootout in Glorious the previous summer. His head ached terribly as he considered his plight. He was stuck in Fort Griffin, Texas, with no money at all.

"Hey, fellow." McLendon looked up and saw two straw-haired men standing over him. They'd been among the onlookers at the saloon. Even fighting his vicious hangover, McLendon took them for brothers because they looked so much alike, except that one was much taller than the other.

"You all right?" the taller man asked. "Lot of money you lost in there. Foolish thing, to take on Doc Holliday at poker. When it gets to the nut-cutting, the Doc never loses."

"Well, I'm too often prone to be foolish and my nuts got cut," McLendon groaned. "This is only the latest calamity I've brought on myself."

The two men laughed. "We're all fools at times," the short one said. "Come with us to get some breakfast. Things will look better on a full stomach."

"I can't afford it. Doc Holliday took my last cent."

The tall one said, "Come along, we'll buy." They led McLendon to a small café and ordered hard-fried eggs, biscuits, and coffee. He introduced himself and learned that they were brothers named Isaac and Jacob Scheidler, though Jacob, for obvious reasons, answered to "Shorty." The Scheidlers were teamsters who used their two wagons to transport freight for clients. They were in Fort Griffin to pick up a load of saddle tack for delivery to Fort Dodge, in Kansas.

"Once we unload there, we'll head a few miles west to Dodge City for recreation," Isaac explained. "We'll spend the next few months taking loads to Wichita and Kansas City; then in the spring, when the hide men in Dodge go out after buffalo, we'll hire on with them to haul their hides back into town. It's decent money and with luck we'll have steady hide-hauling work right through the fall."

When they asked McLendon where he was headed, he said California. "Not that under my new impoverished circumstances I'm going to get there anytime soon. I'll have to scrounge for work here. Have you any suggestions?"

"Can you ride well?" Shorty asked. "Some of the ranchers in the area might be needing a good hand."

"I can stay on a horse if it doesn't move too fast, but no more than that. What I'm good at is talking to people, making arrangements. I can do sums fairly well. I can read acceptably."

Shorty shook his head. "In this part of the country, those are slender talents. I fear all you'll be good for is slop work, washing dishes or cleaning privies and such."

McLendon sighed. "I suppose that's the fate I deserve." He gulped the last of his coffee and pushed back from the table. "Thanks for breakfast. Now I need to commence knocking on doors and find some sort of employment. If I don't find any right away, I suppose I'll be reduced to selling my belongings."

"What you got?" Shorty asked. "We've had steady business and I might be willing to buy."

"There's a fine suit, custom-tailored in St. Louis."

"I doubt it would fit. Besides, I have little occasion to wear a fine suit. What else?"

"A good Navy Colt, only used once. And a book that I'll never sell, for sentimental reasons."

Ike said, "It's gotten too hard to get ammunition for Navy Colts. And even if you wanted to part with the book, you'd find little interest. Not many people in Texas bother with books. That is, if they can even read at all."

"Well, then, I guess I'll find employment here or sleep hungry and on the ground tonight."

Isaac and Shorty exchanged glances.

"Fort Griffin doesn't abound with jobs," the taller brother said. "If you're of a mind, you could come with us to Kansas. Dodge City's a new town and a rough sort of place, but there are jobs of all sorts available. At the very least we could help you catch on with some of the hide men, to work in their camps. When you recover from financial embarrassment, you can go on to California. The train comes through Dodge City, you see."

Anything seemed better to McLendon than being stuck in Fort Griffin, and he thought that Dodge City didn't sound like the kind of place where Killer Boots would come looking for him. "I couldn't pay you for the transportation," he said.

Shorty waved his hand dismissively. "Don't fret about it. We'll be glad of the company, and it won't be the most comfortable journey. We sleep in the wagon beds at night, and beans and biscuits make up the entire menu. Say, I hope you don't mind dogs. Isaac's got this big-ass Newfoundland named Maurice that he treats better than me."

"Because Maurice has got better manners," Isaac said.

"At least I go into the bushes when I feel the need to shit. Anyway, McLendon, you can help with the horses and otherwise make yourself useful. Trip takes about ten days, less we run into Indians and have to scurry to save our hair. Will you join us?"

"I'd be proud to," McLendon said. "And I'm grateful for the chance."

It rained most of the trip, and because of the mud and some flooding they didn't reach Dodge City for eighteen days. McLendon spent almost every day soaked to the skin, and on the one night it didn't rain and they could sit out beside a campfire, the Newfoundland took an unnatural liking to McLendon and kept humping his leg.

"Let loose of McLendon, Maurice," Isaac called as McLendon pried the dog off. Maurice was determined and made several more attempts before he finally retreated under a wagon, where he lay panting and eying McLendon with an unnerving expression of lust.

"I think Maurice loves you," Shorty said.

"The feeling's not mutual," McLendon said. He wanted to rub his leg but thought better of it—Maurice might take it as an invitation. "I'm not fond of dogs anyway. This one eats as much as a man and spooks the horses besides. What use is he to you?"

Isaac lit a clay pipe and puffed contentedly. "Ol' Maurice may have his faults, but I promise you this: If you or anyone raised a hand to Shorty or me, that dog would flat tear your ass off."

"I think he has something in mind for my ass other than tearing it," McLendon said. Later, he tried to wrap up in his blankets as far away from Maurice as he could. Though the dog didn't immediately launch another attack on his leg, McLendon felt certain that it was only a matter of time.

FOUR MONTHS LATER, McLendon lay on his cot in the Olds boardinghouse, brooding as usual about the *if only* regrets in his life. If only he hadn't given up Gabrielle for Ellen Douglass. If only he'd been able to persuade Gabrielle to leave Glorious and come to California with him. If only he hadn't gotten drunk in Fort Griffin and lost all his money to that poker cheat Doc Holliday. Now he was stuck in sorry-ass Dodge City, Kansas, spending his days collecting buffalo bones and his nights anguishing over past mistakes. His life was in ruins and it was his own fault.

McLendon brooded in the dark until Masterson finally stumbled in, rattling on about a whore in Sherman's dance hall who had titties the size of buffalo humps.

"Oh, and Pat Callahan says he spotted Billy Dixon and his winter crew a few days ago just south of the Cimarron," Bat mumbled as he fell onto his cot and pulled the ragged blankets up around his shoulders. "I expect that means Billy's about completed his scout and will be coming back to town anytime. Thrills and excitement are soon to be upon us, C.M."

"Maybe so," McLendon said. Masterson was snoring in seconds. As usual, it took McLendon much longer to fall asleep.

FIVE

Isatai was ready to pronounce the great news to the Quahadi camp: Buffalo Hump was the spirit speaking through him. Though Buffalo Hump had not made his ultimate command for the People quite clear to Isatai yet, that would happen very soon. It was extremely gratifying to Isatai that the greatest of all the People's leaders had chosen him as messenger. Isatai was eager to bask in the additional attention he was bound to receive when he made the announcement.

Quanah insisted that he wait—at least a few days, maybe more. "Everyone needs to be hungry for your words. I'll go about and whisper that the spirits are talking to you again, and you'll deliver their message soon. If everyone has to wait a little longer, they'll be sure to listen better."

"I feel that the spirit of Buffalo Hump wants me to speak now."

"Buffalo Hump and all the other spirits understand the way living people are. Naturally a holy man like you doesn't have the same lowly desires and faults as the rest of us. Our ears need time to get ready to hear. I want to learn Buffalo Hump's message very much; it's hard for me to ask you to wait. Just two days, maybe three."

Isatai was pleased to be referred to as a holy man. "Perhaps you are right. I'll go sit awhile and consider this." A few hours later he informed Quanah that Buffalo Hump did, in fact, want him to wait a little longer.

"I'll stay in camp rather than go out to hunt," Quanah said. "That way, when you tell me the time is right, I can gather everyone to come sit at your feet and drink in your wisdom."

The first hard snow fell that night, and the village awoke to high winds that drove them back into their tipis, where they wrapped themselves up in whatever blankets and fur robes they had and shivered around low fires. They ate sparingly from small stores of food and passed the time wondering when Isatai would next reveal more thoughts of the spirits. Nothing could have suited Quanah better. It would take several days, he thought, for the storm to pass. When it did, when everyone came outside again, when the sense of anticipation was almost unbearable, then it would be time for Isatai to speak.

But on the third morning when the sun came back out and the birds chirped greetings, just before Quanah could gather a crowd and fetch Isatai to address it, the rumble of hoofbeats was heard coming from the southeast. The riders were other Indians; the Quahadis knew this because unshod hooves made a thudding sort of clatter on hard winter ground instead of the clanging of Army steeds with horseshoes.

"It's some Kiowa," a man shouted. "I see Long Branches, Lone Wolf's nephew." Lone Wolf was the chief among those Kiowa who remained off the white man's reservation. Long Branches, named for the astonishing length of his arms and legs, was considered a good fighter by the Comanche—a considerable compliment, since it was understood by everyone that Comanche were the finest fighters of all.

Long Branches and eight other Kiowa men rode into the Quahadi camp and dismounted. They exchanged greetings and asked to speak to the men of the village.

"What's this?" Isatai whined to Quanah, who had just come to the fat man's tipi to tell him that it was finally time to deliver the latest spirit news.

"We have to wait and see," Quanah muttered. He and Isatai joined the crowd gathering around Long Branches and his men.

Long Branches smiled and said, "It's a pleasure to be here among all the great warriors. I have a thought to share. Like you, our people have been cold and hungry. I believe it's time to go out and raid, to bring back horses and maybe guns and blankets and some scalps to decorate our tipis with. I want to do it the old honorable way, riding down among the Mexicans and taking what we please. There are nine of us ready to go. Will any men from this camp join us?"

This was the traditional means of raising a war party from among the People. One warrior developed a plan and invited others to participate. If enough were interested, they rode off with him. If his proposal didn't elicit sufficient interest, he stopped talking about it. Previously it had not been necessary for a man to try to raise a war band outside his own village, but in recent times the various Indian tribes had been so decimated that few camps had sufficient numbers to form complete war parties. Still, Long Branches was taking a chance coming among the Quahadi for recruits. The People were proud of their fighting preeminence. It was understood by the Kiowa and the Cheyenne and the Arapaho that they only lived in the same general vicinity because the People chose to allow it. Any tribes they didn't care to tolerate—the Apaches and the Tonkawa, especially—were driven off to territory that the People didn't want for themselves. It was considered proper for warriors from among the People to come to the Kiowa and the other, lesser tribes to fill out raiding parties, not vice versa.

Long Branches understood this, so his next words were placating.

"I'm here because you are the best fighters of all. With you along, I know the raid will be a success. There must be some men among you who are tired of sitting in the cold. Come and teach us how to fight."

There were murmurs of approval. A half-dozen Quahadi warriors went off to their tipis to fetch their rifles and quivers. Quanah wasn't among them. He remained standing with Isatai in front of the fat man's tipi. Long Branches, scanning his remaining listeners, spotted him there.

"Quanah!" he called out. "Surely you will ride with us. This camp's greatest warrior would enjoy a good fight with the Mexicans."

"This is the wrong way to do it," Quanah said. "You'll have, what, maybe fifteen men? Yes, you may steal some horses, scalp a few Mexicans, but what if you're trapped somewhere? There won't be enough of you to fight your way out, and if you try to run, they'll still get some of you. Even if you get away clean, what is accomplished? A few more horses in your camp won't change anything. The whites will still be coming into our land."

Long Branches didn't want to risk Quanah's wrath. "I honor your words, but I don't agree with them. We need to raid. It's the real joy in life."

"The real joy is in driving away our enemies for good. Wait awhile, maybe a way will be revealed to do that."

"I'm tired of waiting. I want to fight. Who else among the Quahadi feels that way?"

Ultimately, fourteen warriors, almost a fifth of the Quahadi camp's fighting men, rode off with Long Branches and the other eight Kiowa. To Quanah, that was bad enough, but almost as soon as Long Branches' raiding party disappeared over the stark winter horizon, a dozen young men who hadn't gone with him began preparing a war party of their own. Their leader was Cloudy, Quanah's nephew.

"We need you to come with us, Uncle," he told Quanah. "We're not going all the way to Mexico, just down far enough to find some whites to kill. We haven't counted coup for too long." Counting coup was the People's way of measuring the greatest acts of bravery. Warriors came close enough to their enemies to touch them, then whirled away before they could be brought down.

"If you wanted to be in a war party, why didn't you go with Long Branches?" Quanah demanded, sounding and feeling sour. Now, instead of anticipating Isatai's next messages from the spirits, the whole camp was talking about raiding.

"Ah, I'd never ride under the leadership of a Kiowa. Come south with us. It was my idea, but you can lead. We'll bring back many horses and scalps."

"I understand how much a young man like you wants to fight, but you need to think on this. I hear that Bad Hand is lurking just above Mexico. If you encounter him, it will go badly for you." Bad Hand was the name that the People had given to Ranald Mackenzie, a wily Army colonel who had lost several fingers during the Civil War. Quanah himself had survived several fights with Bad Hand and his troops, and even won a few, but they had been near things. Unlike other white officers, Bad Hand tried hard to think like the People and anticipate what they would do next. His troops were guided by crack Indian scouts, Tonkawa and Black Seminole. Once Bad Hand was on your trail, it was hard to shake him, and when he caught you, he was lethal.

"Bad Hand won't know we're near. We'll ride too fast."

Quanah shook his head. "You'd be wise to stay here, just for the present. The spirits have been talking to Isatai again. Soon he'll reveal their plan for the People. I believe that there will be fighting and a lot of it, just in a different way. We'll need you and all our other young men. We can't afford to lose you on foolish raids that accomplish nothing."

"This raid will bring us honor, and spirits talk in their own good time. For all we know, Isatai won't have anything to tell us until we're back with scalps and horses. Maybe some white or Mexican women too. Come with us, Uncle. You know how you love a good fight."

"I can't change your mind? All right, then. Go do what you think you must, but if you see Bad Hand down there, turn and run."

Cloudy grinned. "As you know better than anyone, enemies run from the People. I'll bring you back a fine horse as a gift."

Cloudy's raiding party left the next morning, whooping with anticipation. As soon as they were gone, Quanah went to see Isatai, who was in his tipi fussing with his hair, trying to get the long braids even. Though animal fat was particularly prized during these hard winter months for its nutritional value, Isatai nonetheless rubbed a chunk on the braids to make them shiny.

"I'm about to speak, Quanah. Announce it to the village."

Quanah laid a restraining hand on Isatai's shoulder.

"You need to wait again. All anyone can talk about now are the raiding parties. We need to see what happens to them. Until then, no one is ready to listen to you or the spirits."

Isatai was offended. He drew back his head and regarded Quanah balefully.

"I speak for Buffalo Hump. Of course everyone will listen."

"They won't. They're not wise like you. All they can think about is what's happening now, not what the spirits have to say about the future. You don't want to waste your words, Isatai. People listen best to the spirits when they know that they need them."

"Buffalo Hump commands me to speak."

"Buffalo Hump has chosen you because of your wisdom. If he'd picked someone like me, I'd be foolish and proud and blurt out everything whether or not there were ears ready to hear. You're smarter than that."

"Perhaps," Isatai said grudgingly. "I suppose I should wait until our young men return?"

"You're correct. I trust and accept your judgment. Eager as I am to hear you speak the spirit's words, I'll make myself wait until then."

IN THE DAYS THAT FOLLOWED, Quanah felt torn. As a proud Qua-hadi, he naturally wanted the two war parties to have great success. But if they did, if they returned with many horses and scalps and perhaps some captives, the camp was much less likely to embrace the idea of assembling a single massive fighting force against the whites, even if the spirit of Buffalo Hump urged them to do it. And in that case the time Quanah had invested in Isatai would be wasted. For now, all he could do was wait like everyone else to see what happened to the raiders led by Long Branches and Cloudy. He hoped that Isatai would be able to keep his mouth shut until then.

SIX

Billy Dixon and his scout crew got back to Dodge City a week before Christmas. As with everything else in his life, Billy kept the return low-key. He showed up that night in Jim Hanrahan's saloon and sat quietly in a corner, sipping whiskey for two bits a shot and watching the billiard matches in progress. As always, his red setter bitch Fannie lay by his feet. She was a nervous dog, unlike the rest of the aggressive Dodge pack that roamed the town's dirt streets growling and fighting among themselves. Fannie stuck close to Billy, who often crooned to her in a soft voice that would have invited ridicule for any of the other hide men demonstrating such tenderness. But nobody ever ragged on Billy about it, because for all his quiet ways he was the toughest among them. None of them could have explained precisely why that was common knowledge, but everyone understood it all the same.

Dodge City being a gossipy place, it was soon known that Billy was back and drinking in Hanrahan's. The minute Bat Masterson heard he hustled right over, pausing only to fetch Cash McLendon from their room at the Olds boardinghouse. McLendon didn't want to come. He told Bat that Billy probably just wanted to have a few drinks in peace;

when he was ready, he'd get everyone together and talk about his trip south. But Masterson wouldn't wait.

"The sooner we know Billy's plans, the sooner we can get ourselves right in the middle of them. Haul your ass off that cot, C.M. For all we know, there are fifty others ahead of us, bearding Billy in that saloon and convincing him to take them along when he goes south for his big hunt. We don't hurry, we could lose any chance of places."

"I've told you, I doubt I'll go along with Billy even if I'm invited," McLendon said wearily. "Bat, don't you ever listen to what I'm saying to you?"

"I listen, but I don't credit a lot of what I hear. No man in his right mind would refuse the honor of hunting with Billy Dixon. Now, pull on your boots and we'll be going."

McLendon reached down for the boots. He knew there was no discouraging Bat; his friend would just keep haranguing him until he gave in.

When they got to Hanrahan's, a few others had already joined Billy at his table. They were all hide men, with hair down to their shoulders as a symbol of their profession. Bat's hair was just as long; McLendon's was somewhat shorter because he found long hair too difficult to keep clean.

"Well, looky here," Masterson cried. "We got Heath Lee, Crash Reed, Bermuda Carlyle, Fred Leonard, and Christopher Johnson all in one distinguished group, and who's that stranger among them? Why, can it be the long-absent Mr. Billy Dixon?"

"Sit down, Masterson," Billy said. "And hello, C.M. I hope you're well."

"I am, thank you, and hope you're the same."

"Enough of the social chitchat," Bat said. "What did you find down south, Billy?"

Dixon heaved an exaggerated sigh. "Typical of young Bat Masterson, interrupting when the grown-ups are talking. I pray that he soon grows out of such rude habits." At twenty-four, Billy was only four years older than Bat, but in terms of maturity there was little comparison. Bat huffed to indicate that he was offended, then shut up. The others were content to let Billy choose the time when he'd get to the important subject, and for a time the talk at the table concerned mundane local matters. Another restaurant was about to open, this one featuring French cuisine. The Chinese laundry had started charging a dime a shirt, up from seven cents. The first shipment of the new Colt .45s, popularly known as "Peacemakers," had just reached F. C. Zimmermann's hardware store, and everybody would have to have one. Some of the saloon's women, Tucson Ingrid and Wendy Erica and Hope R. (no further last name known) and Anne Louise, came over to the table to see if any of the gentlemen wanted to dance or maybe something else. Everyone politely declined; they were waiting for Billy to open up about his scout. Bat told the ladies to stay patient: in a while he'd be glad to come and excite them with his company. Heath Lee reached over and lightly smacked the back of Bat's head.

"I'm a gentleman from Virginia and expect white females of every sort to be treated with respect, Masterson," he said. "Mind your tongue around them."

"It's a hard thing to have to watch every word," Bat whined, rubbing the spot where he'd been struck.

"Then try saying fewer of them," Billy suggested. "Well, I suppose Masterson's been patient long enough. I don't want to have too much conversation concerning this yet. The thing of it is, the buffalo really have shifted south in great numbers. We found considerable sign near the Canadian River. I don't doubt hunting down there this summer would far exceed what's left up here. But you all know the problems with that, starting with the Indians."

Everyone nodded. The Cheyenne, the Kiowa, and the Arapaho were ready to annihilate any white hunters who trespassed on what they considered their land—and even so, they were collectively of less concern than the Comanche, who even the most religious among the hide men feared more than Satan himself.

"The son-of-a-bitching treaty favors Indians over white men," Fred Leonard complained. "The Army says we can't go down past the Arkansas, and the Indians come above it all the time. Like a few months back when they got that teenage boy Jacob Dilsey right near here, scalped him and cut off his arms and legs besides. Where was the goddamn Army then?"

"I don't think there's much Army presence along the treaty line anymore," Billy said. "There was no sign of them. I understand most have been pulled out, sent down to South Texas to fight the Indians raiding there. If we mount a large-scale hunt, I don't think the Army will be a problem."

"And it won't," declared a man who walked up to the table.

"Mr. Mooar," said Bermuda Carlyle, putting sarcastic emphasis on "Mr." "Of course you would be coming around, thinking your opinion would be needed or even wanted."

Josiah Wright Mooar was a rangy native of Vermont who found himself in Kansas just as buffalo hides became invaluable as sources of machine belts in the East and in Europe. Outfitting himself with the best guns, horses, and camp crews, he was among the first hide men to decimate the Dodge area herd. In the process he made a lot of money, and the other hide men had to acknowledge both his shooting prowess and business acumen—Mooar was always able to negotiate the best prices for his skins. But he was also given to bragging, and always assumed he was smarter, and better, than the rest. Mooar was the only hide man to consider himself as good a shot as or even a superior marksman to Billy

Dixon. In town he wore gabardine trousers while the other hunters stuck to denim jeans and overalls, and on summer nights in the Dodge City saloons he claimed daily buffalo kill figures that the rest of the hide men felt sure were impossibly high.

Mooar ignored Carlisle and addressed the group as a whole. "I'm certain Billy Dixon here is regaling you with stories of his little trip south," he said, his clipped Yankee accent just as annoying to the men at the table as his condescending tone. "As all of you may know, it lagged behind my own excursion down in that direction. But I'm glad Billy finally found the sand to make the trip and see for himself."

"Billy's got plenty of sand," Bat said angrily, but Dixon held up a hand to silence him.

"J.W., perhaps you can share what you found down there," Billy suggested. "It's certainly possible that you observed things I missed. No man's eyes are infallible."

Mooar signaled the bartender for a drink and pulled up a chair. "Well, there's plenty of buffalo sign. Come late spring, they'll be back along the Canadian, I suspect passing right by that spot where Kit Carson had the big Indian fight ten years back. I forget the name."

"Adobe Walls," Carlyle said. "Called that on account of some of the structures built there by traders. Carson's party barely escaped with their hair."

"Yes, Adobe Walls. The buffs will come through that area. Anyone waiting who has a good eye with a gun and sufficient crews to skin all day will make a fortune."

"That's if the Indians don't get him or the Army don't run him off," observed Heath Lee.

Mooar smiled indulgently. He took a clay pipe from his pocket, tamped in tobacco, and lit his smoke with a match that he struck smartly against the heel of his boot. "Yes, of course, always the Indians. But a smart man can avoid them, and a well-armed man with steady aim can fight them off if needed. They're scattered down there and hungry, no real danger if you stay prepared and alert. And as for the Army, well, I have it on good account that the Army is no longer interested in discouraging white hunters from roaming south of the Arkansas."

"I'd be interested in knowing what you mean by 'good account,'" Billy said. Coming from Mooar, the statement would have sounded like, and been intended as, an insult, but Billy managed to keep his voice neutral. He just seemed curious.

Mooar tossed back his whiskey and gestured for a refill. The bartender rushed over to serve him and was rewarded with a few extra coins.

"Well, young Billy, when I got back, instead of coming straight to a saloon, I paid a visit to Fort Dodge, called on the commanding officer there. I was straight with him, as I always am to everyone. Told him that I knew white hunting was forbidden below the Arkansas, but it was time to be practical, the buffs being virtually vanished from around Dodge. 'Sir,' I said, 'I've just been down all the way to the Canadian River and there's plentiful buffalo sign. Now, we all know that treaty was wrong from the start, all favoring the Indians and so forth. I'm a hide man who wants to make a good living. In my place, what would you do?'" Mooar paused and sipped his drink. He knew someone would soon break the silence.

It was Bat Masterson. "And what was the response?"

"Ah," Mooar said dramatically. "The commanding officer, he said to me, 'Mr. Mooar, if I was hunting buffalo, I would go to where the buffalo are.' Can't get clearer permission than that."

"What he said to you fits with what I've heard," Billy said. "Army's got limited numbers, and they've moved most of them down to the Mexican border. Mackenzie's supposedly leading them."

"I'm gratified that you're trying to keep current. So what about it,

Dixon? In the spring I intend to put together a small, top-notch crew and find my way down by the Canadian, there to shoot record numbers of buffs and enrich myself considerably. Care to hire on? There's always plenty of room for another skinner, though since you're almost as handy with á Sharps as your friends claim, I might bring you along as my backup shooter."

Everyone else at the table stiffened except Billy, who smiled.

"I appreciate the offer, J.W. I've got a lot to ponder before spring, and as I put together my plans, I may well consult you."

"You do that." Mooar nodded to the group, wandered over and whispered to the bartender, then sauntered out of the saloon.

As soon as Mooar disappeared through the swinging doors, Crash Reed blurted, "I can't stand that Yankee bastard. Billy, you ought to have coldcocked him for speaking to you so."

"It's true Mooar's a bastard and a Yankee to boot, but it's also fact that he's a damn fine shot and the best hide-price bargainer among us," Billy said. "Whatever I decide to do, I may need him to be part of, though I doubt the possibilities include one of us being employed by the other. Say, what's this?"

The bartender placed a full bottle of Old Crow bourbon on the table. "Compliments of Mr. J. W. Mooar."

"Now, isn't that a fine thing?" Billy asked. "Let's break the seal." He took the bottle and poured generous drinks for everyone. "It's impossible to detest a man while you're drinking gift whiskey from him."

"Then I'll toss this down fast so I can get back to hating him," Masterson said, and everyone had a good laugh.

They sipped the bourbon appreciatively; it was much smoother than the bar label whiskey they'd previously been drinking. Then Carlyle asked, "Billy, ain't you worried that Mooar will get down there and shoot up all the buffs before any of the rest of us get a crack at them?"

"I'm not, because the sign I saw indicated a herd just as sizable as the ones we used to have up here. Mooar or any other single shooter would need twenty years to make even a tiny dent in it. No, I'm trying to figure how to slim the risk to being down there this coming spring and summer. J.W.'s right with what the fort commander told him. The Army's no longer a consideration. But the Indians could be, especially the Comanche. We go down in the usual way, small groups of six or ten, and half of us won't ever get back. Those Indians will be aware of who's in their land, how many, and where. They'll set ambushes and make sneak attacks and pick us off a few at a time. It wouldn't take that many of them to do it."

"Then you might not go?" Bat protested.

"I want to go, and mean to. But maybe not in the usual way. A lot of hide men are gone from Dodge for the winter. I want to wait on all this until most everybody's back and I can get a sort of general temperature."

"To what end?" McLendon asked. Around the hide men he usually said as little as possible, because he felt he had so little in common with them. But Billy clearly had at least the beginning of a plan in mind, and McLendon's respect for Dixon was such that he was genuinely curious.

Billy furrowed his brow and rubbed his mustache with his thumb. "What I'm thinking is, maybe we need to do this different. Us hide men, we're friendly to each other at night in town, but in the summer daylight we're out there trying to outwit each other, get the best shooting angles, and try to kill all the buffs for ourselves. We do that kind of competing in Comanche country and we're dead men. Six of us in a party, hell, any three or four Comanche braves could take us by surprise and carve us up proper. No, don't argue. In any kind of even numbers, they're the better fighters. But if maybe fifty or a hundred of us went in on the journey down and then out on the hunt together, that might do it. You know how the Comanche and the other Indians never have big war parties—maybe twenty, twenty-five at the most. We put together a big enough group, build us a substantial camp down the Canadian way that we could defend if need be, no twenty Kiowa or Cheyenne or even Comanche could get at us there. They'll be watching us every step of the way and they'll know it would be useless to try. Don't forget, those Indians ain't just good fighters, they're smart."

"You give 'em too much credit," Reed said. "They're little more than animals."

"Well, then, they're smart animals, and we need to be wiser than they are," Dixon said. "All right, boys, that's enough meaningful conversation for one evening. Let's drink up J. W. Mooar's fine bourbon whiskey and then see if some of the ladies in the room care for a dance."

When most of the others were whooping and dancing, McLendon managed to whisper to Dixon, "Your plan makes sense, Billy. Safety in numbers. It's good thinking."

"Don't worry, McLendon. You're inexperienced, but I feel like you're a good man. If I put all this together, I'll include you in the party."

McLendon managed not to laugh. "You misunderstand me. I don't believe I'd want to risk my life in Comanche country for all the buffalo hides south of the Arkansas. I just think you've got an idea that might work. And please, if you do this, let Bat come along. It'd break his heart if you didn't."

Billy looked over at Bat, who was whirling on the dance floor with Anne Louise, the most striking of the girls working at Hanrahan's.

"Hell, I won't be able to keep the mouthy little peckerwood away. I just hope that by then he can shoot as good as he talks."

SEVEN

It was almost two moon cycles before word reached the Quahadi camp about the raiders' fates. The interim was a frustrating time. Besides waiting for the warriors to return, the villagers had very little food and were sometimes reduced to shooting down birds. They only did this when there was real danger of starving.

Then, on two different nights, horses were stolen from their herds. The theft alone was an insufferable insult—the People stole horses, not the other way around—but the shame was compounded when the young boys charged with guarding the herd admitted that the thieves were white men who brazenly cut some of the finest animals away from the rest and drove them away. The Quahadi youngsters were caught completely off guard. Quanah and the rest of the warriors remaining in camp up-braided the boys severely, then took turns guarding the herd themselves. It was considered a menial task, much beneath the dignity of grown men, but the People measured not only their wealth but their power on the number of horses they possessed, and so, for pride's sake, the Quahadi could not tolerate further theft.

Then came the first news of the raids, and the horror of it eclipsed the loss of a few dozen horses.

.   .   .

JUST AFTER DAWN on the coldest morning in camp memory, four of the warriors who'd gone raiding in Mexico with the Kiowa staggered into sight. Three were on foot; the fourth was lashed to the back of a horse that was in just as bad condition as its near-unconscious rider.

The villagers rushed out to help them into camp. Even the three on foot had terrible wounds. They were brought out of the biting wind into a tipi, wrapped in the warmest robes available, and offered the last bites of remaining food. Quanah and a few other senior men asked what had happened to them and what had become of the other Quahadi in their party.

"Dead, all dead," moaned Wide Feather, the most coherent of the wounded men. "Bad Hand's soldiers caught us."

"That can't be," said Bull Bear, an older warrior who'd remained in camp. He was well known for admiring himself and finding fault with everyone else. "Fourteen left with Long Branches and the Kiowa. Bad Hand is clever, but not enough to kill all but four of you."

"All dead," Wide Feather repeated. Shuddering under the robes, choking down gulps of thin hot soup, he told the story.

It had been a good raid—in fact, one of the finest in recent memory. For a Kiowa, Long Branches was a good leader. They made their way down to Mexico completely unimpeded and, once there, pounced on several small villages, raping and killing the women, torturing the men to death, scalping all of them, and gathering up many horses. They thought about bringing some of the Mexican children back to the Quahadi camp, but since food was so scarce even for those already living there, they decided not to add more hungry mouths and slaughtered the Mexican tots instead. This was life worthy of men: conquering enemies, doing what they pleased to them, and then leaving with their hair and horses. Not one Quahadi or even one of the lesser Kiowa suffered so much as a scratch. They sang victory songs as they drove their hoofed booty back north.

But back in Texas, while the triumphant raiders stopped to water their stolen stock at some freshwater springs, Bad Hand's cavalry was suddenly on them, Wide Feather had no idea how they were able to manage such surprise. Several Quahadi and Kiowa fell in the first volley of shots, and of course the remaining Kiowa ran away. Wide Feather emphasized that the surviving Quahadi did not. It was understood among all of the People that their wounded fighters were not to be left for the enemy. They must be picked up and carried away, or at least defended by survivors to the point of their own deaths.

"So why are you four here?" Quanah demanded.

He and the other three were cut off behind a band of trees, Wide Feather explained. They'd lost their guns in the fight and had only their lances and knives. Still, they were prepared to make a counterattack to rescue their fellow Quahadi who were wounded and down, when Bad Hand's soldiers spotted them and fired a volley that drove them back several hundred yards farther. All four were hit, hurt so badly that they were barely able to lose themselves in the tall grass.

"From there, we could only watch what happened," Wide Feather said.

Bad Hand's soldiers were assisted as usual by Tonkawa scouts. The Tonkawa hated the People for being superior and driving them away when they wanted their land. For several generations the People dominated the Tonkawa, taking their horses and their women whenever they wished, and now in response the Tonkawa men were glad to serve Bad Hand. The only great Tonkawa attribute was the ability to track: they could tell from a single bent blade of grass not only how many of the People passed by but their walking speed, their individual weights, and even the condition of their horses. Otherwise, they were the least of humans, all of them weak-limbed and cowardly, and that worst thing of all. The Tonkawa were cannibals.

"And so it happened while we four watched from the high grass beyond the trees," Wide Feather said. "It was terrible, but we could not look away."

As the white soldiers stood idly by, the Tonkawa descended on the fallen Quahadi and Kiowa by the freshwater springs, killing those still alive by slashing their throats. Then they used their knives to cut the livers out of the victims' bodies, roasted the livers over a fire, and ate their disgusting fill. Quanah and the other village men were nauseated by Wide Feather's description.

"I think they saved Long Branches' liver for last," Wide Feather said. "Somehow they guessed that he was the leader."

"The ignorant Tonkawa think that they gain other men's powers by eating their flesh," Bull Bear grunted. "There is much celebration in Tonkawa camps now. They ate livers of the People and now they'll believe they are as great as we are. When our other raiders get back and the weather is better, we Quahadi need to go find them and prove that they're not."

There was general assent, though the loss of ten men severely reduced the Quahadi fighting strength. Everyone waited now for Cloudy and his men to return, no one more than Isatai, who was still eager to announce that the spirit of Buffalo Hump was back in communication with him.

"I think Buffalo Hump's spirit may have allowed the Tonkawa feast because he is angry I'm waiting so long to announce his presence," Isatai told Quanah. "Spirits are very impatient."

"You and Buffalo Hump need to wait like the rest of us," Quanah snapped. He tried his best to tolerate Isatai's prattling, but he was growing increasingly concerned about his nephew Cloudy. If that raid had failed, too—if more camp warriors were lost—maybe the remaining villagers would talk about giving up and taking the white man's road, which is how the People referred to the act of surrendering to live on a reservation.

"Buffalo Hump's spirit won't wait much longer," Isatai warned.

SOON AFTERWARD, the remnants of Cloudy's ten-man raiding party straggled home. Their news wasn't as bad as Wide Feathers', but it was close. Like the Kiowa band led by Long Branches, they'd enjoyed initial success. They'd attacked small ranches in Texas instead of tiny villages in Mexico, but with similar results. Their male victims were tortured to death, their female victims raped and then killed, and all children were slaughtered in deference to the hungry times back at the Quahadi camp. They took some horses, began their return journey, and ran into a substantial white cavalry patrol. The running fight lasted for several days. At times it seemed that the Quahadi might escape. A few were wounded, but none so badly that it was necessary to stand and fight. However, the white soldiers were persistent, and they were being helped by Black Seminole scouts. These men, the products of interbreeding between the Seminole Indians and escaped black slaves who lived among them, weren't cannibals like the Tonkawa but far superior fighters and ever better trackers. Every trick Cloudy and his men tried to conceal their trail was thwarted. Finally they were cornered near the river whites called the Brazos, and though they fought bravely the guns used by the white soldiers and Black Seminoles were better. Cloudy and two others fell down dead; there was no sense in trying to retrieve their bodies. The remaining seven Quahadis ran for it, leaving behind the horses they'd stolen. They felt no disgrace—the raid had been conducted in the honored, traditional way, and they had fought bravely. None of their fallen comrades had been eaten. But, in light of the ten men killed in the earlier raid, an additional three dead Quahadi warriors meant a staggering loss to the camp.

There was much mourning, loud wails from mothers and widows especially. As Quanah feared, some of the villagers, especially the older ones, began talking about going into the reservation. It would be humiliating, but at least everyone left would survive if, for a change, the whites kept their promises and delivered the food promised to reservation Indians. The younger members of the camp, especially the men, would hear nothing of it. They burned to avenge their lost tribesmen on the Tonkawa who'd feasted on their livers. They envisioned a spring raid, when maybe thirty or even forty of the remaining Quahadi men could descend on Tonkawa camps in Texas and butcher everyone living in them.

Only Quanah and Isatai remained apart from the frantic discussions. They spent most of the days roaming on hunts, finding very little game to kill, or else huddled under robes in Isatai's tipi. Quanah avoided his own tipi, because Wickeah couldn't understand why her brave, important husband was keeping to himself at such a critical time. She told him that he had to be a leader, and he told her to be quiet. For a change, she ignored his command and continued to nag, until he had no choice but to get away from her. Any other Quahadi warrior would have soundly beaten a wife who acted so rude, but Quanah never struck Wickeah because he loved her too much.

It was several days after the disastrous news from the raids before Quanah finally told Isatai that it was time.

"I THINK EVERYONE is ready to listen now," he said. "There's much argument and confusion in the camp. Things have never seemed so desperate. We need the guidance of Buffalo Hump's spirit—spoken in your voice, of course."

Lately Isatai had been caught up in confusion himself. Quanah's attitude toward him had become unpredictable. Often he was still the good, humorous friend who understood and respected the great responsibility placed on the fat man by the spirits, but sometimes Quanah was almost as condescending as he'd been before the spirits began speaking through Isatai.

Isatai badly wanted Quanah to continue liking him—with all the bad news about the raids and uncertainty of what the villagers should do next, Isatai's spirit contacts seemed to be forgotten by everyone else. Nobody asked him what the spirits thought that they should do. If anything, Quanah had kept him so far away from everyone else that they might not have been able to find him to ask even if they remembered to.

But now Quanah said that it was time. In the morning he would call everyone together and announce that Isatai and the spirits wished to address them. But first, Quanah wanted to spend the night with Isatai in his tipi, discussing exactly what they spirits would say. Did Isatai still know that he was the vessel of Buffalo Hump? Did he truly feel sure of this, and in the morning would he say so? And why, Quanah wondered, had Isatai decided that it was Buffalo Hump whose spirit called him? Could it be that Buffalo Hump wanted the People to remember his great raid when the whites were driven into the sea? Had Buffalo Hump's spirit reminded Isatai of how all the camps of the People united in a time of desperate trouble, and then reached out to other tribes to join them, until finally they numbered four hundred fighters, maybe five hundred, so many that they were able to sweep the whites before them?

Isatai thought so. He wasn't entirely certain. "Maybe you ought to leave me alone to sleep awhile. Then Buffalo Hump's spirit can blow into me and I'll understand him better."

"What you need besides sleep is something to drink," Quanah said. He produced a bottle of whiskey, the kind the People sometimes acquired from white traders. "Here, have some."

Isatai rarely drank whiskey because he usually had nothing of value to trade. He grasped the bottle and took several gulps, choking as the liquor burned his throat. Quanah thumped him on the back and retrieved the bottle.

"And now sleep," he urged. "When Buffalo Hump's spirit comes, perhaps you might ask if he put it in Long Branches's and Cloudy's minds to make these bad raids happen as a lesson, a way to show us that the old ways of small war parties won't work anymore."

"I'll try," Isatai said. "Can I have some more from that bottle?"

Quanah generously let him drink all he wanted, and then stayed beside him as Isatai passed out.

While Isatai snored, Quanah sat in the fat man's tipi and thought about what might happen in the morning. There was some whiskey left in the bottle but he didn't drink it. That would have felt like celebrating something that made him feel ashamed. Of course, he knew that no spirits, let alone that of Buffalo Hump, were communicating through foolish, trusting Isatai. Quanah was tricking the fat man into saying what he wanted, and it was cruel. In fact, he was using trickery—all right, *lies*— to make the People do something they otherwise never would. But he had to. He'd already tried being honest, using logic. No one would listen, so this was the only way.

Quanah understood what the other People would not accept: if they failed to change, if they didn't attempt something daring and different, they were doomed. There were too many white men and too few of the People. It was impossible to kill all the whites, and when the People lost even one man they were greatly weakened. In Quanah's youth, counting everyone in all their camps, the People numbered twenty thousand or more. Now there were less than four thousand.

The traditional small raiding parties were not suited for present circumstances. Yes, there had been great times, but now more and more whites encroached. If nothing changed, the People would fight in the usual ways and soon be snuffed out, or else give up and live on reservations, where they would be cheated out of rations by greedy agents. In either instance Quanah would stay with his beloved Quahadi and share their inevitable end, dying in useless battle or starving under the white man's rule. But he believed there was still a way to avoid those fates.

If the People, joined by the Kiowa and Cheyenne and Arapaho, gathered all their remaining forces, they could strike the whites in some memorable way that would convince their foes to let them alone, leave them in peace. Then the soldiers could do what they were supposed to: protect the territory promised to the Indians, in particular keeping out the white hunters. This is what Quanah had urged during his recent visits to other camps of the People. No one listened, because he was half white and because they were still too wedded to the old ways. But maybe Buffalo Hump's spirit, speaking through Isatai, could persuade them. And if it did, if the People truly joined together with their allied tribes, then it was a matter of selecting the right target—a fort, perhaps, or one of the bigger white villages like the one just above the Arkansas River where so many of the buffalo hunters gathered. Dodge City, they called it. Leaving the place burning, with mutilated bodies strewn everywhere, might accomplish what was needed. Not long ago, some Cheyenne hungry enough to hunt elk above the treaty river came upon a teenage white boy not far outside Dodge and tortured him to death. No whites from the village heard his screams and came to save him. Apparently the people there believed they were safe from attack and so didn't keep careful watch. It was something for Quanah to think on.

But first he had to gain support not only among the Quahadi but in all the other camps of the People. For that, he needed fat, stupid Isatai. It was a sad thing to take advantage of a fool, and Quanah regretted doing it. But Isatai was the necessary tool at hand and so Quanah would make use of him. In the morning his great plan would either finally take root or else fail completely. Maybe it really was up to the spirits to decide.

EIGHT

In December, McLendon found a project to keep himself busy during the evenings when he didn't feel like staying in his boarding-house room to read and brood. Stephen Geest, an itinerant preacher who traveled around western Kansas, asked for volunteers to build a small Dodge City church in an abandoned building off Front Street to be called Union Church. The building had originally been a saloon, one of the few that went out of business for lack of customers, and only because its proprietor had been caught spiking his barrels of cheap whiskey with snake heads. McLendon was himself a nonbeliever, but he felt that if ever a town needed a church, it was Dodge. Anything that might even marginally stem the constant violence was welcome, so far as he was concerned.

So he joined Geest and a dozen others when they gathered after dinner on the reconstruction project. It was an interesting mix of volunteers—Don and Darlene Burgess, who ran one of the smaller Dodge dry goods shops; buffalo hunter Henry Raymond; Rebecca Travis, a cook at the Dodge House hotel; Hannah Olds, McLendon's landlady; a few working girls from various bawdy houses; and, to McLendon's surprise, a small selection of Dodge City's leading citizens. Druggist Herman Fringer had been a key member of the group organizing county government. Jim Hanrahan, a member of the state legislature, sometimes hired McLendon to do odd jobs around his saloon and billiard parlor, and Fred Zimmermann sold the ubiquitous buffalo hunters most of their guns and ammunition. He and Hanrahan disliked each other, mostly because of Zimmermann's outspoken opposition to any form of alcohol consumption and gambling. But they both favored Christ, and worked amicably together carving and fitting the wood slabs that would form the church altar. McLendon, whose carpentry skills were considerably less advanced, helped the whores pass out tools as needed and occasionally pounded nails. It was a pleasant change to be among company other than Bat, who talked constantly but almost always about the same subjects: getting rich, getting drunk, or dallying with pretty women. Sometimes, if McLendon happened to be working alongside Fringer or Zimmermann, he could even enjoy listening to them converse about non-Dodge topics, often the political scandals in Washington, where the administration of President Grant was apparently awash in corruption. Fringer believed that much was being made of nothing: "All politicians take at least a little." Zimmermann wanted trials and lengthy prison sentences for everyone, up to and including Grant himself: "Even the most powerful men must respect the law."

"That's not been my experience, Mr. Zimmermann," McLendon said, thinking of the days back in St. Louis when he passed around political bribe money on behalf of his influential father-in-law. "The more power men have, the less they think that the law in any way affects or restricts them."

"You're cynical for one still so young, Mr. McLendon," Zimmermann replied. In Dodge City, as in most frontier towns, adult men of limited acquaintance or different social levels addressed each other formally. Zimmermann owned and operated one of Dodge's most successful businesses. McLendon picked up buffalo bones. "I fear you've spent too much time in the company of scoundrels."

"Well, that's inevitable, because at present I reside in Dodge City," McLendon said, and everyone laughed. As always, he was careful not to say anything specific about his past. He'd made that mistake eighteen months earlier in Glorious, and it almost cost him his life.

Everyone sawed and hammered away for an hour until Geest called a work break. They gathered around a kerosene heater to warm their hands and sip hot cider passed around by Rebecca Travis. McLendon liked Rebecca, a middle-aged women with thick, dark hair who was as unwilling to talk about her past as he was. They had a running joke about her marriage prospects. Dodge City's population was overwhelmingly male, and McLendon teased that Rebecca could surely find a man willing to marry her. But when he'd tell her that, with so many single men around, the odds were good, she'd roll her eyes and reply, "Maybe the odds are good, but around here the goods are odd."

While the volunteers drank their cider, Preacher Geest described the wonders Jesus would work in the new Dodge City church. Geest, a thickset, clean-shaven young man, was very earnest in his efforts on behalf of the Lord. He had to be: it was a hard life going from one Kansas town to another, extolling the sinless life preferred by God to the drinking, gambling, brawling, and whoring that sustained most men on the frontier. But he didn't assume the role of judge; one reason McLendon continued to volunteer was because Geest welcomed the participation of Dodge City whores, telling them how much God loved them.

Now, as Geest described the wonders of the first service to be held in the new church—he had hopes the rebuilding process would be finished in a few more weeks—Henry Raymond, the grizzled buffalo hunter, had a question: "Preacher, you going to let any Jews in here?"

"Of course, if they want to come. God's house will be open to anyone."

Raymond spat some tobacco juice. "Jews don't believe in God, do they?"

Geest pursed his lips. "Mr. Raymond, I think that they do, just not in the Christian way."

"Well, ain't this intended as a Christian church?"

"There are many different ways of coming to God, Mr. Raymond. I would hope that our Jewish friends will come here and be persuaded to the Christian faith. But if not, at least they will also praise God. We need a great fellowship of all believers to beat back the forces of Satan. Don't you agree?"

Raymond shrugged. "Hell if I know. I'm just here to drink this lady's cider." He winked at Rebecca, who whispered to McLendon, "See what I mean about the goods being odd?" But when the break was over, McLendon noticed that she and Raymond worked together on sanding long boards for the benches of pews. He hoped that maybe they'd enjoy a romance. His own broken heart didn't prevent him from wishing happiness for others.

Preacher Geest called a halt around eleven p.m. Everyone gathered around as he said a prayer, asking God to keep particular watch over those helping to build the new church. As the volunteers filtered out, Jim Hanrahan whispered to McLendon, "A few of us are going over to Herman Fringer's house for coffee. Come along."

"Not to your place for a drink?"

"Ah, Fred Zimmermann's involved, and he won't set foot in a saloon. So join us. It might get interesting."

DESPITE THE TOWN'S general seediness, there were a few nice homes in Dodge City, all of them built on a hill well above the saloons and whorehouses near the railroad. Herman Fringer, whose drugstore on Front Street was an anchor of town business, had every intention of staying and prospering as Dodge grew. His two-story home reflected this. It was built of the finest wood, with planks brought in by wagon from Wichita. The furnishings were expensive and comfortable; a fire blazed in the front sitting room lit by elegant oil lamps, not the clunky kerosene burners found almost everywhere else in town. Mrs. Fringer, in an elegant dress, greeted her husband and his guests—Hanrahan, Zimmermann, and McLendon—ushering them in and serving coffee in delicate china cups. McLendon hadn't experienced such luxury since fleeing his father-in-law's mansion in St. Louis. It felt odd to once again settle back in a well-upholstered chair and to take real cream and a spoonful of finely granulated sugar in his coffee.

Fringer passed around cigars, sipped some coffee, and sighed with satisfaction. "It's a good thing we're doing, getting this church built. Town needs churches. This little bitty one's just the start. Got to have a solid religious community to attract the investors."

"So they'll see we're not all saloons and whorehouses," Zimmermann agreed. "I long for the day we'll be a civilized place. But it's coming, it's coming. No thanks to you and your ilk, Hanrahan."

Hanrahan chuckled. "Fred, without people like me serving up drinks and girls to dance with—"

"*Dance,*" Zimmermann scoffed.

"Yes, dance, and whatever else. Most men here don't have wives waiting to warm their beds at night. Anyway, it's attractions such as I offer that keep the hide hunters stopping in town at night, and while they're here, that's when they buy their guns from you and their powders and tonics from Herman. We had to start somewhere. And now, with the buffalo scarce, we've got the next step to take. Herman, what are you hearing on that?"

Fringer, a neat-looking man with fleshy cheeks and a double chin, puffed thoughtfully on his cigar.

"Word is, the state legislature's moving the tick line west again by fall. And that means it's going to be Dodge's turn."

Zimmermann grunted with delight, and Hanrahan whispered to McLendon, "You know what the tick line is, right?"

Like virtually everyone else in Kansas, McLendon did. The tick line was critical to the burgeoning cattle industry. Shortly after the end of the Civil War, Texas cattlemen began driving their herds north to Kansas, where the animals could be shipped to Eastern slaughterhouses by rail. It was an economic bonanza for Abilene, the Kansas town where the cattle drives ended. But the Texas cattle soon proved to be infested with ticks whose bite caused Kansas cattle to sicken and die, while the Texas beeves were impervious to the toxin. To keep Kansas animals free of ticks, the legislature began moving a "tick line" gradually west, keeping the ticks away from the majority of Kansas cattle. Texas cattle could not be driven into Kansas east of the line. After Abilene, Ellsworth became the designated cattle town, and when the Texas ticks grew too numerous there, the line moved west again to Wichita. Now, if Fringer's sources were correct—and, given his political connections, they undoubtedly were—Dodge would be the next logical cattle drive town.

"It's perfect timing," Fringer said. "The buffalo go and the cattle come. End of one era for Dodge, the beginning of another."

"I won't be sorry to see those rowdy hide men go," Zimmermann said. "Drunk and carousing, nasty and brawling, good riddance."

"You liked taking their money well enough," McLendon said. He felt offended on behalf of Masterson and his other friends among the hide men.

Zimmermann arched an eyebrow and glanced at Hanrahan, who said, "I have Cash McLendon here with me because I think he's the kind of man we'll need in the days ahead. Good head for business, I believe. He's going to start work for me full-time in the spring, so when they announce the tick line move and I expand my business interests, he'll be in place to help me run my operations."

This was news to McLendon. "Really?"

Hanrahan shushed him. "Thing is, Fred, you've got to accept that we'll be replacing one form of public nuisance with another. You think these hide men are bad, wait 'til you encounter Texas drovers. They'll roar into town, collect their pay from the drives, and set out to spend every cent getting drunk, laid, and loud. Of course, as McLendon points out, we'll all be glad to take their money. And the good thing about the Texans: they'll spend every cent they got and leave town, head home, and instantly be replaced by the next bunch. We'll just need to get the town incorporated, hire some good, tough lawmen."

"That's the key," Fringer agreed. "A sheriff and some deputies to keep things under control. Once the tick line shifts here, we'll get this town set up legally with the state. Hide men, Texans, it doesn't matter, just so long as they spend their money. And as they do, we'll build churches and a school—hell, even have a real cemetery instead of Boot Hill. We'll keep all the rowdiness down below Front Street, and decent people can live up here on the hill. It'll work."

Zimmermann snuffed out his cigar in a fine painted ashtray. It was a costly cigar, and he'd barely smoked a third of it. Mrs. Fringer returned to freshen everyone's coffee. When she swept out in a whirl of bustle and lace, Zimmermann said thoughtfully, "But what about the hide men? If they stay around, and all the Texans come, that doubles our problems."

"Some of the hide men are fine people," McLendon said.

"Even so," Zimmermann said dismissively. He clearly considered McLendon to be both insolent and insignificant. "Herman, another cigar?"

Fringer handed over a cigar and offered a light. "Well, Fred, I don't think you have much to worry about. As I understand it, come spring, young Billy Dixon plans to lead all the hide men south to hunt what's left of the herd down there. Those hunters need hides, and if there are none to be had here, then they'll follow the buffalo."

"Don't dismiss them from sight and mind too quickly, Herman," Hanrahan said. "We've got some prominent people in town who've made their fortunes buying the hides from the hunters, then shipping and selling them back east. Charlie Rath, those folks. If Billy and the hide men hunt to the far south, they'll still have to sell the hides somewhere. Maybe freight them back here by wagon."

"As though the Indians will let them," Zimmermann said. "As soon as they're anywhere near the Canadian, the Comanche will have their hair. Well, no great loss. Texans buy hardware and guns too."

McLendon was pleased to see Hanrahan bristle. "Yes, Fred, you'll continue to make your pile."

"As will you. The Texans will get drunk in your saloon and sleep with your whores."

Fringer said soothingly, "Let's not get our backs up with each other. What we want is what's best for Dodge. What I'm thinking is, let's soon put together a schedule to get the town incorporated, get a tax plan in place so we can raise money to hire lawmen and a schoolteacher. Prepare for progress. Now, who wants to follow up this coffee with some really fine brandy?"

. . .

AFTERWARD, HANRAHAN ASKED McLendon to walk with him back to his saloon. "Let's top off the evening with a beer." Because it was so loud in the main room of the saloon, they took their brimming mugs back to Hanrahan's small office. He gestured for McLendon to take a seat—the chair, though comfortable, wasn't overstuffed like the one in Herman Fringer's sitting room—and took a long sip of beer.

"If you're going to make your way up in the world, you need to mind your tone a bit around the men who can be of some assistance to you," Hanrahan said. "The way you talked to Fred Zimmermann, why, I half expected Herman Fringer would ask you to leave his house."

"I know." McLendon set his beer mug on the corner of Hanrahan's desk. He'd already had brandy at Fringer's, and since the drunken debacle with Doc Holliday in Fort Griffin he'd made it a rule to stop after one drink. He'd only accepted the beer from Hanrahan to be polite. "And it's usually my way to get along with everybody if I can. It was just how Zimmermann talked about Billy and the hide men. Without them, he'd be just another German peddler."

Hanrahan nodded. "But what you need to remember is, the hide men are to Fred what the buffalo are to the hide men: the means to make his living. And he and Herman are right—the buffalo are mostly gone from around here, which means at some point soon the hide men will be too. It's good luck that we're in the right place to change over from a buffalo to a cow town."

"But back at Fringer's, you talked about Billy and the boys hunting to the south, then bringing the hides back here to sell. That'll keep Dodge in the hide business."

Hanrahan drank more beer. An intelligent-looking gray-haired man with deep-set eyes, he had a way of staring up at the ceiling or over a companion's shoulder as he talked. Now he contemplated his dripping mug and mused, "I was being optimistic. Even if Billy does go down south come spring and the buffalo are really there in sufficient number, it's still a long shot that it'll be worth his while. There's just so much risk."

"From the Indians, you mean."

"No, not really. I think the Indians are mostly done for. They're scattered and starving, Comanche and Kiowa and Cheyenne alike. When they do try to ride out and raid, Mackenzie's got his cavalry all over them. From what I've heard, war parties just got whipped twice down Texas and Mexico way. Bill Martin and his boys have been south raiding Comanche horse herds, and Bill says that the Co-manch couldn't do a damned thing about it. He's going after Cheyenne horses next. No, if Billy Dixon puts together a large enough crew—fifty or sixty men, let's say—I doubt that the Indians will be a factor. It's the logistics that could do him in."

Hanrahan explained that the hide men required "quick turnaround" on their hides. "The way it's been, they've set up in camps mostly a day's ride or less from Dodge. They kill their buffs, get their skins, dry them for a bit, load 'em on wagons, and sell them in town right away. Then they use that money to pay their crews and buy their food and ammunition. Down south by the Canadian, they're, what, a hundred twenty or a hundred fifty miles from Dodge, the closest hide market. How do they get those hides back here? It'll take a week by wagon at least. And meanwhile, what do they do for bullets? If their horses throw shoes, how do they get them reshod? Hell, what do they do at night when they want a drink? No, any attempt to establish a base camp down there will be a near-insurmountable challenge, and the Indians are the least of it."

"Will you advise Billy not to go?"

"On the contrary, if he'll have me, I'm going to go with him."

That caught McLendon by surprise. "You? Why? You've already got everything you want. The saloon, plenty of money, and, hell, you're even a member of the state legislature. You could be Kansas governor someday. Why would you want to go out and live rough in Indian country?"

"That's it exactly. You know, I came out here from Pennsylvania because I wanted some adventure. And I got it, and I enjoyed it. Did my share of hunting, had some business dealings, and made my share, got into politics a little. Me and Mose Waters opened this place in Dodge and it's done well. Many of those cowmen from Texas will surely take their nightly pleasures here. But I've got the urge to go out and start over. That's why I thought of you. Say, I hope you don't mind my just assuming you'd come work for me."

"Not at all," McLendon said. "It's nice to have someone looking out for my best interests."

"In this case, I'm looking out for mine too. I head south with Billy and the boys, you stay here and keep track of how Mose is doing, keep in touch with me about that."

McLendon said warily, "Are you asking me to be a stooge? A spy?" He'd heard that request before from other rich men and once, to his eternal regret, he'd agreed.

Hanrahan shook his head. "No, not at all. Mose is my partner and also my friend. It's just that he's not always a good organizer. It's true that I take my investments seriously. My goal is profit. But I do nothing underhanded. Look, I know you hate picking around for buffalo bones. I don't need to know anything about your past to know that you're above that. Helping run a respectable saloon and billiard hall—and despite Fred Zimmermann's slurs, it's respectable—will get you up on a better path. Just help Mose in whatever ways that you can."

"I'm relieved to hear what you require. But honesty compels me to say that I don't intend to linger in Dodge City any longer than necessary. I just want to make enough money to get myself off to California and take my chances there. I guess what I mean to say is, I want to be in charge of my own life for a change. I don't know that I ever really have been before."

Hanrahan drank some beer. "I know the feeling. I'm not asking you to stay long. For all I know, I'll like it down in Indian country so much that I'll sell Mose my share of the saloon and leave Dodge and Kansas behind forever. But while I get that figured out, I'd feel better with you on the job here. Come to work for me in the spring, whenever Billy sets out south and I'm in his party. Then give me three or four months of work after that. That will allow me time to decide whether I want to divest my Dodge business or not. Let's say I'll pay you thirty-five dollars a week. If you're careful with the money, avoid gambling and expensive meals and so on, by the end of the summer you'd have sufficient funds for a train ticket to California, with enough left to tide you over there until you find desirable employment. I know some businesspeople in San Francisco and San Bernardino and could recommend you to them. So this plan would benefit us both."

"It's more than I could have hoped for. Thank you, Jim."

"Ah, what the hell. This arrangement takes a load off my mind. My only concern now is, you'll be overcome by the temptation of adventure, too, and decide to head south with Billy yourself."

McLendon laughed. "No, adventure in Indian country is the absolute last thing I want. Billy couldn't make me come along if he held a gun to my head."

"Well, then, drink down the beer that you've so far left untouched. This has turned into a celebration."

McLendon drank the beer, politely refused another, and whistled on his walk back to the boardinghouse. It still took him a long time to fall asleep, but for the first time since he escaped Killer Boots back in Glorious, he felt slightly optimistic.

NINE

It was sleeting on the morning when Isatai finally addressed the camp. The weather perfectly matched the miserable mood of the Quahadi villagers. They were still in mourning for the warriors lost on the recent raids. Even in their tipis, everyone was cold because the winds howling in from the north were particularly bitter. They were hungry. Their stomachs hurt from being so empty. No game had been seen, let alone successfully hunted, for days. Quanah knew conditions could not be more perfect for the spirit of Buffalo Hump to communicate with the Quahadi.

Before notifying the villagers, Quanah brought Isatai to his tipi and adorned him with his own finest array—the thick wool uniform shirt taken from a cavalry officer Quanah slew in pitched battle, a delicate shawl torn from the shoulders of a sobbing white woman Quanah raped and killed, and a buffalo horn war bonnet decorated with strands of the same white woman's long, flowing blond scalp. Quanah also applied wide stripes of black paint to Isatai's chubby cheeks and down the bridge of his bulbous nose. Wickeah, like other village wives, concocted war paint for her husband. She mixed the juice of dark berries with ground charcoal and bits of clay, adding a little animal fat for binding. When

Quanah was finished adorning Isatai's face with the thick paint, the fat man looked magnificent. He admired himself in a mirror Quanah had obtained from a Comanchero trader as part of a swap for a Mexican child.

"Buffalo Hump is pleased, Quanah," Isatai said. "You are presenting his messenger properly."

Quanah tried not to scowl. It irked him whenever Isatai treated him as a subordinate, but it was a role he was occasionally obligated to play. He needed Isatai feeling pleased and cooperative.

"You remember all that the spirit wants you to say?" he asked.

"Of course. His message has been blown into my heart."

"Well, then, prepare yourself. I'll summon the villagers."

Isatai closed his eyes and began to hum, an irritating habit he'd recently adopted. Quanah sighed and left the tipi. His wife, Wickeah, was outside shivering. He'd sent her to stand there while he dressed Isatai. Wickeah was smart for a woman, and Quanah thought she might see through his scheme if she heard him coaching Isatai. It never occurred to him to discuss it with her. Among the People, men never shared their war plans with women.

"Can I come inside now?" she asked. Glittering bits of ice formed a light coating on her dark hair and the blanket she held tightly wrapped around her.

"No, you must help me tell everyone that the spirits sent messages to Isatai again, and now we must all gather to hear him speak to us."

Wickeah shivered. "Can't it wait until this storm is over?"

"The spirits choose the time, not us. Help me gather the village."

Soon almost everyone in camp clustered in front of Quanah's tipi. Some of the more sickly old people remained in their own tipis, and a few others made it clear that they had no interest in spirits or Isatai. But it was still a substantial crowd, nearly two hundred. After their losses on the recent raids, though, only about sixty were men of fighting age. Everyone looked raggedy, wrapped in whatever robes and blankets they had and suffering from cold and hunger. Some of the men wore bonnets stripped from dead white women; these were always favorite headgear during inclement weather, especially the ones with ribbons that tied under the chin.

"Get ready to listen," Quanah instructed. "I'll bring out the Messenger of the Spirits." He ducked inside the tipi and found Isatai still close-eyed and humming.

"They're waiting," Quanah said. "Come out and speak to them."

Isatai hummed for a long moment more before he opened one eye and peered at Quanah. "Wait a little. Buffalo Hump has one more thing to tell me."

"Buffalo Hump has already told you all you need to know. Come outside."

Isatai said firmly, "The spirits lead me, not you. Wait." He closed his eyes and hummed some more while Quanah fumed. He could hear the crowd outside muttering, wanting to hear what the spirits had to say, but wanting to return to the shelter of their tipis too.

Finally Isatai stopped humming. He said to Quanah, "I need a pouch. Have you got one?"

Quanah rummaged around and found a bag made from a buffalo stomach. It had long straps fashioned from hide. "Will this do?"

Isatai took the pouch and arranged the straps over his shoulder. "It will do. Now give me some ammunition."

Quanah hesitated. Ammunition was so hard to come by. "For my rifle or the small gun?"

"Either, both, it doesn't matter. Just ammunition." When Quanah reluctantly handed him a half-dozen shells, Isatai said that wasn't enough. He wasn't satisfied until Quanah had given him more than fifty cartridges, almost all that he had. Isatai stuffed the shells in the pouch and said, "All right. Now I'm ready."

Quanah pushed the tipi flap aside and led Isatai out into the cold wind and sleet. The crowd sighed at the sight of the fat man in his fine regalia.

"Hear the words of the spirits!" Quanah commanded, and stepped to the side, hoping desperately that Isatai would speak the words that he was supposed to and not improvise.

Isatai spread his arms wide and threw back his head so that he looked up into the falling sleet. "The spirits blow into my heart," he proclaimed. "I feel their thoughts, I understand their commands. One spirit in particular, a great, great spirit, has come back to guide us, to tell us how the People may become powerful again." Isatai looked and sounded impressive.

"Who is this spirit?" he asked his audience. "Do you want to know his name? Shall I tell you?"

"Yes!" someone shouted, then someone else cried out "Yes!" and suddenly the villagers forgot the cold and hunger and lost warriors and everyone chanted "Yes" in unison, faintly at first and then in stronger voices until the whole crowd was roaring.

Isatai let them roar, let them beg him to tell. Finally he raised his arms again and they fell silent, waiting anxiously; the tension grew so great that Quanah almost screamed at Isatai to get on with it, but managed to restrain himself.

"All right," Isatai said, dropping his voice to a near whisper. Everyone leaned forward, determined not to miss a word. Now Quanah recognized the public pacing of a master—Isatai had gifts of showmanship far beyond Quanah's own.

"The spirit speaking through me is—" Isatai hesitated again, then shouted the words: *"Buffalo Hump!"*

Everyone began to howl—not in derision, as Quanah had feared, but in jubilation. Everyone knew and revered the legend of Buffalo Hump, how he'd gathered the largest band of warriors in the history of the People, and for a time drove the white men into the sea. If Buffalo Hump had chosen this man and their village to hear a message, then it must be an important one.

"What does Buffalo Hump want to tell us?" Quanah cried, the prompt that he and Isatai had agreed on back in the tipi.

Thankfully, the fat man responded as planned. "Buffalo Hump wants us to follow his example. He says that it is time to gather a great fighting force and once again drive the white people away, this time forever. It can be done, Buffalo Hump says. Through my mouth, shall he tell you how?"

"*Yes!*"

Say the words as we planned them, Quanah thought. *Just those words.* For all the fat man's theatricality, he didn't think Isatai was intelligent enough to improvise effectively.

"Buffalo Hump was the wisest warrior ever among the People," Isatai said, and the crowd listened raptly. "He saw that only the greatest force would make the whites run away and stay away. One warrior from among the People can defeat a hundred whites, but always there are more of them: they are like the ants and the flies. But all the warriors of the People, united from each of our camps and fighting together—this is a force that cannot be resisted, especially if we bring with us to the fight some others, the Cheyenne and the Kiowa and maybe the Arapaho, fighting as we tell them to, fighting as we do, with fury and skill."

Many in the crowd cheered. This was their vision of the People, powerful and controlling. The world bent to the People's will, as it should be. In their excitement they forgot about the sleet, the cold wind, and the rumbling of their empty bellies.

"Buffalo Hump says what was done once can be done again. Now is the right time, when our white enemy thinks we are weak and defeated. He says, 'Let this be the time.' When the weather warms and the whites think they are finally safe from us, we strike in a memorable way. Buffalo Hump says to gather the People together in one place and then let the warriors together choose where this fight will be. Through me, Buffalo Hump will guide us. And the People will walk proud and strong once again."

Perfect, thought Quanah. *Now stop.*

The villagers shouted with joy and kept shouting. Isatai pushed his arms toward them, palms out in a gesture of benediction.

"Go back to the warmth of your tipis, and soon Buffalo Hump's spirit will return with instructions," Isatai said. "Buffalo Hump watches over us, he blesses us with his wisdom." Smiling triumphantly, the fat man turned to go back into Quanah's tipi, and that was when old Bull Bear's voice rang out.

"How can you be sure that your spirit is Buffalo Hump?" he demanded. "Did he tell his name to you in the same way that a living man would?"

The crowd went silent. Isatai turned slowly toward Bull Bear. His forehead was knotted and he was clearly deciding how to respond.

"When the spirits blow into your heart, you know them, you know who they are," Isatai finally said.

Bull Bear pushed forward so that he and the fat man were face-to-face.

"Then why didn't you know it was Buffalo Hump that first time, when you said that the spirits brought you up into the air among them?" Now the crowd was making noise again. It was a low murmur that made Quanah uneasy. Bull Bear was always fearsome in argument, and Quanah didn't think Isatai could stand up to him.

"It's not for any of the rest of us to challenge Isatai," Quanah said, moving to stand between the self-proclaimed messenger and Bull Bear. "He knows it's Buffalo Hump now because this is when the spirit chose to reveal that to him."

"Ah, we have an explanation from Quanah," Bull Bear said. "Of course, he likes this message from Buffalo Hump. It is exactly the same as what Quanah has been suggesting for quite some time—we must join all the warriors of all the camps together and make one big attack on the white men. No one wanted to listen to Quanah. How convenient for him that now Isatai delivers the same message from a famous spirit. Are you sure you're delivering a message from Buffalo Hump, Isatai? Could it really be from Quanah instead?"

Isatai looked indignant. Before he could respond to Bull Bear, Quanah said, "I was gone from camp when Isatai first talked to the spirits, Bull Bear. You know that. Like everyone else, I wanted to know what they said to him. Because Isatai is so clearly a Spirit Messenger, I have humbled myself to him, assisting him in small ways, helping him with daily tasks so he has more time to think about what the spirits say to him."

There were murmurs of assent. Even though they respected his fighting skills, many in the Quahadi camp liked the idea of proud, half-breed Quanah being humbled.

"I did not know what spirits spoke to Isatai," Quanah continued. "That it is Buffalo Hump, and that he guides us to a certain path, is nothing to do with me. I'm glad about his message, but I'm not bragging that it's the same thing I've been telling you." He turned and addressed the crowd: "Am I bragging? Did I say anything of the sort before Bull Bear rudely challenged the wisdom of the spirits?"

Bull Bear briefly looked rattled. Then he recovered himself and said, "Maybe it's spirit wisdom, and maybe it's not. When Buffalo Hump did this thing in his own life, he won battles for a while and then the white soldiers caught his big war party and drove them away, killing many fleeing warriors. Why would anything be different this time?"

Quanah, who knew the People's history as well as anyone, said, "Buffalo Hump's great attack failed because too many of the men fighting with him began going back to the old ways before the whites were completely driven away. They thought too much about taking trophies and counting their coups. Because of what happened, what he experienced, Buffalo Hump's spirit will keep us from making the same mistakes."

"And there was another time, perhaps ten full turns of the seasons ago," Bull Bear said. "Many Kiowa joined warriors of the People to fight soldiers at a place by the wide river where white houses had been built with stones made of mud. But the soldiers, who were fewer in number, killed many of us and escaped with their hair. What says Buffalo Hump about that?"

Quanah remembered the fight well. He'd been a very young man then, relegated to minor tasks by the older, more experienced warriors. "You say this like we were defeated in that fight. It was the white soldiers who ran. And the only reason they escaped was that they brought with them the very big guns on wheels. They used them to make some lucky shots. But with the spirit of Buffalo Hump guiding us, we'll have the luck this time."

"You're a clever fellow, Quanah," said Bull Bear. The older man turned back toward Isatai. "Let me ask this, then, of the distinguished messenger. Isatai, you say that Buffalo Hump commands us to raise the largest war party possible and make a big attack in some memorable way. One of those white soldier camps with high wooden walls, maybe. But lances can't penetrate those walls, or arrows, either. We'll need to use rifles, which means we'll need bullets. Where will we get all of the ammunition? Will Buffalo Hump's spirit make bullets grow on bushes?"

It was a valid point, and Quanah didn't know how to respond. But, to Quanah's amazement, Isatai did.

"We'll have all the bullets that we need, Bull Bear. Buffalo Hump's spirit has granted me certain powers."

No, Quanah thought. *That's the wrong thing to say.* Isatai was going to ruin everything.

"Powers?" Bull Bear scoffed. "What, the power to eat more than normal men?"

Isatai pulled his shoulders back and stood very straight. Somehow it seemed to Quanah, who was standing next to him, that the fat man was suddenly several inches taller, and when he spoke his voice was deeper, more resonant.

"Hear me!" he commanded, and some in the crowd gasped. "I have the message from Buffalo Hump's spirit, and also as his gift to the People I have magic too. Whenever we go into this battle, I will make it so that the bullets of the white men's guns pass right through our bodies without doing us any harm. And when bullets are needed for our guns, I will supply them; I will vomit them up like *this!*"

Isatai plunged his hand into the pouch at his side and extracted some of the bullets that Quanah had given him earlier. He jammed them in his mouth, then spat them at the crowd. He reached into the pouch again, took more bullets, and tossed them up into the air so that they came down on the heads of his audience. The dramatic gesture had an astonishing effect. Though anyone could clearly see what Isatai had done and where he'd gotten the bullets, a woman still cried out, "It's true! He vomits them up!" and that was when Quanah understood for the first time how truly desperate the Quahadi were, if they took such things for miracles. *People see what they want to,* he thought. *In better days they would have jeered, but right now they believe.* The Quahadi shouted praise for Isatai and allegiance to the spirit of Buffalo Hump. Even Bull Bear was abashed.

"I have my answer," he said, and stood quietly while Isatai blessed the villagers on behalf of the spirit of Buffalo Hump.

"Soon I'll go to visit the other camps of the People to take them the words of Buffalo Hump," Isatai announced. "Quanah will come with me. Be strong and happy while we're gone. Soon the great times will return. If we heed his words, if we accept his guidance, this is what the spirit of Buffalo Hump has promised."

Back inside his tent, Quanah said to Isatai, "They called what you did a miracle."

"Just so," said Isatai, admiring himself again in the mirror.

"That was a smart thing you did with the bullets. You were prepared if you were asked a question like Bull Bear's."

Isatai smiled and patted Quanah on the shoulder. "And why was I prepared? Because the spirit of Buffalo Hump alerted me just before I left your tipi."

For the rest of the winter, Isatai and Quanah went to the other camps of the People, which were scattered about. They visited the main villages of the Penateka, or Honey Eaters; the Nokoni, or Wanderers; the Kotsoteka, or Buffalo Eaters; and the Yamparika, or Root Eaters, as well as some smaller camps. They even sneaked onto the land set aside by the whites as a Comanche reservation and talked to those living there. Not long before, Quanah had been rebuffed in every place, but now he was welcomed, although as Isatai's assistant. Everywhere they went, all their tribesmen had already heard about Isatai and the spirit of Buffalo Hump and the miracle of the vomited-up bullets. This didn't mean that there was universal acceptance of the plan to form a great war party and strike at the whites with unprecedented force. Some of the People couldn't decide, and others still preferred the old ways of small raids. But many warriors pledged to participate in the coming fight—in all, counting fifty or so from among the Quahadi, Quanah thought that the People might muster almost two hundred men to take into battle, more if some of the undecideds eventually chose to participate. It was an impressive number, but not enough.

"We need twice that many, maybe more," Quanah said as he and Isatai turned their horses back toward the Quahadi camp. "We'll have to go to the Kiowa and the Cheyenne next, and after that the Arapaho if we still need others. I hope we don't have to ask the Arapaho. They talk so much, the white men would hear all about it and be waiting for us."

"We'll have all the warriors that are necessary, and whatever white men we attack will be surprised," Isatai said confidently. "Buffalo Hump has promised it."

"You've heard from him again?" Quanah asked. He wasn't certain how much Isatai believed.

"His spirit is always with me now," Isatai said. "You worry too much, Quanah. Soon you'll have your great battle and all of the glory that you want so much."

"I don't care about glory," Quanah protested. "I just want to save our people, help us keep living in the way that we choose, and not bow down to the whites. Did you look inside the tipis of the ones living on agency land? Instead of lances and rifles, they have tools. The white man is making them into farmers. *Farmers!* It's shameful."

"Soon for the People there will be no shame, only glory," Isatai said. He took out a corn cake and ate it as he rode. The grinding of Isatai's teeth on the food reminded Quanah of a horse chewing up particularly thick grass. If anything, the fat man had gained weight since assuming the mantle of Spirit Messenger. Even though food was scarce in all of the camps that they'd just visited, everyone vied to bring treats to Isatai the Spirit Messenger, and he graciously ate all that he was offered. "You need to trust the spirits, Quanah. You need to trust *me*."

Quanah was taken aback by Isatai's self-assurance, which was so different from his old, transparently boastful ways. Sometimes he felt like things were going according to Isatai's plan rather than his. "You're a changed man, Isatai," Quanah admitted.

"Because the spirits have changed me." Isatai gobbled the last bite of corn cake, licked the crumbs from his fingers, then half closed his eyes as he rode and began humming.

TEN

Cash McLendon hoped that in the New Year the general mood in Dodge City might improve, but it didn't. Somehow the drunks seemed drunker, the fights more vicious, and the days so cold as to defy any eventual end to winter.

McLendon himself couldn't wait until spring, when at some point Billy Dixon's hunting party would depart for Indian Territory and his own days of scrounging a living with buffalo bones finally ended. The job Jim Hanrahan promised would be a good one, better suited for a man of McLendon's civilized nature than grubbing around the country-side, keeping one eye out for dead, rotting buffalo and the other for Indians. With steady income in his future, McLendon was able to plan a budget for the first time in the two years since he'd fled St. Louis. Eight or nine months more in Dodge, ten at most, and he'd have enough saved for travel to California and to tide him over for his first few months there besides. After so much time improvising his life on the run, McLendon took comfort in having a set plan. Nothing could disrupt it.

And then something did.

.   .   .

ONE NIGHT IN EARLY JANUARY, Bat Masterson was in a rotten mood. Despite his typical sunny ways, he was occasionally prone to sulks. He'd curl up on his cot in the Olds boardinghouse, turn his back on McLendon, and write furiously in his notebook. When his friend and roommate got this way, McLendon had learned to leave Bat alone and go out for a while. The weather was nasty and there were several fights going on in the Dodge streets, so he wandered over to the Hanrahan and Water's saloon. Billy and some of the other hide men were off at a table in a corner. McLendon was on his way to join them when he heard someone calling his name from a table by the bar. He looked and saw a man waving. There was something very familiar about the fellow, who wore a bowler hat, checked suit and vest. He was still trying to place him when the man said, "McLendon? Cash McLendon? I'm William Clark LeMond—remember me?" And then McLendon did. Nearly two years earlier, he'd shared a decrepit stage with LeMond on a dusty trip from Florence to Glorious. As he now recalled, LeMond was a drummer who traveled Arizona Territory trying to place scented soaps in dry goods stores and other shops.

"Good to see you, Mr. LeMond," he replied, and the salesman gestured for him to sit down.

"Let me buy you a beer or something stronger," LeMond said. After McLendon requested beer, the drummer asked what he was doing in Dodge. Choosing his words carefully, McLendon explained that he'd left Glorious in late summer 1872 to seek his fortune elsewhere and, after one or two stops in Texas, found himself in Dodge for a while.

"Very soon, I'll be helping operate this saloon for a bit," he said. "But I've had enough of the frontier life, and intend soon to make my way to the Pacific coast. And what of you? I thought Arizona was your sales territory."

"It was, but then I heard tell of these great Texas cattle drives coming all the way up to Kansas. That means much higher commissions are possible here."

"And why is that?"

"You get your Texan cow herders up here in Kansas all ready for fun, the one thing they want before whiskey and whores is a good bath to get the trail dust off," LeMond said, polishing off a Jim Beam bourbon neat and signaling for another. "Those drovers want a bit of luxury after their arduous trek, and lemon-scented soap is just the thing. Two months ago I came from Arizona Territory to Kansas. So far I've been mostly doing business in Wichita, but my sources inform me that presently the tick line will move west, and then the Texas herds will be coming to Dodge. So here I am, ready to place my products in local hotels and shops."

"Start with the Dodge House," McLendon suggested. "It has high-class pretensions and is considered the best of the town hotels."

"Ah, these hotels out in the middle of nowhere," LeMond mused. "Remember back in Glorious, Major Mulkins and his so-called Elite Hotel? He was so proud of its few glass windows. Decent fellow, the major. I always liked him."

"He was my friend too."

"You know, I saw him again just before I departed Arizona Territory. He's in a town called Mountain View now, maybe twenty miles east of where Glorious used to be."

McLendon had been contemplating the beer in his mug; now his head snapped up. "Used to be? What do you mean?"

"Ah, you left before the big fight and don't know what happened after."

"Tell me," McLendon urged. "Whatever you know—don't leave anything out."

In late July or maybe August of 1872, LeMond said, there was an Apache raid on Glorious. "I learned after the fact that there'd been some warning that one was coming. Just the day before the attack, the Army came in and evacuated most of the residents. Some, though, refused to leave. According to Major Mulkins, it was him; Crazy George Mitchell and Mary Somebody, the couple who ran the Owaysis Saloon; and Joe Saint. You remember him? The skinny town sheriff. Also a dozen or so prospectors and that rich rancher, Collin MacPherson, plus his gunslinging vaqueros. The major said that Mr. MacPherson believed his gun hands could withstand the Apache attack, but he was mistaken. Many died. Be glad you weren't there."

McLendon nodded. In fact, he had been there, and experienced a night of death and near-unimaginable horror. Determined to own all the businesses in Glorious and prosper in the wake of silver strikes, MacPherson, using his hired assassins, staged the raid to kill off competitors and take over the town. Thankfully, Gabrielle had reluctantly evacuated with the Army and wasn't present when MacPherson's vaqueros systematically cut down the prospectors and came close to killing McLendon, Major Mulkins, Crazy George, Mary Somebody and Joe Saint—only the unexpected appearance of Killer Boots prevented their murders, and Saint's quick thinking allowed McLendon to subsequently escape the clutches of the fearsome nemesis who'd tracked him to Glorious from St. Louis. McLendon still trembled at the memory.

"You make it sound as though Glorious is gone," he said. "Vanished from the face of the earth."

"That's just what happened. A few days after the Apache raid, most of the people came back, but there was no more silver found and the surviving prospectors drifted on. Then there was a solid strike on the other side of the Pinal Mountains, the east side, then another and another in almost the same spot—just loads of silver. So a new town named Mountain View started up there, and unlike Glorious, it was solid from the beginning. Mines got set up and the place has just flourished since. It didn't help Mr. MacPherson. His property next to Glorious was suddenly worthless, and all the ranchland around Mountain View was bought up before he could get any. His reputation was somewhat stained as well. There were rumors that he'd maybe bribed the Apache to attack Glorious for some reason. Nothing of the sort was ever proven, of course. In any event, he's since pulled up stakes and gone elsewhere—the Dakotas, I think, or maybe Washington Territory. I don't know what became of ol' Crazy George and Mary Somebody. Major Mulkins is managing a hotel in Mountain View, though. A very nice hotel. It's called the White Horse and does lots of business. Someone else owns it, but the Major runs it. I had some drinks with the Major there in Mountain View just before I departed Arizona Territory for Kansas."

What about Gabrielle? McLendon desperately wanted to know. But he was afraid that if he asked directly, LeMond might give him news that he didn't want to hear. "Any idea of what happened to other Glorious refugees?"

"You might recall there were some Chinese, but after the evacuation they never returned. Don't know that anyone knows what became of them, where they went after that. And, of course, them being of that race, no white person would care."

McLendon didn't respond, because he had great respect for the Chinese he'd met in Glorious, and hoped very much that they were prospering somewhere.

"Well, Joe Saint, the one who used to be the town sheriff?" LeMond continued. "He's living in Mountain View, too, though he doesn't serve anymore as a lawman. He teaches there. They've got a school of sorts, one room and kids of all ages. Seems Joe was a schoolteacher back east before he came out to the territories."

"Mmm-hmm."

LeMond smiled. "I know who you really want to hear about. I recall you came to Glorious in the first place because you were looking to re-kindle your romance with Miss Gabrielle Tirrito. But she had formed a relationship with Sheriff Saint. Well, she's in Mountain View too. Works at the same hotel, the White Horse, as Major Mulkins, where she runs the front desk and directs the custodial staff. She and her daddy had that dry goods shop in Glorious, of course, but he's gotten sicker and can't do much anymore. And here's the interesting part. Back in Glorious, espe-cially after she spurned you, everybody figured she would soon marry Joe Saint. But here it's, what, a year and a half or more gone, they're both in Mountain View, and still no wedding."

"Oh?"

"I have this from Major Mulkins, who, as you remember, didn't mind passing along a bit of gossip. Joe Saint still pays court to Miss Gabrielle, he truly wants to marry her, and she keeps putting him off. The Major couldn't say why."

"Really?" McLendon had trouble choking out the single word.

"So it seems. You know, you might still be in with a chance if she weren't in Mountain View and you all the way out here in Dodge City, Kansas. The Major suspects that Mr. Saint will wear her down eventu-ally. But it hasn't happened yet. Now, what do you think of that, McLen-don? Wait—where are you going?"

As HE HURRIED BACK to his room at the Olds boardinghouse, Mc-Lendon considered his options. He loved Gabrielle as much as ever, and simply letting matters play out between her and Joe Saint was no longer acceptable. If she hadn't married Joe Saint yet, maybe it was because she'd finally realized that she loved McLendon more. He had to make another try for Gabrielle. But how?

McLendon's first impulse was to leave for Mountain View immediately, his obligation to Jim Hanrahan be damned. Despite his impatience, it wouldn't be a quick trip. There were two choices. He could spend long weeks riding horses and, later, mules that could handle the rough ascent to the Arizona Territory high desert, or else take the train to Kansas City, then transfer to another train heading west to Denver. From there he'd have to go by stage, Denver to Tucson, Tucson to Florence, Florence to Mountain View. He didn't know Mountain View's exact location, but LeMond said it was on the other side of the Pinal Mountains from where Glorious used to be, and there had been daily stage service between Glorious and Florence. Factoring in train and stage transfers and inevitable delays for mechanical failures and weather, the trip would take at least ten days, maybe two weeks or more. But money was an issue.

McLendon had about $110 saved, possibly enough for train and stage fare. But he'd arrive in Mountain View flat broke, and when he got there he wanted to focus his complete attention on Gabrielle and not waste valuable time doing odd jobs for room and board. But if he waited any longer, working in Dodge City until he had enough to cover living expenses as well as travel to Mountain View, in the interim Joe Saint might very well talk Gabrielle into marriage. Saint, McLendon ruefully recalled, was a man whose innocuous appearance belied a sharp, calculating intellect. Gabrielle, not without cause, considered him a better person than McLendon. But he'd changed; surely if he saw her again, he could convince her of that. Yet even then, if she agreed to come away with him this time, he'd still need a lot more money for train fare to California for two, or for three if her father came with them. And then living expenses for three while he looked for a job. . . . Of course, he could find work in Mountain View for a while. But he certainly wouldn't find a job there that paid the same thirty-five dollars a week that Jim Hanrahan had promised him in Dodge. Still, he had to go, and right away. It was Gabrielle. He'd take the train and figure out the rest of the money issues when he had to.

McLendon charged into his room at the boardinghouse. Bat was gone; he'd probably shaken off his sulk and headed to Tom Sherman's place for beer and dances with whores. So he couldn't tell Bat good-bye—well, too bad.

He began jamming clothes in his valise, then stopped with a shirt half-way packed. Once before he'd tried shocking Gabrielle by turning up unexpectedly, but when he surprised her in Glorious she tried sending him on his way. Maybe this time it would be better to give her some warning. A letter, maybe. He would send her a letter at the White Horse Hotel in Mountain View, where she worked, telling her that he was going to come, and why. Meanwhile, he'd work as planned for Hanrahan and Waters, saving the money he—*they*, hopefully—would need in California.

Bat might be out, but he'd left his notebook on his cot. McLendon tore a blank page loose. Then he took a pencil and, resting the paper on the rickety dresser, began writing. It wasn't easy. When he and Gabrielle met back in St. Louis, McLendon, who'd been orphaned early and never attended a single day of school, was completely illiterate. Gabrielle taught him to read, which he grew to love, and to write, which he didn't care for at all. He had trouble expressing his thoughts in print. His communication skill remained exclusively oral; McLendon had a talent for talking people into things with spoken rather than written words. In particular, his spelling was spotty. Sighing, squinting in the limited light provided by the kerosene lantern, he tried to make his best case to the woman he loved.

January 1874

Dearest Gabrielle:

I am in Dodge City, Kansas, and have word of you from William Clark Leemond, the salesman of soap. He tells me you live in a place called Mountain View now, still in Arizona Territory but on the other side of the mountains from where Glorious was. He also says your father is sick and I am sorry for that, I hope he is better soon.

Since I left Glorious I have been in Texas and now Kansas still with hopes of getting to Californeya soon. Mister Leemond says that you have not married Joe Saint yet. This is very happy news for me. I still think of you all the time and am sorry for what I did to you back in Saint Louis. I want to come see you and tell you again that I love you and want to marry you. I am still trying to be a better man, the kind you dezerve. I will come as soon as I save enough money to take you to Californeya with me and your father also if he would like to come. I will take care of him and you there, I promise. You know I don't write nearly as well as I talk or read, if you marry me you could help me learn to write better. I would like that so much. You used to laugh at my poor spelling, and you are so pretty when you laugh.

I am coming to Mountain View no matter what and hope it will not be very long, by the end of fall maybe. I have a good job promised here and will save every pennie. I will come as soon as

*I can. No matter how long it takes I will come, don't marry Joe
Saint until I can talk to you again face to face. It's not that I hate Joe
but I love you and can make you happier than he can. Don't say no
right away, wait and see me first. Meantime if you want to write
to me you can, care of Hanrahan and Waters, Dodge City Kansas.
Pleaze dont tell that to anyone else. I dont want Killer Boots to
find out, though I hope he isnt after me all the time anymore and
I think we would be safe now in Californeya. Well I guess you can
tell Joe Saint, you are truthfull and may want him to know that I
am coming. But if you do I hope you tell him to keep where I am
secret to.*

I love you
Cash McLendon

The next morning, McLendon took the letter to A. C. Myers's Pioneer
Store. He bought and addressed an envelope to Miss Gabrielle Tirrito in
care of the White Horse Hotel, Mountain View, Arizona Territory, then
sealed the letter in it and gave the envelope to a store clerk who served
as the town postmaster. He paid three cents postage, plus another dime
in return for the clerk's promise to personally see that the letter went out
on the noon train. It would take at least two weeks to reach Gabrielle,
the clerk noted, but in McLendon's quest to win her back, every hour
counted. Then McLendon sat on the windswept Dodge City sidewalk,
leaning back against the wood frame wall of the store, trying to calculate
how many months it would take before he saved enough to go to Gabrielle in Mountain View. Even if he ate only one meal a day, he couldn't see
any way to do it in less than ten.

ELEVEN

The main Kiowa camp was north of the Quahadi village, high up in what the whites called the Texas Panhandle. As they rode there, Quanah cautioned Isatai about Kiowa customs.

"They have a chief, Lone Wolf, who leads them, and also a medicine man they believe has great power to prophesy. We, of course, are of the People and in all things know better than they do, but we must appear respectful."

"Their medicine man is a fool," Isatai scoffed. "I hear that he claims to talk to animals both living and dead. That's how he says he gets messages. Buffalo Hump says that this Kiowa faker should tremble before me."

"I'm sure Buffalo Hump is wiser than that," Quanah said. "He knows we need the Kiowa to cooperate with his great plan to drive away the whites."

Isatai's eyes narrowed. "Remember that Buffalo Hump speaks through me, not you. Don't presume to tell me what he knows."

"You're right, of course," Quanah said. He had resigned himself to Isatai's pomposity. "But when we reach the Kiowa camp, perhaps it would be best for you to stand quietly and impress them with the power of the spirits. I'll explain everything to Lone Wolf. If you talk much, they might be so afraid of Buffalo Hump—and, of course, of you—that their ears would not listen properly."

Isatai grunted in agreement. "But I'll correct you if you say anything wrong."

There was birdsong; the end of winter had arrived. It was still quite cool in the mornings and evenings, but in early afternoon Quanah and Isatai felt comfortable in shirts without blankets or fur robes wrapped around their shoulders. Some green shoots had popped out in valleys and along the tops of rolling hills. A few rabbits skittered in the brush, but no snakes slithered there. It was still too chilly for them to emerge from their snug winter holes.

As Quanah and Isatai approached the Kiowa village, they heard laughter and singing. Everyone was outside enjoying the weak sunshine.

Isatai sniffed the air. "They're roasting meat, probably deer, since it's still too early for the buffalo. I hope that they invite us to eat with them."

The Kiowa camp was much more colorful than the Quahadi's. The people living there wore breechclouts and dresses dyed rich browns and crimson with berry juice. Their buffalo-hide tipis were decorated with many designs rendered in yellows and blues. Besides the usual clays and berry juices, the ingredients of their paint also included moss, pollen, and buffalo fat, all of which contributed brighter pigmentation. Kiowa men wore these same paints into battle. Warriors among the People would have considered such garishness weak and effeminate, but the Kiowa did not.

It was easy for visitors to identify the dwelling of the chief, whose tipi was adorned with the most pictures of all. Quanah and Isatai rode straight to it. They dismounted and handed their horses over to an old woman who led the animals off to graze. Lone Wolf emerged from his tipi. He was impressive looking, like many Kiowa men taller than the average warrior among the People, but still a bit shorter than Quanah. His hair was cut in the traditional Kiowa manner, short on the right side to display bone pendants dangling from his ear, and long on the left side. The long hair was twisted into an intricate braid.

"We welcome our visitors," he said courteously. "Come in and smoke." Quanah followed him into the tent, taking care to let Isatai enter first. The portly Spirit Messenger glanced around the interior, taking in the thick robes arranged around a low fire, and various weapons stacked against the sides of the tipi. War shields hung from loops on poles, and caches of dried food, some stored in captured white Army packs, were stacked off to one side. Isatai sniffed, dropped down cross-legged on the finest robe, closed his eyes, and hummed.

Quanah said quickly, "That's Isatai's way. He does that so he can hear the spirits."

"He's making so much noise himself, I wonder that he can hear them at all," Lone Wolf said. "Well, we've heard about his great magic. Such special people often have strange ways about them." He sat on a robe opposite Isatai and gestured for Quanah to sit beside him. There was rustling outside, and two more men entered the tent.

"I've asked them to join us," Lone Wolf said. He gestured toward a short man wearing a headdress and shirt decorated with owl feathers. "This is Mamanti, our medicine man." Mamanti nodded to Quanah, then fixed his eyes on Isatai, who paid no attention to the newcomers. His eyes remained closed and he continued humming. Lone Wolf pointed to the other man and said, "This is Satanta," and even though Quanah considered himself the greatest of all warriors, he was still impressed. Satanta was legendary; he'd fought the whites for many years, plaguing soldiers and settlers alike. He was also famous for his oratory, and for the Army bugle he blew when leading his warriors in battle. The bugle notes often confused the white soldiers and contributed to Kiowa victories. For a while he'd made peace and tried to follow the white man's way, only to be betrayed and sent off to one of their prisons in Texas. Lone Wolf, leading a Kiowa delegation to meet with the Great Father Grant in Washington, promised to ask the rest of his people to lay down their weapons if Satanta was released. Of course, Lone Wolf meant only that they would stop fighting for a little while, though maybe Grant didn't understand that. Still, he let Satanta go.

"It's good to see you back in your own land," Quanah said politely. He studied Satanta carefully, trying to discern what made him such a great fighter. Satanta stared back. His forehead was narrow and his jaw-line was wide, making his face the image of a triangle with a wide base.

"My heart never left, just my body," he said.

"Because he promised the whites to never fight them again, Satanta joins us to listen and give counsel only," Lone Wolf explained.

"Of course," Quanah said, but he immediately felt less respect for the old Kiowa. In the same position, Quanah would have gleefully promised the whites anything, then reneged the moment he was out of their clutches and back among the People. It was all right to lie to whites, because white people lied all of the time. They couldn't help it because that was their nature.

"Let's smoke, and then you can tell me what you want of us," Lone Wolf suggested. They passed the pipe around, each man taking a few ceremonial puffs except for Isatai, who sat closed-eyed and humming as though he were the only one in the tipi. Mamanti, the Kiowa medicine man, smoked in his turn but never took his eyes off Isatai, obviously try-ing to take the measure of a rival shaman.

When the smoking was done, Quanah spoke. He explained how the spirit of Buffalo Hump had communicated through Isatai that it was time for a great action to drive the whites out of Indian land. The old ways of small, unconnected raids no longer worked. A collaborative effort between the People, the Kiowa, the Cheyenne, and perhaps the Arapaho would convince all the soldiers and settlers to leave for good. The magic granted to Isatai by Buffalo Hump would render white bullets useless in the battle. A rout would ensue, and afterward the Indians would live uninterrupted by white intrusion. It would be a victory for all.

Lone Wolf and Satanta listened carefully. Neither interrupted with questions or observations, and for several moments after Quanah was finished the only sound inside the tipi was Isatai's incessant humming. Finally Lone Wolf asked, "Does your medicine man have anything to add?"

Without opening his eyes, Isatai murmured, "I'm not a medicine man. I'm a Spirit Messenger and I have magic."

Lone Wolf exchanged glances with Satanta and said, "We've heard about that. I'm told that once you seemed to vomit up ammunition. Can you do that now for us?"

Quanah nervously tried to think of how to respond, but before he could Isatai opened his eyes and said calmly, "The magic must be saved for when it is really needed."

Mamanti made a cawing, insulting sound, but Lone Wolf said politely, "You know best about such things. I think Satanta wants to say something."

The renowned Kiowa rolled the end of his long braid in his fingertips for a moment, then stared hard at Quanah. The gray-eyed Quahadi was hard pressed not to blink. He did his best to calmly gaze back. Finally Satanta said, "It's interesting that two Comanche come with this request for the Kiowa to fight alongside their warriors. I'm an old man, Quanah.

I've known the Comanche since your father's time and long before that. You call yourselves the People, as though no one else is a human being. Comanche always believe that they are the best fighters, that they don't need anyone's help. You trade with us, but from the earliest time any Kiowa can remember, you made it plain that we live here only because you let us. You drove away the Apache; they went west to live in the dirt and dung where of course they, being too bandy-legged and untrustworthy, belong. You fought the Tonkawa and they ran away to serve the white men. If we try this thing that your medicine man's spirits suggest, one great battle instead of many small ones, and it works—if we join you and the whites are driven away forever—how do we know, once they're gone, that you won't turn on us next? Isn't that the Comanche way, to always find someone to fight?"

Quanah knew better than to disagree. "Before this, maybe. The times have changed. After we get rid of the whites, you'll live beside us as equals."

"Perhaps," Satanta said.

Lone Wolf leaned forward. "The Comanche have no single chief. You say that you and Isatai speak for all of your people, all the different camps."

"That's true," Quanah said.

"This has never happened before."

"As I said, times have changed."

Mamanti whispered something to Lone Wolf, who said, "Our medicine man wonders if it's really Buffalo Hump's spirit speaking through this man who sits and hums. There are bad spirits too. He might be possessed by one of those, Mamanti thinks."

Isatai's eyes flew open. Mamanti, who'd been watching him carefully, jerked back. He raised a stick decorated with more owl feathers and shook it in Isatai's face. Isatai squared his shoulders and Quanah feared that he was about to attack the Kiowa shaman, but instead Isatai smirked. "The spirit in me has no time to waste on fools like this feathery idiot," he said. "Lone Wolf, Buffalo Hump wants you to listen to Quanah. He says that you should do what he asks." Isatai closed his eyes and resumed humming. Mamanti shook his stick again, but when Isatai didn't respond further he tucked it back in his leggings and sat down, shaking his head in exaggerated disbelief.

"Well," Lone Wolf said, "I don't know anything about spirits and magic. Like Satanta, I do know about the Comanche. I'll think about what you've said, Quanah. I have no answer for you today."

Quanah said desperately, "Not long ago, your nephew Long Branches came to the Quahadi village and asked us to fight with him in the old way. Some of our warriors did, and you know what happened. If you join us, if you help us do this thing that Buffalo Hump wants, you can have revenge on the whites for the death of your nephew. Don't you want that?"

Lone Wolf looked into the fire, then at Quanah. "In that raid, I didn't just lose a nephew. My youngest son died too. He had fifteen summers. He was a good son."

"And Bad Hand's Tonkawa scouts ate his liver."

The Kiowa chief glared, and Quanah feared he'd pushed too hard.

"Yes," Lone Wolf finally said. "The Tonkawa are evil people, and you Comanche were right to chase them away from this land. Long Branches and your boy weren't looking for a fight with white soldiers. They were just raiding Mexicans."

"They were being good warriors," Quanah agreed.

"The whites say we can't fight anyone, but they fight whoever they please without respect to any promises they made," Satanta said. For the first time, he sounded angry. "I told them I would live at their agency and wouldn't fight them, though other Kiowa might. They said that they understood, but when something happened, they blamed me anyway. They put iron bands on my arms and legs and they put me in their prison. Lone Wolf had to beg the white chief Grant to set me free. It was a sad thing. I felt great shame. And before they let me go, they made me promise one more time to never fight them again, and I'm not a liar, I'll keep my word just as I did before they put me in their prison. But I won't be sorry if everyone else fights them and makes them run away for good."

"We can avenge your son and Long Branches, and also the honor of the great Satanta," Quanah said to Lone Wolf. "White blood must pay for these insults."

The Kiowa chief stood and stretched. "Let's go outside."

Quanah leaned over and grasped Isatai's arm. "Come on," he whispered. Isatai opened his eyes again and stopped humming. He went outside with the others, though he ostentatiously avoided any contact with Mamanti.

"You see your Spirit Messenger, how he acts superior to our medicine man," Lone Wolf said to Quanah. "I think this is still the way all of you Comanche feel about the Kiowa. You trade with us, but you mock our medicine men and our sun dances and all of our ways that are different from yours. We can sometimes be of use to you, but we're not as good as you. I said I would think on your words and I will. I ask that you think on this—do something to show me that if we join you in this fight and win, afterward we're all the same, not Comanche and, beneath you, everyone else. The Kiowa must stand beside the Comanche, not be ruled by them."

"If the way to fight must be different, then the Comanche must be different too," Satanta added.

Quanah said, "If we prove it, will you fight with us?"

Lone Wolf smiled. "First, show the proof. Then the Kiowa will decide. Meanwhile, I wish that your Spirit Messenger had made some of his famous magic. Besides vomiting up bullets, I've heard that he can fly."

AS THEY RODE AWAY, Isatai said, "They didn't offer us any food. If they had, I might have summoned a little magic for them."

Quanah didn't reply. He was thinking hard.

TWELVE

Around mid-February, some of the hide men and their hangers-on who'd gone off to spend the winter in warmer climes returned, but not nearly as many as Dodge business leaders had expected back. In the buffalo hunting peak of 1872, almost ten thousand hide men and crew members either lived in or camped near the town. But now, with word spreading that most of the buffalo were far to the south, fewer than half the anticipated crowd of hunters came back. Town merchants consequently sold far fewer goods. Saloons still did good business, so drunken brawls were just as frequent. The merchants were frustrated and the hide men were nervous: What if, come spring, the buffalo didn't return at all? There was an abiding sense that Dodge was at a critical, in-between stage. Its days as a buffalo town were numbered, if not already over, and there was still no assurance that the state legislature would move the tick line west and give Dodge a new, thriving economy.

McLendon could not have cared less. He spent virtually every waking minute thinking of Gabrielle. She surely had received his letter. Had it made her weep with joy to learn that he was still alive, that he still loved her? Or had she sneered, crumpled the paper in her hand, and tossed it disdainfully away? He couldn't make up his mind which extreme action she was more likely to have had, and never considered Gabrielle's response falling anywhere in between. He yearned for a return letter from her and swore to himself that even a flat refusal of his love wouldn't keep him from traveling to Mountain View anyway, just as soon as he was financially able. But that would take so long. Until Billy Dixon announced some kind of formal plan for a hunt down south, McLendon didn't even know when he would start working at the saloon and drawing a good salary. For the moment, he still could barely cover living expenses by gathering buffalo bones. That frustration, combined with his eagerness and uncertainty about Gabrielle, kept him in a constant foul mood.

No one noticed. Everyone else in Dodge was testy too. Hannah Olds, when McLendon joined his landlords for a beefsteak supper, complained throughout the meal about the dearth of boarders she expected when the tick line moved. Texas cow herders would arrive in town and stay only for two or three days, she predicted, and even then they'd get so drunk every night that, instead of renting rooms, they'd pass out in the streets. Her husband William's constant belches seemed somehow indicative of sour temper as well as excess gastric juices. McLendon felt nervous and off balance because he wanted to start his full-time job at Hanrahan's, and besides, his chronic insomnia was growing worse. He spent sleepless hours alternately feeling guilty about the death of his wife and castigating himself for losing Gabrielle to Sheriff Joe Saint back in Arizona Territory. If he'd only been smarter, done one or two crucial things differently, how much better his life would be. Even Bat Masterson, when he and McLendon went out to collect buffalo bones, groused more than he joked. Since Billy Dixon still hadn't announced formal plans for establishing a hunting base south in Indian Territory, Bat now feared that Billy never would.

"He's being too damned closemouthed, C.M.," Masterson grumbled.

It was around noon, and some of the winter chill still hung in the air. Because most of the area within a ten-mile radius of Dodge had been picked clean, he and McLendon had to range much farther afield for bones. That meant they could bring fewer wagonloads a day back to town to sell—sometimes only one—and their incomes dropped accordingly. Some nights Bat couldn't afford a beer or even a single dance in Tom Sherman's saloon.

"Billy's *always* closemouthed," McLendon said. He was handling the reins while Bat scanned the horizon for piles of bones or sign of Indians. Some Cheyenne had been spotted in the area, though they reportedly looked like a hunting rather than a raiding party—no war paint and bows instead of rifles. "If he hasn't said for sure that he's going, at least he hasn't said that he's decided not to."

"What's got me concerned is the identity of the few that he has been talking to," Masterson said. "Instead of enjoying convivial evenings of beer and good conversation with fellow adventurers such as myself, Billy's been huddling with the likes of A. C. Myers, Fred Leonard, Charlie Rath, even your good pal Jim Hanrahan—businessmen all. If I didn't know better, I'd swear Billy Dixon is thinking of giving up the hunt and becoming a merchant."

McLendon pulled his coat a little tighter around his shoulders. Though the wind wasn't as cold as it had been just weeks earlier, it still had considerable bite. "Bat, I understand your impatience, and I promise you, I share it. But you know very well that hide men are businessmen too. They're concerned with profit and loss, same as the store and saloon men. I'm sure Billy's just trying to get a handle on how the most money can be made in an Indian Territory hunting camp. He wants a good, solid plan in place. In a way, you ought to be glad that he's taking his time."

"Well, I'm not. I've had enough of gathering stinky bones and fetching them back to Dodge to sell for pennies. You and I need our own chance for some riches. He can't let us down."

"I've told you, even when Billy does head south—you'll notice I said 'when,' not 'if'—I'm staying in Dodge. I'm going to work for Jim Hanrahan pretty soon."

Masterson heaved an exaggerated sigh. "We both know that ain't true. Deep down, you ain't a figure-fiddling clerk. You've got ambition beyond that. You talk about how you're eventually bound for California, and maybe so. But you've got an eye for opportunity and turning a quick dollar. When the time comes, you'll be right beside me, riding down toward the Canadian with Billy Dixon."

"You'll see, Bat."

"Yessir, I will."

It grew increasingly dangerous to walk Dodge City streets at night. While many of the hide men observed what they called town manners, leaving their weapons back in their boardinghouse rooms or camp tents, some of them took pride in parading about, armed and ornery. Dutch Henry Borne and Brick Bond in particular looked for trouble and found it. Henry savagely beat a whore he claimed took his money but left him unsatisfied. When two other working girls from the same saloon tried to save their friend from his fists, he beat them, too, and dared those watching to try and stop him. They didn't. Bond shot and killed a man just outside the Rath and Company store. They'd both reached for the same bandanna on a shelf, and that made Bond feel disrespected. By the time Ford County sheriff Charlie Bassett was summoned and arrived, Bond had ridden out of town. He lay low for a few days and then came back, nasty and aggressive as ever. His victim was buried on Boot Hill. No one knew his name, so the flimsy wood marker simply read "Shot Dead 2-22-1874." He was the forty-sixth anonymous shooting victim buried there. Three had been dispatched by Brick Bond.

Near the end of the month, Jim Hanrahan quietly confided to McLendon that Billy Dixon would announce his plans any day now: "There'll be some surprises."

"You're still going with him, aren't you, Jim? I need to be starting that job for you."

"Wait and see. I promised Billy to keep his confidence. But don't fret."

WHAT WAS DUBBED the Union Church opened in the renovated saloon. McLendon went to the first service, hoping it might take his mind off Gabrielle for a little while. It didn't, even though Stephen Geest delivered a rousing sermon on how God was in Dodge City to stay.

"If you have God in your heart, everything else falls into place," Geest promised. "And, now with a house of God here in its midst, Dodge City on this morning—this very morning—comes into its holy own."

He had to talk loudly to be heard over a fistfight just outside. A half-dozen skinners from various hide men's crews, drunk at ten on Sunday morning, cursed and rolled in the dirt street. Their imprecations cut cleanly through the morning sunshine. A few of Dodge's high society families—the Fringers, the Zimmermanns, Charles Rath and his wife—had come to Geest's first service. The fine ladies looked uncomfortable at all the swearing outside, but Geest's other congregants, whores and some middle-class shopkeepers like Rebecca Travis, paid no mind. They heard cussing all the time. Hide man Henry Raymond came, too, sitting beside Rebecca and trying to hold her hand while Geest preached. After a while, she let him.

When Geest finished his sermon, he said, "And now let's raise a joyful noise unto the Lord. I'm sure that everyone knows 'Bringing In the Sheaves.'"

It turned out that only Geest, one of the rich women, and three of the whores did. The Union Church as yet had no hymnals, so everyone else tried to hum along while the other five sang. McLendon thought that it might not be joyful, but it certainly was noise. Remembering how Gabrielle had loved attending church, in a fine St. Louis cathedral and later in a hotel back room in Glorious, McLendon put a dollar he could ill afford to lose in the collection plate when Geest passed it around. He noticed that was two bits more than Herman Fringer contributed.

BY LATE FEBRUARY, the plains began to abound again with game—deer, quail, turkey. Even a few bears lumbered out of hibernation. But there was not the slightest sign of buffalo. It was early days yet, some of the hide men noted. Even back in the heyday of '72, the main herd didn't head Dodge's way until May or even June. All you ever got around early spring was an early buff or two. But as February 1874 gave gradual way to March, not a single buffalo was seen.

That was when Billy Dixon finally called a meeting in Hanrahan's billiard parlor and saloon.

JUST ABOUT ALL the main hide men came, and many of the town merchants. They crammed inside, got their whiskey or beer—now served mostly in bottles rather than mugs—and waited impatiently to hear what Billy had to say. He was closeted back in Jim Hanrahan's office with Jim, A. C. Myers, and Charlie Rath. That inspired considerable speculation, since it was well-known that Rath and Myers didn't get along. Rath & Company by far dominated the town hide purchasing, but Myers also did some hide dealing at his so-called Pioneer Store. He didn't have as much trade volume, but most people liked him better than Rath, who drove hard bargains.

McLendon came to hear Billy because he was curious, not because he had any intention of joining in whatever expedition was about to be proposed. Bat stood by McLendon's side, gulping beer at a furious pace, three bottles in the twenty minutes they'd been in the saloon, with a fourth already ordered from the busy bartender.

"You might slow down that rate of guzzling," McLendon advised. "If you don't, you'll be potted before Billy gets out word one."

"I can't help it," Masterson said. "What if Billy's already cut deals with the ones he intends to take with him? I don't want to be left behind."

"That's foolish, Bat. You know how people talk in this town. If Billy had been recruiting, we'd have heard."

"But what if he has been, and we haven't? If he don't offer to take me, I swear—" But Bat didn't elaborate, because Billy, Hanrahan, Myers, and Rath emerged from the back office and took up places in front of the long bar. They blinked a little from the tobacco haze. The merchants smoked hand-rolled cigarettes, while the hide men favored their clay pipes.

"This is Billy Dixon's party, so he'll be the main one to address you," Jim Hanrahan said. "I'll ask that you refrain from interrupting."

Billy nodded and took a step forward. Some of his long hair fell in front of his face and he brushed it back. As always, he got right to the point: Everybody knew the buffalo were about hunted out north of the

Arkansas River. There was plenty of sign of a large herd down around the Canadian, maybe one as big as had roamed around Dodge in the summer of '72. Billy said it seemed to him that he and the other hide men had no choice. They had to either hunt south where the buffalo were or else get out of the business.

"If we choose to stay in Dodge, there's a limit on possible professions," Billy said. He took a sip of beer and let that thought settle on his listeners. "We can try our hands at shopkeeping. But there are already enough shops in town, and plenty of folks to work in them. We're fairly sure, I might even say certain, that the tick line's going to be moved west and Texas cattle drives here will follow. So we can get into the cattle business, maybe herding or branding or some such. Then there's the obvious. Dodge will continue to grow, and more people means the need for more food—not just meat, but bread and vegetables and forage for animals and so forth. So we could become farmers."

But hide men, Billy said, were unsuited to such pursuits. "It's our nature to crave challenge. We want excitement. None of us came this way to end up merchants or cattle hands or farmers. I'd die before I was a farmer. So sometime in March, mid-month hopefully but surely not much later, I'm going to head south to down around the Canadian, where the great herd will surely pass. If I have to, I'll go alone with whatever shooters and skinners and cooks I can recruit."

"Count me in!" Bat hollered, and Billy grinned at him.

"Okay, now I got one who wants to come with me for sure. But the thing of it is, what we need to do is all go together, one big group, a hundred or more. If we go in another three weeks or maybe in a month, that will give us time to pick a site and build a permanent camp, one with solid sod buildings that can't be burned down, and a stout corral. A defensible place if need be. Then in late April, early May, or even into June, whenever the herd arrives, we can go out during the day in our individual parties and return at night with our hides. It'll be safety in numbers, as some like to say. We can make our livings and be the kind of men we want to be."

Heath Lee waved his hand. "So, Billy, who are you inviting?"

Billy grinned again. "It ain't a matter of issuing invitations. All who care to come are welcome, so long as they're willing to be part of the general group."

"How we going to handle the Indians?" Bermuda Carlyle demanded. "I want hides, but not at the expense of my hair or my privates."

Billy said that as far as he could tell from his recent scout south, the Indians had backed off considerably. The Army had recently administered some ass whippings to them.

"Don't mistake me, they're still dangerous," Billy said. "But that's why we'll have the big permanent camp. The Co-manch, the Cheyenne, the Kioways—their way is to attack in small raiding parties, maybe two dozen braves at the most. That size bunch won't dare take on all the guns we'd be able to muster, particularly as the Indians are always short of ammunition."

A voice with an unmistakable Yankee twang rose from the back of the saloon: "Might I pose a question or two?"

"Pose as many as you like, Mr. Mooar," Billy said politely.

Mooar smoothly maneuvered through the crowd until he stood beside Billy at the bar. "So you're asking us to go down south under your command? Is that the case? You are the boss?"

"I'm not boss. I don't think anybody is going to be. Just a bunch of hide men working together for the common good."

"Precisely," Mooar said, and he smirked. "So let's consider once again what you term the nature of hide men. We're business folk, wouldn't you say?"

"Of course. We look to our efforts for profit."

"So in the strictest sense, whether here or down south, we compete with each other to shoot the most buffalo, get the most hides?"

Billy looked annoyed. "I guess, if you put it that way."

Mooar turned slightly so he that addressed the crowd rather than Billy. "I believe I can safely rate myself as the senior hide man here. My brother and I came to this area early on. I take credit for bringing down more than twenty thousand buffalo since. As a result I'm well positioned financially, and intend to remain that way. I will not go down to be part of some group that shares equal chances to kill buffalo and shares the money besides. I don't believe any of the rest of you who are *real* hide men will want to do that, either. In our profession it's every man for himself, and let the best shots thrive the most. Don't you all agree?" Because everybody liked Billy, and most of the other hide men didn't care for Mooar, there wasn't much reaction. But there was still a sudden restlessness; this was an issue that no one seemed to have previously considered, Billy included.

Billy took a moment to think through an appropriate response; he finally settled for: "That's not the point of a big group. During the day's hunting, we go our own ways with our crews and test our skills. But afterward at night we bunch up together at the settlement. You come on down with us, Mr. Mooar, and you can kill all the buffs you want. No man among us will try to horn in on your share, whatever it may be."

"Ah." Mooar seemed so easily mollified by Billy's answer that McLendon knew the Yankee hide man was about to spring his main attack on the proposed expedition. Mooar drew the moment out by scratching his head and looking reflective while everyone waited to see what he'd say next. He was a showman. Finally he said pleasantly, "And all of the hides, Billy. What of them?"

"Why, we'd sell them, of course. That's the purpose of the hunt, to take and sell hides."

Mooar smiled. "Sell them to who, Billy? The Indians who'll be surrounding you down there? Perhaps to the buzzards who'll circle your great big camp? You'll be some hundred fifty miles from Dodge City, so I suppose you could interrupt your hunts every so often and take another four or five days to bring the hides back here to sell, then another four or five to get back to camp. Even if the buffs decide to lie down along the Canadian and take long summer naps, you'll still miss most of the passing of the herd. Meanwhile, everyone left behind in your camp will have to survive on buffalo chips and water, and if they go out to hunt, they'll have to shoot the buffs with pebbles, for your supplies of ammunition will soon run out."

Jesus, McLendon thought, *Mooar's got Billy.* But Billy simply smiled in his own turn.

"You're a smart fellow, Mr. Mooar," Billy said. "You think of everything. But some other smart people have helped me solve those very problems. Jim Hanrahan, A. C. Myers, Mr. Rath, would any of you care to step forward and address Mr. Mooar's concerns?"

"I'll start," Hanrahan said. He stuck his thumbs in the waistcoat of his expensive suit and nodded in Mooar's direction. "First thing is, Billy Dixon and I are going partners in his part of the hunt down south. I'm going to bankroll his initial supplies, the best guns and horses and gear to be had, and those who sign up for his crew will have free use of it all." That got the crowd excited—basically, Hanrahan and Billy would subsidize the rides and equipment of everyone who hired on with them. Their crew's share of the profits would be free and clear.

"You hear that, C.M.?" Masterson said exultantly. "You and me are going to make a pile of money!"

"Further, after a day's hard shooting and skinning, we'll have something better on offer than buffalo chips and water," Hanrahan continued. "I'm going down with Billy and the boys, and wherever they choose to settle I'm going to open a saloon. Beer, whiskey, sarsaparilla, bitters—whatever your drinking pleasure, we'll have it on hand."

"And there's more," A. C. Myers put in. "I'm going to open up a general store, with all the ammunition and amenities in constant stock. We've got some teamsters signed on, like the Scheidler boys—you back there? Give a wave, Isaac and Shorty—who'll keep me constantly resupplied. Fred Leonard's partnering up with me in this endeavor, and Fred's going to be right there with Billy and the rest. Oh, and don't fear inflated costs. I intend to charge about the same for all goods as I do here in Dodge. Cheerful, friendly, and reasonably priced service, as has always been the custom of the Pioneer Store ownership."

Mooar flinched as though he'd been struck. He was a proud man and hated being shown up in public. For a moment it looked as though he'd stalk out of the saloon, but then he caught himself and said, "But what of us selling the hides in a timely manner? All the liquor and luxuries in the world are of no use if you lack the coin to buy them."

Billy said calmly, "I believe that Mr. Rath can speak to that."

Charlie Rath knew he wasn't especially popular with the hide men; he'd bargained all of them down too many times on prices for the skins they brought him. So, unlike A. C. Myers, who emphasized congenial customer relations in the new south camp, he spoke directly to business issues.

"I'm going to open a hide dealership wherever Billy chooses to stop down there; also a café of sorts. I don't have a cook yet, but I'll hire one. And every day I'll buy the skins brought in, unless they're chock-full of holes from faulty marksmanship. Fair prices as always. The teamsters will haul the hides back here to Dodge. It'll be business as usual. Oh, and I'll have a general store too. Best goods available"—he nodded at Myers—"and competitive pricing."

"Tom O'Keefe is going to come with us and operate a blacksmith shop," Hanrahan added. "All we'll lack there by the Canadian'll be dancing girls, and we may bring in some of those by midsummer if we can find any who are willing."

"Well," Billy said, sounding pleased. "If that resolves your concerns, Mr. Mooar, I hope you'll consider throwing in with us. As you know from your own scouting, the buffalo will be coming along the Canadian in great numbers. Of that, there is no doubt. We'll have the firepower to discourage the Indians, and the means to keep ourselves paid for our skins and stocked up with supplies on a daily basis. Everything's been thought of. Come take advantage." Mooar waved a deprecating hand in Billy's direction and shouldered his way out of the crowded saloon.

"All right, I'll be glad to talk to anybody with a mind to join my crew," Billy said. "I guess that's it—wait, Jim Hanrahan wants to say something more."

Hanrahan clapped his hands together sharply to get the crowd's attention. Everyone was buzzing excitedly. "One last thing. You heard me say I'll be going south with Billy next month. For those who remain behind, don't fear—Waters and Hanrahan's Occident Billiards Hall and Saloon will remain open for business here in Dodge, under the guidance of my partner Mose Waters and, after my departure, new assistant manager Cash McLendon. And now, to celebrate, one free round of beer for all. Don't try and hornswoggle a second one, for I'm keeping a sharp eye on the bartender."

There was a surge toward the front of the room, with some men moving toward Billy and others pushing to the bar. A few paused briefly to slap McLendon on the shoulder and murmur congratulations. Masterson looked at him sorrowfully for a moment, then burrowed into the crowd around Billy. McLendon watched the merry melee for a few minutes, then went back to his room at the boardinghouse, where he tossed and turned for the rest of the night and tried, for perhaps the millionth time, to calculate how long he would have to work at Hanrahan's before he had enough saved to get from Dodge City to Mountain View, and from there to San Francisco with Gabrielle and, maybe, her father.

BAT MASTERSON NEVER got back to his room that night. In the morning McLendon found him slumped outside Hanrahan's. He roused his bedraggled friend and said, "Bat, surely you didn't sleep in the street."

"I believe that I did. Are all my parts intact, or did stray dogs dine on me?"

"You got that drunk?"

Bat shrugged, then moaned as though the brief flexing of his shoulders hurt him. "I suppose so. I was celebrating. Billy said I could be part of his crew: skinner to start, but I'll be allowed to kill five buffs of my own during each day's hunting. So I figure five skins sold for, say, three dollars each, and also two bits for each of Billy's kills I skin, maybe ten of those at a time. Seventeen and a half dollars a day, less a little for food and reviving drink—that ain't bad. Plus, I'll so dazzle Billy with my marksmanship that he'll eventually promote me to full-fledged shooter. I'll be rolling in riches by summer's end."

"I'm happy for you. That was what you wanted. Now let's get you cleaned up and ready to go out and work. Billy's not leaving for at least a couple of weeks, so you'll need money 'til then. Those buffalo bones won't collect themselves."

"Give me a minute. I feel so bad, I'd have to get better to die. I can't wait to be done with buffalo bones. Pretty soon I'll be selling their hides instead, and the profits will be overflowing my pockets. God bless Billy Dixon."

McLendon chuckled. "We should seek out Mrs. Olds, see if she might spare you a cup of coffee before we set off. That'll perk you up."

"Maybe so." Bat took a deep breath, straightened up, and blinked in the sun's glare. As they made their way slowly toward the boarding-house, McLendon gently leading Masterson by the arm as though guid-ing an elderly invalid, Bat said, "And don't think I forgot Jim Hanrahan's announcement about you, C.M. But mark my words, you ain't going to spend a minute working for him here in Dodge. You're meant to come south with Billy Dixon and me. I know it in my heart."

McLendon didn't argue, because he knew his friend's throbbing brain wasn't up to it. "We'll see, Bat. We'll see. Right now, let's just get you some coffee. We've got a long day ahead."

DODGE FINALLY HAD its own newspaper, and the *Dodge City Messenger* split space between predictions of when the tick line would move west and listing the latest locals to join Billy Dixon's southern hunting expedition. This was smart journalism, Cash McLendon reflected, be-cause those were the two subjects everyone was talking about.

Rumblings from the state legislature indicated that a tick line deci-sion would be coming by late summer or early fall. Factoring in time for Texas ranchers to get official notification and change their herds' route accordingly from Wichita to Dodge, many in town anticipated the first influx of cattle and cash-flush drovers by November or, at worst, March 1875, since cattle drives were routinely suspended during the harshest portion of winter.

That news as reported in the *Messenger* impacted the newspaper's other main topic, since some of the hide men and potential crew mem-bers who planned going south with Billy decided they had new, attrac-tive career options. Bat Masterson was disgusted that his brothers Ed and Jim anticipated better prospects by staying in town and working in saloons. Heath Lee said he would "stick around town—the hide business is just about done, so in one way or another I'm going to find a place in the cattle trade." Gruff Henry Raymond astonished everyone by announcing he was staying on in Dodge too. His decision was dictated not by professional concerns but by romance.

"Me and Becky Travis are hitching up," he told his stunned friends. "Becky don't favor a life of waiting around for me to return from long trips out on the hunt. So she's got me a job making repairs and such at Dodge House, where she does the cooking. We'll spend our days working shoulder to shoulder and our nights—well, a gentleman don't speak too plainly of that."

"Jesus, Henry, you can't mean it," Masterson protested. "That kind of life will never suit you. You were born to hunt by day and sleep out under the stars at night."

"Perhaps up to now, but my present nightly choice is between wrapping up in a blanket on hard ground, listening to other men snore and fart, or snuggling in a warm bed with my honey. And that's no choice at all."

But many other veteran hide men and workers threw in with Billy Dixon. Bermuda Carlyle, Charley Armitage, Jim Campbell, Billy Ogg, Sam Smith, Hiram Watson, Ed Trevor, and Mike Welsh were among those committed to going. Several signed on to work directly for Billy and Jim Hanrahan. Brick Bond and Dutch Henry said they would come, too, but not as anybody's partners or employees. They'd put together independent crews to kill and skin their own buffalo. That was fine with everyone else, since Bond and Henry weren't to be trusted beyond being crack shots. That marksmanship would come in handy if there were any Indian battles.

"This is the intended spirit of the place," Billy said. "Come in the main bunch, come on your own, just stay close to the compound, and stick together in case of trouble."

J. W. Mooar made it clear that he'd be somewhere around the Canadian, but not in any way part of the Dixon settlement.

"I'll have my own substantial crew," he said. "I'll hunt in the vicinity and sell my hides to Charlie Rath at your outpost, but otherwise I'll range and sleep where I damn please. Woe betide the man who tries to horn in on my shooting area. And I'm fully capable of defending myself if the Indians care to tangle."

"Fine," Billy said. "The size of the herd I anticipate is so vast that there'll be plenty of prime shooting space for everyone. And if you change your mind about being part of the main hunting community, there would certainly be room for you and your men."

"Don't count on it, Dixon. I still regard your plan as foolishness. Jim Hanrahan is going to weary of the hard life quicker than a blink, and he'll take himself and his money back to civilization, leaving you broke and desperate. You'll be swamping out privies in Dodge before summer's end."

Billy refused to be drawn into an argument. "You're allowed your opinion, Mr. Mooar. I wish you good hunting down along the Canadian, and the best possible prices for your hides."

Some other Dodge residents also made plans to come south with Billy, though not as hide men or members of their crews. With plans for a store, saloon, blacksmith shop, and food services at the new settlement, there was a need for support staff—shop clerks, hide stackers, at least one bartender, bookkeepers for A. C. Myers and Charlie Rath, and several cooks.

Hannah Olds shocked McLendon and Masterson by telling them that she and her husband had signed on with Rath.

"I'm to be a cook, and William will help keep Mr. Rath's books," she said. "This means, of course, that you and our other Dodge boarders will have to presently find other accommodations. We're selling this building to Miss Mollie Whitecamp."

Bat whistled sharply. "Mollie Whitecamp? You mean the madam who calls herself Dutch Jake? Why, she's going to turn this building into a brothel. I guess her first cathouse is doing such brisk business that she requires additional space."

"That's of no consequence to me," Mrs. Olds sniffed. "Mr. Olds and myself require you to vacate the premises by the time we make our journey to the south."

"Well, I'm going in the same direction, so I had plans to pack up and move out anyway," Bat said. "Though the thought of continuing my residence here in the company of Dutch Jake's finest girls has considerable appeal. Did you know this was happening, C.M.? Working girls in these rooms? Is that your real reason for staying behind?"

"Hardly," McLendon said. "Thanks for the notice, Mrs. Olds. I'll make new arrangements."

Later he pulled Hannah Olds aside and said, "Ma'am, have you considered the situation in which you're about to find yourself: out in wild country with rough men, and danger everywhere? You've told me often enough that Dodge City is too much for your nerves. And your husband isn't a well man. Down south, he'll be beyond the reach of doctors."

Mrs. Olds blinked, and McLendon noticed the deep stress lines at the corners of her eyes and mouth. "It's a gamble that we're willing to take. My husband's health continues to deteriorate. I've got family in the East if we can only get together the money to go to them; he could die in more comfort there, and afterward I'd not be alone in the world.

This boardinghouse earns us very little. Mr. Rath has offered generous salaries. If we can survive down there through this single hunting
season, we'll be in a financial position to depart this awful frontier for
good."

Billy Dixon set the departure time for the third week in March. Masterson was too excited to continue picking up buffalo bones, and Mc-
Lendon couldn't gather enough of them alone, so they spent the days
in town. Bat had several flings with saloon girls, telling each that she
was his one true love and he wanted a last night in her arms before he
left to risk death down south. McLendon looked for a new place to live,
and found a room in the boardinghouse operated by the Burgesses, who
he'd met helping to build Union Church. They charged $1.50 a night,
considerably more than he had paid Hannah and William Olds, but the
room was bright and clean and the $35 weekly salary he'd make at Han-
rahan and Waters allowed the additional expenditure. *September,* he
thought. *I ought to have sufficient funds by September, and then I'm going to Gabrielle.*

McLendon also spent time with Jim and Mose Waters, discussing his
new duties in the saloon. Mostly he would be expected to keep books,
track inventory, and place orders for liquor, beer, and billiard equipment. McLendon hadn't previously had much to do with Hanrahan's
business partner, but Waters seemed like a decent fellow.

"I can't promise you much more than a few months, Mr. Waters,"
McLendon said. "By that time I hope to have put aside enough money to
head out to California."

"Call me Mose. Jim's told me of your plans, and that's fine with me.
Meanwhile, I'll be glad of your assistance. I understand that Jim and
Billy Dixon and the rest are setting off south next Tuesday. What say we
make that your first day on the job?"

.   .   .

ON A SUNDAY NIGHT two days before the expedition was to depart, McLendon sat with Billy Dixon and some of the other hide men in the Hanrahan and Waters saloon. The hunters sipped whiskey and talked about the good shooting they anticipated down south. Figuring an average of three dollars per hide, the money they expected to earn was considerable—at least sixty dollars a day for the worst shots, and a hundred or more for marksmen like Billy. Even their lowliest crew members could anticipate hefty wages.

"If my backup shooters have any skill at all, together we'll surely take down a hundred fifty or two hundred buffs each day," Billy said. "I pay my skinners two bits a hide. So they might earn twenty-five or even thirty dollars on a daily basis if they demonstrate sufficient stamina with the knife."

"Don't say that where McLendon can hear," Jim Hanrahan joked. "He'll turn his nose up at the wage I'm paying him to stay in Dodge, and insist on coming south with us instead."

McLendon laughed with the rest. "Jim, you have my word that I won't change my mind. I'm reporting for work on Tuesday, right after you boys set out south."

On Monday morning he packed his belongings so he could move into his new room the next day. It didn't take long. He hadn't accumulated much during his time in Dodge, just a few shirts, denim jeans, and long johns. Then McLendon went over to Hanrahan's to ask Mose Waters when he should report for work on Tuesday.

"Early afternoon, I expect, or whenever Billy and Jim and the boys have departed," Mose said. "Meanwhile, this letter came for you."

Just the sight of the handwriting on the outside of the envelope thrilled McLendon. He ran to his room in the Olds boardinghouse and read what Gabrielle had written:

March 1, 1874

I am in receipt of your letter, and was pleased to learn that you are well. Given the circumstances of our parting back in Glorious and your subsequent departure from there in haste, I remained concerned for your well-being. Thus your message has afforded me considerable relief.

So far as your offer to resume a relationship, I am frankly confused. Since last we met, things in my life have changed. As I believe you learned from the salesman Mr. LeMond, I now live in Mountain View not far from the old site of Glorious and work at a hotel here. My father, who is in ill health, lives with me. My own health is good.

No, I have not married Joe Saint. This is not to say that I will not, only that as yet I have not felt it was appropriate for me to do so. You have brought me so much pain and he has been constantly kind and loving. But back in Glorious you swore to me that you had changed, and based on my observations there I believe that this may be true, at least to some extent. I respect you for working hard to become a better person. You are right in one thing, it is time for me to make my choice. I do not know what it will be.

If you still wish it, come to Mountain View and we will talk. Let me emphasize that I make no promises. Also, I would never do to Joe Saint what you did to me in St. Louis, simply walk away with someone else without regard for the feelings of the other. I have shared your letter with Joe, and will show him this one before I send it to you. When he noted the return address on your envelope, he commented that he has heard of Dodge City and it is said to be a fearsome place. Joe says he will somehow convince me to marry him rather than go with you, and I will continue to give him that opportunity. When possible, please contact me with the presumed date of your arrival here. Mountain View is a growing town and you might find it even more to your liking than California. (And if you do go to that state, you must learn to spell its name correctly.)

I will wait to hear from you.

With kind regards,

Gabrielle

THIRTEEN

It took almost five days of hard riding for Quanah and Isatai to reach the main Cheyenne camp, which was well north of the Kiowa village. They briefly detoured to meet with the leaders of the Arapaho, who, as Quanah expected, were glad to talk about attacking the whites but declined to participate. They'd watch this great fight Quanah described, they promised. If it was successful, their people might join in a second one.

"The Arapaho want others to do the fighting, and the Kiowa want proof that we consider them our equals," Quanah said. "Now everything depends on the Cheyenne. They have the greatest numbers and, next to the People, are the finest fighters. If they don't agree to join us, our plan is ruined."

Isatai corrected him. "Buffalo Hump's plan, you mean."

"Yes, Buffalo Hump's."

"Don't worry. His spirit promises me that the Cheyenne will agree, and so will the Kiowa, at least some of them. Buffalo Hump has nothing to say about the Arapaho, so I guess they'll just stand aside and watch after all, being no better than Mexicans. But we'll get all of the warriors that we need."

"I'm glad to hear it. Now, do you think Buffalo Hump's spirit might be willing to tell us exactly where the Cheyenne are?"

All the Indian tribes moved their campsites frequently, sometimes to follow the buffalo or other animal herds, other times to escape detection from the white soldiers. The Cheyenne camp Quanah and Isatai were seeking had been recently established. Many of the Cheyenne had wintered on an agency south of the Cimarron, hoping to subsist during the cold months on the white man's food. As usual, far less was provided than had been promised, and, additionally, they were harassed by white rustlers who ran off many of their horses. That caused a rift in the Cheyenne leadership. Little Robe, Stone Calf, White Shield, and Whirlwind argued that, since everyone was settled, it made sense to stay on at the agency until the snow melted. But Medicine Water and Gray Beard were too furious, and led about half of the two thousand people away to the north, losing the meager agency rations but maintaining their pride. So while Quanah knew roughly where their new camp was located, the region was still vast.

"I believe that if we keep going in this direction for just a while longer, we'll find the Cheyenne and they'll welcome us," Isatai said. "You worry too much. Trust the spirits like I do."

Quanah was sick of hearing Isatai tell him to trust the spirits, but because he didn't have any other ideas, he kept riding in the direction Isatai wanted. As the sun began to sink behind a mountain range, he saw wisps of smoke rising from behind some hills just ahead.

"That will be the Cheyenne camp," Isatai said. "We're going to arrive in time for the evening meal. I hope they're better hosts than Lone Wolf and the Kiowa."

They were. The Cheyenne greeted their two visitors like long-lost brothers, and soon Quanah and Isatai were seated beside a warm outdoor fire, smoking a pipe with Gray Beard and stuffing themselves with dog stew. It was a happy camp. Recent hunting had been good, and everyone was glad to be free of the agency workers and their endless demands for the Cheyenne to wear white people's clothing and learn to plant crops.

"They even wanted us to pray to their god," Gray Beard said, popping a hunk of dog meat into his mouth and smacking his lips at the fine taste. "They only have one, though they say confusing things about his son and how the father and the son are the same thing. These whites at the agency call themselves Kway-kers. They say we have to pray to their god, or else he'll send us to some other agency called Hell. It's supposed to be very hot there, with evil spirits who will prod us with pointed weapons."

"Ah, the Cheyenne dog soldiers can beat any Kway-kers or their evil spirits," Quanah said, complimenting the elite fighting force of the Cheyenne nation. "But it's better not to be at any agency at all. We were meant to live on this land in whatever way we choose, not how the whites tell us that we must. And Isatai and I have come here on behalf of the People to tell you about a way we can make that happen."

Gray Beard listened attentively as Quanah explained. Isatai didn't talk at all. He ate several helpings of stew, then closed his eyes and hummed. Quanah felt more comfortable with Gray Beard than he had with Lone Wolf and Satanta in the Kiowa camp. The Cheyenne chief seemed more interested in war strategy than in the spirit of Buffalo Hump, but he didn't make light of the spirit choosing a very odd fat man as his messenger. When Quanah was finished talking, Isatai opened his eyes, said, "Buffalo Hump's spirit promises that the Cheyenne will prosper once you join us," and resumed humming.

"This is interesting," Gray Beard said. "Of course, I must talk about it with the ones still at the agency. They're getting ready to leave, since the cold times are finally over."

"So they might join us too?" Quanah asked hopefully. Stone Calf, Little Robe, and the other chiefs at the agency were all great fighters.

"Maybe," Gray Beard said. "They are very angry at the whites and I think they would like to fight. Meanwhile, we're glad to have you and Isatai here as our guests. Can you stay awhile? Tomorrow we're going to have some contests led by Medicine Water, and after that a dance—not the sun dance, which I know you Comanche don't care for."

"The sun dance, any of your dances or customs, we respect them all," Quanah said quickly. "We'd be honored to stay."

"Will there also be feasting?" Isatai inquired.

"Of course," Gray Beard said without the slightest hint of mockery. "Communicating with spirits must be hungry work."

The two visitors spent the night in Gray Beard's tipi. Like those of the People, it was made from buffalo hides, but the Cheyenne tanned their hides much longer, until they were bleached almost white. Then they decorated the pale hides with pictures in bright colors, mostly reds, yellows, and blues. As a result, they were much lighter inside, even at night when only a low fire smoldered, its small, darting flames reflecting off the white, scraped skins. Gray Beard and his three wives all slumbered peacefully, and Isatai snored like ten bull buffalo in full rut. Quanah, though, tossed on his robes. The too-bright interior contributed to keeping him awake, but mostly he couldn't sleep because he was so excited. Gray Beard seemed prepared to enthusiastically become a partner in the Great Fight. If he helped Quanah convince the agency chiefs to do the same, and almost all the available Cheyenne warriors participated, why, that was maybe five hundred fighters right there! And added to that might be two or three hundred Kiowa, and surely the same number of warriors from among the People. A fighting force of a thousand or more—no whites could withstand it, not even if Bad Hand gathered all his soldiers to oppose them. Though Quanah couldn't sleep, he still passed the night happily, imagining what was going to happen.

THE DAWN WAS GLORIOUS, perhaps the first morning since winter that the air was pleasantly warm. Birds sang and the sun rose in an especially bright blue sky. Gray Beard's wives served fresh hot corn cakes smeared with honey for breakfast. After enjoying the meal, Quanah asked Isatai if he wanted to come with him to a nearby creek to wash. Isatai crammed another corn cake in his mouth and shook his head.

Quanah walked through the camp toward the creek. He and most of the villagers he passed exchanged greetings. Quanah thought to himself that they were an especially good-looking tribe. Men among the People tended to be short, with thick chests; Cheyenne men were taller and much less bulky. The physical contrast between the women of the two tribes was even greater. Comanche females were usually squat, with wide waists and heavy haunches. Quanah's wife, Wickeah, was a rare exception. Some of the Cheyenne women Quanah passed on his way to the creek came close to matching Wickeah in willowy beauty.

Several villagers were performing morning ablutions at the creek, splashing their faces and cleaning their teeth with twigs. A half-dozen men used sharp-edged rock fragments to scrape whiskers from their cheeks and chins. A few dozen yards farther down, some women of the camp were washing clothes, swishing calico shirts and deerskin dresses in the water, then vigorously wringing them out and spreading them to dry on nearby bushes. Quanah watched for a few moments, enjoying the domestic bustle, and then he noticed her. She was so perfect—face, figure, a kind of sensual glow and confidence emanating from her—that for a moment Quanah forgot to breathe.

She was still young, but more of a woman than a girl. Her eyes flashed, her thick black hair hung loose around her shoulders, and she wore a thin cotton shift that Quanah guessed must have been stripped from some white woman during a raid. The sun shone through the shift, and her breasts and legs were deliciously silhouetted. She stood shin-deep in the creek, washing clothes with the other women, chattering and laughing with them. Quanah saw that some of the things she rinsed were men's apparel: a breechclout and leggings and some shirts. Maybe a husband's, but hopefully a father's instead. Already Quanah was calculating how many horses it might take to buy this woman as his second wife. Wickeah would be jealous of the newcomer's superior beauty, but at this moment Quanah didn't care what Wickeah would think. True, this woman who he instantly coveted was a Cheyenne, but surely she would feel pleased, even honored, to become the second wife of the greatest warrior among all the People and, as such, a member of the People herself, the ultimate elevation in life. In fact, after he married her, Quanah thought he might take a third and even a fourth wife from among the Quahadi. That way, if Wickeah tried to assert herself as senior wife by assigning chores, the work would be done by wives three and four while Quanah spent many hours lying with his lovely, ripe Cheyenne.

Spotted Feather, a Cheyenne man who Quanah knew slightly from trading, washed his face nearby. Quanah went over and greeted him.

"I heard you were in camp, also that you have some new plan to fight the white men," Spotted Feather said. "White raiders took four of my horses back at the agency. I'd be pleased to be part of any war party."

"A fighter like you will be welcome," Quanah assured him, even though he had no idea what kind of fighter Spotted Feather was. "Say, can you tell me something about that woman over there—the one leaning down to wash that red shirt?"

Without glancing up, Spotted Feather spit out some creek water and said, "Her name is Mochi."

"Mochi? Are you sure that's who I mean?"

Spotted Feather dried his face with a handful of grass, briefly looked over at the women washing clothes, and said, "Of course, Mochi. All the men notice her. The way she looks, how could they not?"

"Is she married?"

"A woman that fine, of course she is. And not to just any man. Her husband is Medicine Water, the leader of our dog soldiers."

"Ah. Medicine Water." This complicated but did not entirely crush Quanah's hope. Any Cheyenne dog soldier was a formidable warrior— Quanah couldn't take his wife away without anticipating a bruising battle. As their leader, Medicine Water was unquestionably the finest fighter among his tribe. Still, Quanah believed that he would win—he was one of the People, after all. Of course, if Quanah wanted the cooperation of the Cheyenne in his efforts to drive away the white men, he could hardly alienate them at this early stage by forcibly taking Medicine Water's wife. That would have to wait until the great battle was over and the People were reestablished as the rulers of the land, with all other tribes subordinate to them. But eventually Mochi would be his.

Spotted Feather seemed to read Quanah's mind. "Twice before, men tried to take her away from Medicine Water."

"Oh?"

"They died."

Quanah shrugged. "Medicine Water killed them?"

"Oh, no. Mochi did."

"Mochi? How?"

Spotted Feathers grinned. "Are you staying for the contests?" Quanah nodded. "Good. Then you'll see."

. . .

THE CONTESTS STARTED when the sun reached its highest point. The villagers gathered, chattering happily. As senior camp chief, Gray Beard seated himself on a thick buffalo hide and gestured for Quanah and Isatai to join them. Isatai was in one of his closed-eyes-humming moods, but Gray Beard didn't seem offended.

"First, we'll watch the children," he explained.

Small boys competed in short races, then fired blunt-tipped arrows at hide targets marked with red paint circles in the center. The winners received small prizes—beaded moccasins, small pouches of sugar purchased or purloined from sutlers before the band escaped the white agency. Then teenage boys still too young to raid with grown men had their competition—racing and target shooting and wrestling—since skill in hand-to-hand combat was crucial in combat. The winners here received the coveted right to go out on the next raids. They would hold horses and only fight themselves if the full-fledged Cheyenne warriors found themselves in desperate straits, but it was still an honor and the final step before official manhood. The youngsters who won this privilege strutted in front of the girls, who called out appropriate compliments.

"Now the real contests," Gray Beard said. The crowd shifted into an elongated horseshoe shape, with the creek marking the other boundary about four long bowshots away. A tall stake was pounded into the ground about a yard before the creek's bank, and hide targets were set up near the stake. Two dozen men, all painted in full battle colors, pushed through the horseshoe and stood proudly in front of where Gray Beard and his guests sat on the buffalo robe. Quanah knew that most of them were dog soldiers, elite warriors and obviously proud of their status. All of the men wore deerskin shirts and leggings. They stood straight, with knives and pistols on their belts, quivers and bows slung over their shoulders, and rifles in their hands. They all had good rifles, Quanah observed, mostly Winchesters, but also some Henrys like the one Quanah himself carried.

Medicine Water, the most impressive among them, stepped forward and said to Gray Beard, "We are ready." Gray Beard nodded and Medicine Water snapped out commands. The dog soldiers laid their handguns, bows and arrows, and rifles to the side, drew their knives, and paired off.

"They're going to fight without wounding," Gray Beard said. "Their challenge is to demonstrate the skill to win and also the skill not to cut. There are occasional wounds, but only by accident. To win, one must disarm the other or at least get his knife to his opponent's throat."

The paired dog soldiers began to maneuver for position, flicking with their knives, lunging unexpectedly. Quanah couldn't watch them all at once. His eyes were drawn to a pair scuffling off to the left. One was much larger, but the smaller man seemed to *flow*, every movement quick and smooth. There was something about him that seemed very familiar, and then Quanah realized with a start that it wasn't a man, it was Mochi.

"W-what?" he stammered.

Gray Beard saw where Quanah was looking and laughed. "Mochi is one of our best fighters. In camp she is Medicine Water's wife, but when we raid, she goes with the men."

Among the People, women might fight if their camp was being overrun and there weren't enough men left to oppose the enemy. But they were never allowed to take up weapons and participate in raids or full battles. "She's going to be hurt," Quanah protested. Mochi was steadily giving ground to her opponent, who swung his knife in hard arcs, barely missing her.

"Just watch," Gray Beard suggested.

Mochi fell back a few steps at a time, and the man fighting her gained considerable forward momentum. But just as it seemed that Mochi had to lose, she ducked under a particularly vicious swipe of her opponent's knife. Suddenly she was completely behind him. Before he could turn around, Mochi leaped on his back, wrapped her legs around his waist, and placed her knife against his throat. All the onlookers cheered, the camp women loudest of all, as the man dropped his knife in a gesture of surrender.

"That was very skillful," Quanah said. Something dripped in his eye and he wiped his brow. He discovered that he'd broken out into a hard sweat.

"Indeed," Gray Beard said. Isatai just hummed.

The winners broke into new pairs. Mochi won that round, too, and then the next, always defeating her opponents with speed and guile. Finally, there were just two remaining—Mochi and Medicine Water. When Quanah said that she surely wouldn't fight her husband, Gray Beard said, "Mochi will fight anyone."

It was thrilling to watch. Mochi continued moving adroitly, never presenting a direct target, but Medicine Water was quicker than her previous opponents and she couldn't evade his knife thrusts as easily. They sparred, their blades missing by the smallest possible distance. Then Medicine Water's arm was nicked, and a trickle of blood ran down his biceps to his hand. Mochi stopped, giving him time to determine whether the wound was serious. Medicine Water examined his cut and said he was fit to continue. He lunged forward, looking clumsy for the first time, and Mochi ducked underneath his arm to dart behind him. But it was a ruse. Medicine Water whirled and, as Mochi tried to leap on him, pressed his knife against her throat. She glared, then smiled and dropped her knife to the ground. Amid considerable cheering, husband and wife embraced. Then, arm in arm, they walked to where Gray Beard, Quanah, and Isatai sat. Even Isatai watched as they approached.

"Medicine Water wins," Gray Beard announced. He stood up to congratulate the leader of the dog soldiers. Quanah stood too. He couldn't resist looking at Mochi instead of Medicine Water, and she looked right back at him. Worn-out as she had to be from such extended, violent exercise, there was still something impudent in her gaze.

"You fought well," Quanah said.

"It's kind of the Comanche chief to say so," she said. Her voice was musical. Still, Quanah noted the veiled insult. Surely, Mochi knew very well that, unlike the Cheyenne, the People did not designate formal chiefs. Her words were intended to remind him that he was just another warrior. Up close, with her hair piled atop her head instead of flowing down her back, he noticed a physical imperfection. Mochi had a scar on the left side of her neck. Somehow it made her even more alluring.

Quanah realized that Medicine Water knew he was staring at his wife. Forcing himself to look away from Mochi, he turned to her husband and said, "My congratulations to a great fighter."

Medicine Water said, "I couldn't let her beat me. Then she'd want to be in charge of our tipi. But she doesn't fight badly, for a woman. So I'll keep her."

Gray Beard gave Medicine Water his prize, a butcher knife whose handle was decorated with intricate carving. "Now a race for the women," he announced. Medicine Water went off with the other dog soldiers to put their weapons back in their tipis, but Mochi walked over to where several dozen women had lined up. At a command from Gray Beard, they sprinted toward the creek, racing around the stake near its bank and running back toward a finish line someone had scratched in the dirt. It wasn't much of a contest. Mochi won easily. She came back to Gray Beard, finally breathing hard, and Quanah was transfixed by her breasts heaving underneath her shirt. He thought everything about her was magnificent, and he wanted her even more than he had when he first saw her washing clothes in the creek.

There was no prize for winning the women's race. Gray Beard told Mochi that she had run well. Quanah said, "Congratulations again," but Mochi ignored him. She looked at Isatai and asked, "Are you staying tonight for the dance?"

For once, Isatai forgot about the spirits and humming. "Yes, I'm staying," he said.

Mochi told the fat Spirit Messenger, "I'll see you there." She shot a brief, arch glance at Quanah, then walked away.

ALL THE TRIBES DANCED—the Cheyenne, the Kiowa, the Arapaho. Even the cannibal Tonkawa danced, and so, of course, did the People. They danced for all sorts of reasons: to thank the gods for good hunting seasons, or to convince them to send game, or to take away cold and snow. There were dances to win the spirits' favor for planned attacks, and others to simply allow men and women to have a good time. Everyone would sing and gyrate to drumbeats. Sometimes there was also music from wooden flutes. Satanta had begun the Kiowa tradition of blowing bugles taken from white soldiers. But all dances were community occasions. Sometimes all the scattered camps of tribes converged in one place, the Cheyenne and Kiowa often, but the People almost never.

The People were disgusted by the self-inflicted mutilation that was part of the Kiowa and Cheyenne sun dances. In these, always held over a multi-day period, a high pole was erected inside a roofless compound and hide thongs were secured to the pole. Then, usually after fasting, warriors used sharp bone or wooden skewers to attach these thongs to their chests and sometimes with help from others to their backs, driving the skewers behind the tendons and muscles beneath the skin. Then they would dance around the pole, leaning back hard so that, eventually, the skewers tore free, leaving great bleeding holes on their bodies. The hope was that the agony, plus light-headedness from hunger, would result in their seeing visions from the spirits. This made absolutely no sense to the People, who saw no advantage to their best fighters wounding themselves. If Gray Beard's Cheyenne camp had held a sun dance, Quanah would have felt uncomfortable staying to watch it. His tribe abhorred the practice, and believed it was just one more way that the Kiowa and Cheyenne demonstrated their inferiority to the People.

But the dance that night was a simpler, safer one, simply an occasion when the villagers in Gray Beard's camp celebrated the new, warmer season and their newfound freedom from the white agency. There was feasting, which Isatai especially enjoyed, and flute and drum music. Everyone dressed in their best. Many of the Cheyenne wore feathered headdresses. As the camp leader, Gray Beard had the most elaborate of all. It went partway down his back, double rows of eagle feathers held in place by hide lacing and beadwork, and then trailed behind him as he walked. Though warriors among the People preferred simpler headgear, usually buffalo hide caps with the horns still attached, Quanah made a point of complimenting Gray Beard on his impressive headdress.

"Something like this can be hard to keep on, especially in battle, but I wear it anyway because it is a sign to the other men that a leader is there among them," Gray Beard said. "Eagles are hard to find sometimes, so when we do, we pluck all their feathers and store them until the next time they're needed for headdresses; also for decorating shields and lances. Of course, we use other sorts of feathers for arrows."

"It looks very fine," Quanah said. "I know that you're proud to wear it."

Everyone gathered around a large campfire. Stewpots lined its edges.

The food was distributed and the villagers and guests ate their fill. They washed down the meal with bottles of whiskey. On agency land, white traders always made liquor available even when food was scarce, and Gray Beard's followers had built up a good supply before they left. Now the men drank the most, but the women had their share. As the whiskey warmed everyone's veins, the dancing began. At first the men danced alone, acting out exploits from past battles, shaking their fists and howling. When it was the turn of the women, they swayed more gracefully. But gradually their gyrations grew more blatant. Their hips twitched toward the watching men. This was the signal for mixed dancing. The boldest women chose their male partners instead of waiting to be asked. Some wives chose men other than their husbands, but this was not considered in any way wrong. Flirting was part of the fun. It was understood by the men that they should not consider this an invitation to do anything more than dance.

Mochi, eyes shiny from drinking, made her way to the robes where Gray Beard, Quanah, and Isatai sat. Quanah's heart leaped—she was going to choose him. But instead she held out her hand to Isatai, who grunted as he struggled to his feet. He tried to dance, and everyone laughed at the sight of his jiggling flesh. Mochi moved seductively beside him; Quanah, disappointed and jealous, still couldn't take his eyes off her.

Isatai could dance only for a few minutes. Then he was out of breath and had to sit down. When he did, Mochi said to Quanah, "It's your turn." She took his hand and led him toward the fire. Her fingers felt very warm. They danced, mostly not touching, but sometimes Mochi brushed him with an arm or a hip, and when she did, Quanah's whole body tingled. He tried to think of something smart to say, but all he could manage was "You run very fast."

"Yes, I do." Looking over Mochi's shoulder, Quanah could see Medicine Water dancing with a woman, laughing with her and not paying attention.

"I'd like to run with you," he said to Mochi, wondering how she would react.

She giggled, a marvelous sound. "You couldn't keep up with me."

"You know what I mean."

"Yes. You want to race me. All right. The stake is still there, down by the creek." To Quanah's astonishment, Mochi shouted, "This Comanche wants to race me. Clear a path," and the drums stopped beating and the flutes went silent as everyone else drew back. Medicine Water came over and clapped his wife on the shoulder. Obviously, he approved.

"My wife and the Comanche, to the stake and back," Medicine Water said. "It will be a fine thing to watch."

Quanah turned to Gray Beard. "I can't do this. It wouldn't be fair."

The Cheyenne chief said, "Maybe not. We'll see."

Quanah tried to reason with Mochi. "I'm a man. You won't be able to keep up. I don't want to embarrass you."

"Oh?" She slipped off her moccasins. "I like to run barefoot."

Medicine Water said to Quanah, "Let's wager, if you're so confident. You rode a good horse into our camp."

"It's a very good horse. I took it from Bad Hand's herd." Quanah felt slightly disoriented, and wished he hadn't drunk quite so much whiskey. His head buzzed. Still, it was going to be a race against a woman. "Do you have a good horse too?"

Medicine Water looked over at Mochi, who was stretching, preparing to run. She was wearing a short deerskin skirt and her bare legs were shapely. "Yes, I have several. If you win, you can pick one, though of course Cheyenne don't keep as many horses as the Comanche."

"Let's agree on the rules," Mochi suggested.

"What rules?" Quanah said. "We're racing. Trying to see who runs fastest."

"Around the pole by the creek and back?"

"Fine."

"No other rules? Just whoever gets back to the campfire first?" Mochi asked. "You're sure?" Quanah nodded impatiently, wanting to get it over with. It was exciting to be standing next to Mochi, but her husband was there, too, and Gray Beard and Isatai and the rest of the Cheyenne camp were all watching. "All right," Mochi said. "Gray Beard, will you give the order?"

"Of course," the chief said. "Both of you get ready. *Go!*"

Quanah wasn't the fastest runner among the Quahadi, but he was good enough to come close to winning some of their camp races, and that was against other men. He sprinted toward the stake by the creek. It was hard to see in the dark. The flames from the large campfire made it barely visible. Quanah was surprised to find Mochi keeping up, her legs pumping furiously. She was just behind his shoulder and he had to turn his head to see her. That slowed him slightly and she pulled even. That didn't worry Quanah. As they made the turn around the stake, Quanah moved ahead again—not by much but enough. Just as he knew he had the race won, Mochi lunged from behind and smacked her foot against his heel. It knocked Quanah off balance and he went sprawling. Mochi ran on, raising her arms in victory as she reached the campfire.

Furious, Quanah got to his feet and ran to her. "You tripped me!"

Mochi was accepting congratulations from some village women. She turned to Quanah. "So?"

"You cheated!"

Medicine Water walked over to Quanah. He said very quietly, "She didn't cheat. The only rule was to see who could run around the stake and get back to the campfire first. My wife did, and now I own your horse."

Quanah wanted to argue, but he saw that the whole Cheyenne village was watching. He needed their friendship and, more importantly, their cooperation. He swallowed hard and said, "He's yours. I'll go get him."

"It can wait until morning," Medicine Water said. "Come on, let's drink together." He and Quanah and a few of the other dog soldiers emptied two full bottles of white man's whiskey. Mochi had one drink with them, then retired along with the rest of the camp women. Quanah completely lost track of Isatai. He supposed that the fat man had gone to sleep in Gray Beard's hut. After a while, Quanah passed out on the grass near the campfire.

When he woke in the morning, someone had covered him with a blanket. Though he had a terrible headache, he got his horse from the meadow where it had been grazing along with the village herd. He led the horse by its hackamore to the tipi of Medicine Water and Mochi, and tethered it in front. Mochi stuck her head out of the opening, saw him, and asked, "Will you eat something with us?" Despite how she'd tricked him the night before, Quanah still wanted her so badly that his loins ached, though not as much as his pounding head. He was the furthest thing from hungry.

"Thank you, another time," he said politely, and went to Gray Beard's tent to fetch Isatai. The Spirit Messenger and their host were just finishing breakfast. The sight of greasy meat slices made Quanah's stomach lurch. Gray Beard joked about the perils of drinking, and Quanah did his best to smile.

"Since you lost your horse, I'll lend you one," Gray Beard said. "On the way home, I don't want you to have to ride double with your prophet."

"No, Isatai and I can take turns riding," Quanah said. It would be too humiliating for one of the People to have to ride a Cheyenne horse. "Have you considered what we talked about? Will you join us?"

"Your war plan sounds good," Gray Beard said. When Isatai looked offended, the Cheyenne chief added, "Of course, the support of the spirits is also impressive. I'll talk to the other chiefs who remained at the agency. They have to agree. I think that they will. You'll have our answer soon. We'll find you in your camp."

As they made their way out of the village, Isatai riding and Quanah walking alongside the horse, some of the Cheyenne waved. Quanah had made a positive impression when he was a good sport and gave up his horse after losing to Mochi. He hoped to at least glimpse her as they departed the camp, but apparently she was still in her tipi.

Quanah passed the first hours of the long trip home imagining himself under the blankets with Mochi. It was very exciting. Isatai hummed for a while. It was annoying but Quanah was getting used to it. Then the fat man said, "That woman back at the camp? The fighter?"

"Yes, what about her?"

"If her Cheyenne husband could in some way be persuaded, don't you think she would make a worthy wife for a Spirit Messenger?"

A new, disgusting image flashed in Quanah's mind. "Absolutely not," he said. "You need to be concerned only with Buffalo Hump's spirit and prophecy and magic, on the success of our plan. You can't be thinking about women, even that one."

"I suppose," Isatai agreed. He sounded regretful.

FOURTEEN

McLendon went looking for Bat Masterson, and found him sound asleep in a whore's crib behind Tom Sherman's saloon. The cramped room stunk of sweat and cheap perfume. The woman who lived in it had apparently left Bat there in an obviously drunken stupor. McLendon shook him awake. It took several minutes for Bat to become coherent.

"What the hell, C.M.?" he complained. "I only got this last day to sleep in. Billy intends for us to pull out south early tomorrow. Can't you leave me to my shut-eye?"

"Sorry, no," McLendon said, and began firing questions at Masterson. What, exactly, was his work agreement with Billy Dixon? Was he certain that, besides twenty-five cents for each buffalo he skinned, he'd also be allowed to shoot five each day for himself? Was Bat certain that A. C. Myers would pay about three dollars per skin, if it didn't have too many bullet holes or other rips and tears? Above all, did Bat swear that a big migrating herd was so thick with buffalo that it was almost impossible not to hit one with every shot?

Bat grumbled, "What's the purpose of this interrogation? Why the hell do you care?" But he answered everything. Then McLendon, multiplying sums in his head, told Bat to go back to sleep and rushed out of the room.

McLendon spent the rest of the morning and early afternoon finding and quizzing veteran hide men who'd decided not to go south with Billy's expedition. He got no useful information from Henry Raymond, who was staying in Dodge for love, but Heath Lee, Christopher Johnson, Crash Reed, and Pat Callahan all told him pretty much the same thing.

"Sure, I was worried about the Indians, but it ain't the reason I'm staying behind," Callahan said. "I'd'a made plenty good money down there with Billy this season, but who knows after that? I'm looking long-term, is what it is. If I read you right, I think you've got it in mind to join up with Billy and throw away that fine job Jim Hanrahan's giving you at his place. You'd be a fool to pass that up."

"Maybe so," McLendon said. "But the money will be good for everybody in Billy's party, even the crews, the skinners, and so forth? Sometimes as much as twenty, even thirty dollars a day for those on the low end?"

"If they strike a big herd, then that's the money involved, without question. But we've seen right here around Dodge how even the biggest bunch of buffs soon gets hunted out. This summer they'll thrive, but after that, Billy and his boys'll have to find other means of making their livings. The ones like me and you who stay behind in Dodge will get a whole year's head start on them. If you're thinking twice about that job in Hanrahan's bar, well, I'm of a mind to buy myself some grazing land just south of town. The herds driven up from Texas'll need grass and water while waiting for sale and rail shipment east. We could partner up, if you've got some money to invest."

"Sorry, Pat, I've got no money at present," McLendon said. "And as soon as I do, I intend to invest it in something else."

McLendon found Heath Lee at the Chinese laundry, where he was leaving some shirts to be washed. He spoke with the Tennessean for several minutes. After that, McLendon went back to Hanrahan's and asked the bartender if Jim was in his office. Told that he was, McLendon made his way to the back of the building, knocked, and asked Jim if he had a minute.

"Have a drink with me, C.M.," Hanrahan said. "I'm just doing some last-minute paperwork, putting together a liquor order schedule for Mose. I suspect making those orders will be part of your job. Mose does tend to be forgetful about such things."

"About the job," McLendon said, seating himself in a frame chair on the other side of Hanrahan's desk. "I need to talk to you about that."

"Oh?" Hanrahan said. "Well, let's have that drink." He produced a bottle of whiskey and two glasses from a desk drawer and poured generous tots.

McLendon briefly touched his lips to the liquor. "Jim, I hope you'll understand."

Hanrahan's eyes narrowed. "C.M., I'm a man of my word, and I've always assumed that you were too. We agreed on thirty-five dollars a week. That's a fair wage, about as good as anyone employed here in Dodge earns. Don't try to hustle me for more, knowing that I'm about to leave with Billy and need you at work here in the morning."

"No, it's not that. The salary is more than fair."

Hanrahan gulped down his whiskey and poured himself another shot. "What, then? Have you found something objectionable about Mose? I know he's a bit rough; I took him on as a partner because he had money to invest when I needed it. But he's a good man. You can work out any differences with him, I swear."

"Please, let me explain. There was this woman I loved, in Arizona Territory. I thought she was going to marry someone else—that was one of the reasons I left, and eventually found myself in Dodge. Like you and I discussed, my plan was to work for you this summer and fall and save up enough money to get myself out to California, probably San Francisco. But I've learned that the woman was still unmarried, that I might have a chance with her after all. But I need to get to her soon, and for that I need more money faster than I could ever make it working here."

"So?"

"I'm thinking I might go south with you and Billy after all, on the same financial agreement with Billy that Bat Masterson has. You know, working mostly as a skinner, but also getting the chance each day to kill a few buffalo and sell the hides. Bat expects to make maybe twenty or thirty dollars a day, and if I did, too, by the end of the summer I'd have the money to go to Arizona Territory, win the love of my girl, and take her with me to California. I hope you understand, Jim. Surely you've been in love yourself."

Hanrahan shook his head. "C.M., I thought better of you. You're throwing away a fine opportunity for some female? Didn't I say that if you did a good job for me in Dodge, I'd recommend you to business friends in San Francisco? Don't you remember that?"

"I do, and I appreciate it. But as I've tried to explain—"

"Damn you and any explanations. We had a deal, still have a deal, and you're going to honor it." Hanrahan's eyes glistened with a fury McLendon hadn't realized could ever be in him. The saloon owner's hands trembled with barely suppressed rage.

This was a side of previously affable Jim Hanrahan that McLendon hadn't seen before. It threw him off balance. "Jim, I never thought that you'd react this way. Can't you understand—"

"There's nothing to understand. You're trying to renege. I won't have it. If I let you out of our deal, there'd be nobody with sense to help

Mose, and, for all I know, this saloon will be out of business before I get back at the end of the summer. If I wanted to sell it, there'd be nothing to sell, nothing left a buyer might want. All right, forty dollars a week, but don't expect me to laud you to my California friends anymore, for you're a chiseler and I despise such men."

McLendon leaned forward, reminding himself to smile and sound soothing. "Jim, I wouldn't leave you in such straits. I know you need someone with sense to help Mose. That's why I've made arrangements for you to talk later today with Heath Lee. Heath's a smart man, and an honest one. In the past summers he's led hunting crews of as many as twenty men, handling all the finances and equipment purchases, the very type of organizing Mose is weak at. As you may know, Heath has decided against going south and is looking for an opportunity in Dodge. He could be your man, and one better qualified than me. Talk to him and see if he doesn't perfectly fit your needs."

"Heath Lee. Well, I expect that I could talk to him." Some of the anger left Hanrahan's eyes.

"And here's another thing. I told Heath that, so far as salary, you might go as high as twenty-five a week. So you'd not only get a better man, you'd save money. Hell, offer him twenty. I believe that he might take it. He's concerned about making his living away from the hide hunting."

"Well," Hanrahan said again. He was suddenly calm. "It seems you've thought of everything, C.M. Why don't you go find Heath Lee and ask him to come see me. Say, how did Billy Dixon react when you told him that you wanted to join his company?"

"I confess that I haven't spoken to Billy yet. I wanted your blessing first."

"Assuming Heath Lee is acceptable, you have it. And you'll be a pleasant companion in our new surroundings down south. And after you

send Mr. Lee my way, go make your arrangements with Billy, mention-
ing of course that I concur with your plan. I believe Billy can be found
at Fred Zimmermann's shop, making some final purchases of lead, powder, and loading tools."

Billy was indeed at Zimmermann's, picking through samples while
the store owner looked on impatiently.

"Choose what you want, Dixon, and let's be done. My wife expects
me for dinner."

"You could go on, Mr. Zimmermann," Billy said. "I'll make my selec-
tions, leave you a list of them, and come back to pay you in the morning
just before we depart." Billy's reputation for honesty was such that even
the perpetually suspicious Zimmermann trusted him enough to nod and
leave the store.

"Fred's not really a bad sort," Billy told McLendon after the door shut
behind the gun shop owner. "There's many a fellow out here who has no
regard for the law, and who will steal anything he can. Fred's just encountered a few too many of them. What can I do for you, C.M.? Forgive
me if I continue to work while we talk. Nothing's more important to a
hunting party than ammunition, and of course many of the boys are
particular about what they use to put together their loads."

McLendon knew that most veteran buffalo hunters started out with a
few boxes of factory-made ammunition. But they saved the cartridge
casings after they fired, and afterward reloaded them themselves, using
powder and lead bullets that they'd purchased separately. The cost of
handmade ammunition was much cheaper. Billy was trying to determine
the finest powder and lead currently available at Zimmermann's, carefully rubbing powder grains between his fingers to test granulation and
composition.

McLendon launched into the same explanation that he'd offered
Hanrahan. Billy listened and frequently nodded. He knew all about love,

he said—there had been a girl back in Missouri that he still dreamed about sometimes.

"You never can be sure that you've found the right one, or at least that's been my experience. Are you certain about this girl in Arizona, C.M.?"

"I am, Billy."

"Well, hell. What do you think Jim Hanrahan will say about this?"

"We've already talked. He's good with it. My question to you now is, can I have the same arrangement with you as Bat Masterson? I don't pretend I'm a great shot, or more than an adequate skinner, Billy. But I'll work hard, and I'll be very loyal. Whatever you need to be done, ask and I'll do it. And at the end of the summer, when the herd has moved on, I'll thank you, take my earnings, and head to Arizona Territory to win my girl."

Billy grinned. "What's her name?"

"Gabrielle."

"Gabrielle. That's pretty, and I'll bet she is too. Well, let me remind you. The work is going to be constant and hard. Every hunting day you'll be up to your elbows in blood and buffalo guts. You only get to try and shoot your allotted five after my main shooters and I are finished for the day. No one can ever promise how many buffs there will be. We may get down there only to find that the main herd is somewhere entirely different and beyond our reach. Then nobody makes any money, and we wander back to Dodge penniless. Nothing's guaranteed like the certain salary you'd earn staying back here and working for Jim in his saloon."

"I know."

"Then there's the Indians. You never know what they might be up to. Myself, I'm fairly certain they'll present little threat if we're watchful, but they might. And if they do, you'll have to fight to preserve your scalp, not to mention all your other parts. Those Co-manch in particular, they do things to the white men they capture that defy belief. Are you willing to risk it?"

"I am," McLendon said, though it was something he didn't want to think about.

"All right, then. Jim Hanrahan and I will furnish the basic equipment, rifles and skinning knives and so forth. You're responsible for buying your own food, clothing, and personal items. You're signing on for the whole summer. If you up and quit, you're on your own finding your way back to Dodge City or wherever else. You're one of my skinners at two bits a hide, plus a chance to shoot up to five buffs on your own each day, the profits from those hides to be strictly yours and not shared with me or Jim. Same deal as Bat's. Are we agreed?"

"We are," McLendon said, and the two men shook hands.

"Well, then," Billy said. "I surmise that the rest of the boys are spending their final town hours drinking and whoring. My advice to you is, go off to your room and sleep all you can. You'll want to be rested and have a clear head in the morning when we start out. It's going to be rough going under the best of circumstances. But what the hell, C.M., you're coming south, and may God watch over and protect you. I sure hope that this gal Gabrielle is worth it."

"She is."

Billy piled boxes of cartridges, cases of lead, and casks of gunpowder near the door of the shop. "I've got one of my wagons outside, C.M. Will you assist me in loading it up?"

Billy's dog, Fannie, was tied to one of the wagon wheels. When she saw Billy she capered and licked at his hands. Billy crouched to pet the red setter, then looked up at McLendon.

"I know you've done some skinning and a little hunting right outside of Dodge, but you haven't ever been on a full expedition, living in camp and so forth. You're going to find it's a vastly different experience, never easy in any way, but the sense of yourself you'll get—a feeling of freedom, I guess it is—there's just nothing like it. For all the hardships you're about to endure, C.M., you still have my word that you're about to embark on a great and wonderful adventure."

FIFTEEN

Quanah walked for a long time after he and Isatai left the Cheyenne village. The sun was about halfway across the sky when they approached the first landmark on their journey back to the Quahadi camp. The Cimarron River was, as always, wide, sandy, and treacherous. There was a strong current, and its mushy bottom sucked in the feet of men and the hooves of horses. Men and animals were often known to get caught in the quicksand and drown. When they reached its banks and Isatai had to dismount to lead his horse across, Quanah suggested that this was a good time for them to switch so that he could ride awhile. But the Spirit Messenger refused.

"Buffalo Hump wants me to keep riding."

"Why would he want that?"

Isatai straightened his mount's hackamore, making sure to stand between Quanah and the horse. "If I walk, I have to watch out for stones and roots that could trip me. Buffalo Hump wants me to constantly be listening for him in case he has a new message. Since I need to pay attention to him above all other things, I have to ride. What if I missed something important that he wanted to tell me?"

Quanah's feet hurt. There were a lot of small rocks on the ground, and his moccasins didn't cushion the impact when he stepped on them. "You wouldn't have to walk very long. I just need to rest my feet for a while. Maybe Buffalo Hump would understand."

"No, I have to ride." Grunting with the effort, Isatai hauled himself back up on the horse. He closed his eyes and hummed for a moment, then said, "I have good news. Buffalo Hump says that you're going to get a horse soon. For now, just keep walking."

"How will I get this horse?"

"The spirit didn't say. You should feel honored that Buffalo Hump has concerned himself with such a small matter. Let's see how the spirit makes this happen."

The going was hard. Quanah gave no credence to Isatai's promise of a horse for him. The terrain was very uneven. The hills were steep and valley inclines were often precipitous, almost like the walls of gorges. The sky was cloudless and the air was still, so there was no shade or breeze to cool the sweat on Quanah's body. He tried to distract himself from the physical discomfort by thinking about Mochi, but that only made him feel frustrated. His irritability intensified when they stopped at a spot well known for its pool of clean water. They'd emptied their water bags along the way and needed to refill them, but instead of plenty of water, there was only a small trickle—enough to wet their throats, but not sufficient for hearty drinks and water bag replenishment.

"There's another place a full day ahead," Quanah said. "We'll have to go thirsty tonight."

"That place will be almost dried up too," Isatai said. "Buffalo Hump says so, and that there will be no more rain for a long time."

"Does Buffalo Hump ever have anything good to tell you?"

"He says you'll have your horse very soon. Water too. Let's keep going."

They were in a place of abrupt hills that often made it hard to see very far ahead. But as they topped a rise, Quanah saw movement about five bowshots in front of them and slightly to the right. He stopped and cupped his hand over his eyes to block the glare of the sun, and saw three white men making their way up another hill. They were on foot, leading a horse laden with packs. It was odd that they had only one horse between them, but perhaps they'd lost others to injury or snakebite. All three men had rifles, but Quanah saw that these were older models, not the big, long-barreled guns that could send bullets straight over very long distances.

It wasn't surprising, two moons or more before the buffalo returned, to see a small party of whites this far into Indian land. There were always some white hunters around, even in the cold months. Only fools like the one Quanah had killed several months before came alone. Usually they came at least in pairs, and often more than that. Whenever they encountered these white men and their own numbers were sufficient, Indians had a choice. They could attack and kill the interlopers or, if they didn't feel like going to so much trouble or risk, they could make it clear that they expected gifts—usually whiskey, tobacco, or sacks of sugar and coffee—in return for safe passage. Then the whites had to choose between handouts and possibly fighting for their lives if they refused and the Indians took offense. They almost always chose to hand over whatever the Indians wanted. In this case, Quanah wanted the horse. That was clearly more than these whites would be prepared to give, especially since there were three of them and the only other Indian besides Quanah was a very fat man who even stupid white men could tell was not much of a threat. So it would be a fight, then. That pleased Quanah. It had been too long since his last one. He quickly formulated a strategy.

"We'll approach them like we're looking for small presents," Quanah told Isatai. "Here. You take my rifle. Hold it down at your side, not pointed at them."

"Will you want me to shoot them?" Isatai asked nervously. Spirit Messenger or not, he knew he wasn't very good with guns.

"No, you won't have to do anything. Just sit calmly on your horse and I'll do what's necessary."

"There are three of them," Isatai said. "Are you sure? I'll ask Buffalo Hump."

"Don't bother him. The spirit can leave this fight to me."

Quanah grabbed the hackamore of Isatai's horse and led the way down the rise toward the white men. He did nothing to hide and soon the whites saw them. The three hunters leaned together and talked briefly. Obviously deciding that the two approaching Indians didn't pose a serious threat, the white men got their rifles ready and waited. When he was close enough, Quanah waved. One of the hunters waved back. Quanah stopped a short distance from them. He let the white men see how fat and useless Isatai was up on his horse, and how Quanah had no rifle or bow and quiver, only a knife and also the claw hammer in the waist of his breechclout.

One of the whites said something in the incomprehensible gabble of his race. Quanah nodded and held out his hand. The other two hunters went over to their horse and took a few twists of tobacco from one of the packs. They gave the bits of tobacco to the first man, who stepped forward and handed the crumbly stuff to Quanah. He said something that sounded stern, probably a warning to take the tobacco and go before they shot him and Isatai, too, but it didn't matter. Quanah stepped forward to meet him, reaching out for the tobacco with his left hand but dropping his right hand to the hilt of his knife as he did, and then he thrust the knife forward so quickly that it was in the throat of the first hunter before the man could sense what was happening. Blood shot up in a high arc as Quanah moved right past him, leaving the knife buried in his victim's neck and snatching the claw hammer. The remaining two hunters were a pace or two away, one on either side of the horse. Because they'd let themselves relax and dropped the muzzles of their guns toward the ground, they had to raise them up to shoot, and the split second it took was all the time that Quanah needed. His claw hammer smashed against the temple of one, and the man dropped without a sound. The other hunter managed to get his rifle up, but Quanah knocked the barrel aside with his left forearm. The rifle went off and the sound of the shot echoed among the hills, but the bullet flew wild and Quanah clubbed the man's shoulder. He screamed in agony and dropped the rifle. Quanah had him then and they both knew it, but the white man tried to run. His arm dangled and he moved slowly. Quanah could have caught him immediately, but he chose to lope behind for several moments, listening to his prey gasp and whimper. He reached out and tugged at the hunter's coat, deliberately letting him wrench free and run a little more. Finally Quanah caught the man by his good arm, swung him around, and pushed him to the ground. He knelt on his victim's chest and listened to the man babble. He might have been begging or praying to his god; Quanah wasn't sure and didn't care. What mattered was that he had triumphed, as the People always should. The man squirmed a little under the pressure of Quanah's knees, but he knew there was no hope of escape and no one to save him. Helpless, he had to accept whatever Quanah wanted to do with him.

This, to Quanah, was the essence of being a man. In such situations, the People showed no mercy. Small in number, they did horrifying things to their victims not just to celebrate their superiority but to intimidate future foes. Many more white hunters, Quanah knew, would soon be coming south to hunt the buffalo. Maybe some of them would stumble upon the body of this man. Quanah meant to send them an unmistakable message. When he'd killed the lone white hunter months ago, he had to hurry because the band of hide men was nearby. Now he could take his time.

Almost casually, he raised the claw hammer and slammed it into the hunter's face, cracking bones and breaking teeth. The man, too injured or terrified to shriek, uttered a low moan. Quanah got up and dragged him back to where the other two hunters lay. Isatai, after laboriously dismounting, rummaged through the packs on the white hunters' horse. The hunter with Quanah's knife in his throat was clearly dead. The one Quanah had hit in the head with his claw hammer twitched a little as he lay on the ground. Quanah threw his third victim down, pulled his knife from the first man's throat, and cut the throat of the second man, who choked briefly and stopped breathing.

Then Quanah turned his attention again to the surviving hunter. Isatai found some hard candies in one of the white men's packs. He sat on the grass crunching the candy in his teeth and watched as his companion went to work. First Quanah built a small fire of sticks. When his victim tried to crawl away, he hauled him back and prevented further escape attempts by severing his hamstrings. The man groaned but didn't scream. He was too injured and petrified for that.

While the sticks burned down to hot ashy lumps, Quanah passed the time cutting things off the hunter—a few fingers, one ear, and finally a testicle. He did this very deliberately, letting the man see the knife in his hand, allowing him to wonder what body part he would lose next. Though he suffered greatly, he was not yet near death. When the white man passed out from the pain, Quanah pinched his remaining earlobe until he came to.

When he judged that the fire was ready, Quanah scalped the man, making a good job of it, cutting along the hairline and finally yanking the scalp from the skull. As he wrenched it loose, there was a tearing sound, like a piece of cloth being ripped violently in half. By this point, there was no resistance at all from the victim. He felt the pain but lacked the strength to react in any way to it. Quanah held the dripping scalp at arm's length and shook it to dislodge the wet gobbets of blood, then stuffed the clotted hair into his waistband. When he got back to the Quahadi village, he would weave strands of the scalp into his best war horse's hackamore, so they would stream attractively when he rode into battle. If any strands were left over, Wickeah would sew them onto the hems of her skirts as decorations.

Quanah reached down and yanked the hunter's shirt completely away from his chest and abdomen. Then he used the point of his knife to make a slit from below the man's breastbone to his pubic bone, taking care to cut just deeply enough so that he could pull back the skin and expose the entrails beneath without killing his victim on the spot. Then, using a platter of bark cut from a nearby tree, he took the glowing coals of the fire and dumped them into the hunter's exposed body cavity. The man jerked hard, spasmodically, and emitted a thin, keening howl that went on for some time, gradually sinking in volume. Quanah stood over him and savored the moment, the smell of burning flesh and guts, the sense of absolute power. When the hunter was finally dead Quanah went back to the other two white corpses and cut them up, too, taking both scalps and tearing off their trousers to castrate them. He pried the dead men's mouths open and stuffed in their penises, cutting out their tongues to make room. He placed the severed tongues on their chests.

"You do that very well," Isatai said. "I suppose we ought to be going now. It will be dark soon." They left most of the hunters' belongings by the bodies. Quanah's rifle was better than any of theirs, and Isatai said that he didn't want or need a gun, since he had the magic granted to him by the spirit of Buffalo Hump. There were some boxes of ammunition—

nothing that would fire from Quanah's Henry, but they took the bullets anyway. They might work in some of the other Quahadi guns. There were three canteens, two filled with water and one with whiskey. They took these, and also some dried beef and the remaining hard candies that Isatai hadn't eaten. They put everything in one of the packs on the horse, discarded the other packs, and Quanah mounted. It wasn't a very good horse, splay-legged from age and overwork, but riding it was better than walking. Isatai mounted his horse and they headed south, leaving the white men for the vultures and coyotes. Even after the scavengers ate their fill, Quanah knew, there would still be enough left of the corpses to serve as a warning to whatever whites came this way next.

As usual, Isatai hummed as he rode. Quanah exulted in what he had just done, and imagined the great battle and victory that surely were coming. The People, the Cheyenne, some Kiowa, all joining together. Quanah didn't know where they would launch the great attack. That had yet to be determined. But of this he was certain: soon, very soon, would come the spilling of more blood, a flood of it. Somewhere, in an Army fort or even in a town, maybe—someplace where there were many of them gathered and feeling safe—white men should be singing their death songs.

PART TWO

March–June 1874

SIXTEEN

Just after dawn on Tuesday, McLendon reread the letter he was sending to Gabrielle. He'd spent most of the night laboring over it. After several failures to convey his feelings in lengthy, heartfelt fashion, he'd decided brevity would be best.

Dearest Gabrielle:

Your words are pleasing and I thank you for this chanse. You are always fair so of course you will be so to Joe Saint. He is a good man but I swear I will make you happyer. I am better than I was. I gess it would be hard to be worse.

I beleeve I have found a way to make enough money to get to you faster, I think maybe by summers end. I hope you will hold me in your heart untill that time.

I will send word when I am on my way.

All my love
Cash McLendon

He took the letter to the Pioneer Store to mail. McLendon expected a lengthy wait in line behind many of the hunters leaving that morning with Billy. Undoubtedly they'd be making last-minute purchases of necessaries. But when he got to the shop, he found only a clerk behind the counter.

"I expect the boys are either sleeping it off or else having one last coupling with the whores," the clerk said when McLendon remarked on the lack of customers. "You folks are going to Indian country, after all. Not everybody's coming back."

"The word is, the Indians have backed off," McLendon said. "Billy Dixon says it's likely we'll be left to hunt in peace."

"So Billy would have to say, since he was trying to convince others to come with him. Do you have plenty of ammunition for that shiny new Peacemaker you're carrying?"

"I do, thanks." McLendon gave the clerk his letter. "Please be certain this goes out on today's train." He put three pennies on the counter for postage, and added a dime tip.

The clerk pushed the dime back to him. "No gratuity necessary. I admire a man who's about to risk his life."

"Well, I hope that I'm not," McLendon said. He walked out of the shop with Indians much on his mind. Surely Billy wouldn't lie about such things to facilitate recruitment.

McLendon found Billy in front of Hanrahan's saloon. He was arguing with Bat and Shorty Scheidler. McLendon hadn't seen Bat since the night before. He'd whooped when he learned that McLendon was coming on Billy's expedition after all, and urged him to come along for a last-night-in-Dodge revel with whiskey and women. When McLendon declined, Bat went ahead without him. From his disheveled appearance as he yammered with Billy, Bat had overindulged considerably.

"I told you no, and that's the end of it," Billy said to Masterson and Scheidler. He sounded frustrated.

"It makes all the sense in the world," Bat pleaded. "Me and Shorty, we'll be in charge of it. You can have a share of the profits."

"Absolutely not," Billy said. "We're going down south on serious business. Last thing we need's some women for you tomcats to get to fighting over."

"It won't be that way," Bat pleaded. "We'll have it under control. And I personally think I shoot straighter in the daylight if I've had a woman on the night before."

"Well, since you don't shoot straight at all, I assume you're still virgin and have yet to test your theory. No women."

"Mrs. Olds is a woman, and she's coming," Shorty argued.

Billy glared at him. "Mrs. Olds is going to be one of Mr. Rath's cooks. Anyway, none of the Rath people are part of this first bunch. They're going to follow along in a month or so, after we pick a site and get the camp going. Enough—you two have my answer. Masterson, go get your gear before I change my mind about having you on my crew. Scheidler, find your brother and start loading crates on your wagon. I hoped to leave by seven, and at this rate it will be nearly noon."

Bat and Shorty stumbled off, trailing whiskey fumes in their wake. "Those two," Billy said to McLendon. "All they care about is drink and whores. By the smell of their breath they've had plenty of the one, and now they want to take the other along on the expedition."

"What? I miss your meaning."

Billy sighed. He took off his hat and wiped his brow with a grimy handkerchief. "Young Bat and Shorty just came to me with a scheme to bring a dozen or so whores with us. They said they'd set up a tent at night and handle all the money arrangements. Lord save us from fools. The sooner we're away from Dodge and all its temptations, the better."

Despite Billy's impatience, it was just past noon before the massive wagon train finally set out. Much of the town turned out to see them off. Best wishes for a profitable hunt and dire prognostications of Indian massacres were called out in about equal number as whips cracked and horse and mule teams surged forward. In all, there were a hundred and ten men and seventy wagons, most of these belonging to the hide men. During hunts, they were used for transporting hides, but now they were loaded with every kind of foodstuff, tool, and ordnance. A. C. Myers was paying the hide men for the use of their wagons to convey his store stocks down south. Two dozen wagons were owned and driven by team-sters, who hired on for general transport during the trip. Another three wagons belonged to Tom O'Keefe, who intended to open a blacksmith shop at the new campsite. His massive anvil alone took up one whole wagon bed. About twenty men rode horses, with spare mounts tethered to wagons. A small herd of cattle was driven along—these would furnish beef and, in the case of four cows, milk for those who wanted it. Two dogs came along, too: Billy's red setter Fannie, who trotted alongside her master's horse, and Maurice, Isaac Scheidler's black Newfoundland.

Cash McLendon was pleased to be invited to ride with the Scheidlers on their wagon. He could have mounted one of Billy Dixon's spare horses, but he was never comfortable in the saddle. When he prepared to climb up on the wagon bench beside Isaac, though, Maurice yelped with excitement and leaped to attach himself to McLendon's leg.

"He still fancies you, C.M.," Isaac said.

"He's like your brother and Bat Masterson with their whores," Mc-Lendon joked as he pried the dog loose and shoved him back down in the street. Maurice took the rebuff as coyness rather than outright re-jection, and launched himself at the leg a second time. McLendon, who was nervous about going south and also on edge thinking of Gabrielle, didn't have the patience to keep the determined animal at bay. "Isaac, I believe I'll hitch a ride elsewhere," he said. There was space on the bench of another nearby wagon, and McLendon asked the teamster at the reins if he might sit there. Receiving a nod in response, he climbed up. There was no time for immediate introductions. Billy finally had everyone ready, and hollered for them to move out. The wagons lurched forward over the bridge spanning the Arkansas River, and McLendon settled in for a long day. Billy had said it would probably take six or seven days to get wherever they were going in Indian Territory. Everything depended on finding just the right spot, which would include lots of water, good grazing, and proper sight lines for defense.

Despite Billy Dixon's problems getting everyone under way, McLendon thought that he was a good leader. Even during the first miles of the trip, there was a certain organization to the long procession. Billy, Bermuda Carlyle, and Mike McCabe, Billy's head skinner, rode out in front, with Bat Masterson tagging along. The other riders were spread out up and down the wagon train. Jim Hanrahan rode on a middle wagon, making sure that all the drivers kept in tight formation. Fred Leonard and Tom O'Keefe, both armed with Winchester repeaters, brought up the rear. The procession kept up an even pace. It helped that there weren't any hills or draws to speak of. Looking ahead, all McLendon could see was an endless mass of gray-green grass swaying in the breeze, and a few scattered trees. Because of the sameness up ahead, after a while there was little sense of actual progress.

McLendon thought about Gabrielle, imagining how she might react when she received his latest letter. Perhaps she'd write back the very same day. Freight service between Dodge and the new south camp would be in place almost immediately, and Heath Lee had promised he'd send along any mail directed to McLendon care of Hanrahan and Waters's saloon. It was going to be hard working for Billy, no doubt about it, but if he made the kind of money he was anticipating—surely fifteen dollars a day, probably twenty—by the end of the hunting season, McLendon could travel in style to Mountain View in Arizona Territory.

He squirmed a little on the wagon bench. The hard wood plank was in itself uncomfortable, and there was an additional irritation. Just before leaving Dodge, Bat had talked McLendon into buying one of the new Colt Peacemakers. He traded in his old Navy Colt as part of the transaction. Bat said it was easier getting ammunition for the Peacemaker, and also it was a more reliable weapon in a fight: "If Indians come howling after your hair, you'd best be prepared to give a good account for yourself." McLendon hated parting with the money—fourteen dollars for the gun, plus a small screwdriver that was included in the purchase for reasons that gun shop owner Zimmermann was unwilling to explain, took a considerable bite out of his current grubstake—but he couldn't win Gabrielle back unless he survived his Indian Territory sojourn. He wore the gun now on a holster attached to his belt, and the handle poked into his midsection. He tried to push the holster to an angle where the gun lay flat against his hip, but he couldn't manage it.

"Shovit round front," someone said, and McLendon turned to see the driver smiling at him. This teamster was a portly man with very bad teeth.

"Beg your pardon?" McLendon said politely.

"Shovit round front." The words sounded somewhat familiar, as though the fellow was speaking an alternative form of English.

"I don't understand."

"Youkin unnerstand." The man dropped the reins and grabbed McLendon's holster. "Shovit round *front*." He yanked the holster along McLendon's belt until the gun rested between his legs. So long as McLendon's legs were slightly spread, the handle didn't poke into him anymore.

"Yew geddown, yankit back t'thuh sahd."

McLendon began to discern parts of words jammed together. "Yes. When I get down, I'll return the holster to its original position. Meanwhile, this is much more comfortable. Thank you."

The driver nodded amiably. "Mirkle Jones," he said, drawing out the *s* in his surname like a lingering *z*. "Good ta meecha."

McLendon gave his own name, and they shook hands. Jones's heavy paw was thick with callus, which McLendon suspected came from decades of handling wagon reins. "My pleasure, Mr. Jones. Thanks for letting me ride with you."

Jones grinned again. His teeth were very yellow and crooked. "Dahg humpt ya on t'other one."

"That's true. Its name is Maurice and it's had at my leg before. But now that I'm riding with you, Maurice can direct his romantic intentions elsewhere."

Jones chuckled companionably and then jostled along in silence. McLendon sneaked surreptitious glances at the hefty man, whose skin didn't seem entirely white but wasn't dark enough to mark him as a mulatto. His features didn't strike McLendon as Mexican or Indian. He very much wanted to know Jones's ancestry, but felt it would be rude to ask. Perhaps, he thought, he could inquire about the man's name instead.

"Mirkle," McLendon said. "Now, that's an unusual name."

"Niverherd uv anuffer."

"Me, neither," McLendon said. He was catching on to Jones's unique phrasings. "Can I ask how you came by it?"

"Mumma. She uz old whin I come, dint espek havin a chile. So aftah, Mumma alluz called me her mirkle baby."

"Ah," McLendon said, and amused himself with that until Billy Dixon called out for everyone to take a break and rest the wagon teams. They'd been on the trail for about three hours. While Mirkle Jones watered his horses, McLendon wandered off to a spot a few dozen yards

away where many of the other men, including Bat Masterson, were relieving themselves. The men took turns pissing and standing guard.
Even this early on the journey, they worried about Indians.

"It's a grand day, isn't it?" Bat exulted as he and McLendon stood side
by side, splashing the grass. "Adventure and riches, C.M., ain't nothin'
like it. You ought to hop down off that wagon bench and get up on
horseback, ride in front with Billy Dixon and me."

"Thanks anyway." McLendon finished pissing and buttoned his
pants. "I'm an adequate horseman at best, and better off on the wagon.
Are we making good progress, Bat?"

"I'll say we are. Only mid-afternoon, and Dodge City is already almost out of sight."

McLendon looked back north and saw the grainy silhouette of Dodge
on the apparently endless horizon. "It's like we've hardly left."

"It's a trick of the terrain, being so flat and all. I'll bet we're averaging
four miles an hour. Keep it up, we'll be deep in Indian Territory sometime tomorrow."

"Not exactly a comforting thought."

"The thing is, be vigilant but not afraid. We've a hundred guns in our
party. The Indians would be wise to fear us."

McLendon shook his head. "Well, then, I hope someone tells them
how they should feel."

On the first night, they stopped at a place Billy Dixon called Crooked
Creek. There was water to refill barrels and canteens, and plenty of grass
for the wagon teams and livestock. To McLendon, the expedition took
on what seemed to be a party mood. Everyone was jolly, exulting about
the great times ahead. Men gathered around a dozen different campfires, where they cooked bacon and biscuits, brewed coffee in battered
tin pots, and exchanged tales of past adventures. McLendon found him-

self in a group that included Billy, Jim Hanrahan, Mirkle Jones, a dozen other hide men and their crew members, and Bat, who seemed determined never to be far from Billy's side. Fannie, Billy's dog, lay quietly at her master's feet. Billy fed her bits of bacon, then checked her paws for thorns and cuts. Brick Bond was in the group, too, which concerned McLendon, but even Bond seemed caught up in the spirit of good fellowship. He'd fought in the Civil War, for the South, and regaled the group for a while with stories of great battles. A couple of crewmen had served the Union, and they told war stories too. McLendon feared that Bond would take offense, but he didn't. In contrast to all the arguments McLendon had heard back in Arizona Territory about the war and politics, the men around this campfire seemed content to recall the conflict as an experience worth remembering but not regretting.

"They're not at each other's throats about North and South, Billy," he whispered to Dixon.

"Of course not. We're all men out making our livings now. None of us give a damn about politics or who was at fault in the war. We just want to shoot buffalo."

When the stories were told and the coffee was gone, McLendon thought that everyone would turn in. Instead, Mirkle fetched a fiddle from his wagon and began playing a sprightly tune. To McLendon's absolute astonishment, most of the grizzled hunters and crewmen jumped up to dance. Some of them formed couples and whirled arm in arm. Even Billy stood and bounced a little, though he rebuffed Bat when Masterson tried to dance with him. McLendon stood but didn't dance. He felt a bit uncomfortable.

When Mirkle stopped sawing on his fiddle, Jim Hanrahan recited a poem as the others listened. Then one of the skinners sang a mournful song about being alone on the prairie. When he was done, Hanrahan said, "Well, I guess that's it for tonight. Some of you others will step up tomorrow."

"What's that mean?" McLendon asked Bat.

"Rule of the hunting trail. Everybody has to take turns entertaining. That includes you, C.M. You better start thinking of an appropriate performance."

"Hell, Bat, I don't think I know any poems, and I sure can't sing."

"Refusal's not allowed, so come up with something. Ever'body else will."

All around, McLendon could hear singing, and a few other fiddles. Someone was wailing on a harmonica, which the hide men called a French harp. But soon the night grew quiet. Billy posted guards— everyone would take a nightlong turn sometime on the trip south, he said—and the remaining travelers rolled up in blankets by the campfires or under the wagons. McLendon knew he wouldn't sleep, so he volunteered to join Bat on guard duty.

"What am I looking for?" he asked.

"Just any movement out of the ordinary. I don't expect any Indians. We're not that far south. If there's to be trouble, it won't come now. That's why we're wise to pull first night duty. Stay alert all the same."

"I will."

"That's good, because I've had a long day and not much sleep last night, what with saying good-bye to some of Dodge's finest working girls. Nudge me if you have occasion, but not otherwise."

"But Billy said we're all supposed to stay awake."

"Well, don't tell him, then. I'm a light sleeper and will snap to instantly, should circumstances so require."

It seemed to McLendon that Masterson didn't take guard duty seriously enough, but Bat was asleep before he could debate the point.

. . .

By late morning of the second day, they reached the Cimarron River. Billy called a halt and walked up to the riverbank, staring down into the water. McLendon jumped down from Mirkle Jones's wagon and joined him.

"This is commonly called the Dead Line," Billy said. "When we cross over, we're truly in Indian country. I notice a couple of the boys have thought about it some and are pulling their wagons around to return to Dodge. If you're of a mind to do something of that sort, now's the time. After this, you can be certain that the Co-manch and their other red brethren will be watching every move, eager to pick off anyone who strays."

McLendon reflexively looked around. "I said I'd come work for you and be loyal. I'm not turning back."

Billy chuckled. "You want to, though."

"I want the money more."

"Because of your girl. I swear, she must be delightful. Well, take a piss and eat a cracker. Getting across here won't be easy, and we'll need every available man in the water helping guide the animals."

"It doesn't look very deep."

"It isn't, but it's not the water itself that's the problem. The sand underneath it is soft and shifty. It can suck something down without a trace. A box of tools tips in off a wagon, we're like to never find it. Horse puts a hoof wrong, it's in up to the withers and done for if we can't pull it out. Trick is, take off your boots and keep your feet moving at all times."

It took almost three hours. One of the cattle got stuck in the sand and couldn't be extracted. Old Man Keeler, coming along to be cook in the Myers and Leonard store, took a long knife and cut the bellowing animal's throat. He tried to hack off some meat but was stymied by the river's soft sand bed and constant current.

"Waste of good beef," he complained. He rinsed the blood off his knife and plodded to the far bank.

The men were still in reasonably good spirits that night, but the overall mood was subdued from the day before. Everyone gathered around campfires to eat, dance, and sing, but this time guards were posted as soon as the expedition stopped. McLendon managed to avoid having to entertain, and also tried to quiz Mirkle Jones on his ancestry.

"I don't know much about my forebears, Mr. Jones," he said. "I was orphaned early on the streets of St. Louis and so never heard family history. But what of yourself?"

Old Man Keeler had baked huge, crusty biscuits in a Dutch oven and slathered them with honey before he passed them around the campfire. Jones had one jammed in his mouth, rendering his speech even more incomprehensible.

"Ahm fruh Loozyanna," he said. A few wet crumbs popped free past his lips. "*Kree*-ole." McLendon wasn't certain of the term, though he'd heard the word before. Whatever race or culture it described, he felt that he liked it, if its people were all as friendly and kind-spirited as Mirkle Jones. He bid the bulky teamster good night and rolled up in a blanket near the fire. The combination of fresh air and a long, hard day wore McLendon down sufficiently so that he slept most of the night.

ON THE THIRD DAY, they saw their first Indians. The land was broken up now by banks of hills, and suddenly Bermuda Carlyle whistled shrilly and pointed ahead toward a far-off crest. Everyone stared in the direction. Seated on the bench of Mirkle Jones's wagon, McLendon, squinting, made out the figures of three men on horseback. From such distance, he couldn't discern many details. They leaned comfortably forward on their mounts, like hunters determining if recently sighted prey was worth pursuing. McLendon couldn't tell if they wore feathers in their hair. Both had something long and narrow in their hands—lances? Rifles? He wasn't certain. The Indians didn't try to disguise their presence. They remained stock-still as the long procession of whites passed about three-quarters of a mile east from where they watched.

"Figure a few us of should ride over there, run 'em off?" Fred Leonard asked Billy. "Arrogant bastards is what they are."

"Nope, it wouldn't do any good," Billy said. "Those are just the ones we can see right now. There are bound to be more in the vicinity. You've not yet spent much time out in this country, Mr. Leonard. There will always be Indians about. We need to remain vigilant so that they only watch rather than attack us."

The sight of the Indians made McLendon so nervous that he didn't wander off with the other men to relieve himself during trail breaks. Despite the pressure from his bladder, he stayed on the wagon bench the entire day, occasionally checking his Colt Peacemaker to reassure himself that it was loaded. He doubted he could hit any Indian he shot at, but he wanted to be ready in case he had to try. That night, Billy made a point of reminding everyone that the Indians were unlikely to attack such a large, well-armed party. But McLendon noticed that Billy also assigned the most experienced hide men and crew members to guard duty. Nobody sang or otherwise entertained around the campfires. The company was on alert.

NO ONE SAW OR HEARD anything suspicious that night. The next day, Friday, they moved forward warily. Billy sent scouts ahead; they periodically reported back that there were no Indian sightings, even at a distance. Still, everyone in the wagon caravan remained tense. Even Bat

Masterson seemed anxious. During a short trail break, he passed Mc-Lendon a canteen of water and said, "We're smack in no-man's-land now." McLendon gulped the water. It was warm, much like the slight breeze. Everyone said the weather now was warmer than usual, in contrast to the harsh winter just concluded. But McLendon had spent time out in the high desert of Arizona Territory and knew what real molten heat was like. "What do you mean, 'no-man's-land'?"

"We're far enough away from Dodge and any Army posts so that we're on our own. We get into something with the Indians, we'll have to fight our own way out of it."

"You knew that all along."

Bat took a long drink from the canteen. "What we know in town and what we feel out here are two different things. I'll be glad when we get where we're going and put up some buildings with stout walls. Billy says it'll be maybe three, four more days. And then we can— Jesus Christ, look over there."

McLendon looked. A hundred yards to the west, on a low ridge where nothing had been just moments before, stood a half-dozen Indians. Each held a lance in one hand and the reins of a pony in the other. Most of them had bows and quivers of arrows slung over their shoulders. There was paint on their faces and bodies, yellow and blue mostly. All around him McLendon heard metallic clicks as the hide men and their crews cocked rifles.

"Stand easy but watchful," Billy called. "Probably just some young bucks looking for a handout."

For several long moments, the Indians and white men stood watching each other. Then, at an almost stately pace, the Indians walked toward the wagons. McLendon was mesmerized. These wild Indians were real human beings; he could see drops of sweat on their brows.

Billy, Bermuda Carlyle, Jim Hanrahan, and Fred Leonard walked out a few paces to meet them. One of the Indians said something—to McLendon, it sounded more like guttural grunting than actual words. Billy spread his arms in a universal signal: *I don't understand.* The Indian nodded as though this was the response that he expected. He gestured toward the wagons.

"Them's Kioway," whispered Old Man Keeler, who was standing near McLendon and Masterson. "You can tell from the hair, all cut on one side and long on t'other. Nasty pieces a work."

Billy extended a hand toward the Indians, palm up: *Wait here.* He walked to a wagon, rummaged in the bed, and extracted some small packets of coffee and sugar. The Indians waited; McLendon could see them glancing up and down the line of wagons and riders.

"Shit, Billy, the sonsabitches are counting our guns," a teamster hissed.

"Be glad that they are," Billy said quietly. "Now they can pass the word among their people that we're too well armed to attack." He went back to the Indians and gave the sacks to the one who seemed to be the leader. Then he gestured: *Go away.* With considerable dignity, the Indians turned and led their horses back toward the ridge where they had first appeared. Then they dropped the reins of their horses. For one panic-stricken moment, McLendon thought they were reaching for their bows to shoot, but instead they turned their backs, yanked down their breechclouts, and exposed their buttocks to the white audience. Then, uttering derisive shrieks, they disappeared down the far side of the ridge. Most of the expedition members couldn't help but laugh.

"Cheeky bastards," Bat cracked, and that evoked a second round of laughter.

ON THE FIFTH DAY they reached the mouth of Palo Duro Creek. The land was harsh now; there were steep slopes instead of gentle hills, and precipitous canyons rather than gracefully curved arroyos. Billy said that they were very near where he'd seen the sign of all the buffalo during his winter scouting expedition. "Tomorrow, Monday at the latest, we'll strike the Canadian and find ourselves just the right place to roost." McLendon was glad to hear it. His ass ached from the hard wagon bench, and as much as he liked Mirkle Jones, the teamster from Louisiana was too hard to understand when he talked. McLendon was used to Bat Masterson's more comprehensible yammering. Still, Jones was a generous traveling companion, sharing with McLendon little snacks he had tucked away in his wagon bed. McLendon especially appreciated the gift of hard candies to suck. That was a much better-tasting way to alleviate thirst than gulping down brackish canteen water.

Besides serving as a landmark that the trip was almost over, everyone was glad to arrive at the creek because it was surrounded with high green grass. As a result of the harsh winter and intemperate spring heat, much of the grassland they'd crossed so far was stunted and sparse. The saddle horses, pack animals, and wagon teams hadn't grazed well. Now there would be an opportunity to crop their fill, giving them plenty of strength for the final leg of the expedition. The animals sensed the bounty ahead; their nostrils flared and they surged forward.

Billy asked Bermuda Carlyle and Jim Hanrahan to ride ahead and pick a prime campsite by the river. They came back with disturbing news.

"Somebody's already got a camp in place," Hanrahan said. "If you look close over there, you can just see a thread of smoke from a small fire. We heard some ponies whickering."

"Indians?" Billy asked.

"We didn't go close enough to see. Thought we'd come back, tell you, then maybe go forward again with a few more guns, just in case."

Billy pulled his Sharps "Big Fifty" from the scabbard on his saddle.

"All right, then. Brick Bond, Mike McCabe, get your guns and come with Bermuda, Jim, and me. Ever'body else, stay back. You hear shooting, come on fast, but remember to leave behind enough men to guard the wagons."

Bat said, "Billy, I'm coming too. I want some action."

"It's your hair," Billy said. "And if it's Indians and trouble starts, don't go using me for cover."

The six men rode toward the river, then eased down a slope and were lost to sight. McLendon waited nervously, expecting to hear gunshots. After ten minutes, Masterson came racing back.

"Everyone come on to the river!" he cried. "It's the Cator brothers—they're camped on the water!"

Bat rode beside Mirkle Jones's wagon as it lurched forward. "The Cators are hide men who came over from England," he explained to McLendon. "Jim and Bob are fine fellows, crack shots and the canniest of frontiersmen. Turns out they made winter camp all the way down here, so they're well versed on the area. We'll have ourselves a fine time with them tonight."

McLendon found the Cators to be especially congenial. Both had long dark beards that tapered to points just above their waists. Their camp by the creek consisted of a half-dozen tents for the brothers and their ten-man crew. Over mugs of tea, Jim and Bob explained that they chose to winter so far from civilization because the Indians had apparently abandoned the area.

"It seems that the majority of red fellows are drifting somewhat north and east, toward the reservations set aside for them," Jim Cator said in an English accent that fell pleasantly on McLendon's ear. "The Army under Mackenzie must be wearing them down. You say that a few Kiowa came begging a few days back—well, that's what those remaining must be reduced to. We've camped out here and ranged where we pleased, and never once have we suffered any attacks. As soon as the great herd arrives, which might be anytime now, what with this early heat, it's clear sailing for a fine season of shooting and skinning, with great profits for all."

Hearing that was a tremendous relief. The Cator brothers were veteran hide men. When they downplayed any Indian threat, they could be trusted.

"You and Bob ought to come with us," Billy suggested. "It's our intention to set up somewhere near the Canadian and build a considerable camp. We'll have every amenity, and merchants who'll buy your hides on the spot. And, of course, there will be so many guns behind stout walls that the Indians will leave us alone."

"With respect, Billy, that sounds a little too crowded," Bob Cator said. He was heavier than his brother and had a longer beard. "But we certainly wish you well, and promise to drop in to your new settlement from time to time."

"Do that. You can sell your hides to A. C. Myers, who's opening a store wherever we light, and enjoy drinks from the bar of our mutual friend Jim Hanrahan."

Hanrahan clapped Bob Cator on the shoulder and said, "In honor of this meeting, I think I'll just bring out a few bottles right now. Let's have a drink all around, and then some entertainment."

The singing and dancing lasted long into the night. At one point, Bat insisted that McLendon stand up and sing. "It's your turn, C.M. Give us your finest tune."

"Bat, you don't want to hear me sing."

"Oh, but I do. Everybody does. Get up and provide some entertainment. It's required, if you truly wish to be one of the boys."

McLendon looked hopefully at Billy, but Dixon was deep in conversation with Jim Cator. "This is a mistake, Bat. I'm the worst singer in the world."

"Sing, damn it. Mirkle Jones has his fiddle at the ready."

"Wachu sangin'?" Mirkle asked.

McLendon tried to think of a song, any song, that he knew the words to. There was one . . .

"'Buffalo Gals,' I guess," he said. Jones nodded enthusiastically and set his bow on the fiddle strings. Taking a deep breath, McLendon sang. *"Buffalo gals, won't you come out tonight, come out tonight, come out tonight? Buffalo gals, won't you—"* and then he stopped. All around the campfire, men stared at him with expressions of pain and even horror. "I said I couldn't sing," he said defensively.

"You're a truthful man," Bat said.

"So do I have to finish my song?"

"We'd all rather you didn't, C.M.," Billy said. "I believe that, from now on, you can remain part of the audience."

Mirkle Jones resumed playing "Buffalo Gals." Somebody else stood up to sing. McLendon slumped down next to Billy. "At least I tried."

"Yes, you did. And now, never sing again."

On Sunday, they were deep in the Texas Panhandle and reached the South Canadian River. It was wider and deeper than the Arkansas and Cimarron. McLendon thought that they would make permanent camp on its bank, but Billy said no, what they needed was a place with streams of clean water and good grazing—maybe a valley if they could find one—with sufficient trees to provide lumber for building.

"When the herd arrives, it'll move parallel to the river," Billy said. "We can't have the skinned bodies turning rotten right where we sleep and get our drinking water. We'd all get sick. We'll rest here tonight, and tomorrow I'm sure we'll find a suitable site."

. . .

EVERYONE WAS UP EARLY and eager to go. The end of the trip was imminent. No one lingered over coffee and breakfast biscuits. Billy led the way along the creek bed, following its bends and turns. McLendon didn't see the sense of it. There were plenty of inviting hills nearby; surely some of them surrounded valleys containing the kind of stopping place required. When they made a brief stop to water the animals, McLendon asked Bermuda Carlyle where in the hell they were going.

"Oh, Billy's got a spot in mind," Carlyle said. He reeked of the cheap plug tobacco that he chewed constantly. His teeth and shirtfront were stained with brown juice. "You're about to learn a little history." McLendon was intrigued, but Carlyle wouldn't say more.

After almost a dozen miles, Billy stopped and gestured toward a flat plain dotted with what seemed to be the ruins of low walls. "There you are, boys. Go take a good look."

The walls were weathered brick, formed from some sort of clay. They were very old and some were crumbling at the edges. McLendon guessed that they were all that remained of about a dozen buildings.

"Adobe Walls, this place was called," Carlyle told him. "Built some forty years ago by men who thought they'd set up a trading post for white hunters and Indians. Didn't work out that way, of course. Owners got run off by the savages and then, ten years ago, Kit Carson and an Army bunch had a considerable clash here with about a thousand or more Co-manch and Kioways, the biggest war party just about ever, I expect. The Army boys took cover behind these walls as the Indians swarmed at 'em. Lucky for the soldiers, Carson had insisted that they bring four howitzers with them. It was enough firepower to hold off the Indians until nightfall, and then Carson and the soldiers escaped under cover of dark. The Battle of Adobe Walls—I doubt that there'll ever be another fight like it. All those Indians, and so few white men up against them. But the soldiers fought smarter, and so they survived."

Several men had grabbed shovels from wagon beds while Carlyle was talking. As soon as he stopped, they began digging frantically around the base of the surviving walls. "What are they doing?" McLendon asked.

Carlyle sent a lazy arc of tobacco juice in the direction of the diggers. "Oh, there's said to be some kind of treasure buried here. Not so, of course. But some will believe anything."

McLendon walked over to Billy. "Is this where we're going to make permanent camp?"

"I'd like to, if nothing else than to honor old Kit Carson. But look around—still no decent grazing. I think we're close to the right place, though."

Billy called everyone together. "For the moment, let's keep all the wagons and livestock right here," he said. "What I'd like is, let's have some scouts, maybe three or four to the bunch, spread out and take a long look around, maybe to the north a bit. There seem to be some streams running off that way. Remember, we want grass and some timber as well as water. We've come so far, let's be certain to pick just the right place."

Riders set off, Bat Masterson among them. The teamsters fed their animals oats from barrels. Some of the men kept digging; no one found treasure. After a few hours, the scouts began drifting back. One bunch, led by Billy's head skinner Mike McCabe, was excited. They swore that they'd found the perfect spot not a mile and a half away. Their enthusiasm was contagious. Everyone wanted to go and see. Billy passed the word to get ready to move, and after a hasty lunch of jerky and canteen water, the caravan set out. They passed through some low hills, topped a rise, and there, ahead of them, was a lovely long meadow framed by higher hills and, off to the north, a flat-topped mesa. A rippling stream

helped form a natural boundary to the north and west. There was another to the south, and along the banks of the streams grew clusters of
trees. Even McLendon could tell it was an idyllic spot. Some of the men
cheered. Billy, grinning so hard that it seemed his face might split, announced what everyone knew already.

"We've arrived, boys!" he shouted. "Look around at your new home."

"What shall we call it, Billy?" someone asked.

"I have just the name," Billy said. "Let's show our respect for the ones
who came before us and tried to settle in not a mile from here. In their
memory, I say welcome to the new Adobe Walls, and may our luck be
better than theirs."

SEVENTEEN

Quanah was arguing with Wickeah when the Kiowa rode into the Quahadi camp and stood outside Quanah's tipi, calling for him to come out and talk with them. He was grateful for the interruption. The argument was a foolish one and entirely the fault of his wife. Wickeah always expected a great deal of Quanah's time and attention, so she bitterly resented his trips from the village with Isatai. Ever since he'd returned from the visit to the Cheyenne camp, she'd been particularly irritable, claiming that he never thought about her anymore. It was true that he was constantly preoccupied. He had to think of some way to make the Kiowa and Cheyenne believe that if they fought together with the People and drove off the whites, then afterward they would be considered equals. And, as well, Isatai was a constant concern. The fat man truly believed that he was the spokesman of the spirits, and was liable to say foolish things if Quanah wasn't constantly on hand to stop him. In particular, he kept insisting that no one kill any skunks, because skunks were precious to the spirits. Such prattling detracted from the dignified Spirit Messenger pose that Quanah wanted Isatai to maintain in public.

If he gabbled about skunks too much, everyone might be reminded why Isatai had once been the camp laughingstock.

Collectively, these concerns were already too much for anyone but the strongest man to bear, and Quanah was doing his best. How dare Wickeah add to his burdens? Maybe he often did imagine himself with Mochi instead of Wickeah when they coupled in their blankets, and perhaps he seldom spoke to her anymore because he was so worn down from his other responsibilities. She was his wife and should sympathize. He told Wickeah that it was her obligation to make him feel better, not worse. But she turned that around and insisted that husbands had to make their wives happy too. She was loudly insisting on this when the Kiowa arrived.

Quanah called to them, "I'll be right there." Though he had no idea what they wanted, he was relieved to have an excuse to escape Wickeah. She was a very stubborn woman and could argue for hours when given the opportunity, especially since she knew her husband was tender-hearted and would never beat her.

"Let the Kiowa wait," she snapped. "Put your wife first for a change."

"Enough," Quanah said, trying to sound commanding. Wickeah, fists jammed on her hips, glared as he ducked down through the tipi's entrance flap.

Five Kiowa awaited Quanah. He recognized one of them. Iseeo was a hotheaded young warrior who often counted impressive coup in battle. "Welcome," Quanah said. "Do you bring a message from your chief, Lone Wolf? Are you ready to join us in the great fight to come?"

"No, we have news of white hunters who have come into our land," Iseeo said. "We thought we should inform the Comanche's Spirit Messenger at once, and learn his thoughts about it."

"He's communicating with the spirits right now," Quanah said carefully. In fact, he felt sure that Isatai was either gorging himself on food brought to him by camp admirers or else asleep. But the Kiowa didn't need to know that. "You and I can talk about this, Iseeo. You others, if you'll go inside my tipi, my wife will have food for you." This was common courtesy, and an easy offer for Quanah to make. No matter how angry she might be with her husband, Wickeah was always a gracious hostess who would find something to serve guests.

Quanah and Iseeo wandered out of camp toward the Quahadi horse herd. "So what is there to tell about these white hunters?" Quanah asked. "It's no surprise that some have come down here. With the cold season over and the buffalo on their way, what did you expect? Don't you think we have more important concerns?"

"These hunters are different," Iseeo said. "We first saw them five days ago, coming south. There were many of them, ten times at least the number of fingers on your hands, and almost that many wagons. Next to the soldiers following Bad Hand into battle, I have never seen so many white men riding together. My four friends and I went right up to them and let them think we wanted gifts, which they gave us. What they call coffee, and also the sweet white powder. And that was when we counted them, and saw their guns."

"These were good guns?" Quanah asked, thinking of the old, battered weapons carried by the three hunters he'd recently killed.

"Yes," Iseeo said grimly. "They were the new long guns that shoot straight and far. All of them had those, or at least the small guns they carry on their belts. And in the wagons—every kind of food, and all sorts of other things."

"But they gave you gifts and didn't threaten you?"

"No, they acted like superior beings and not in the least afraid. As we left, we bent over and showed them our bare asses just to see what they would do. We knew we could outrun them if we had to. But they didn't do anything. Of course, after that we followed them, and didn't let them see us."

"They kept coming south?"

"Yes. And at the mouth of the river by the deep canyon, they stopped and camped for the night with another small party of hunters who'd been there all through the cold months. You probably know the ones. They're led by two men with long face hair down almost to their bellies. We've been watching them and expect to kill them soon. There was much rejoicing when the big party of hunters arrived—I think they knew each other and were friends. But the next morning, the big party left, still coming south, and now they are camped in a meadow not far from the Great River. It's also near the place of the old walls. You know the one, where some seasons ago my people and yours lost a fight to white soldiers with guns on wheels."

"We didn't lose," Quanah said. "The white soldiers ran away after it got dark. But that's not important. So this big party of white hunters has made a camp?"

Iseeo nodded. "I think they mean to stay. They're building their usual tipis of wood."

Quanah thought for a moment. "Iseeo, you were right to come and share this news. I'll repeat it to the Spirit Messenger."

"Can't I see him?" Iseeo asked plaintively. "I hoped he would give me a blessing."

"I'm sorry, but he can't be disturbed when he's talking to the spirits. I'll tell him about this good thing you've done, though if you really want his blessing, convince your chief to join in the great fight with us. That's what the spirits command."

"I'm trying. Lone Wolf says that you Comanche don't respect the Kiowa."

"Fight with us. That will assure our respect. Gather your friends, go back to your village, and tell this to Lone Wolf. We need his decision soon."

AFTER THE FIVE KIOWA rode away, Quanah went to Isatai's tipi. As he expected, the fat man was sprawled out snoring on his blankets. Both of his old, ugly wives squatted nearby, sorting through the latest presents brought by the other Quahadi. Some were small trinkets—beads and ribbons—but most of the tributes were varieties of food. Someone had just killed a deer, and given Isatai a haunch. There were corn cakes and fruit jellies and also several skinned rabbits. The villagers felt that such an important Spirit Messenger shouldn't have to waste his time hunting.

The wives gestured for Quanah to let their husband alone, but he shook him awake anyway. "Come on. We have something to do."

Isatai protested, "Let me alone, I'm tired." His voice was thick with sleep. "Maybe I was receiving a message from the spirits in a dream."

"Well, were you?"

Isatai rubbed his eyes. "I can't remember now. Why are you bothering me?"

"Some Kiowa came to the village. They told me about a big new camp of white hunters near the Great River, close to those old ruined walls. We need to go see."

It took a while to get Isatai up and out of the tipi. He wanted to eat first, and then he had to apply new face paint, which he said demonstrated respect for the spirits. Quanah waited impatiently. He hadn't been out of the village for several days as he waited for word from Lone Wolf of the Kiowa and Gray Beard of the Cheyenne. He hated any sense of being hemmed in, and he always felt that way if he stayed in

camp too long. It would have been simpler to go spy on the newly arrived whites by himself, but he couldn't depend on Isatai not to say or do
something foolish while he was away. It was better to drag the pompous
fool along.

They packed some food, because they knew they would be gone
overnight. Quanah didn't inform Wickeah that he was leaving. Let her
wonder if maybe he'd gotten so tired of her sharp tongue that he was
deserting her for good. Wickeah's unwomanly assertiveness, Quanah
thought, compared unfavorably to high-spirited Mochi's attitude. Mochi
could fight better than most men, but she still deferred to her husband,
Medicine Water, as a respectful wife should. Soon, maybe, Mochi would
set a proper example in Wickeah's own tipi.

IT TOOK A FULL DAY to reach the ruins that marked the old battle
site. Isatai hummed most of the way. When they stopped for a meal and
a few hours' sleep, he complained about the pemmican that Quanah
had brought. "There was some tasty fresh venison in my tent. You could
have brought that."

"Eat what we have."

"You shouldn't speak so rudely to me. I'm the Spirit Messenger and
deserve respect."

Quanah struggled to keep his temper in check. It was important
to keep Isatai placated and cooperative. "Forgive me. I'm worried about
the Kiowa. I believe the Cheyenne will be with us, but we need the
Kiowa too."

Despite his complaints about the pemmican, Isatai gobbled it down.
"The Kiowa will join us. Buffalo Hump's spirit says so."

"Does Buffalo Hump's spirit explain how to make certain that
happens?"

Isatai stopped chewing, closed his eyes, and hummed. "All right. The spirit says, dance."

"What?"

Isatai opened his eyes and shook his head. "Sometimes the spirit just says a word or two and that's the message."

"Can you ask him to tell us more?"

"No, I think the spirit feels that you have your answer."

"Dance," Quanah said. "The spirit wants me to dance, and then the Kiowa will do what we want?"

"I don't know. This message was for you and not me, so you have to interpret and obey it." Isatai resumed stuffing his mouth with pemmican.

AFTER THEY REACHED the battle site, it was easy to track the white hunting party. They had made no attempt to cover their tracks—there were the marks of wagon wheels and many hoofprints, all going north. Quanah and Isatai carefully used the rolling hills to hide themselves from any scouts the white hunters might have left behind. They soon reached some streams emanating from the Great River and followed the most promising one. Almost immediately, they heard sounds peculiar to white men making permanent camp—pounding and sawing on wood, metal smashing on metal.

The Indians ground-tethered their horses and proceeded on foot. They crept up the side of a medium-sized hill and dropped on their bellies just behind the crest. Peering over, they saw a low grassy meadow rimmed by creeks, other hills, and, almost a mile away on the left, a flat-topped mesa. Down in the bowl of the meadow, swarms of whites were hard at work putting logs and boards in place for three buildings. The two farthest from the hill where Quanah and Isatai watched were medium-sized. Nearest to the Indians, the whites constructed a big corral. They had many animals down in the valley and obviously needed a place to keep them together. Inside the corral, using part of it as an outer wall, was the skeletal wooden outline of the third building.

"They intend to stay," Isatai whispered. This was the first sensible observation Quanah had heard him make in many days. "They will build a whole town, maybe."

Quanah burned at the thought. It was bad enough the hunters came to kill buffalo that belonged by natural right and even white treaty to the People. But now, a town? Such an insult. He forced himself to remain calm. He counted the men in the valley and decided Iseeo the Kiowa was probably right. They numbered about ten times the fingers on his hands, and they moved with the confidence of men who knew what they were doing. Many had the long, dangling hair that identified them as the hunters of buffalo. All had guns close to hand, pistols on their belts, and rifles propped within easy reach. They were clearly on guard, which was only to be expected. These were seasoned fighters, not fools. Quanah studied them carefully, picking out clues to their intentions. Some were digging a well, another sign they meant to stay. In a temporary camp, they would have been content to fetch water from the nearby creeks.

One of the long-haired men walked away into the high grass to take a shit. A red dog romped along behind him. Both the animal and the man looked familiar, and then Quanah remembered. This was the young man he'd seen many months earlier, the one scouting for buffalo sign. The longhair squatted with his pants tangled around his boots; Quanah thought he could probably rush him and cut his throat, but there was also the dog to consider. It might scent him, start barking, and then the rest of the whites would come after him. Quanah could easily escape, but Isatai wouldn't. Killing this longhair would have to wait for another time.

"Can we go back now?" Isatai asked. "We've seen the white men. I want some of the good food back in my tipi."

"I want to watch a while longer," Quanah said. "You can go back down the hill and wait by the horses. There's more pemmican in the pack on my pony. Why don't you go eat some, then keep watch on our mounts. Alert me if any whites are coming that way."

For the rest of the day, Quanah watched the activity down in the meadow. Most of what he saw was to be expected: trees being cut along the banks of the creek and hauled into the white camp, where they were trimmed, cut to size, and used on the buildings. The well was completed, and buckets of water drawn up. Then something astonished Quanah. One of the buildings had sides of logs, which was what he'd expected. But some of the whites hitched a strange-looking machine to a horse team and proceeded to cut out huge chunks of earth and grass. They fashioned these into thick bricks and began piling them all along the wood-frame sides of two buildings, gluing the bricks together with handfuls of mud. Buildings of dirt and grass? Who would want to live in them? It was a very curious thing.

It grew dark. Isatai wormed his way back up the hill and insisted that it was time to leave. "Just a little longer," Quanah said. "I want to count their fires, see how many stay and how many leave."

None of them left. Instead, they built some half-dozen fires, slaughtered a cow, and cooked the beef—Isatai's stomach rumbled so loudly when he smelled the roasting meat that Quanah feared the whites below would hear it. After the men had eaten, Quanah prepared to creep away. Surely the white men would send out guards to patrol the area around their camp. But that didn't happen. The young longhair who was the leader placed a few men at the edges of the meadow, but no farther out. There was no need to move Isatai and the horses away, or for Quanah to move from the crest where he lay so comfortably.

He watched idly as the white men cleared away the pots and plates from dinner, rinsing them with buckets of well water. As he watched, he thought again of the message Isatai claimed to have received from the spirits. *Dance.* Of course, Isatai was a fool and a liar, and he had probably just blurted the first word that came into his empty head. Still, the word seemed to have some meaning. *Dance.*

One of the men below was a white man and yet wasn't, his skin an off color. Like Isatai, he was big and fat. He rummaged in a wagon and produced a thing with strings. Then he grasped another long, narrow thing with a single string—it looked like a very fragile bow. He rubbed this skinny bow across the thing with strings, and this made musical sounds that Quanah liked very much. So did the other white men, who began to hop about, some singing along and others linking arms and whirling—*dancing.*

"So white men dance too," Isatai whispered, startling Quanah, who had been so absorbed in the scene below that he hadn't heard his rotund companion coming back up the hill. "I suppose everyone dances. The People have ours, and the Kiowa and the Cheyenne have their bloody sun dances. I wonder why the white men are dancing tonight."

And then, in an instant, Quanah had it, the way to make everything work. Of course the word "dance" was key to gaining the cooperation of the Kiowa and assuring the continued support of the Cheyenne as well. It was so obvious—why had he not have thought of it sooner?

He dragged Isatai back down the hill and, once they were mounted, set the fastest pace possible back to the Quahadi camp.

EIGHTEEN

Cash McLendon considered himself smarter than most of the men he met in the West. From his time in St. Louis society, he knew how to waltz, which utensils to use when during multicourse dinners, and the surest, least detectable methods of stealing industrial secrets from competitors. With the exception of Jim Hanrahan, a seasoned businessman who'd served in the Kansas state legislature, such things were certainly beyond the ken of almost everyone else at the new Adobe Walls site. But they far surpassed McLendon in skills required for frontier construction. Left to his own devices, McLendon would have struggled to put up a tent that wouldn't immediately fall over. He had no idea which type of tree furnished the best wood for ridge logs, as opposed to an entirely different type of lumber required for fences. It astonished him that great bricks of sod could actually be cut from the meadow using a special plow, and that these earth-and-grass bricks could be used to form thick walls. Two of the structures taking shape in the undulating meadow actually had glass windows. Whatever social skills they might lack, these rough-and-tumble frontiersman used the materials at hand to construct honest-to-God buildings.

At first, as soon as they'd picked the site and spent a full day resting after the trip from Dodge City, everyone pitched in. Deep trenches were dug; then thick cottonwood logs were laid down in them to provide a foundation to which slimmer upright logs could be nailed. It was hard, sweaty work, but required sure hands all the same. A single misplaced log would weaken an entire wall. Just constructing the two-hundred-by-three-hundred-foot corral for the Myers and Leonard store took almost two weeks. Its log fence stood eight feet high, and the wood had to be cut and hauled back to the meadow from groves of cottonwood about six miles away. The walls of the three buildings that bordered the corral—a store, a mess hall, and a stable—were what the building crew called picket, logs chinked with mud, pocked occasionally with shooting slots so gunmen could stand inside and fire in case of attack. There was a heavy double door in front, also made of wood. The door faced east so that it could be open on cool mornings to let in breeze and sunshine. There was also a smaller, lighter back door.

Tom O'Keefe's blacksmith shop was much smaller, a square fifteen by fifteen feet, and also had wood picket walls. But unlike the Myers and Leonard store, there were wide gaps between the logs. O'Keefe would spend most of his days laboring by the roaring fire necessary to bring metal to molten heat, and so he required constant fresh air blowing through.

Hanrahan's Saloon, twenty-five by sixty feet, had sod walls three feet thick at the base and two feet thick at the top. They could be penetrated by bullets, but defenders could also easily poke holes in the walls with tools or gun barrels and fire out. The great advantage was that sod bricks were virtually fireproof.

All three structures had the same roofs: in each, a thick central ridge-pole supported a framework of smaller supporting poles. When these were in place, they were covered by several layers of sod and dirt. Though bullets could penetrate, rain couldn't. There was some space between the buildings, almost thirty or forty yards. The meadow was deep enough so there was no need to cram one on top of the other. All of the buildings faced east.

After the first few days, most of the construction was done by crew members rather than the hide men themselves. They felt themselves above such menial labor, even though prior to leaving Dodge they'd agreed to lend a hand. Fred Leonard, O'Keefe, and Hanrahan hadn't expected free labor: every man was paid four dollars a day plus meals—not bad wages for hunting camp skinners and cooks—but this was a pittance to hunters accustomed to making that much from the sale of one or two hides. So, one by one, the hide men announced that they needed to scout the area, and rode out for days at a time, often bringing some of their crewmen with them and slowing camp construction accordingly. The three businessmen argued that they were breaking their word, but the hide men responded that they were heading out for the long-term benefit of the camp. For maximum hunting success, everyone needed to know all the freshwater springs in the area, and where the draws and hollows were where significant numbers of buffs might try to shelter in case of bad weather. Of course, they would also be on the lookout for Indians. None had been seen since they'd been accosted by the butt-baring Kiowa; apparently the Cator brothers were right, and most of the Indians had drifted away. Still, it was important to be sure.

Even Billy Dixon quickly got bored with camp construction and rode out with Frenchy, Mike McCabe, and Charley Armitage, three of his most veteran crewmen. Bat Masterson begged to come, but Billy, being less tactful than usual, said no because it was to be a long, wide scout, with a pace so blistering that an inexperienced hand like Bat could never keep up. That sent Masterson into a prolonged sulk; after Billy and his three companions rode off, Bat disappeared too. McLendon found him on the banks of the northernmost creek several hours later. Bat was slouched in the shade, scribbling away in his notebook. As usual, he refused to let McLendon read what he'd written.

"It's private, C.M. Now, tell me, is the camp work all done for the day? I swear I'll puke if I have to help secure one more ridgepole into place."

"You're in luck. I think the last nail was driven not too long ago, and tomorrow we'll commence putting in shelves for the store and saloon."

Bat tucked his pencil behind his ear and snapped the notebook shut. "Glad to hear it. Once they've got an array of items for sale, we can have some relief from the monotony of bacon and beans for dinner, washed down with water. I'm parched for beer or something stronger."

"Water will continue to suit me fine, since Jim Hanrahan's bound to charge at least a nickel a beer. I'm down here to make and save every cent that I can. You ought to be too."

Bat waved his hand dismissively. "In a few weeks, C.M., maybe a month at most, these hills will be crawling with buffs and echoing with the sound of gunfire. A few beers ahead of that won't cause either of us to go financially amiss."

"I need every cent, Bat."

"Ah, you have no idea of the amount of money we're about to come into."

Still upset by the snub from Billy, Bat stalked rather than strolled the half mile back into camp. McLendon followed at a more leisurely pace, thinking again about Gabrielle. Now that construction was almost complete, some of the teamsters were heading back to Dodge City in the morning. Charlie Rath would be waiting there to load their wagons with his own supplies prior to setting up shop in newly built Adobe Walls. The teamsters would carry letters to mail in Kansas, too, and bring back any missives addressed to denizens of the camp. Perhaps there'd be a letter coming from Gabrielle—she'd had time now to receive the latest one from him and decide how to respond. The slightest hint of further encouragement would help McLendon get through what he knew would be a summer of hard, messy work.

It was two full weeks before Billy Dixon and his three crewmen returned. They reported that they'd ridden east and encountered a few stray buffs here and there, but not the main herd.

"It's early yet, only April," Billy said. "They'll surely show by month's end, or the beginning of May at the latest."

Everyone at Adobe Walls was restless. They did some hunting, held shooting competitions, which Billy Dixon invariably won, and played cards. Since nobody had much money—and wouldn't until the great herd arrived and sales of hides could commence—they played for markers to be redeemed at a later date. A few of the men ran up considerable debts, a hundred dollars or more. Markers were also used to purchase food and dry goods at the Myers and Leonard store, sit-down meals prepared in the store mess hall by Old Man Keeler, and libations served in Hanrahan's saloon. Crew skinners and cooks drank liquor, but to McLendon's surprise most of the hide men limited themselves to beer and an odd concoction known as "bitters." Masterson explained that bitters, named for a somewhat unpleasant taste, was believed to promote good digestion and bowel health. Curious, McLendon squandered two bits for a glass and nearly gagged on the first sip. So far as he could tell, besides tasting bad, bitters had the kick of pure alcohol.

Inevitably, there were physical flare-ups. Brick Bond got into several near brawls, which were broken up by Billy Dixon, Jim Hanrahan, and a few of the other men. Mike McCabe and Dutch Henry Borne had a fistfight over who was first in line for a rabbit hash breakfast served up by Old Man Keeler. Bat Masterson, who'd been so sunny-natured back

in Dodge City, now acted touchy much of the time. He found insult in
the most innocuous comments, and once when McLendon kidded him
about his black mood, Bat challenged him to fight right then and there.

"What the hell, Bat, I'm your friend and you know it," McLendon
protested. "Why in the world would you want to fight me?"

"I really don't," Bat admitted. "But ever since Billy put me down a
few weeks back, ever'body's been treating me like the camp buffoon. I
won't stand for it."

"That's foolishness. It's true the others like to josh with you, but they
did that back in Dodge, too, and you always joshed right back."

"It's just that I want to prove myself here," Bat said. "I don't want to
be the goddamn kid brother anymore."

McLendon patted Masterson's shoulder. "You'll feel better when the
herd arrives and there's plenty of action to keep you occupied."

"Well, I wish those damn buffs would get here. This waiting is
tedious."

IN EARLY MAY, Charlie Rath came down from Dodge at the head of
a dozen wagons loaded with dry goods. He brought with him a dozen
employees, including a Swede named Andy Johnson who would be in
charge of the Rath store, and also William and Hannah Olds. William
Olds's cough was more wracking than ever, and his wife's nerves were as
shaky as McLendon remembered. Rath hired members of the hunting
crews to build him a sod structure about the same size as Jim Hanrahan's saloon. Since the men had nothing else to do, it was completed in
three days. Its attic-like storage area, which included glass windows commanding a view of the meadow, could be reached only by ladder. The
Oldses slept up in the attic to preserve Hannah Olds's privacy. As the
only woman in Adobe Walls, she was afforded great courtesies by all of

the men. She was always addressed as "Mrs. Olds," never "Hannah." They went out of their way to ease her obvious discomfort in such rough surroundings. They built a spacious outhouse so, unlike the men, Mrs. Olds wouldn't have to relieve herself in the brush. A pregnant mare gave birth, and the skinner who owned her gave the tottery colt to Mrs. Olds as a pet. A special stall for the foal was built in the Myers and Leonard stable, and in the mornings and evenings Mrs. Olds went there to feed it by hand.

A well was also dug just inside one of the walls. That meant, during inclement weather or in the event of a siege, it would be possible for anyone in the Rath store to get all the water they needed without going outside.

Once his store was ready to open for business, Rath and Andy Johnson took Fred Leonard aside for a private chat. The hunters and their crews had hoped for store price wars, with each trying to undercut what the other charged for popular goods. But what happened was the opposite. Prices in both stores were identical—and, in almost every case, higher than what had been charged for the same items back in Dodge. A can of tomatoes that went for thirty cents in Kansas cost forty in both the Rath and Myers and Leonard stores. The hide men and their crews were accustomed to spending a dollar for each pound of tobacco they smoked in their clay pipes. Now the charge was a dollar twenty-five.

"That ain't fair, Fred," Frenchy told Leonard. "With my own ears, I heard you promise back in Dodge that you'd keep prices down here the same."

"I don't deny that," Leonard said. "But what I failed to realize, until Andy Johnson and Charlie Rath pointed it out, was that I got to factor in shipping costs now. These teamsters charge exceeding high for every wagonload of goods they haul. There's where the extra few cents comes in. Surely you can understand."

"I understand that I'll have one or two less pipefuls to smoke a day," Frenchy groused. "There better be a damn sizable herd of buffs about to arrive here. I'll need the extra money to buy your outrageously priced tobacco and make you a rich man by so doing."

Almost everyone in camp ran up extensive bills at the stores and saloons. One of the few who didn't was McLendon. He only imbibed at the saloon when someone else was standing drinks, and his meals consisted of the cheapest fare available, usually crackers and cheese sliced from a mighty wheel in Myers and Leonard's. Hannah Olds couldn't give him occasional free suppers as she had in Dodge. Charlie Rath watched everything like a hawk, and when he went back to Dodge after two weeks in Adobe Walls, Andy Johnson exhibited the same watchfulness.

The days dragged, growing increasingly warmer. Some of the men gladly volunteered to help when Andy Johnson added a small bastion to the corner of the Rath store. Inside the bastion, they dug another well, so that water was available indoors as well as from the outside well and nearby freshwater springs. Billy insisted on everyone taking turns on guard duty at night, but eventually even he conceded that there didn't seem to be any Indians to guard against.

"Damndest thing," Billy mused. "Still, I want one or two sets of eyes alert ever night. Indians got to be out there somewhere. They can't all have moved on from the region."

Most mornings, some of the hide men rode out, most of them going southeast in hopes of catching the first glimpse of the approaching herd. A few went in other directions, hunting or else simply avoiding camp tedium. During the third week in May, there was considerable commotion when almost twenty men rode into Adobe Walls. Their leader was J. W. Mooar, who announced that anyone who wanted was welcome to leave the camp and come with him.

"The buffs may come any day now, but it appears to me that you've been too quick to pick this location," Mooar said. "The main herd might pass by close, but then again it might not. You may sit here all summer and not see a single buffalo. My boys and I, on the other hand, will remain mobile and find and hunt them wherever they may be."

Most of the Adobe Walls hide men told Mooar that they felt fine right where they were. Mooar made disparaging remarks about the camp— "It looks like the ground took a couple of craps and those things you call stores and a saloon resulted." Then he bought his crew members and anyone else who was thirsty some beer in the saloon. As everyone drank, Mooar repeated that all the "Dixon" hands willing to come with him instead would be welcome. When he and his men rode out an hour later, four of the Adobe Walls contingent—two skinners, a cook, and hide man Buck Firth—went with them.

Afterward, Billy Dixon, Fred Leonard, Andy Johnson, and Jim Hanrahan conferred, then called the camp together. They began by offering everyone another free beer.

"We can't have attrition," Hanrahan said after passing out the bottles. "Our best chance for not only success but safety rests in staying together. Nobody here should be so green as to conclude that there are no Indians about just because we haven't seen any. Now, we've all allowed ourselves to get into quarrelsome moods, and that has to cease. It's going to, starting now. Anyone who absolutely wants to go, well, pack up. Some of the teamsters are heading back to Dodge in the morning to fetch additional supplies, and you can travel with them if you like, or else you can set out on your own and hope to join up with J. W. Mooar or the Cators or whoever. Everyone else, we're going to liven spirits by giving ourselves a few days of festivity, with all kinds of tests of skill. Fred, Andy, and me are going to put up some prizes, tobacco and knives and such. Right now, drink down your beer, and for the rest of the night the price per bottle is reduced from fifteen cents to ten."

.   .   .

THE NEXT TWO DAYS were much more pleasant. Everyone enjoyed the games, especially the footraces and the marksmanship events. In one of those, Billy Dixon even lost to Bermuda Carlyle, who shouted with joy after his victory and proudly accepted a pint of bitters as his prize. Old Man Keeler and Hannah Olds served up especially tasty stews, offered at half price, and at night Mirkle Jones and his fiddle had everyone dancing. Being the only woman in camp, Mrs. Olds was everyone's choice as a partner. For a while, she stopped acting nervous and spun and giggled like a young girl. Only afterward, as they lay in their blankets under wagons or else on the floors of the stores and saloon, did most of them remember that it was now late May, and still the buffalo had not come.

NINETEEN

It took Quanah some time to set the newest aspect of his plan in motion. First, he and Isatai had to convince their own Quahadi camp. Bull Bear and the other older men were especially stubborn, but eventually they gave in. Then Quanah and Isatai had to travel to all the other places where bands of the People camped—the Yamparika, the Nokoni, the Penateka, and the Kotsoteka, and also those among the People who had taken refuge on the white man's reservation. In each village they heard the same objection, had to respond with the same logic: No, of course Kiowa and Cheyenne aren't the equals of the People. But we have to make them think that we believe they are. It's the only way they'll join us in the fight that Buffalo Hump's spirit wants us to make.

Afterward, Quanah thought that if he'd been by himself, he could never have made all of them see the sense of it. Though he still considered Isatai to be a pompous fraud, the fat man proved to be an invaluable ally. Drawing himself up, exhibiting a sort of thoughtful dignity Quanah would have previously considered beyond him, Isatai gravely lectured about the importance of obeying the spirits, and that ultimately made the difference. In the end, they had what they needed—an agreement among all the scattered camps of the People to convene in one place at the end of the current moon cycle and, once there, to arrange things in the way that the spirit of Buffalo Hump required.

And that was just the first step. Next, Quanah and Isatai traveled to see the Kiowa and Cheyenne, including again the members of those tribes living on the reservations. They invited them to join the People at their great convocation, which would be held along the banks of the wide red river dividing the places whites called Oklahoma and Texas. Everyone greeted this news with surprise: never in living memory had all of the Comanche gathered together in one place. But when they inquired as to why this was happening, Quanah was coy. Something special would take place, he promised, something that would prove that the People now accepted the Kiowa and Cheyenne as equals, and would even after the whites were finally driven from Indian land.

Lone Wolf and Satanta of the Kiowa were doubtful. They said that the Comanche would never consider anyone to be full partners. There must be some trick involved. But Quanah and Isatai persisted: They should come and see, then decide. Mamanti, the Kiowa medicine man, howled at his leaders to stay away from the Comanche gathering, but in the end curiosity overcame them.

"We will come, but we make you no promises," Lone Wolf told Quanah. "And we'll expect to be your guests in matters of food."

"All of our men are out hunting," Quanah promised. "There will be every kind of meat except for buffalo. The herd is late this season. But the feasting will please our Kiowa friends."

Lone Wolf said that the Kiowa would be there, and Quanah and Isatai departed for the camp of Gray Beard and the Cheyenne. It was a long ride, several days, and Quanah spent it alternately imagining the great battle with the whites and fantasizing about rolling in his blankets with

Mochi. Isatai, as usual, closed his eyes and hummed as he rode. By now Quanah was so used to the annoying sound that he could block it out.

The Cheyenne camp was still in the same place, but larger than when the two Quahadi men had last visited. After Gray Beard greeted them and invited them into his tent for food and a smoke, he explained that many more of his tribe had come to the village from the white reservation.

"They're tired of the lies," Gray Beard said. "The Kway-kers said more meat was coming and it never did. They ordered all of the men to bury seeds in the ground and grow plants to eat."

"Plants," Quanah said dismissively. "They wanted your men to be farmers."

Unlike the Kiowa chiefs, who immediately demanded to know why Quanah and Isatai had come, Gray Beard made friendly conversation with his Quahadi guests for a while. Stone Calf, White Shield, and Whirlwind, tribal leaders who'd recently arrived from the reservation, were summoned and introduced. Medicine Water, leader of the Cheyenne dog soldiers and Mochi's husband, came into the tipi too. Everyone continued to chat and smoke for a while. Quanah appreciated the courtesy. Finally he said, "We're here with an invitation." The People were coming together for a gathering, and wanted their Cheyenne brothers to attend. A great thing that Quanah could not reveal would happen.

"But it will prove to you that the People want to be one with the Cheyenne," Quanah said. "And after that, we will plan our attack on the whites."

"Buffalo Hump's spirit promises that the time for this fight has come," Isatai added. "He has given me medicine to protect us, and his wisdom will guide us to victory."

The Cheyenne chiefs looked at each other, and Stone Calf whispered something to Medicine Water, who glanced at Isatai and then whispered back.

"It would be a hard thing to take everyone here and move our camp all the way down to the wide red river," Stone Calf said. "You should tell us more about what we'll see there."

Quanah shook his head. "I can't. But when you see it, you'll understand."

Stone Calf looked again at the other Cheyenne leaders and said, "Then we're sorry, but if you don't tell us more, we won't come."

Before Quanah could respond, Isatai stood up, his great bulk filling an entire side of the tipi. "Listen to the spirit. He says, 'Come,'" and for that single word, Isatai's voice took on a sort of guttural majesty that made the hair on Quanah's arms stand up. The Cheyenne chiefs cringed. They whispered frantically among themselves. Isatai, arms folded across his thick, flabby chest, glared at them, daring them to disobey.

Finally, very quietly, Lone Wolf spoke for them all. "We will come."

TWO DAYS LATER, the Cheyenne camp was packed and ready. Every tipi was pulled down, and each family's possessions were tightly tied to a travois. They set out in a long procession, with the tribal chiefs, Quanah, and Isatai riding in the lead. The pace they set wasn't brisk. Though there were enough horses for the men to ride, all of the women and children were on foot. Much to Quanah's dismay, Mochi walked among them. He was able to catch only occasional glimpses of her. He'd hoped to spend at least some of the march regaling her with tales of his prowess in battle, which surely eclipsed that of her current husband. Medicine Water and the other dog soldiers spent most of their time riding ahead as lookouts, so he wouldn't have been there to object. But apparently it was traditional with Cheyenne on the march for men not to mingle with women, a foolish thing in Quanah's mind and further evidence so far as he was concerned that this tribe was vastly inferior to the People.

When they stopped that night, the women immediately spread out blankets, lit fires, and cooked meals for their families. Because camp was always made beside streams, they had to fetch water too. Then men who weren't posted as guards sat and smoked while their supper was prepared. After they ate, they smoked some more and played simple gambling games with sticks and cards made from squares of dried animal hide while the women cleaned up. Everyone turned in early.

Quanah was too restless to sleep. He sat by one of the fires, staring into the flames and brooding. Much depended on the People properly preparing the big new camp; for maximum effect, it had to look perfect when the Kiowa and Cheyenne arrived. Anything less, and the plan would fail. Maybe some of the Cheyenne would still agree to fight, but the Kiowa never would. Quanah had instructed Yellowfish and Wolf Tongue of the Quahadi to guide the Kiowa in. He'd warned them both not to bring these visitors until all the construction was complete. What if they arrived too early? He'd emphasized they had to wait until the moon was whole in the sky. It was so frustrating when he had to rely on anyone other than himself. Isatai, at least, was doing surprisingly well. The way he'd said the word *"Come"*—it really seemed like the voice of a spirit, not of a man.

Quanah's moody reverie was interrupted by Spotted Feather, his Cheyenne trading acquaintance. "I've just been on watch," Spotted Feather said. "I saw nothing stirring, but many are worried about the white soldiers."

"Before Isatai and I came to your village, we sent out scouts from our own camp, who went very far in all directions," Quanah said. "There are no white soldiers anywhere near. Bad Hand is still down toward Mexico."

"I'm glad to hear it." Spotted Feather squatted by the fire and offered a hand-rolled cigarette to Quanah. "I'd also be glad to hear what kind of surprise you have for us at the big Comanche camp."

Quanah sucked the sweet smoke deep into his lungs. "You know that I can't tell you."

"Some think it will be a great thing, others that this is a trick so we'll join you and do most of the fighting against the whites while the Comanche watch."

"Surely you know better. The People are always fierce fighters. We take pride in it."

"I didn't say this was what I thought. I said that others did."

Quanah exhaled a cloud of smoke. "Well, you and everyone else will see. Three days' ride, maybe four. Then the Cheyenne will have a great surprise."

"Ah. That will be good."

They smoked awhile in silence. Then Quanah said, "I want to talk about Mochi. My words are not to be repeated, of course."

"If you think you might take her away from Medicine Water and make her your wife, don't even try. It will never happen."

Quanah said testily, "I'm a man of some importance among the People. I have killed more whites and Mexicans than anyone else, and I own many more horses than are in the entire herd of your camp."

"That would impress other women, but it won't matter to Mochi. Only one thing is important to her. She loves killing white people with her own hands."

"Why? How did she become such a great fighter?"

Spotted Feather tossed the butt of his cigarette into the fire, then reached inside a pouch to get the fixings to roll another. "You remember many seasons ago, what happened to Cheyenne chief Black Kettle and his people?"

"A little. The white men killed them in the place called Sand Creek."

"It's a terrible story. Black Kettle had made peace with the whites. He trusted them; he even liked them so much that he took their country's flag with the stripes and the stars and put it up on a pole above his tipi. The whites never had a truer Cheyenne friend than Black Kettle. He stopped fighting them and took his people—there were many of them—into winter camp by Sandy Creek in a place the whites named Colorado. They were ordered there by the whites and Black Kettle didn't argue. It was a happy camp, even though there was very little game and the men had to go very far away to hunt. They kept to themselves, as they'd agreed when they made peace. But some of the white men wanted to kill them anyway, and one cold morning soldiers rode into Black Kettle's camp when the warriors were gone hunting, and they attacked. Besides killing the few men who were there, they went after the families. The whites were on horseback and they chased these women and children, who screamed as they ran, and when they came up beside them they leaned down and swung long knives to cut off their heads."

"The whites are devils."

"Mochi was there. She was a little girl. She saw her father shot and her mother and two brothers cut apart by the soldiers. She ran up a hill and a soldier chased her. He cut her with his long knife. Today you can still see the scar on her neck. They must have thought she was dead, because they left her there. Later some Cheyenne from another camp came by and they found her. Ever since, she has wanted nothing more than to kill all the white people that she can. She would rather do that than breathe. Mochi trained alongside boys to learn a warrior's skills, and eventually surpassed them. She'll never go with you, Quanah. Comanche men don't let their women join them in battle, and Mochi couldn't stand that. No matter what else you might promise her, she'll stay with Medicine Water and the Cheyenne."

"We might let her fight," Quanah said, imagining the disgusted response of other warriors among the People if he asked.

"Well, if you want any chance with Mochi, you would have to," Spotted Feather replied.

THEY RODE SOUTH AND EAST for three more days, swinging wide to avoid the big new camp of the white hunters. Word of it had already spread among the Cheyenne. Quanah broke away from the group for a little while to take a look. Everything seemed the same, except for one more building. A lot of the whites seemed to be milling aimlessly around. They clearly didn't have much to do, since the buffalo hadn't yet come. The presence of the camp annoyed Quanah greatly. It was an affront to the People and ought to be obliterated. Perhaps this was a possible target for the great attack. The more he thought about it, the more sense it made.

FINALLY THEY APPROACHED the wide red river. As they drew near, Quanah asked the Cheyenne to wait while he rode ahead. "I want to make sure that everything is ready," He said. "Call back Medicine Water and the dog soldiers. All of you should see it first at the same time."

Once all the Cheyenne scouts had returned, Quanah rode forward. He took Isatai with him. The fat man hadn't said anything foolish for days, and Quanah wanted to keep it that way.

"Everything has to be right," Quanah said as they pushed their mounts into a trot. "If it isn't—"

"It will be," Isatai promised. "The spirit says so."

Then they topped a rise and Quanah looked down and there everything was, even better than he'd hoped. "Wait here," he told Isatai. Then he turned his pony and raced back to where the Cheyenne were waiting.

Quanah took the chiefs ahead with him, Gray Beard and Stone Calf and Medicine Water and Whirlwind. When they looked down, they gasped, because the sight was unprecedented in the history of the Comanche.

Spreading out along the banks of the wide red river were Comanche tipis in almost countless number, and beyond them were tipis of the Kiowa, distinctive for daubs of bright paint. A few hundred yards away on a low bluff was a mock white fort built from cottonwood logs, and also a wide lodge of wood with buffalo skulls spread across the brush roof and a high pole extending up beyond the roof, with the largest buffalo skull of all adorning it on top.

"What *is* this?" Gray Beard asked.

Quanah grinned. "Why, it's something new for the People. In honor of our friends the Cheyenne and Kiowa, to prove we respect all of your customs and beliefs as we do our own, we invite you now to join us in our first sun dance."

TWENTY

In the last week of May, Billy Dixon called everyone at Adobe Walls together and tried to rally them. "The buffs are coming, we all know that," he said. "It's just that winter was especially hard and spring came late. We need to quit bitching and scrapping among ourselves while we wait. Let's have some more games or something."

"I'm tired of shooting at paper targets," Brick Bond growled. "I came here to shoot buffalo. Or, failing that, any fools who annoy me."

"Well, then, goddamn go back to Dodge City," Billy said. "We got some wagons heading there this very morning. But afterward you won't have any better luck hunting. Nobody's seen any buffs around Dodge, either. If we'd stayed up there, we'd still be waiting on a herd just the same."

"Billy's right," Fred Leonard said. "A bit more patience is what is required."

"It's all right for you to be patient, Fred," Jim McKinley snapped. Premature baldness had left him the only hide man without long hair. "Every day, you take more of our markers for your food and notions. Same with Hanrahan for his beer and bitters, and with Jimmy Langton and his pricey goods at the Rath store. If the herd never shows, what's it, really, to you? You're still making money every day that we wait."

"Nobody makes you buy cans of soup or peaches or tomatoes for your meals. Go out and shoot a deer, get your own dinner instead of paying me for classier sustenance. If you've run up bills at my store, it's your fault and none of my own."

"I'll not tolerate this situation much longer, and neither will a lot of the other boys," McKinley said. "Billy Dixon, we all think you're a fine man. But we're approaching our limits here. You can't blame us for that."

Billy's head bobbed in a rueful shake. "I know, Jim, I know. Tell you what—if there's no buffalo sign today, I'll take a few of my crew and ride east and south tomorrow. I won't stop this time until I find the herd, and then I'll ride back here pronto to report. That'll give everyone time to be set up just right as they finally arrive, so the shooting can commence at once and the hide sales immediately after."

LATER THAT DAY, McLendon found Bat slouched in the shade by the bank of the north creek, scribbling in his notebook.

"Are you going to ask Billy to ride along with him tomorrow?" he asked. "You could maybe work off some of your restlessness that way."

Bat shrugged. "I'd like to, but my pride won't allow me to be told for a second time that I'm too inexperienced for such responsibility."

"Go on and ask. Billy's sure to take you along."

"Maybe so. Now I need to go off a minute and piss. It's sad when taking a piss is the highlight of a man's day."

Bat wandered off into the brush. He left his notebook on the creek bank, and McLendon couldn't resist. He opened it to a random page. Bat's handwriting was surprisingly neat.

"At night the sky turns first from bright blue to pink and then deep violet. The colors so much resemble flowers that a floral fragrance seems to perfume the air. Against this colorful backdrop stand the hide men, all of them with long flowing hair and steely, determined gaze. There is about them a sense of resolution. These are men of considerable grit and experience who never tremble in the face of danger. Foremost among them is—"

"What the hell are you doing, McLendon?" Masterson screamed. Still fumbling at his trouser buttons, he dashed out of the brush and snatched the notebook from McLendon's hands. "What I write is private, goddammit. You know I don't want you reading it."

"Why, it's really good, Bat. Jesus, you ought to be writing books or for a newspaper or something. I believe that you demonstrate evidence of real talent."

Bat's attitude instantly shifted from aggrieved to bashful. He ducked his head and mumbled, "You think so?"

"I do, and I'm a man who likes to read a lot. When the hunting season's over and you're back in Dodge or wherever, you should send some of this off to one of those magazines that have stories about the West. Bet you anything they'd buy what you've written, get it into print as fast as they could."

"Really?" Bat said. "Well, then."

"Will you let me read some more?"

"Another time, maybe. Meanwhile, don't tell any of the others about this, all right? They'd consider writing stories to be girlish."

"What do they know? This is such a surprise. What you really want to be is a writer?"

"Who knows? For now, all I really want is to see the buffalo coming this way. I guess I *will* ask Billy to ride along."

. . .

BACK IN CAMP, McLendon considered his own situation, which wasn't good. He'd spurned a job with good, steady pay in Dodge to gamble on making much more money working for Billy Dixon. The expedition had left Dodge almost nine weeks before. Thirty-five dollars a week at nine weeks—even with a dollar and a half a day for a boardinghouse room and, say, another four or five dollars a week for meals and other necessities, why, he'd still have more than two hundred saved up for his journey to Gabrielle in Arizona Territory, with several more months of savings to come. Plenty of money. The reverse was true at Adobe Walls. He had absolutely no income and, try as he might, he still had to spend some of his remaining, dwindling funds each day—two bits, at least, for cheese and crackers, and every now and then he had to vary that bland fare with a can of soup or some of Old Man Keeler's stew. He liked and felt sorry for Hannah Olds, but her cooking didn't compare to Keeler's. Anyway, he was down to about eighty dollars, barely enough for his train and stage fare from Dodge to Mountain View, let alone a sufficient stake to stay awhile in that town and then get him and Gabrielle and maybe her sick father from there to California. Coming along with Billy Dixon instead of remaining and working in Dodge had been a mistake, just the latest in the long string that he'd made. It had all started back in St. Louis, when he'd abandoned Gabrielle for the chance to marry Ellen, the daughter of his rich boss Rupert Douglass. If only, back then, he'd done the decent thing, the right thing, how different his life now would be.

McLendon's plunge into recrimination and self-pity lasted into early afternoon. Bat bounced up and announced gleefully that Billy had given him permission to come along. He insisted on buying McLendon a beer in Hanrahan's saloon to celebrate. McLendon didn't particularly feel

like drinking, but Bat badgered him and it was something to do. Oscar
Shepherd, Hanrahan's bartender, uncapped two beer bottles and shoved
them across the counter. Bat gulped down his beer and called for another; McLendon sipped slowly.

"You need to come with Billy, too, C.M.," Bat said. "Get out of camp
for a while. It'd do you good."

"I think I'll stay behind and wait for you to come back with good
news. Anyway, the Scheidler brothers and some other teamsters are due
in from Dodge anytime now. They might see sign of the herd on their
way in. Then Billy won't need to ride out tomorrow after all."

"I almost hope they don't. I'm eager for some adventure, and it would
be a thing to be the first who spots the herd."

"Well, then, I hope it's you. But somebody better see something."

A HALF-DOZEN WAGONS arrived late in the afternoon. They brought
more supplies for the camp stores and saloon, and mail forwarded on
by the Dodge City postmaster to those at Adobe Walls lucky enough to
get some. McLendon was startled when Isaac Scheidler came looking
for him with an envelope in his hand.

"C.M.? Here's something addressed to you."

McLendon tore the envelope open and his hands trembled as he un-
folded the single page inside. Gabrielle wrote,

April 12, 1874

*I am in receipt of your new letter, and am pleased with the
thought that you are coming, though apparently not as soon as
I would wish. The end of summer seems a long way away.*

You should not obsess so about money. It need not be an immediate consideration when you arrive here. Major Mulkins, who you will remember from Glorious, manages the hotel where I work. He is delighted that you are coming to Mountain View, and says that upon your arrival you may share his room at the hotel until you are able to otherwise situate yourself. Your meals may be taken free of charge with us at the hotel staff table, he adds. And, of course, it will cost you nothing but your time to share my company.

I repeat that I am making no promises. But I am eager to see you.

> *Fondly,*
> *Gabrielle*

McLendon's immediate impulse was to ride along on the next wagon heading back to Dodge City. From there, he'd go as far by train and stage as his remaining stake would take him, and walk the last miles if necessary. It would mean quitting Billy Dixon when he'd promised Billy back in Dodge that he wouldn't. But if Billy went out on the latest scout and didn't find the big buffalo herd, the expedition would be called off anyway. That would free McLendon from his obligation to Billy without requiring him to break his word. In the past, McLendon had broken promises as easily as he'd drawn breath. He'd promised Gabrielle that he'd changed for the better—now he had to prove it to himself, too, even if it meant delaying his rush to Gabrielle for another week or so.

Still, if the herd wasn't coming, McLendon wanted to be among the first to know it and get on his way. He found Billy in the Rath store and asked to come along on the final scout for the buffalo.

"It'll be a hard ride," Billy said. "As I recall, you're none too comfortable in the saddle."

"I don't care. I want to go."

"All right. We leave at dawn."

DAWN ARRIVED EARLY. The first muted paling of the eastern sky came about four-thirty in the morning, and by five it was light enough for Billy, McLendon, Bat, Frenchy, and Charley Armitage to ride out of camp. They brought with them enough provisions for a week—coffee, bacon, a few cans of tomatoes, and the ingredients for biscuits that Frenchy would bake in the Dutch oven strapped to his saddle. Billy said they'd vary their diet with game; there were plenty of deer and birds about. Billy and Charley had Sharps Big Fifties. Frenchy had an older, smaller-caliber Sharps. Bat had a shotgun. McLendon had only his Colt Peacemaker. The other four carried Peacemakers too. Because they needed to maintain a steady pace without distractions, Billy left his red setter closed up in a stall at camp. Fannie's howls followed them as they left.

All morning they rode through alternately rugged and undulating country, always moving east and a little south. McLendon did his best to ignore the chafing of his legs against the sides of his horse, and the occasional bruising of his tailbone when he bounced in the saddle. Someday soon, he might never have to ride a horse again. It was something to hope for.

He and Bat brought up the rear, keeping alert for Indians, while Billy, Frenchy, and Charley scanned the horizon ahead for buffalo. No one saw anything, so their brief pause for lunch included tomatoes and cold bacon but little conversation. There seemed to be nothing to say. With every mile, Billy's expression grew grimmer.

They made almost thirty miles that day, and made camp for the night in a gully near a water hole. They refilled their canteens, ate Frenchy's biscuits and more bacon, then curled up in their blankets by the campfire. Billy assigned Bat and Charley to night guard duty, Bat for the first four hours and then Charley until they broke camp at dawn.

"Co-manch love nothing more than absconding with horses from white camps," Billy said. "Be alert for any noise. But, Bat, that don't mean go blasting off ever' time you think you hear something."

"I'd rather shoot right away than delay to my eventual regret," Bat said. "I know how to stand watch, Billy."

Accustomed to bedding down on the trail, Charley and Frenchy fell asleep right away. McLendon sat up for a while with Billy, who sipped coffee from a tin cup and stared into the campfire.

"I've been wondering," McLendon said to him. "You don't know exactly where the big buffalo herd is, but you're pretty sure it's south and east of here?"

"That's correct."

"Well, why do we stick at the Adobe Walls camp, then? Why not just pack everything up and everybody keep moving in this direction, and we keep going until we find the buffalo? At some point we would, and then we can set up permanent camp and kill them to our hearts' content."

Billy swished coffee in his mouth. "It ain't that simple, C.M. You got to remember the distances involved. Now, tell me—if we keep on going in this direction, how far until we strike the nearest town with a railroad?"

"Let me think. Well, I'm not sure that there is one."

"And that's the problem. It's not enough to kill bunches of buffs and take their hides. From there, we got to get the hides to the railroad for shipment east. The companies there, the manufacturers who turn the hides into machine belts and the like, they need to get fresh hides in a timely manner. If they can't, they'll use other materials. Adobe Walls is absolutely the farthest we can hunt from Dodge, which is the nearest railroad hub, and still get the hides shipped back there in time to get them east and satisfy the manufacturers."

"And if we keep riding this way and never see any buffalo at all?"

"You already know. That's why we got to pray that very soon the buffs make their tardy way along the Canadian near our camp there, or else we'll all head home with empty pockets. Now, let's get some shut-eye. Long day tomorrow."

AS THEY RODE ALONG late the next morning, Frenchy let out a whoop. McLendon thought that maybe he'd spotted buffalo, but instead the crew cook pointed excitedly at what appeared to be clumps of wild grass.

Billy smiled for the first time that day and said, "I believe we'll have ourselves a scrumptious lunch."

"What?" McLendon asked. His ass ached and he was feeling cranky. For the last hour, he'd been imagining arriving in Mountain View only to find that Gabrielle had married Joe Saint the day before.

"Those plants are called lamb's-quarter, and they're tasty boiled up in water and served with a little salt, of which I happen to have a small amount in a pouch in my pocket."

Frenchy built a fire, filled a metal pot with water from his canteen, and boiled the greens. Everybody took forks from a pack on Frenchy's horse and ate the greens straight from the pot. Billy was right: they were delicious, and a welcome change from biscuits and bacon.

After everyone ate their fill, Billy stood and stretched. "All right, boys," he said. "I figure we ride the rest of today, maybe a few hours tomorrow. If we don't sight buffs by then, perhaps we never will. Might be they've gone in some unexpected direction, and we're just out of luck."

"That's not a message I'd care to deliver back at camp," Bat said. "We do, and most of the men will be on their way back to Dodge."

"Honesty compels," Billy said. "I'm just baffled. Even with the late spring, that herd should have come this way long since."

They mounted up, and shortly afterward Charley Armitage began to sing. He had a pleasant voice, and sailed through "Buffalo Gals" and "Jeanie with the Light Brown Hair." His performance soothed the troubled men who rode with him. Charley said, "Here's a new tune I learned just before we left Dodge. Its subject is appropriate, you'll agree." He sang,

"Oh, give me a home
Where the buffalo roam . . ."

"Hush, Charley," Billy commanded. "I think I hear something." He stood up in his stirrups and cupped a hand to his ear.

"What?" McLendon asked.

"Quiet," Billy said. "Listen. Yes—there it is!"

Moments later Frenchy said, "I hear it. Praise Jesus!" Charley and Bat said that they heard it too.

"Hear what?" McLendon demanded. "I don't hear anything."

"Listen a moment longer," Bat urged. "It's long and low, easy to miss at first."

Then McLendon heard it: a subdued sort of noise that rolled at them from just beyond a range of hills, punctuated by slight ground tremors that caused their horses to twitch nervously.

"What is it?" he asked. "It's almost like a train, but I know that it's not."

"Up the hill," Billy said. "We're about to see a most welcome sight." He urged his horse up the sloping grade, with Bat, Charley, and Frenchy hard on his heels. They reached the crest well ahead of McLendon, who had trouble getting his horse pointed in the proper direction. He saw the other four dismount, look ahead, and begin capering like school-boys. When McLendon finally reached them, he dismounted and looked off in the same direction. There, dark against the gold and green grass, was a vast brown cloud moving slowly but steadily west. It took a mo-ment for McLendon to see that the heaving mass was composed of indi-vidual animals, all packed tightly together. The rumbling sound was a cacophony of mingled bleats, grunts, and bellows. There was seemingly no end to it—the great moving wave extended as far back toward the east as McLendon could see, over a dozen hills or more and still pour-ing over the horizon. McLendon had come to Dodge near the end of the previous year's hunting season, and seen only stragglers. He'd as-sumed, when the hide men and their crews described unimaginably huge herds, that they were indulging in the frontier tradition of gross exaggeration. Now McLendon understood what Bat had been telling him—that even a terrible marksman could blast away and feel certain of hitting something with every shot.

"There's millions of them," he said. "I never thought there could ever be this many."

"And all moving west, right toward our camp," Billy said. "Jump back up in the saddles, boys. We got to ride hard and deliver the glad tidings. The buffalo have returned, and in greater numbers than ever we could have guessed. Five days from now, six at most, and the shooting can commence."

THEY RODE ALMOST straight through, stopping that night only for a few hours to rest the horses. The other four couldn't stop talking; even Billy babbled with joy. McLendon was quiet. He tried to convince himself that the herd arriving was a good thing. It would delay his reunion with Gabrielle for months, but at least he could come to her with full pockets as well as a full heart, and not have to depend on the charity of Major Mulkins. That meant that as soon as he won her from Joe Saint, there would be money for immediate departure to California, giving Gabrielle no time to change her mind.

As they paused for a while just after midnight, a comet burned in the night sky, a curious comet that took its time passing across the darkness above them.

"It's a sign that this will be the greatest summer hunt ever," Charley Armitage said. "There's celebration even in the heavens. All of our troubles are over, and there's nothing but fine times ahead. That flaming star guarantees it."

TWENTY-ONE

Quanah was worried that some of the Indians at the sun dance might attempt to thwart his plans, but he never expected interference from the sky.

Things began so well. On the night of their arrival, the visiting Cheyenne and Kiowa were treated to a lavish feast, with so much meat and so many other assorted treats (plum pudding, marrow bones) that everyone could and did cram their stomachs full to bursting. When the last bite was consumed and all were replete, White Wolf, Otter Belt, and some of the other most veteran Comanche warriors officially welcomed their guests to the sun dance. Quanah chose, at this point, to remain in the background, the better to convince remaining skeptics that the People were united in this celebration. Isatai wanted to offer the formal greeting, but at Quanah's insistence he stayed out of sight in a tipi during the opening moments of the ceremony.

"Our sun dance will go on for five nights," White Wolf explained. "Tonight we celebrate the arrival of our Kiowa and Cheyenne brothers. Tomorrow we demonstrate to Buffalo Hump and the other spirits that we have heard and understood the command to unite and drive the white men away forever. On the final three nights we will dance and ask the spirits to send us visions."

"And we watch while the Comanche dance?" Satanta asked. "As usual, you take the lead and we are to follow like stupid children?"

Quanah shot a sharp glance at Otter Belt, who he'd prepared to answer this predictable question.

"All who wish to may dance," Otter Belt said. To Quanah's great satisfaction, the old man sounded as though he'd thought of this response himself. "In fact, should our friends wish, they may even impale their own flesh and hang from hide lines as they do. While Comanche men will not, we respect your customs, too, and will gladly allow you to follow them."

"Such courtesy is appreciated," Gray Beard said. "Since we are your guests, we will honor the sun dance rules of the Comanche." He paused, then added pointedly, "At least the Cheyenne will. I cannot, of course, speak for the Kiowa."

Satanta and Lone Wolf bent their heads together and whispered. Finally Lone Wolf said, "We will dance like the Comanche too."

Quanah spoke for the first time. "Excellent! Now let us gather together. Isatai the Spirit Messenger is ready to speak."

The gathering took some time. Not all of the People had come to the sun dance, and it was the same with the Kiowa and Cheyenne. Among each of the tribes, there were skeptics about the spirit of Buffalo Hump or else those who doubted the wisdom of attempting a mass attack on the whites. But more than a thousand of the People were in this camp, and an equal number of Kiowa. There were even more Cheyenne, perhaps a thousand and a half again that many. Counted among the entire group were some eight hundred warriors able to fight if they chose— plenty, Quanah thought, to sweep the white people back to wherever they came from. They were well fed now to the point of being almost logy, and it was time for Isatai to seal the bargain.

"Come out, Spirit Messenger," Quanah called, and everyone gasped in surprise as Isatai emerged from the tipi. He wore a headdress of woven white scalps, mostly the long yellow hair of women, and the tresses streamed behind him as he walked to the campfire. The only clothing on Isatai was a beaded breechclout; his exposed flesh, all the mountains and jiggling rolls of it, was covered with splotches of yellow and blue paint, the favorite decorative colors of the Kiowa and Cheyenne. In his left hand, he carried a lance with a six-foot shaft, and he held his right palm flat in front of him in a gesture of blessing.

"I speak for the spirits," Isatai announced, and everyone fell silent, impressed by his commanding manner as well as his memorable appearance. "They have come to me and, through me, to you. And they welcome you to this celebration."

The fat man paused; everyone leaned in, eager to hear what he would say next. Quanah worried that Isatai would pause too long and lose his audience. But just as it seemed that the delay would become unbearable, Isatai spoke again.

"The spirits are pleased tonight. They summoned us and we came. Tonight and the next four nights they will be with us. If we honor them enough, they will speak some more, and if we listen, we will once again know victory. The People and the Kiowa and the Cheyenne once were happy in this land. When there were other tribes less worthy—the Apache and the Tonkawa—we drove them away. And then we lived here and there was plenty of game, and when we wanted to fight, we did. The Mexicans and the lesser tribes feared us, as they should. Then the white men came. They believed that any land they wanted was theirs, and they wanted what we had and told us we had to go. We fought, and fought very well, of course, but the whites were like the blades of grass and soon there were too many to count. They said that if we stopped fighting, there could be an honorable peace, and the People and the Kiowa and Cheyenne could stay on their old land and hunt as usual, unless we wanted to go to live under white rules, and if we did they would give us plenty of food and everything else we would need.

"And these words were lies. Those who went to live on what the whites call 'reservations' did not get the food that was promised. Instead they were given seeds and told to grow plants to eat. This was not and can never be our way. For the rest of us, we tried to stay on our land and hunt, but many white hunters came where they had promised not to and began killing all the game for themselves, the buffalo especially. Also, we were told not to fight the Mexicans anymore, though we had no peace agreement with them. White soldiers, especially the ones led by Bad Hand, make cruel attacks on us. We are never safe, we are often hungry, and though things are bad now they will only get worse so long as we try to live in the presence of the white men. They will never be satisfied until they have everything and we have nothing, they will not rest until they are everywhere and we are gone. You know this is true."

There were shouts of assent.

"In this bad time when we are desperate, the spirits have chosen to share their wisdom. For too long, the People and the Cheyenne and the Kiowa have fought the white men separately. Now, the spirits say, we must put aside any differences and fight together. The whites are many and strong, but we can also be many and even stronger. So tomorrow it begins. You saw when you came that we have built a thing that looks like a white man's fort. We will attack it, destroy it to show the spirits that, yes, we hear their words and will obey. Then for three more nights we will dance, and at the end of the last night the spirits will come to us and tell us where we should make our great fight, and when."

Isatai drew himself up and raised his arms to the sky.

"And now we thank the spirits, who—" And then it happened.

The night sky was dark and studded with bright stars. Isatai's gesture caused everyone to instinctively look up, and when they did, one of the stars suddenly burst into flames and began to move. It seemed to the Indians that it was about to fall directly on the camp. They had seen stars unexpectedly move and appear to fall before, but never one as bright, as frightening, as this one. Some of the women and children began to shriek, and the volume of the screaming increased as the burning star continued to cut through the blackness.

"The sky is falling because the spirit speaking through you is evil!" some warrior shouted, and Quanah's heart sank. He tried to yell something more encouraging, but there were too many other voices being raised in panic. What was this flaming star? Why had it appeared now?

"Be calm." Even though Isatai had not raised his voice, somehow it cut through the screaming and confusion. Everyone grew quiet, though they continued to stare at the star on fire above them.

"This star is not a bad thing. There are no evil spirits here, only good ones." Isatai's tone was soothing. "A burning star is a decoration of the spirits, the way our friends the Cheyenne and Kiowa decorate our tents with pictures to celebrate great victories. This star is a sign that the spirits are pleased with us. It will remain in the sky for a while, we will see it every night until our dance is completed, and then it will disappear. I know this. The spirits have told me. So don't be afraid. Sleep well." After making his blessing gesture again, Isatai walked to his tipi. Gradually, everyone else drifted off, some still looking fearfully up at the star, which trailed its flames above them. A few hundred people were so frightened that they left camp immediately, frantically riding through the dark toward their home villages. But most stayed.

Quanah hurried to Isatai's tipi. The fat man reclined on thick robes made from the finest pelts of winter buffalo. His eyes were closed and he was humming.

"That was very good," Quanah said. "You were clever."

Isatai paused in mid-hum and opened one eye. "I said what the spirits told me."

"About the star?"

"Especially about the star. Now let me rest. I have to be ready to hear the spirits again tomorrow."

ON THE SECOND DAY, all the men of fighting age made a mock attack on the model of the white men's fort. The women and children and old men watched and cried out their approval as the combined force of the People, Cheyenne, and Kiowa charged the wooden structure, loosing arrows from horseback—bullets were too valuable to waste outside of actual battle, even for such an important exercise—and dismounting to clamber over the walls and pretend to annihilate all the defenders. The warriors were gifted mimics. They grimaced and contorted their bodies as though they were in actual combat. In every instance they eventually raised their arms in triumph over dead enemies. Not one attacker fell to the invisible foe. It was late afternoon by the time all of the imagined corpses were mutilated and scalped. Then the warriors trooped back to the main camp, where they enjoyed a rapturous greeting from their families. There was another feast, and after dark the fort was set ablaze. The fire star seared the night sky again and it made almost everyone nervous. Isatai reminded them that it was a sign of favor from the spirits, one that would last through the entire sun dance. Then he retired to his tipi, saying he would speak to them again on the fifth and final night of the gathering.

On the third, fourth, and fifth day, the warriors danced. The interior of the lodge with the tall skull-topped pole in the center was swept clean, and then the old men from all three tribes entered, sat along the walls, and pounded drums in a simple, hypnotic rhythm. Women and children surrounded the structure, waiting outside while all the men of fighting age went in. None had eaten since the night before, and now all would continue to fast and dance until they collapsed. When they did, they hoped that the spirits would favor them with visions. Whatever they saw in these virtual trances would be indications of the future.

Almost seven hundred men danced, all of them naked except for breechclouts. The lodge was massive but they were still packed tight. They moved as best they could. The air was hot and soon thick with the smell of sweat. Even a well-fed man standing still would soon have felt faint. The old men with the drums took turns playing, going outside for fresh air and food whenever they felt the need. The dancers swayed and chanted, and by the end of the first afternoon the first ones began passing out. When they collapsed, some of the drummers put down their instruments and dragged the fallen dancers outside, where they were left to lie there and twitch. There was no honor in falling down so soon— everyone knew the best, truest visions were reserved by the spirits for the dancers who lasted longest. The families of these first collapsed men felt a degree of shame.

Inside the lodge, space was created each time someone fainted and was carried out, but still conditions worsened. The dancers weren't willing to stop for a few moments and go outside to relieve themselves, so they pissed where they were and the stench of urine mingled with the stink of sweat. A few of them shit, too, and that smell was added to the unsettling mix. By the end of the first day almost half of the original dancers were gone. Those who remained were determined to keep going on. Now they had more room to move, but they conserved their energy and didn't indulge in wild gyrations.

When morning came, light filtered in through wall cracks and it was possible to see one another in the remaining gloom. Quanah, willing himself to keep dancing, noticed Medicine Water swaying nearby. It was permissible for the dancers to talk quietly among themselves, so he inched over and said, "It's hard going."

Medicine Water muttered, "Of course. The spirits reward us for it."

"I thought your wife would dance too. Isn't she a full Cheyenne warrior?"

"You Comanche aren't letting your women dance. We're honoring your customs."

"So she won't fight in the great battle, either?"

"That's different. In battle, we will honor our own ways."

When the second day was over, only a few dozen men were still dancing. Quanah remained among them, but he was fading fast. Though his competitive instinct demanded that he be the last one standing, the combination of hunger and fatigue was too much. By mid-morning he was overcome by dizziness and dropped to his knees. Two of the old men grabbed his arms and dragged him outside. He sprawled on the ground and took deep, rasping breaths of fresh air. He wanted a vision, felt that he deserved a vision, but nothing came. He lay there awhile and then Wickeah dropped to her knees by his side and gave him water from a clay pot. Quanah gulped it and rested his head in her lap.

"You danced a long time," Wickeah said. "You were the last of the People in there. I'm proud of you."

"Just Kiowa and Cheyenne left?" Quanah moaned.

"We have more practice." Quanah looked up over Wickeah's shoulder and saw Mochi standing there. "You did very well, for a Comanche."

"You didn't dance," Quanah said.

"No, because Comanche don't respect their women enough to let them do such things. While we're here, we must follow your foolish rules. But if I had danced, I would have lasted longer than you. Meanwhile, my husband, Medicine Water, is still in there. I think he will be the final dancer."

Mochi turned and walked back toward the lodge. Wickeah glared at her back and hissed, *"Witch."*

Medicine Water was one of the final four dancers, but in the end Iseeo of the Kiowa danced alone. He kept on into late afternoon, lasting almost three full days before he finally toppled over. When he did, he was carried out more tenderly than any of the others, and lay twitching for some time while everyone else looked on. Finally Iseeo sat up and croaked a request for water. After he drank, he got to his feet with some difficulty.

"The spirits came to me," Iseeo said. "Because they want us to obey Isatai the Comanche Spirit Messenger, they granted me this vision. I was among so many warriors that I could not count them, and then there was a camp of white men with very long hair. We flowed over this camp like water over the banks of a stream, and after we passed, all the long-haired white men lay dead and not one of us attacking was even wounded. It was the finest of all victories."

The crowd murmured approval. Then Otter Belt and White Wolf said that everyone should go back to their tipis. All the dancers should rest. When it was full dark, there would be one more feast. Just before the five-day sun dance ceremonies concluded it would be time to talk about the great attack to come.

In their tipi, Wickeah fed Quanah strong broth and complained about the rude Cheyenne woman. "She should be beaten for her insulting words. If there had been a stick nearby, I would have done it myself."

"It was good that you didn't try. Among the Cheyenne she is considered a great warrior."

Wickeah sniffed. "Any woman of the People can beat two Cheyenne women at a time. She thinks she's a man, and in some ways she looks like one."

Quanah almost said that, no, Mochi didn't look anything like a man, but thought better of it. After he finished his broth he felt well enough to go see Isatai in his tipi. The fat man was preparing for his special moment and Quanah wanted to be certain that he was ready.

"Yes, I'm going to say the thing about the camp of the white hunters. We've talked about this many times."

"Remember not to say it until I speak about Bad Hand. That is your signal."

Isatai raised his eyebrows. "It is unless the spirits say otherwise."

"Just do as we discussed. Please. The others have to think that it is their idea, not mine."

"Why must it be the white hunters?"

"The spirits give us commands and we must decide the best way to obey," Quanah said. "The land rightfully ours is vast, but there is only one large settlement of whites in it, and that is where those hunters are camped. Bad Hand has most of his soldiers down near Mexico. It would mean nothing if we attacked a fort with very few white soldiers in it. If we kill all of the white hunters at their camp, maybe Bad Hand and the rest of his people will stay away from here. I don't care where else the whites want to be, as long as they leave us and our land alone."

Isatai yawned. "Maybe you think too much. Now, why don't you look outside for me? It's just getting dark. Is the fire star still up there?"

Quanah looked and came back into the tipi. "It's there. Everyone is getting used to it, I think."

"They'd better look now, because very soon it will be gone."

. . .

THE MEN OF ALL THREE TRIBES gathered back in the medicine lodge. After the defections of the first night, and with some too weakened by the sun dance experience to leave their blankets, about six hundred remained. Quanah noticed that now Mochi was among the Cheyenne warriors. The entrance had been left open so that the air inside would clear, but there were lingering smells. The chiefs and leaders sat close to the fire and smoked pipes while the other men gathered behind them. After a while Isatai came in, again painted yellow and blue and wearing his bonnet of scalps.

"The spirits have spoken and we've listened," he said. "We've had the sun dance and even a star on fire."

"Which is still there," Lone Wolf said pointedly.

"Only for a short while longer. Right now we must prove to the spirits that we're going to act. All three of our tribes will unite and make a great attack that drives away the white men. The People are ready for this. Are the Cheyenne and Kiowa agreed?"

Gray Beard, Stone Calf, Whirlwind, and Medicine Water all nodded.

"We are with you," Medicine Water said.

"And the Kiowa?" Isatai asked.

"This was a good sun dance," Lone Wolf said. "But we still aren't sure. The fire star concerns us. There has never been one like it in memory. We think we'll go back to our main camp, where our medicine man Mamanti chose to stay instead of coming here. We want to ask Mamanti what he thinks about the fire star."

Quanah suppressed a groan. He knew Mamanti, who hated Isatai, would insist that the star was a sign for the Kiowa not to join the alliance. "That will take too long, and also insult the spirits," he said.

Lone Wolf waved his hand dismissingly in Quanah's direction. "You're a warrior, not a Spirit Messenger, or medicine man."

"So only the fire star prevents your agreement?" Isatai asked. When the Kiowa chief nodded, Isatai stood up and said, "Then let's go outside." He led the way, and when they were all standing among the women and children, Isatai pointed up.

"There is the fire star," he declared. "Look—do you see it?"

"Of course we do," Lone Wolf snapped. "This is five nights that it's burned."

"And what did I say of the fifth night?" Isatai asked.

"That it would be gone, but there it still is."

"Yes. There it is." Isatai threw back his head, spread out his arms, and began to hum. He hummed louder and louder and then his body began to shake and everyone stared at him in wonder, even Quanah. Every eye was on the fat man. Then, suddenly, Isatai raised his right arm, pointed dramatically toward the sky, and shouted, "Look!"

They did, and as they watched, the fire star vanished.

"As the spirits promised," Isatai said solemnly. "Now, all warriors come back inside."

Everyone was staggered, especially Quanah. He told himself that it was just incredible luck, that there were no such things as genuine signs from the spirits. But the disappearance of the fire star was such a perfectly timed coincidence that he couldn't help wondering. He'd heard about the white man's Christian religion. Its single god mostly told them what they were not allowed to do. Indian faith was better because it offered so many possibilities instead.

When the tribal leaders were around the fire again, their followers grouped behind them, Isatai asked Lone Wolf and Satanta with great courtesy, "Are you with us?"

"Yes," Satanta said, and Lone Wolf added, "The spirits are indeed with you, with us."

"They are," Isatai agreed. "Now we must ask the spirits for more guidance. We will make a great attack. But where?"

That was Quanah's cue. "It must be a place all the whites know about. Not a little camp. I think maybe we should go see where Bad Hand is, which white man's fort he and his soldiers live in right now, and attack him there. A big victory over Bad Hand with many dead soldiers—that would scare away the whites. Let's surprise Bad Hand."

For a moment everyone talked at once. There was significant support for choosing Bad Hand. All the warriors respected him—many feared him, though they would never say so—and it was true that if he and his soldiers were wiped out, the other whites would be very afraid.

Then Isatai spoke again. "The spirits are telling me that they don't agree with you, Quanah. Bad Hand may have his soldiers divided so that they are in several places, all of them far away. The spirits want something different. Think: Where, closer to our land, is there a large group of white men all together?"

"There is one not far from the place of the strange walls," Otter Belt said.

"I saw them as they came," Iseeo said. He was not a Kiowa chief, so he had to push his way into the circle by the fire. "There were a hundred of them, maybe more, the white hunters with the long hair. I think that's what my vision means. I saw us killing white men with long hair. We should attack their camp."

"Wait," Quanah said. "Lone Wolf, Bad Hand's soldiers killed your son. If we lead this war party down to where they are near Mexico, we can have revenge."

The Kiowa chief thought for a moment. "I would like to see Bad

Hand dead and my son avenged, but I think he would have all his soldiers spread out in many places and it would be hard to catch them all together."

"Yes, that would be hard, and the white camp is also much closer," Quanah agreed. "Still, are these long-haired white hunters the right ones to attack? I'm not sure."

"The spirits are sure, Quanah," Iseeo insisted. "Think about it, these hunters coming here to kill all the remaining buffalo, which is an insult to us all, and now I've also had my vision."

"Well," Quanah said doubtfully, "I thought you said these hunters had many guns."

Isatai said, "The spirits say not to worry about that, Quanah. They are giving me magic. Here are the things I will do. First, I will make it so that when we attack, all of the white hunters will be asleep and we'll take them by surprise. The spirits don't care about how many guns they have. If any are awake and shoot at us, I will bless all of your bodies with magic so their bullets cannot harm you. Finally, if we need to shoot a lot, I will belch up ammunition. Kiowa and Cheyenne friends, ask among the Quahadis here. They have seen me do this."

Quanah thought, *They saw what they wanted to see.* All his skepticism about spirits and signs came flooding back. Still, he spoke in support of Isatai's contrived miracle. "It's true, Isatai vomited forth bullets." He paused, then said, trying to sound grudging, "All right. I suppose I must submit to the wisdom of the spirits and to the judgment of everyone else here. We will kill all of the hunters and that will chase away the rest of the white men."

Everyone was excited, and there were shouts of "When? When do we fight?"

"I'll ask the spirits," Isatai said. He closed his eyes and hummed while everyone else waited. After a moment he smiled broadly and said, "The last full moon is just past. We must prepare, and we will make this fight with the hunters on the next one."

"Agreed, then," said Gray Beard of the Cheyenne, and all of the men in the lodge cheered.

TWENTY-TWO

When Billy and his scouting party announced the good news, the mood of the Adobe Walls camp instantly transformed from torpor to frenzy. The hide men summoned their crews, telling them to hurry and grab their gear so that they could stake out the best possible shooting sites along the line that the great herd was expected to follow as it made its slow, majestic way through the area. It seemed to McLendon that any sense of camaraderie had vanished, replaced by an atmosphere of cutthroat competition. Just as in Dodge, the philosophy of the buffalo hunters was every man for himself. Brick Bond even announced that he and his men were leaving camp for good—they'd ride a day or two east and commence shooting that much sooner. When they had a few wagonloads of hides, they'd freight those back to Adobe Walls and sell them to Myers and Leonard. The Bond teamsters would use some of that money to buy supplies and ammunition.

"I'm personally shut of this boring place," Bond declared. "I'll send my crew in here to sell our hides, but when next you see me, Billy Dixon, it'll be back in a Dodge City saloon this winter with a plump whore on each side and a third on my lap."

"Don't do that," Billy pleaded. "You know our plan for the camp.

Everybody goes out to shoot during the day and comes back here at
night. That provides security against Indian attack."

"To hell with the Indians. There ain't been any savages seen of late,
and if some do intrude on my hunt, I'll blow them away like buffalo.
Now, stand aside."

Bond wasn't the only separatist. Dutch Henry Borne took his crew
east, too, as did Sam Smith and Jim McKinley. When they did, members
of Billy's own crew began to fret.

"As we sit here twiddling thumbs and waiting on the appearance of
the herd, them others is out shooting and skinning already," Mike Mc-
Cabe said. "Billy, we got to get out there too. We lose money every hour
that we delay."

Billy gave in. He told McCabe, Frenchy, Charley Armitage, Bat, and
McLendon to pack their gear. After promising Jim Hanrahan and Fred
Leonard that they'd return in a few days, he led his crew east for about
ten miles, following the twists and turns of the Canadian. Billy, Charley,
and Masterson were on horseback. McLendon and Frenchy took an
empty wagon. When they found a promising spot, Billy said to set up
camp. That took several hours. It was easy to pitch tents about a mile from
the sloping hill that Billy intended to use as a shooting perch, but there
was also a latrine to dig and space to be cleared for pegging and drying
hides. Frenchy wanted a fire pit so he could slow-cook meat, and McLendon had to help dig that. By the time they were done, it was almost dark.

"Reckon the buffs will reach here tomorrow, Billy?" Bat asked as the
six men reclined around the campfire drinking coffee.

"I expect so, probably before noon," Billy said. "I think I heard some
reports not that far east of here—probably Brick Bond or one of the others taking their first turns."

"If they shoot the leaders of the herd, won't the rest of the buffalo
turn in some other direction?" McLendon asked. After the others had a

good laugh, Billy explained that the momentum of the huge herd was such that, no matter what, they'd keep on going in the same general direction.

"That's the odd nature of buffs," he said. "You can shoot them by the dozens, and all that may happen with the others right around them is that they run a little in the same way that they've been going. They never scatter, never turn abruptly unless you make them as the Indians sometimes do. The Co-manch, for instance, get on their horses and try to run buffs over cliffs. They have their women waiting underneath to do the skinning. We could do that, too, but such falls often tear the hides too much. There's greater profit in shooting them one by one and preserving almost all of the skins for sale."

AS BILLY HAD PREDICTED, the first surge of buffalo reached his shooting site by mid-morning. Billy and Charley were ready, their Sharps Big Fifties in hand and small mounds of cartridges heaped at their feet. They fired methodically, pausing between shots. McLendon, stationed at the bottom of the hill with Bat and Mike McCabe, watched as buffalo almost a hundred yards away fell to the ground. The other buffalo simply moved around them. There was no real sense of panic or stampede. Sometimes the fallen buffalo writhed in agony. Then there would be the sound of a second shot and the beast jerked, then lay still.

After perhaps an hour, the herd's path swung slightly north and Billy and Charley moved to another hill. As soon as they did, McCabe, Bat, and McLendon rushed in to skin the two dozen or so dead buffalo. It was a tedious task. Each man took an individual buffalo. First, a razor-sharp skinning knife was used to make long cuts along the belly and up the inside of each leg. Then, after another cut across the neck, fingers were inserted along the cuts and, with a hard yank, the hide was loosened. A cut was made near the top of the hide and rope pushed through. The rope was pulled hard until the skin tore loose. By this point, the skinner's hands would already be covered with gore, but there was more messy work to do. The hide had to be scraped and set aside while the rest of the buffalo were skinned. After that, the hides were loaded in the wagon, brought back to camp, and pegged out to dry. As soon as that was done, it was time to go back out to skin the next batch of buffs shot by Billy and Charley.

There was no break for rest or lunch: each buffalo shot and skinned meant more money in everyone's pockets. By late afternoon, McLendon was filthy and exhausted. At twenty-five cents per skin, he calculated that he'd made about six dollars; Billy and Charley had probably shot a hundred buffs between them, and both McCabe and Masterson were much faster skinners than he was. The money had been hard-won, but at least for the first time since leaving Dodge he'd earned a few dollars. To his vast relief, Billy and Charley were packing away their rifles. That was when Masterson said, "Move smartly, C.M. Billy's done, and that means it's our turn to do some shooting."

McLendon had forgotten Billy's promise that, at the end of each day's hunting, he and Bat had the right to each shoot five buffalo too. "I don't know, Bat. I'm pretty weary."

"As you shoot your buffs, you'll perk right up. See, I put two Sharps forty-fives in the wagon bed, along with cartridges. Haul ass, we've got our own set of hides to procure."

The shooting part was easy. Masterson and McLendon guided the wagon to a spot two or three hundred yards from where Billy and Charley had stopped shooting. They climbed out, got the rifles, aimed, and fired. A few minutes later, nine buffalo were either dead or kicking on the ground, and Bat snapped off a final shot and felled a tenth.

"*Yee*-hah!" Bat crowed. "We are looking at a fistful of dollars, C.M. Come on, let's peel those hides."

When they did, McLendon saw that two of his five hides were likely unsellable. One buffalo he'd felled had some sort of disease that left thick scabs all along its hide. Another had long scars creasing its skin from previous wounds, and when McLendon attempted to yank the hide loose, it tore in too many places. But three hides, he knew, would fetch three dollars each from Myers and Leonard back at Adobe Walls. Added to the six dollars or so earned from skinning Billy's buffs meant that he was fifteen dollars closer to Gabrielle. Two or three more months with similar earnings would provide all the money he needed.

BILLY AND HIS CREW hunted from the same camp for three more days. The herd kept drifting by and they kept shooting. There was no particular challenge to it. By the end of the last day, they broke camp not because of a lack of targets but because the wagon bed was overflowing with hides.

"We'll take these back to sell at Adobe Walls, re-kit ourselves, perhaps stay overnight, and then return promptly to the hunt," Billy said. "I believe we'll set up next a bit farther west, just for variety's sake."

It was a merry ride into camp. Charley Armitage sang some more songs, and normally grouchy Mike McCabe regaled the others with stories of whores in far-flung frontier towns. Along the way they met Sam Smith and his crew, who'd enjoyed similarly good hunting.

"I believe the size of this herd exceeds any that we set eyes on around Dodge," Smith said. "We may run out of bullets before we even begin to thin this excess of buffs."

"Probably not, but if our luck holds, this migrating herd may satisfy our needs for several more seasons," Billy said. "Perhaps the hide business has some future after all."

The good moods lasted right up to the moment when they presented their hides to Fred Leonard for purchase and learned he'd pay two dollars apiece.

"Goddamn it to hell, Fred, in Dodge we were getting three dollars and sometimes three twenty-five!" Bat bellowed. "How can you in good conscience offer us just two?"

"Calm down and think it through," Leonard said. "I got freight costs here that make my blood boil. The goddamn teamsters, once word spread about the arrival of the buffs, promptly upped their rates for hide transport back to Dodge. They know these hides are worthless unless they're brought up to the railroad in a timely fashion. They charge me more, I got to pay you less. Nothing personal, it's just business."

Bat blustered some more before Billy told him, "I hate what Fred's telling us, but I understand why. Stand down, Masterson. We'll just have to kill that many more buffs to make up the difference. You and C.M. can increase your end-of-day shoots from five buffalo to eight, all right?"

"I'm not entirely mollified," Bat said. "Perhaps my temper will cool further with the aid of some beer in Hanrahan's saloon. Are you buying?"

Billy sighed. "I expect that I am. But there seems to be a considerable bustle about the place, so you may have to wait in line a bit before wetting your whistle."

Almost all of the hunting crews out in the field had chosen the same afternoon to come in and sell their first loads of hides. As they drank beer and bitters and, in a few cases, Jim Beam bourbon, the men bitched about Fred Leonard's miserly purchase prices and enthused about the number of buffalo in the oncoming herd. McLendon was both pleased and worried by widespread speculation that the hunting season might extend into early fall, September or maybe even the first week of October. He'd figured on the season ending sometime in August. He didn't want to wait any longer to go to Gabrielle. Every day he delayed meant that much more opportunity for Joe Saint, his rival. He had, of course, promised Billy Dixon to stay for the entire season. He wondered how Billy might react to an early resignation. Well, time to think about that later.

Everyone was three or four drinks into it when J. W. Mooar came in. He ordered a round for the house, boasting that he'd just concluded the best five days of hunting in his entire career.

"I told Freddy Leonard that I'd have two twenty-five per hide or else his head would feel the force of my fist," Mooar said.

"And did you get the two twenty-five?" Jim McKinley wanted to know.

"Well, Freddy's head is intact and I'm standing drinks for this mob. What do you think? Of course, I got my two twenty-five."

"Shit," Bat said. "Fred told us that two was as high as he'd go."

"Well, next time act the man, Masterson," Mooar said. "Try using your backbone as much as your mouth for a change."

Later, McLendon passed Leonard on his way back from the outhouse. He asked, "Fred, why did you pay J. W. Mooar a higher rate than the rest of us?"

"What do you mean? He got two dollars a hide, just like you." By then Mooar and his crew had already ridden out of camp, and McLendon decided that telling Bat would just cause trouble. He kept the information to himself.

THE NEXT TIME that the Dixon bunch came in to sell hides around the end of the first week in June, they found Adobe Walls swarming with newly arrived crews. Word had reached Dodge about the monster herd to the south, and most of the hide men remaining in western Kansas left at once. McLendon knew some of the newcomers. Antelope Jack Jones, Anderson Moore, and Blue Billy Muhler were mainstays among the Dodge City hide men. They'd worked together for years and had no ambition beyond killing as many buffalo as possible.

"It's a man's trade, C.M.," Jones said. "These last months up in Dodge, waiting and praying for the buffalo to come, and then every day, nothing—why, you can't imagine it."

"Actually, I can," McLendon said. "We had the same experience here."

"Maybe for a while, but now you got a different result. I'm gonna kill me a hundred buffs a day, and shoot 'til the barrel of my rifle melts."

McLendon was astonished to see Mirkle Jones packing his wagon to join another hunting party. Hide men Joe Plummer, Dave Dudley, and Tommy Wallace had coaxed the portly Creole into joining their crew.

"You're a teamster, Mirkle, and you can make steadier money freight-ing hides back to Dodge than hauling them back here to Adobe Walls," McLendon said. "Have you really thought this through?"

"Ah bin gettin' tard a tha ushewl," Jones said. "Ah wahn me sum advenchoor." He brandished his fiddle. "Doan worry. Ah'll play fah ya plenny in da daze ahid."

IN ALMOST EVERY WAY, at Adobe Walls there was cause for optimism. Though the price of individual hides wasn't what had been expected, there were still so many to sell that profits were guaranteed for everyone involved. Tom O'Keefe couldn't keep up with blacksmith tasks—every crew had wagon wheels that needed refitting and horses that threw shoes. The merchants did a brisk daily business. Besides necessities—bacon, beans, coffee, and canned foods for the trail, lead and gunpowder for bullet making, shirts and denim jeans to replace torn clothing—the hide men and their crews had plenty of money for luxuries and the urge to spend it when they came into camp. Candy, brand-name liquor, and top-quality tobacco were in constant demand. Old Man Keeler at Myers and Leonard and Hannah Olds at Rath and Company couldn't cook enough meals to satisfy crews that arrived ravenous after days out on the hunt. There was some grumbling about a lack of whores. Bat Masterson and Shorty Scheidler were the most constant complainers. Andy Johnson, who ran the Rath store, told McLendon that he was thinking of adding a few whores' cribs behind his shop, then importing a half-dozen girls from Dodge.

"They could bring five dollars a turn, easy," Johnson said.

"Last night Bat told me that he's so desperate, he'd pay a hundred dollars for a woman," McLendon said.

"Well, then, maybe I'll charge six. The problem will be finding acceptable whores willing to rough it out here. The diseased ones would come readily, but I doubt the boys would thank me if their peckers fell off."

ON JUNE EIGHTH, Jim Hanrahan and some teamsters returned from a trip to Dodge with fresh supplies and news that was possible cause for concern.

"Maybe seventy-five miles out, a bunch of Indians came at us," Hanrahan said. "I guess there were a dozen. Looked like Kiowa. We had enough guns to drive them off. It seemed more like they were testing us rather than mounting a serious attack."

"It looked pretty damn serious to me," said Billy Tyler, one of the teamsters. "Any time an Indian looses an arrow or bullet in my direction, I feel properly threatened."

"If it's just an isolated incident, I don't think it's anything of real consequence," Hanrahan said. "We still haven't seen any Indians in this camp's vicinity."

Billy Dixon, standing next to McLendon, said that he'd pass the word about the attack to everyone in the area.

"We all need to be alert anyway," he said.

"Try not to raise unnecessary alarm, Billy," Hanrahan cautioned. "Some are too jumpy to begin with. You know how, with that comet, a few of the more superstitious boys thought it was a sign from God that we were in the wrong place and ought to leave pronto. I'm glad it burned out after a few nights. Hey, we're all doing well here. As for you and me, this partnership is particularly profitable. Don't be messing things up with too much Indian talk."

"No life is worth any amount of money, Jim."

"I know. I know."

BILLY'S CREW SPENT that night in Adobe Walls. McLendon stayed up late. He'd just figured out why screwdrivers were sold in tandem with the Colt Peacemakers. The six-gun's trigger guard was held in place by a series of small screws that gradually loosened. They periodically needed tightening, especially after long days in the saddle or other spells of physical activity. So McLendon wielded his screwdriver in a corner of Hanrahan's saloon, squinting in the light of a flickering candle. Hanrahan sat in the doorway smoking a cigar. Everyone else was outside, sleeping under wagons or in blankets spread out on the ground. In this warm weather, it was too stuffy in the buildings to sleep inside.

There was a quiet crunch of boots on pebbles. McLendon, bent over his gun, heard J. W. Mooar, who'd come into camp late that evening, speaking softly to Hanrahan.

"Indians, like you said. They didn't jump us, but they were watching."

"Kiowa? This is somewhat south for them."

"Shit, these were Comanche."

"Keep quiet about this. We can't have everybody running off."

"If I do, what's in it for me?"

"Two twenty-five a hide instead of two. I'll pay the extra two bits out of my own pocket."

"Four bits, not two."

"You're a bastard, Mooar."

Mooar chuckled. "Never said I wasn't. But I'll keep mum."

ON THE MORNING of June ninth, as the Dixon crew prepared to head out again, McLendon told Billy what he'd heard. Billy looked troubled and said, "All right. Let me take this into consideration. I know it sounded bad, but likely Jim Hanrahan's trying to look after everyone's best interests. Still, let me go have a quick word with him."

A few minutes later, Billy was back. "It's as I thought. Jim doesn't feel there's reason to get everybody bothered. We're all making good money, and if one Indian attack far from here and one glimpse somewhat closer is the extent of it, then we're not in any particular danger. Hell, we knew the Indians had to be around somewhere. Jim said he knows what J. W. Mooar is like: he'd exaggerate those Comanche he saw until we all thought there were a thousand red men about to descend upon us. So he's going to pay Mooar a few pennies extra for hides to keep his trap shut. He hates the additional expense, but in the end it's good business. Rest easy, C.M. If we're reasonably watchful, there's probably no cause for concern."

TWENTY-THREE

The tribal alliance was unwieldy from the start. The Kiowa and Cheyenne chiefs indicated to Quanah at the sun dance that if their tribes joined in the great attack, their warriors would first have to return to their home villages and prepare themselves for war. Arrows had to be fashioned, knives honed, war paint mixed, and all available ammunition collected. When properly equipped, the Kiowa and Cheyenne would come back south and meet Quanah and the fighting men of the People along the Canadian near the white hunters' camp. This was why, after Quanah suggested it was the wish of the spirits, Isatai delayed the assault on the white hunters' big camp until the next full moon.

But as soon as the allied tribes departed for home and the People returned to their various villages, Quanah realized that he had made a mistake. Almost immediately, most of the Nokoni men changed their mind about participating. One told Quanah, "Those other tribes aren't our equals. It was disgusting to hear you address them as brothers." Half of the Yamparika who promised to return never did. Nobody among that branch of the People ever had the stomach to fight well anyway, Quanah thought sourly. They were cowards. At least the Nokoni stayed away out of principle.

Word reached him from the north that many Kiowa were having second thoughts. Quanah immediately rode to see Lone Wolf and Satanta. The problem, they told him, was not that the Kiowa men didn't want to kill white men. They did, very much. In fact, the Comanche sun dance had so inflamed the fighting instincts of the Kiowa braves that they couldn't wait until the next full moon. Several war parties had already formed with the intent of finding and attacking any white wagon trains or smaller hunting camps that appeared vulnerable.

"You can't allow that," Quanah protested. "We want the hunters in the big white camp to think that they are in no danger from us. That way, when we make our attack, they'll be surprised."

"If our young men want to fight, they will, even if it isn't what you want them to do," Satanta said. "Talk to them if you want. I don't think you can change their minds."

Quanah tried. He called the Kiowa warriors together and explained why they should wait. Responding for their tribesmen, High Forehead and Buffalo with Holes in His Ears replied that they had agreed to join the People and the Cheyenne in one fight, but that didn't mean they were giving up their right to fight on their own as well.

"Your Spirit Messenger says he's been given magic so we can win the fight at the big camp easily," High Forehead said. "If the spirits already promise us victory there, what does it matter if we kill some more whites before that?"

This was a question that Quanah couldn't answer. He waited nervously with Lone Wolf and Satanta while a Kiowa war party of about a dozen warriors rode out. They'd heard that wagons loaded with supplies had left the white town above the main treaty river and were coming south, probably with supplies for the big white hunting camp. The Kiowa meant to intercept the wagons, kill all the white men, and take the supplies. They hoped their booty would include good guns and lots of ammunition. Most of the firearms carried by the Kiowa were essentially useless—ancient muzzle-loaders and antiquated pistols. None of the warriors had more than a few bullets.

But the raiders returned empty-handed. They'd ambushed the wagons as planned, but the white men all had the rifles that shot long and straight, so the Kiowa couldn't get close enough. In retrospect, they should have waited to attack at night, when most of the white men would have been asleep.

"That's our plan at the full moon when we fall on the big white hunting camp," Quanah said. "If you'll only be patient, after we kill everyone there, you can take their guns for yourselves."

"Yes, we'll take their guns, but until then I don't want to be patient," said Bear Mountain, a Kiowa who honored Satanta by blowing a bugle as he rode into battle. "Any white man I see, I'm going to kill."

Iseeo, who hadn't joined the raiders in the attack on the wagon train, supported Quanah. "At the Comanche's sun dance, we all heard the words of the Spirit Messenger. We should trust him and trust Quanah."

"Trust who you want," Bear Mountain said. "I promised I'd fight with them at the white hunting camp, and I will. But otherwise, they're not my leaders."

Lone Wolf and Satanta told Quanah that he should go. When the time for the attack on the white camp neared, they would bring the Kiowa warriors south. Until then, they'd do what they could to keep their young men under control.

NOW VERY WORRIED, Quanah went to the Cheyenne camp, where, to his relief, things seemed better. The chiefs assured him that Medicine Water and the dog soldiers were maintaining strict discipline.

"None of our warriors will fight too early," Gray Beard assured him. "If they try to, they will have to fight the dog soldiers instead, and none of them want to do that."

"The Cheyenne have wisdom," Quanah said, feeling and sounding grateful. "If we win the fight with the white hunters, most of the glory will be yours."

"Others can have the glory. What we want afterward are the white hunters' guns, because they are so much better than the ones we have."

"You'll have them all," Quanah promised. "No one among the People or the Kiowa will get any. Every one of the white guns will belong to the Cheyenne."

THOUGH HE'D HAD DOUBTS regarding the Cheyenne, the Kiowa, and even some of the bands of the People, Quanah was certain he could count on his own Quahadi to show sense and leave the whites alone until the great attack. But when he returned to his village, he was disgusted to learn that some Quahadi braves had also gone out on a raid. Fortunately, they scouted the white hunting party they encountered instead of attacking on the spot. They decided that there were too many guns among the hunters and rode away.

"Did they see you?" Quanah demanded as he angrily confronted Wild Horse, the warrior who'd led the would-be raiders.

"I suppose so," Wild Horse said. "We were on a hill about five or six bowshots away."

"You met them too close to the big white camp. They probably rode back there and warned them."

"So what? Isatai's spirit magic is going to let us kill everyone there anyway."

.   .   .

QUANAH'S INFLUENCE was now such among the Quahadi that there were no other raids while they waited for the full moon. The days dragged, and then Iseeo rode in to announce that the Kiowa were on their way.

"We didn't think you would be back this early," Quanah said. "There is still some time before the full moon."

"Too many of our warriors are impatient," Iseeo said. "They didn't want to wait and started talking about attacking the big village whites call Dodge instead of waiting to fight with you at the hunters' camp. So Lone Wolf and Satanta decided to bring them down here now."

"How many warriors are coming?"

Iseeo flexed all of his fingers a dozen times. "That many, perhaps a few more."

"What happened to the rest? We need every man."

"They decided that they liked making little fights, not one big one. Lone Wolf argued with them."

"What about Satanta? Did he try to persuade them?"

"He said that each warrior had to do what he thought best. If they didn't want to come fight beside the Comanche, they shouldn't. But when Bear Mountain asked Satanta if he was going, Satanta said that he was, and then Bear Mountain said all right, he would come too. So Satanta helped you."

THE KIOWA CAMPED near the Quahadi village. At night they sat around their campfires and drank whiskey. Quanah thought that they drank too much. He spoke to Lone Wolf and Satanta about it. They told him that he should be happy their warriors were getting drunk. When they woke up in the mornings feeling soreheaded and queasy, it kept them from riding out, looking for trouble. Since the buffalo had arrived in the area, lots of small hunting parties left the white camp for days at a time, and these parties were the traditional targets of Kiowa raids.

"Many of our men don't want to wait for the big fight," Lone Wolf said. "You saw that for yourself when you came to our village. Now every day they're close to the small groups of white hunters who think only of killing buffalo, not of keeping watch for us. Of course, they are tempted. Aren't you?"

"I control myself," Quanah said. "Why can't the Kiowa do the same?"

Lone Wolf's eyebrows arched. "Are you saying that Comanche are better?"

"No, I just don't want our plan to be spoiled."

"Be sure to remember that it is *our* plan, that it belongs to all of us. But the white hunters' guns will belong to the Kiowa."

A FEW DAYS LATER, Lone Wolf and Satanta told Quanah that they needed to talk. Some of their young braves insisted on forming a war party to attack one of the small bands of white hunters who slept at night away from the main camp.

"There will only be four or five white men, probably, easy to kill," Lone Wolf said. "That will let the most eager young men get some scalps. I think it will keep them happy until it's time for the big attack."

"It's a mistake," Quanah said. "The other white hunters will see what happened and prepare to fight. We need them to think only of the buffalo. Tell your young men not to do this, Lone Wolf."

"If I tell them that, they will ride back north. You won't have any

Kiowa left, except maybe Iseeo, because he loves your Spirit Messenger so much. We must let them do this small thing, Quanah, if you want their help with the big thing."

"I'll have Isatai speak to them. Perhaps they'll listen to him."

The young Kiowa listened politely to Isatai when he told them that the spirits didn't want any premature attacks. Quanah thought that the fat man might have persuaded them, but then he began ranting that besides waiting to kill white hunters, the spirits also commanded that skunks must not be shot. The Kiowa thought that was foolish, and a few of them said so. Isatai was offended and stalked off. After he did, some of the Kiowa daubed on war paint and prepared to leave.

"Will you stop them?" Quanah pleaded to Lone Wolf and Satanta. They shook their heads.

"It would be wise for you to ride along with them, Quanah," Satanta said. "Lone Wolf is. The young men are going to do this anyway. They'll be pleased to have you and Lone Wolf along. That will make them feel better about following you in the great fight that's coming."

Quanah saw the sense in that. He put on his own war paint, the black style traditional to the People, and got his Henry rifle. Mounting one of his best horses, he joined the Kiowa as they rode southeast.

THE SUN WAS SETTING when the war party approached the buffalo herd. There were scattered *crack*s in the distance—some of the white hunters were getting in last shots.

Bear Mountain had assumed informal command. Now he impressed Quanah by saying, "We need to be careful. I think that there will be several small parties of white hunters all along the river here." Bear Mountain told everyone else to graze and water their ponies while he and High Forehead went ahead to scout. It was completely dark when they returned to report that there were four separate groups in small camps within easy riding distance.

"There are plenty of hills between them and the main white camp," Bear Mountain said. "I don't think the sounds of fighting will be heard all the way there. But when we attack, we don't want the noise to alert the other small camps nearby. So we'll have to kill quietly."

"But we want to play with them before they die," complained a Kiowa named Good Talk.

"I know," Bear Mountain said. "I think maybe we will kill the whites in one of these groups tonight, and then tomorrow, when the buffalo are back on the move and making noise, we'll kill some more and then it won't matter if they scream."

Quanah wanted to say that killing one of the groups was plenty, but as he took a breath to speak he saw Lone Wolf staring at him. The Kiowa chief shook his head, and Quanah kept silent.

High Forehead and Bear Mountain thought the most likely victims for the night attack were camped farthest below the river. "There were just three of them. But they each had good guns and long hair." White Goose, the youngest in the war party, stayed behind with the horses while the rest went ahead on foot. It took a while because they had to circle well beyond the other three camps. Finally they saw flickerings of yellow and orange in the distance—campfire flames. The raiders approached with caution, crawling on their bellies over the last yards.

"I only see two," Quanah hissed to Bear Mountain. "Is the third out standing guard?" Bear Mountain motioned for High Forehead to creep around the entire periphery of the camp. When he came back, he said there was no sign of the third white man.

"I looked in the bushes to see if he'd gone there to shit," High Forehead whispered. "But he wasn't anywhere. I think that he must have gone back to their big camp."

"Then let's kill these two," Bear Mountain said. At his signal, the raiders rose, rushed the camp, and fell on the white hunters sprawled in their blankets by the fire. Quanah and Lone Wolf lagged behind. In the few extra moments it took them to come up, one of the white men's throats was slit and his heels kicked against the ground in death throes. The other woke up and tried to run. High Forehead caught him and dragged him back to the fire. The white man was too frightened to scream. The only noise was his bootheels dragging in the dirt. High Forehead strangled him. His victim's eyes bulged and he shit himself just before he died. The Indians ripped off the two scalps. Bear Mountain claimed one of the big rifles for himself and handed the other to Quanah.

"You didn't want us to do this, but you came along like a good friend anyway," he said.

Despite his misgivings about the attack, Quanah was pleased. "Thank you, but I have a good gun," he said, patting the stock of his Henry repeater. "Give that one to whoever needs it most." High Forehead got the second rifle and nodded his thanks to Quanah.

They wrapped the dead men in their blankets, then hid themselves in the shadows for a while, waiting in case the third white hunter came back. When he didn't, some of the Kiowa dragged the bodies back into the open and systematically dismembered them. They laughed among themselves as they severed finger joints and genitals. After they finished, everyone enjoyed some dried fruit and bread that they found in the dead men's packs. By then it was almost dawn, and Bear Mountain reminded the others that they wanted to attack another small camp.

"Soon the buffalo will start moving, and then we won't have to worry about noise," he said.

. . .

THERE WERE FOUR MEN in the second group of victims. The raiders crept up on them quietly, but they could have been noisy and the whites still would never have noticed, so obsessed were they in killing and skinning buffalo. Two of them fired rifles, one ran to where the buffalo fell and skinned them, and the fourth, a very heavy man, carried the skins to a wagon. Quanah had never actually seen the white hide men at work and he found it interesting. There was no wasted time or motion—they were just as efficient as Indian women. The hides were removed with a minimum of fuss. He could have watched for a long time, but the Kiowa were impatient to kill again. Bear Mountain was just about to give the signal to attack when the wagon bed became full of hides and two of the white men, the heavy man and a skinner, began talking loudly, though not quite arguing, beside it. After a few moments the heavy man laughed and the skinner got up on the wagon, shook the reins, and urged the two-mule team forward. Some of the Kiowa twitched, but Bear Mountain held up a cautioning hand: *Let that one go.* The heavy man was picking at something on the bottom of his boot, but the other two remaining white men still had their rifles in hand and were looking back at the wagon as it rattled away. If the raiders charged at that moment, they would overwhelm the whites, but probably not before the riflemen got off shots. It was better to let the white man on the wagon get away than to have any warriors severely wounded or killed. There were always more white men to replace any that fell in battle. The Indians did not share that luxury.

When the wagon was out of sight, the white shooters laid their guns aside. As soon as they did, the raiders burst from cover, shrieking and brandishing lances, knives, and war clubs. Quanah and Lone Wolf again stayed back. The white shooters went down fast, gore gushing from dozens of wounds. The heavy man took longer because the Kiowa played with him, leaning in to prick his body with knife- and spearpoints. Mostly he screamed, but sometimes he yelled a strange-sounding word, "Bruddas," over and over. Finally Man Who Walks Above the Ground tired of the sport and rammed his lance through the heavy man's heart, having to push hard because the chest wall was so thick. Then all three dead men were scalped and mutilated. High Forehead, yelping with glee, tore a branch from a tree, sharpened one end to a point, and pushed the branch up the anus of one of the shooters. The point eventually emerged from his belly. They took the guns—two very good rifles, one older one, and four pistols—as well as some canned goods and blankets. The canned goods were special prizes. Back in the Quahadi village, they would be opened and whatever juice was inside would be shared around. Then the cans themselves would be cut up and the sharp metal pieces used for arrow points. Lone Wolf found a wooden device with four taut strings along one side and up the handle, and also a long, thin thing that looked like a bow, but one too fragile to shoot an arrow. The four strings on the wood thing made pretty sounds when they pulled at them. Everyone wanted the wood thing. Lone Wolf kept it for himself.

"Was that enough?" Quanah asked Bear Mountain as they rode back west.

The Kiowa smiled. "Enough for now," he said.

TWENTY-FOUR

The Billy Dixon crew moved its camp north of the Canadian. For several days they enjoyed the finest shooting yet. The buffalo herd was expansive, more than a dozen miles in length. The hides they took were thick and relatively unscarred. At night the sky was clear, and they drank coffee and gorged themselves on Frenchy's fine cooking. One night Charley Armitage walked out to take a shit and came back with several plump quail. He said they came up near where he was squatting and practically begged to be shot. Frenchy served them with boiled greens, and there were canned peaches for dessert.

As much as Cash McLendon wanted to be on his way to Arizona Territory and Gabrielle, he still found himself enjoying the hunt, mostly because he was making fine money. With Billy and Charley knocking down a buff with every shot, and with Bat and himself killing seven or eight each day, McLendon averaged twenty dollars a day. He calculated that by mid-July he would have enough to quit, hitch a ride back to Dodge on one of the freight wagons, then travel by train and stage to Mountain View. Billy would understand, he felt certain.

On June eleventh they had enough hides to overflow the wagon bed. Billy said that he'd run them back to Adobe Walls. "You come with me,

C.M.," he said. "Two of us can get the wagon unloaded quicker. We'll take a nice meal from Old Man Keeler or Mrs. Olds, enjoy some fellowship in Hanrahan's saloon, then set out on the return trip at daylight. We'll be back here in camp by mid-afternoon."

"You ought to take me instead, Billy," Bat argued. "I'm far more sociable than McLendon, and I'm eager for a drink besides."

"No, you'd end up talking so much that I'd waste additional hours tearing you away from conversations. I mean this to be a reasonably prompt trip there and back."

Billy and McLendon set out, with Fannie the red setter trotting alongside. Billy put his Sharps Big Fifty in the wagon bed, and McLendon did the same with the older rifle that Billy had lent him. McLendon had his Colt in a holster on his belt, and had his razor-sharp skinning knife too. Billy took up the reins of the two-mule team. It was a hot day, and McLendon felt sweat trickling down his chest and sides underneath his shirt. Billy didn't seem especially talkative, and McLendon didn't mind. He'd decided to send another letter to Gabrielle, this one promising to be in Mountain View by the end of July, or early August at the latest. McLendon was mentally composing just the right romantic message when Billy said, "Lord, look at the water rush in the Canadian."

When they'd moved the camp north of the river, they found a relatively shallow spot to cross. But now the water was deeper, and there was rippling evidence of a fast current.

"We try to ford it here, this wagon's liable to tip over," Billy said. "We best go along a bit farther, see if there isn't a better place."

They picked their way along the river for another mile or so, but didn't find a place that looked more promising.

"Well, damn," Billy said. "What do you think, C.M.? Shall we attempt it?"

McLendon didn't think so. He remembered the cow that had been

caught in quicksand on the trip down from Dodge City, and it seemed
to him that the swirling current was suspiciously flecked with dirt. But
before he could reply, there was the sound of hoofbeats, and two riders
raced into sight.

"It's Jim McKinley and Dutch Henry," Billy said. "Those two hate
each other. If they're riding together, something's happened."

It had. McKinley and Henry said word had reached Adobe Walls
that one of the scattered white hunting parties had been slaughtered by
Indians.

"Joe Plummer left their camp to bring a load of hides in to sell,"
McKinley said. "Joe goes back and finds the other three in the crew all
cut up to hell."

"Left in pieces is what they were," Dutch Henry added. "Joe says it
was so cruel that he was too repulsed to vomit."

"Wait a minute," McLendon said. "Joe Plummer—was he with Tommy
Wallace and Dave Dudley? Does that mean that Mirkle Jones—"

"Yep," McKinley said sorrowfully. "That fat Creole was just the finest fiddler. But they carved him up, too, Joe reports. A few of the boys
have gone out with Joe to collect what remains that they can, so we can
give them a decent burial. Dutch Henry and me are trying to find all the
outlying camps to spread the warning."

"Everybody needs to come in," Billy said. "If the Indians are on the
attack, we're better off sticking together."

"Jim Hanrahan says perhaps not," Dutch Henry said. "Jim's thinking is, if everybody's warned and alert, then maybe there's no need to
break off the hunting, what with it being at its peak just now. Plenty of
time to come in later if it appears there are Indians in any significant
number."

"That's still to be determined," Billy said. "C.M. and I need to head
on in and dispose of these hides. We don't want to get caught out in

between if any raiding parties are still about. Jim, you and Dutch go on
and get the word spread."

McKinley and Henry galloped off. Billy said to McLendon, "There's
no time now for further exploration. We'll cross the river right here. Pull
Fannie up into the wagon and then hold on tight."

"Whatever you say." McLendon was grief-stricken by the news of
Mirkle Jones's death, and petrified that some lurking Indian band might
be creeping up on them in the brush along the bank.

Billy clucked at the mules and yanked the reins. The braying team
balked at the river's edge. McLendon had always found Billy Dixon to
be the calmest of men, but now he swore and slapped the reins sharply
on the mules' backs. The animals reluctantly plunged into the water, and
the wagon dropped in behind them. As soon as it did, McClendon felt
the conveyance tugged hard by the current. "Keep *going!*" Billy shouted
at the mules, and Fannie added a series of panicked yelps from the
wagon bed. The river was about twenty yards wide, and they were almost halfway, when one of the mules lost its footing and collapsed with
a splash. The other mule lost momentum and stumbled, briefly disappearing under the water. As both mules struggled desperately to get
back up, the wagon tipped precipitously. Billy and McLendon tried to
keep their balance, but couldn't.

"It's going over—jump!" Billy yelled, and they did. McLendon was
surprised that the river was so cold on such a hot day. His boots hit the
sandy bottom and he pulled them up quickly, fearing quicksand more
than drowning. He found solid footing and stood up. "Use your knife to
cut the mules free," Billy called, and McLendon tried. He got one cut
loose and it worked its way to the south bank. The second mule's eyes
were wide with hysteria, and it jerked its head from side to side. The
water was up to McLendon's chest as he waded to the stricken animal,
grabbing at its harness. His left foot hit soft sand and he felt his boot

being sucked down. Involuntarily wailing in panic, he tried to extricate his boot but couldn't. Taking a breath, he plunged his face below the surface, reached down, and yanked his foot out of the boot. Then he cut the second mule loose and hung on to its bridle as the long-eared beast pulled them both to the south riverbank. Fannie met them there, barking loudly. Then the mule that had pulled McLendon clear heaved a great sigh and dropped dead.

McLendon lay on the bank, trying to catch his breath. After a moment he remembered Billy Dixon and looked for him. Billy was still in the river, frantically yanking at the part of the capsized wagon still above the surface.

"Help me, C.M. We got to get the rifles out of there if we can!" he yelled, and McLendon reluctantly went back into the water. But try as they might, they couldn't retrieve the weapons, which apparently had been swallowed up by the sand of the riverbed.

"We lost the hides, but that's a small thing," Billy said when they'd finally given up and climbed out onto the Canadian's south bank. "The guns are what matter if there's fighting ahead. After we clean and dry your Colt, I expect that it'll work again. We don't have time to do it now, and even if we did, all your ammunition is soaked and ruined. Should the Indians fall upon us now, we'd have to throw rocks. Come on, we'll ride double into Adobe Walls on our surviving mule." McLendon had trouble staying in the saddle of a well-trained horse. The six- or seven-mile ride to Adobe Walls seated behind Billy Dixon on the bony spine of a nervous, irascible mule was agonizing, but at least they didn't encounter any Indians.

ADOBE WALLS WAS in an uproar when they arrived. Dozens of men, all shouting and gesticulating, were gathered in front of the Myers and

Leonard store. Billy hopped down from the mule; McLendon, crotch and ass aching, gently eased himself to the ground. He limped behind Billy, who shouted to Brick Bond, "Is there fresh information on the killings?"

"Anderson Moore just rode in," Bond said. "He reports finding his partners butchered."

"Anderson Moore?" Billy asked. "I thought it was Joe Plummer who discovered them."

"That's yesterday's news," Bond said grimly. "Dave Dudley and Mirkle Jones and Tommy Wallace were the ones Plummer found. No, there's been a second attack. Moore rode off from his camp night before last, looking to fetch up with Sam Smith's crew and enjoy some card playing. Billy Muhler and Antelope Jack Jones, the two Moore was camped with, considered themselves too Christian to play a few hands of poker. So Moore rides back to their camp the next day and finds them just tore to pieces. Goddamn Indians actually poked a stick up Antelope Jack's ass 'til the pointy end come out his throat. Some of the boys is fixing to head back there, try to clean up what's left of the bodies, and get them properly in the ground."

"C.M. and me are going to get some guns and shells, then turn right around and go fetch the rest of our crew, if in fact they aren't already on their way back here," Billy said. "We passed Dutch Henry and Jim McKinley on the way in. They were bent on informing all the outlying camps."

Inside the store, Fred Leonard was busy selling guns and ammunition. Billy grabbed McLendon's arm and dragged him to the counter. He told Leonard that they each needed a Sharps Big Fifty and a box of shells. McLendon needed new boots.

"That would run you about eighty dollars each for the rifles, and another ten for the ammunition, Billy," Leonard said. "McLendon, the boots is seven dollars. You'll both understand that I require payment in cash."

"Fred, I've surely got several thousand dollars in credit with you," Billy said. "My crew's brought in three loads of fine hides, and you've purchased them and entered the transaction in your books."

Leonard shook his head. "In light of the current situation and also the present demand for weaponry, I'm not selling anything against accrued credit just now. Should the decision be made for all of us to flee, some of my ledgers might be lost and then there's no accounting for credit balances. Unless you've got actual money, Billy, please step aside. I've got cash customers standing behind you."

McLendon thought the veins in Billy's neck would burst. He roared, *"I got to go bring in my crew, and you deny me the means to protect myself and them, if necessary?"*

Leonard looked past him and said, "Next."

Billy was about to lunge, but McLendon stepped in front of him. "Billy, arguing will only waste time. We've got to get back to the others. Look, I've got cash money—not much, but some." He fished in his pocket and extracted some soggy bills: seventy-six dollars all told. He hated giving up even a penny, but he handed the bills to Billy. "See what Andy Johnson or Jim Langton over at the Rath store will give you for this."

Langton sold Billy a secondhand .44 caliber Sharps and twenty shells. McLendon got some serviceable footwear. After making the purchases, they briefly ducked back into Myers and Leonard's store. "One day soon, we'll discuss this, Fred," Billy said. "Meanwhile, be damned straight to hell." He and McLendon got some bread and bacon from Old Man Keeler, who didn't charge them a cent, then went to the stables and saddled two of the extra horses that Billy had stabled there. They were shocked to see Brick Bond saddling up too.

"You might need another gun," he said. "My crew is in here safe, so let's go collect yours."

"I thought he said he'd never come back to Adobe Walls again," McLendon whispered. "Guess the Indians changed his mind."

"Don't provoke him," Billy whispered back. He said loudly, "Thank you, Bond. This is a fine thing."

They raced back east along the Canadian, gnawing makeshift bacon sandwiches as they rode.

BAT MASTERSON, Frenchy, Mike McCabe, and Charley Armitage were surprised when Dixon, McLendon, and Bond came clattering into the camp. They said they'd been shooting and skinning buffalo. Nobody had come to warn them about Indian attacks.

"Maybe the Indians got Dutch Henry and Jim McKinley too," Frenchy said.

"More likely they just went around to the crews that they found and missed some," Billy said. "All right, our wagon was lost in the Canadian, so take what you can carry while mounted and let's be going."

"Christ Jesus, Billy, we got about a hundred fresh hides perfect for selling," McCabe said. "Let me stay with them. When you get back to Adobe Walls, send another wagon out this way."

"I know how you like to argue, Mike, but this is no time for it," Billy said. "Leave the hides stacked as they are. Maybe if this blows over, we can come back for them. Now let's ride."

THE NEXT NIGHT, some sixty hide men, crew members, and camp merchants gathered in Myers and Leonard's because it was the biggest Adobe Walls building. Jim Hanrahan led the meeting.

"We've got to decide what to do next," he said. "I already know of three, maybe four outfits who've already lit out for Dodge City. I know more of you are ready to do the same. But let's think for a minute of our circumstances."

"Ain't much to think about," Billy Tyler said. "There's bunches of Indians about, and a man has to care more for his own hair than a buffalo's hide."

"Self-preservation is a powerful thing," Hanrahan said. "But it's also true that we've a mighty crowd of buffalo right here, and so far as we know there's not another herd like it to be found anywhere. We go back to Dodge City, there are no buffs there. You boys are making fine money here."

"At least we'll be alive back in Kansas," skinner Mike Welsh said. "I went out with the group that wanted to bring back the remains of the Dudley crew. Time we got there, all the bits and pieces left of them had scattered about and we couldn't find enough to retrieve. And the other camp where they got chopped up, the ones went to fetch them back found that the bodies got swept up in the Canadian, which was rising high at the time. Dudley, Tommy Wallace, Antelope Jack—were they here, they'd tell us running away poor beats dying with money. I see no disgrace in shedding this place at once—Brick Bond and his boys just left for Dodge. At least Kansas is safe."

"Not necessarily so," said Hanrahan. "Shorty and Isaac Scheidler are just back from hauling some hide loads there. They inform me that just a week or so ago there was an Indian attack right outside of Dodge. Isn't that so, boys?"

Isaac rubbed his temples. "Well, Mr. Hanrahan, the fellow that told it to us was pretty drunk, so he might have been seeing Indians around Dodge when there weren't any."

Shorty said, "Well, Indians around Dodge or not, the important thing is, we didn't come across any on our way here. Left Dodge six days ago, got here yesterday, not a red man to be seen."

"That's my point," Hanrahan said. "We've lost some good men to the savages, I admit. But it's been a few days since, and there have been no other attacks. My thought is that this was the work of a small band just coming through the area and jumping crews that weren't sufficiently alert. These Indians are probably far removed by now—heading farther into Texas to raid in Mexico would be my guess. No reason, if we take additional precautions, that we can't continue on, take advantage of this great buffalo herd while there still is one. This is the end of our time, boys, we all know it. When this herd's gone there won't be another, and all of us will have to find other means of making our livings, and probably not in ways that pay as well. What we can do is, go out in hunting parties of fifteen, maybe twenty. Have five or six guns on watch while the rest take the buffalo. No Indian raiding party will have sufficient numbers to risk further assaults. Back here in camp, you can sell your hides for honest profit, have all the necessities and even enjoy some luxuries. Surely you won't let the Indians spook you out of that."

It was a persuasive speech. Afterward, even Billy Dixon admitted Hanrahan had made valid points.

"What do you think, C.M.?" he asked as they drank bottled beer in Hanrahan's saloon.

McLendon considered his current plight. He'd given Billy all the money in his pockets to buy the old Sharps. So far, from the buffalo he'd shot and the hides he'd sold, he had about $250 in credit with Fred Leonard, but for the moment Fred wasn't honoring credit with hard cash. Even the two bits per skin that Billy paid him was accounted for in credit with Myers and Leonard's. If McLendon went back to Dodge City now and Leonard never redeemed the credit he'd accrued, then McLendon would be flat broke and in no way able to get to Gabrielle in

Arizona Territory for months to come, maybe longer if he had trouble finding a job in town. True, he was very much afraid that if he stayed south in Adobe Walls, he'd be killed by Indians in some particularly horrible way. But if he stuck it out, if he survived and Fred Leonard paid out after the current crisis was past . . .

"Let's stay, Billy," McLendon said. "I know that some, like Bond and his outfit, have headed back to Dodge, but Jim Hanrahan's probably right. The Indians are long gone."

TWENTY-FIVE

After the two raids on their outlying camps, the remaining white hunters did exactly what Quanah anticipated. Some fled north; the others barricaded themselves in the big camp in the meadow and posted guards. This would make the coming attack more difficult. Quanah didn't believe that Isatai's magic would make the whites fall asleep at the crucial moment. Still, he thought the camp could be taken. For a change, the Indians would enjoy a huge advantage in numbers: five hundred warriors against maybe a tenth as many whites. If they didn't kill all of the hunters in the first rush, they could surround the four buildings that made up the camp and overrun the few survivors. It would be over before the sun was halfway across the sky.

Then the white hunters went out again, but this time in larger numbers than before, maybe twice all of the fingers on Quanah's hands. There were enough white men to withstand assault by raiding parties, and even the brashest young warriors didn't want to risk attacking them. The hunters took precautions, too, stationing men to watch in all directions while the rest of them shot and skinned buffalo. They were ready to fight if they had to, and the Indians respected the deadly accuracy of their rifles.

While the hunters roamed, the whites remaining behind in the big camp were careful too. They posted guards at each end of the meadow. They stopped going to the well outside the buildings. Quanah wondered what they had to drink—maybe whiskey. He hoped they didn't drink it all before the attack at the full moon. Whiskey would be a fine reward for the triumphant warriors, especially since there was only one white woman in the camp, and she looked too old and scrawny to survive more than a few rapes.

THREE DAYS BEFORE the full moon, runners arrived to announce the imminent arrival of the Cheyenne. Quanah was relieved. The Kiowa were again growing restless and resented any attempts by the People to be pacified. With Gray Beard and his strict Cheyenne dog soldiers on the scene, it would be much easier to keep things under control.

Quanah and Isatai rode out to greet the Cheyenne and to escort them to the war village set about a half day's ride north of the white camp. It was far enough away so that white hunters would be unlikely to reach it, but still close enough to the camp so that the great war party could easily move into position for attack.

Gray Beard and Whirlwind rode at the head of the Cheyenne procession. Quanah was surprised to see that their medicine man, Mamanti, had made the trip too. Mamanti and Isatai eyed each other warily as Quanah made a short speech of welcome.

"We're ready to fight," Gray Beard said. "Are the whites still in their great camp?"

"At night they are," Quanah said. He surreptitiously scanned the Cheyenne, hoping for a glimpse of Mochi, but apparently she was somewhere at the back of the group with the other women. Her husband, Medicine Water, though, was prominent in the first ranks, riding with the rest of the fierce-looking dog soldiers. "We're happy to see our Cheyenne friends."

"I heard you had some trouble with the Kiowa," Gray Beard said. "Don't look surprised. We've been watching. We wondered if all the remaining whites might have run away after the Kiowa killed some of them. You should have kept the Kiowa away from the white hunters, Quanah. They could have ruined everything."

"I did what I could. It doesn't matter now. The whites are still there."

THAT NIGHT the People, the Cheyenne, and the Kiowa enjoyed a feast. They ate great quantities of buffalo—the whites weren't the only ones enjoying fine hunting—and especially enjoyed cracking and sucking clean the marrow bones. Afterward, chiefs and war leaders from all three tribes gathered to discuss the coming fight. Isatai and Mamanti were there too.

"In two more nights it will be the full moon," Quanah said. "We'll take the warriors down to a good place by the wide river, and there we'll prepare, then, when all is ready, ride quietly along a creek that runs into the meadow where the white camp is. It will be easy to conceal ourselves in the trees and brush on its banks. That will bring us very close, and then we'll surprise and kill their guards. Just at sunrise, we attack."

"Before the attack, I will say words and my magic will make sure all the white men are asleep," Isatai said. "There is no magic so great as spirit magic. It is stronger than the weak powers of those who talk to dead owls." He glared at Mamanti, who glowered back.

"Yes, the magic will be important," Quanah said hastily. He feared that any squabbling between Isatai and Mamanti would distract from making battle plans. "I thought that tomorrow a few of us might ride down toward the white camp to scout it one last time."

The scouting party included Quanah, Lone Wolf and Iseeo of the Kiowa, and Medicine Water of the Cheyenne. To Quanah's delight, as they were leaving, Mochi ran up and insisted on coming too.

"We're going to kill many white men," she said. "My knife is very sharp."

"Mochi likes to use her knife on white men," Medicine Water said. "That way she can look into their eyes as they die."

The five Indians rode south much of the day, taking care to approach the meadow after dark. Quanah knew the way well. He pointed out various landmarks, especially the high bluff north of the white camp, a fine vantage point. When they reached the creek that flowed just above the camp, they tethered their horses and walked the last mile. Easing their way up the side of the bluff, they crawled on their bellies along its flat top until they reached the edge and could look down into the camp. Since the moon was almost full, it offered some illumination on the buildings below—a big grass-and-mud one with a picket corral was closest to the creek, and then a small picket structure, another of sod, and finally a second picket building. There were lights in all of them. The sharp sound of metal banging on metal came from the small picket building, and raucous male conversation and laughter emanated from the others.

"The white men are happy," Lone Wolf observed to Quanah. "They aren't mourning their dead anymore."

"Soon they'll be dead themselves," Mochi gloated. Her voice, so close to his ear, made Quanah start; she had moved very silently to his side. "I want to do it now. It will be very hard to wait another day and night."

"Patience," Medicine Water said. "This looks like a good place to fight." But after a moment he said, "There's something wrong down there. Do the rest of you see it?"

"Yes," Quanah said. "Where are their guards?"

"Did they never have any here?" Medicine Water asked.

"After the Kiowa killings they did, always one at each end of the meadow and also one or two who walked from one end to the other. I have watched here on four other nights, and it was always the same."

"Isn't this a good thing?" Iseeo asked. "We can surprise the white hunters more easily now, since they're fools and no longer keeping watch."

"Maybe they still have guards and we just can't see them," Lone Wolf suggested. "They could be hiding themselves in new places. I've known white men to dig holes in the ground and pull branches on top."

Medicine Water said he and Mochi would creep down into the meadow to look around. The others should stay on top of the bluff. Quanah said he would come with them, but Mochi told him that they would be fine by themselves. Quanah and the two Kiowa listened to the white men whooping it up down below while they waited. Finally, Mochi and Medicine Water returned.

"I'm sure that there are no guards," Medicine Water said. "We looked carefully and would not have missed them."

Iseeo was pleased, but Lone Wolf expressed concern.

"I have little respect for the whites, but I can't believe that they would not have someone watching. Maybe this is a trick. They guessed we're going to attack, and they want us to believe they are not prepared."

"This is possible," Medicine Water said. "Quanah, how many of the white hunters are left down there?"

"I think maybe three times my fingers, or four if some more came in while I was away greeting you. Not enough to fight all the warriors we'll have with us."

"That closest hut is very big," Medicine Water said. "Lots of white men with good guns could be hiding in there. You're right, they could have come when you weren't here to see them. There could be more than you know about—many more. If there are twice as many as you think, and they all have good guns and they're not asleep like your Spirit Messenger promises, then it will be a harder fight than you promised."

Quanah said crossly, "I think that these hunters are just stupid people and no longer think that they need guards."

"Maybe. But until we know how many white men with guns are down there, the Cheyenne will wait to fight."

Quanah felt a surge of panic. His plan was in jeopardy. "But you've come here. The Kiowa are ready, and the People too. We're going to have a great victory and drive away the white men forever. The spirits are guiding us."

"Unless we can count the white men, the spirits will have to guide the Kiowa and Comanche without the Cheyenne," Medicine Water said.

"What do you want me to do, walk down there among them?" Quanah asked. "Should I go in all those huts and ask them to stay still while I do?"

"Wait until morning," Lone Wolf suggested. "When the sun is up, maybe any white men who are hiding inside will come out."

"Maybe they won't," Medicine Water said. "If they're trying to trick us, and if they think that we're watching, they'll keep hidden."

"What, then?" Quanah asked. "Are the rest of us supposed to walk away like the Cheyenne?"

"If the Cheyenne don't fight, then the Kiowa may not," Lone Wolf said. "I think we need to ride back so I can talk about this with my people."

"No one has to walk away," Mochi said. Quanah had forgotten about her. Now she pulled at her husband's shoulder and said to Medicine Water, "Come with me." They withdrew to the back of the bluff and talked quietly. It seemed to Quanah, as he anxiously watched and tried unsuccessfully to hear what they were saying, that Mochi was trying to convince Medicine Water of something. Finally, he shrugged, and they came back to where Quanah, Lone Wolf, and Iseeo waited.

"I need to go to the stream," she said. They followed her down the side of the bluff. When they reached the creek, Mochi did a curious thing. She cupped water in her hands and dripped it on herself, taking care not to make any splashing sounds. Then, when her hair, exposed skin, and deerskin dress were wet, she rolled on the ground, splotching herself with the resulting mud. When she was done, she walked to her husband and told Medicine Water, "Tear it." He made rips in the sleeves and along the hem of her dress. "Do I look all right?" she asked him. Medicine Water wet his own hand in the river, scooped up some dirt, and wiped the moist sludge on her face and hair.

"Yes, now," he said. There was sadness in his voice.

"I'm going to count the white men," Mochi told the others. "You better hide, because when they see me, they may come looking for more of us." She embraced Medicine Water, pushed her way through the brush along the river, and walked toward the buildings in the meadow.

TWENTY-SIX

On the night of June twenty-fifth, most of the men in Adobe Walls got drunk to some degree. Earlier that day, Billy Dixon and Jim Hanrahan had called everyone into the saloon to make an announcement.

"The main part of the herd is above and west of us now," Billy said. "We've had a bad patch and lost some friends, but in general the hunting has been good, the best in more than a year. We're all making money. Now we got to think ahead a little. Going out in one big group has worked well. There's been no further sign of Indians. So maybe it's time to stop this going out and coming back in on the same day. Repeated trips cut down on shooting time."

Billy suggested that all the remaining hunters and their crews buy supplies for a month and follow the herd north and west, making temporary camps as they went along. The teamsters would come as well. In two weeks their wagons would bring the hides back to Adobe Walls, where the merchants and their staffs kept the stores and blacksmith shop in operation. Fred Leonard would purchase the hides, crediting each hunting crew for its share. Then the teamsters would haul the hides back to Dodge, drop them off at the railroad for shipment east, and return west to wherever the hunters were. Because the merchants would still be in place at Adobe Walls, the teamsters would stop there on the way back and pick up additional supplies for the crews. In two more weeks the cycle would be repeated. After that, the herd would probably turn back toward the east, and they'd kill all of the buffalo that they could before fall turned into winter and hunting season ended. Then everyone would close up Adobe Walls, return to Dodge City, and enjoy a comfortable winter spending their hard-earned money.

"This makes all the sense in the world," Hanrahan added. "We're all businessmen here, and smart businessmen look for ways to maximize profit. We do it the way Billy just described, and everyone's pockets will be overflowing, because you'll always be right where the buffalo are."

"Jim, I agree that you and Fred Leonard and the other shop men will have overflowing pockets, but the rest of us still haven't seen an actual coin," Bermuda Carlyle said. "I think I speak for at least a few of the others when I say that there remain hard feelings about Fred's actions following the attacks. He acted like our credit with his store mattered for nothing. How can we be sure that while we're out in the wilds for all this time, he won't one day just skedaddle away with his ledgers and leave us empty-handed?"

"Why, I'd never—" Leonard said.

Carlyle snapped, "Yes, you would," and took a threatening step toward him.

Billy stepped between them. "I had my own hard feelings with Fred about this, and we've come to a satisfactory agreement. After we head out—I think we'll need tomorrow to prepare; let's go on the twenty-seventh—Fred will travel back to Dodge with the teamsters and the first load of skins under the new arrangement. He's going to go to the bank there and withdraw in cash all that's owed to everyone, then bring it back here to Adobe Walls. This means that, by the middle of July, any man who wishes can demand in cash all that he's got coming. Will that provide you with sufficient peace of mind?"

"It will," Carlyle said. "I'll rest easy on it now."

McLendon's heart gave a happy lurch. In mid-July he could quit Billy's crew, collect his earnings in cash from Fred Leonard—about five hundred dollars, he estimated—join the teamsters on their next trip to Dodge City, and then make his way to Mountain View and Gabrielle.

"Good thinking, Billy," he yelled. "A fine solution!" McLendon's pleasure didn't extend to joining in the general rush to the bar to purchase celebratory drinks. He needed every cent to finance his trip to Arizona Territory and, hopefully, two fares to California after that. As McLendon watched the crowd descend on bartender Oscar Shepherd, he heard sniffling behind him. Hannah Olds was weeping into a linen handkerchief.

"Why, what is it, Mrs. Olds?" he asked.

"Oh, it's just that I'd hoped Mr. Dixon would say we're closing up this dreadful place now and going back home. My husband, William, is feeling even more poorly, and I haven't slept soundly since those men were butchered by the savages. This is no fit place for decent people, Mr. McLendon. There's the smell of death to it."

McLendon patted her bony shoulder. "That's just the smell of hides. The stacks outside are easily fifty feet high, and the wind is blowing the stink in this direction. Don't despair. You heard Billy—in a matter of months you'll be back in Dodge."

Mrs. Olds dabbed at her eyes with the handkerchief. "I'm not so sure. This is an evil place. Well, these men may want some supper. I'd best get back to my kitchen."

.   .   .

A FEW OF THEM did buy supper for a dollar a plate. Despite her fatalistic mood, Mrs. Olds prepared a savory venison stew and hot, flaky biscuits. But most of the men wanted to drink. It was a relief to have a new plan, one that not only made sense but provided a time frame for leaving Adobe Walls for good. No one had really felt comfortable there since the raids on the outlying camps. Jim Hanrahan told Oscar Shepherd to pour with a liberal hand. By midnight almost every man in camp was at least tipsy, and a few were stumbling drunk. The only completely sober ones were William Olds, who'd long been in bed, and McLendon, who asked Billy Dixon, "Who's supposed to be out on guard tonight?"

Billy rarely took more than a few drinks, but tonight was an exception. After thinking for a moment, he replied, "I guess Masterson and Shorty Scheidler. You see them around?"

Bat and Shorty were seated at a table in the far corner of the saloon, passing a bottle back and forth. There was only about an inch of whiskey left in it.

"You two need to go out and stand watch," McLendon said. "Let me take that bottle back to Oscar."

Bat jerked the bottle out of McLendon's reach. "Don't be interrupting us, C.M. Me and Shorty are discussing opening our own whorehouse back in Dodge."

"So we never have to do without women again," Shorty said. "My pecker's so itchy, I can't hardly think straight." He took the bottle from Bat and drained it.

"I doubt it's your pecker that's got you in this present condition," McLendon said. "How can you two be watchful, drunk as you are?"

"Well, we can't," Bat said. "Go tell Billy that we're indisposed." He pronounced it "indishposhed."

McLendon saw that Bat's eyes were glazed. Shorty's weren't. They burned with glassy intensity. Liquor turned Bat clownish, but Shorty, McLendon realized, was a mean drunk. "You two sit there," he said. "I'll go speak to Billy."

To McLendon's surprise, Billy wasn't concerned. "Ah, well, it's a party tonight. I expect that we're okay unguarded. There's been no sign of Indians. Let Shorty and Bat have their fun. In a little while, maybe you and I can go out and take a look. Meanwhile, have a drink."

"Thanks anyway."

"You're trying to save all your money to go see that girl in Arizona. Have something anyway. I'm buying."

McLendon saw no reason to refuse Billy's generosity. He had a beer, and then another. They tasted good and Billy was willing to continue treating him. After a while he got caught up in the general hilarity. When some of them started singing "Buffalo Gals," he sang, too, and then joined in the general merriment at how terrible he sounded. It occurred to him that these were fine people—even Shorty Scheidler, who kept drinking hard and looking meaner. If he hadn't had to rush off soon to Gabrielle, he might have been glad to remain in their company.

SOMETIME AFTER MIDNIGHT, Billy Tyler went outside to take a piss. A few minutes later, he stuck his head back inside the saloon door and yelped, "Looky here! See what we got ourselves!" Then he hauled in a cringing Indian woman, dragging her by the arm. She was crusted with filth and wore a ragged deerskin dress. Most of the men got up, clustered around her, and leered.

"The rest of you can look all you like, but I'm going first," Bat Masterson announced. He was unsteady as he stepped forward and reached for the woman's arm.

Tyler tugged her back. "I'm the one that found her, Masterson. You can damn well wait."

The Indian woman shrank away. Her head was bowed, and McLendon, watching from the fringe of the crowd, saw that there was a long scar on her neck. "Billy, what is this?" he asked Dixon. "They can't do what it looks like they're about to."

"It's going to happen," Billy said. "Stray squaw comes up on a camp like this, it means she's hungry and wants a handout after ever'body's done screwing her."

"It's not right. If she's hungry, let's just give her some food."

Billy looked past McLendon to where Masterson, Tyler, and now Mike McCabe were squabbling over the first turn. "It wouldn't do to deny the boys, C.M. This is just the way it is. She knew what was going to happen when she came here. What worries me more, she might not be all alone. Come on, you and me'll go out and take a look."

"Billy, we can't let this happen."

Billy nodded toward the others. Mike McCabe had apparently prevailed over Tyler and Bat. He grabbed the Indian woman by the hair and dragged her behind the bar. "Move out, Oscar," he said to the bartender. "I need some room."

"It's happening already, C.M.," Billy said. "Let's get going. This is something we don't need to see."

McLendon and Billy took their rifles—Billy had the .44 Sharps, and McLendon a Winchester. They walked cautiously out into the meadow, squinting into the darkness. McLendon was slightly drunk and Billy more so. Still, for about an hour they explored the camp perimeter, occasionally tripping over roots and rocks and falling on their faces.

"Think we ought to follow the creek for a bit, maybe look up on the bluff?" McLendon asked.

"Maybe the creek. Bluff's almost a mile away; don't want to go that far." When they didn't see anything along the creek, Billy said what the hell, they ought to go back.

"Do you think they're finished with her?" asked McLendon.

"I hope so. But most of the boys seem to be possessed by rutting fever. That squaw's had a hard time for certain."

WHEN THEY GOT BACK, the saloon was mostly empty. Some of the men were sprawled out asleep in front of it; it was too hot to sleep inside. Oscar Shepherd paused as he stacked glasses to say that "the party" had moved over to the Myers and Leonard's store, where there was more room.

"Some more of them wanted to have at that squaw, and I told them I needed to get back behind the bar 'cause I had work to do," he said. "She's such a pitiful thing too. Dirty and bad smelling. But they didn't care about that."

"I believe I'll just turn in outside," Billy said to McLendon. "I'm going to sleep under my remaining wagon. You ought to do the same, C.M. Whatever they're doing with that woman, you got to let it go."

"I know you're right. I'm just thinking that if they're done with her, I'd make sure that she got something to eat."

"Do as you think best, but if they're still sporting with her, don't interfere. That's how you get shot."

IN THE MORE EXPANSIVE Myers and Leonard's store, McLendon saw that in a back corner some of the men had made a rudimentary mattress from gunny sacks of rice and beans. The Indian woman was splayed on her back there, and Shorty Scheidler grunted as his body heaved between her legs. She emitted occasional mews of discomfort. A few drunks watched. Bat Masterson sat on the floor, his back propped against the store counter.

"You come to have a go at her, C.M.?" he asked, struggling to stay upright.

"Oh, Bat," McLendon said. "Did you have to use her like that?"

"She's just a goddamn Indian. It wasn't even all that good. She just lay there." Bat slumped forward and for a moment McLendon thought that he'd passed out. But then he raised his head again and mumbled, "I prefer white whores to red ones."

McLendon shook his head in disgust as Shorty Scheidler gave a long, loud groan and collapsed on top of the Indian woman, who lay limply beneath him, her deerskin garment crumpled near her feet. McLendon thought she might have passed out, but then it seemed to him that although her body was still, her eyes were flitting everywhere, and the expression in them was anything but submissive. It was only an impression, and the next moment, when he looked again, her eyes were closed.

"Come on, Shorty," McLendon said. He reached down and shook Scheidler's shoulder. There was a raw, gamy odor of sex. "You can get off her now. You had your fun. Let's give her some food and let her go."

Shorty pushed himself up on his knees. His grimy pants and stained drawers were lowered down around his ankles, and his limp member glistened in the glow of a kerosene lantern on the counter. "Not yet. I want some more." Beneath him, the Indian woman lay passive. Her bare body was splattered with sweat and semen. "For a dirty squaw, she ain't bad looking, even with that neck scar. Pretty good titties, don't you think?" There was satisfaction in Shorty's tone, and threat too. McLendon still had his Winchester in his hand and wondered if he might need to use it.

"From the look of you, you won't be able to do anything for some time," McLendon said, trying to sound reasonable rather than confrontational. "Come on, let her go. We've got a big day tomorrow, packing up for the long trip and so forth. You need your sleep."

"That's my concern and none of your own. I'll keep her here as long as I please." The woman stirred and tried to sit up. Almost casually, Shorty struck her in the face with the back of his hand, and there was a thud as her skull bounced off the floor. "Go away, McLendon." The woman moaned, and Shorty pulled his hand back to hit her again. As he did, McLendon smashed the butt of his rifle against Scheidler's skull and knocked him off her. He was sure that the blow would knock the diminutive teamster unconscious, but Scheidler rolled over and lurched to his feet. Screaming incoherently, he tackled McLendon and they tumbled over Bat Masterson, who screamed in his turn and reached for his pistol. McLendon's rifle was knocked from his hand. Scheidler punched McLendon twice in the face, hard, and was about to do it again, when Masterson pushed the barrel of the gun against his neck.

"Don't be hitting my friend, Shorty," Bat said in a voice that sounded almost sober. "I think you'll go outside now and find someplace to sleep."

"I won't forget this, Masterson," Scheidler snarled.

"Sure you will. We all will. We've had whiskey and a woman to boot. It's been a fine night. Let's not ruin it."

Scheidler stumbled outside. McLendon said, "Thank you, Bat," but Masterson was already snoring. McLendon's face smarted, and blood dribbled down his chin from a split lip. He turned to where the woman lay on the gunny sacks and gestured for her to get up. She did, slowly. He picked up the dress from the floor and handed it to her. She put it on and stood looking at him, her gaze an unsettling combination of disgust and curiosity.

"Let's get you some food," he said. He went to a shelf and took down a package of hard candies and a small loaf of bread. The bread had been baked that morning by Old Man Keeler and was surely going stale. It wasn't much for her to eat, and he briefly considered going to the kitchen in the Rath store to see if any of Mrs. Olds's venison stew was left over. But that would take several minutes at least, and he wanted to get the woman out of camp before any of the other men came after her. She took the candy and bread from him; he noticed that she avoided touching his hand. "You should go now," he said. "Come on." He motioned toward the door. She moved gingerly; he thought that she must be very sore. McLendon walked beside her, not making any physical contact but guiding her between sprawled hunters and their crews where they lay sleeping on the ground. When they were clear of the buildings, on the north side of camp in the direction of the creek, McLendon said, "I'm sorry. I know that you don't understand what I'm saying, but I'm sorry. Go on, now." He thought that she would try to get away as quickly as she could, but she stood for just a moment longer, studying him in the dim moonlight. He noticed that her right eye was swelling from Shorty Scheidler's blow. Then she whirled and he heard the soft crunching of the brush as she pushed through it toward the water.

TWENTY-SEVEN

Soon after one of the white men pulled Mochi into one of the huts down in the meadow, two others emerged with rifles and began walking out toward the river, taking their time and sometimes even flattening themselves on the ground, dropping quickly when they did.

"These are very wise men," Lone Wolf whispered. "They get down close to look for signs."

Still, the four Indians were able to move about along the bluff and river and avoid the two whites, who might have been wise but were also loud, talking to each other and stepping on brittle twigs that snapped under their feet. After a while the white men went back to their camp and the Indians regrouped on top of the bluff. As they regained that vantage point, they saw Mochi being dragged into the largest hut. Her dress hung around her waist and several men pawed at her before she was thrown inside. Medicine Water, crouched behind Quanah, gasped as he saw the battered state of his wife. Quanah thought for a moment that Medicine Water might lose control and bolt down the bluff to her, but the leader of the Cheyenne dog soldiers stayed where he was, though his body trembled.

Then they waited for a long time. Some of the white men came out of the big hut and lay down on the grass to sleep. It gradually grew quieter. Finally a white man, one of the pair who'd scouted the valley earlier, emerged, and he had Mochi with him. She carried some things in her hands. The white man walked with her toward the river, and the Indians dropped down the side of the bluff and moved that way, too, Medicine Water well ahead of the others, practically sprinting to the thick brush along the banks. Quanah briefly considered going out to kill the white man with Mochi, but didn't want to risk making too much noise. Then the white man stopped and Mochi did as well, but only briefly. Then she continued on to the river, while the white man returned to his camp.

The three other Indians hung back as Medicine Water rushed to Mochi's side. She said something to him, then gently pushed him away. She walked down along the river and threw the things in her hand into it. She pulled off her dress and got into the water, ducking completely under the surface, then emerging. Ever since he had met her, Quanah had imagined the glory of Mochi naked, but now that he could see her he felt no sexual tug, only astonishment at what she had just done. She scrubbed every inch of her body with handfuls of sand, rubbing so hard that it seemed her skin must tear off, and then she put her dress back on. Finally Medicine Water went to her and wrapped his arms around her. He guided Mochi away from the others and they sat together on the riverbank for a while. Quanah, Lone Wolf, and Iseeo kept a discreet distance from them.

"She is a woman of real courage," Iseeo said. "I have never seen such bravery."

After a while Mochi and Medicine Water stood up and gestured for the other three to join them. "We need to ride back," Medicine Water said. "We know what we need to do now."

Quanah looked at Mochi. Her right eye was swelling shut. "Are you all right?" he asked.

The familiar insolent glint was back in her left eye. "Of course I am. Are you?" But Quanah saw that she winced as she mounted her pony.

As they rode, Mochi shared her report. There were, she estimated, white men in the camp in the number of three times her fingers. There weren't any more hidden in the big hut. There were guns, lots of them, rifles and also the small guns—all of the white men wore those on their belts. Best of all, in the big hut there were many fine things, ammunition and knives and the curious white war clubs with blunt metal ends. There were sacks and sacks of food, things grown in the ground that were not as good as fresh meat but still would prove most welcome during the next cold season when it was hard to find game.

"After the great fight, we'll have so much," Mochi said. "Everyone will walk away with many things."

Mochi had also noted useful things about the huts themselves. She said that in two of them the walls were very thick and made of squares of grass and mud. The roofs of all the huts were the same, packed dirt held up by a crosshatching of log poles. These huts wouldn't burn, but she thought bullets fired from close range would penetrate the walls. Arrows wouldn't, so they should be aimed through the openings on the sides of the buildings, the ones protected with the shiny thing white men called glass. Arrows could break through that. All of the huts had the wooden doors favored by whites, and these were stout and could be barred from the inside. It would be best for the attackers to catch all of the whites outside. If any of the white enemy managed to get into the huts and shut the doors, it would be difficult, though certainly not impossible, for the Indians to get at them.

"Oh, we don't have to worry about that," Iseeo said. "The Comanche Spirit Messenger is going to use his magic to keep them all asleep. They'll be lying on the ground outside their huts and we will just walk up and kill them. Afterward we'll speak of Isatai as the greatest ever among us."

"Perhaps," Mochi said, and Quanah thought she sounded doubtful. She must not believe Isatai any more than he did, proving herself a woman of sense as well as courage.

"They have horses and mules in their corral, and also some cattle," she continued. "I heard dogs, not many. Maybe two or three."

"And one woman," Quanah said. "Where was she?"

"I didn't see her."

They rode in silence for a while. Then Mochi said, "In the fight, there is one of the white men that I want to kill myself. He's easy to know because he's a small one, almost like a child. There will be confusion and everyone will want to kill any whites they can reach, but if it is possible, this one is mine." She looked hard at Quanah, glaring with her good eye. "I know you're going to lead the attack. I want to ride in front with you."

"You've earned that right."

Mochi said firmly, "Yes, I have."

WHEN THEY REACHED the war camp late in the morning, they summoned the warriors. Quanah, Medicine Water, and Lone Wolf described the white camp, the four main buildings all in a line, and how many enemies they would find there. They explained how the mighty war party would ride out soon and go almost all of the way before nightfall. After it was dark, they would make their way along the bank of the wide river, then follow the creek that broke off toward the meadow where the white men had their camp. They would spend the rest of the night far enough away so that the white hunters couldn't hear them. Just before dawn they would go the rest of the way down the creek, a very short ride, and then they would attack.

Isatai insisted on speaking then. He reminded everyone that the magic given to him by the spirits would cast the white men into sleep so deep that it would be easy to ride up and kill them all. He would person-ally be there, staying just beyond the fight itself and communicating with the spirits, Buffalo Hump especially.

"Through me, they will guide and bless you," Isatai said. "Believe, and everything that happens will be a good thing." To Quanah's immense relief, Isatai seemed done talking; but as he was stepping back he caught himself, came forward again, and added, "Remember not to kill any skunks. The spirits say so." There was some muted chuckling. "Don't do it," Isatai repeated. Quanah quickly tugged him back and changed the subject, telling the assembled war band about all the fine things in the white hunters' biggest hut. They enjoyed hearing about the ammunition most of all.

SOON AFTERWARD, the procession of nearly five hundred warriors rode majestically out of camp. There were so many that it took a very long time. A man could have fletched a dozen arrows or a woman might have cooked a big meal from start to finish before the war band was completely beyond the circle of tipis and the horse herd just beyond. The barrels of their rifles and the blades on their spears glinted in the sun. The women, children, and old men remaining behind were dazzled by the spectacle. No one in living memory had seen so many fighting men in a single war party. The warriors were supremely confident. Even those who doubted Isatai's magic felt that the assembled fighting force was invincible. Quanah let Lone Wolf and the Kiowa take the lead. Though he would not participate in the fight, Satanta rode with them. Then came the warriors of the People, with Quanah and Isatai at the forefront. The Spirit Messenger closed his eyes and hummed, a much better thing in Quanah's estimation than babbling about skunks. The Cheyenne, at Quanah's suggestion, brought up the rear, with Medicine Water and his dog soldiers hurrying along any stragglers and keeping the formation relatively tight. Mochi rode at Medicine Water's side. She was dressed in the same regalia as the other dog soldiers: leggings, a breechclout, and a war bonnet made from the feathers of predator birds. In addition, she wore a bone and hide breastplate. A bow and quiver of arrows was slung over her shoulder, she balanced a shotgun in front of her, and a long, wicked knife hung in a hide sheath at her side. Mochi's right eye was swollen completely shut, but her face glowed with anticipation.

TWENTY-EIGHT

Cash McLendon was reluctant to stir from his blankets when Bat Masterson woke him shortly after sunup. As usual, he'd had trouble falling asleep, though this time not because he was troubled by mistakes in his past. Instead, he felt haunted by the suffering inflicted on the young Indian woman, and his head ached and his split lip stung from Shorty Scheidler's punches.

"For God's sake, Bat, leave me alone," McLendon grumbled. The spot in front of Hanrahan's saloon where he'd chosen to lie down was soft with thick grass that was almost as good as a mattress. "Drunk as you were last night, I'd have thought you'd be slow to arise yourself."

"Bad as we both might feel, some mornings require early activities," Masterson said, prodding McLendon in the ribs with his boot until he groaned and sat up. "There's some fences to mend if we want to avoid future conflict, as we surely do."

"Shorty, you mean."

"Correct. Lingering grudges tend to fester, especially out in the country where we can't much escape each other's company. Go wash up and then let's get this over with."

Masterson and McLendon found Shorty Scheidler where he usually was in the early morning, sleeping beside his brother, Isaac, in their wagon, which they habitually left on the north side of the Myers and Leonard picket corral. The brothers, covered with thin blankets, were stretched out snoring in the wagon bed. Maurice, Isaac Scheidler's massive black Newfoundland, lay between them. When he heard Masterson and McLendon approaching, he raised his heavy head and growled low in his throat. Then, when he recognized McLendon, he yelped happily and hopped down from the wagon. McLendon gave the dog's head a brief pat and pushed him aside. Maurice barked some more, which woke the Scheidlers.

"Quiet, Maurice," Isaac commanded, and the dog backed away. The taller Scheidler brother rubbed his eyes. "Boys, what brings you around so early in the day? Shorty and me always find it difficult to wake up."

"We want to talk with your brother," Bat said. "Shorty, are you feeling at all sociable this morning?"

"God, no," the younger Scheidler moaned. "How much whiskey did we get on the outside of last night?"

"A considerable amount is what I recall," Bat said. "Which, of course, led to some regrettable events. C.M. and I are wondering as to your recollection of them, and your current disposition in regards to us."

"Ah," Shorty said. He thought for a moment. "I've got the damndest lump on the side of my head, McLendon. It was impolite of you to smash me with that rifle butt."

McLendon almost pointed out that it was much worse to beat and rape women, but thought better of it. Bat was right. What was done was done, and now it was important to avoid any additional trouble. "I'm sorry for that. If it helps, this apology is particularly painful as a result of your blows to my mouth."

Shorty leaned down from the wagon bed and inspected McLendon's puffy split lip. "Well, I'm glad to see I got in a lick or two of my own. After all, it was only a squaw. Do you admit that now?"

McLendon nodded because he couldn't choke out words.

Shorty smiled. "All right, then I'm regretful too. When I take a few glasses, it's my tendency to become irritable. Pals again, fellows?" He reached out and shook McLendon's and Masterson's hands in turn.

"Well, if that's settled, let's all go back to sleep," Bat suggested. The Scheidlers rolled back up in their blankets in the wagon bed; Maurice whined mournfully as McLendon followed Masterson away. Bat went back to sleep, but McLendon knew that he couldn't. He wandered over to Myers and Leonard's, where Old Man Keeler fixed him a breakfast of coffee and bacon. His split lip stung as he chewed and swallowed.

THE DAY QUICKLY TURNED uncomfortably warm. By the time everyone was up, the slightest movement brought perspiration. But the camp mood was good. Everyone was ready for the next big stage of the summer. Both stores did brisk business as the hunters and their crews stocked up on ammunition and other supplies. They stacked these things in corners and along the store walls, everybody knowing where his pile was and each respecting the property of the others. There was a great deal of excited conversation. Everyone seemed glad that there was a plan in place, one that virtually guaranteed both profit and personal safety. Despite his throbbing head and lip, McLendon got caught up in the camaraderie, only stepping back from the chatter and laughter when others made reference to the squaw they'd diddled the previous night.

Around noon, Jim Hanrahan announced that he'd found some weaknesses in the sod roof over his saloon. He could see daylight through parts of it, he complained, because there wasn't enough dirt on top.

Oscar Shepherd and Mike Welsh, who worked in the saloon, began digging a fresh supply, and Hanrahan promised two bottles of beer to anyone who'd help with the repairs. Billy Ogg and Jim McKinley took him up on it. With his headache easing, McLendon helped, too, though he intended to pass on the beer.

The work was harder than McLendon had anticipated. Not just any dirt would do for the roof. Hanrahan wanted the dark, denser earth near the banks of the creek. Shepherd and Welsh dug it up, and McLendon was given the task of hauling the dirt in a wheelbarrow from the creek bank to Hanrahan's saloon, where he dumped the load on the ground. Ogg and McKinley filled buckets and clambered up a ladder to the roof, where they painstakingly spread the dirt from one side to the other in a thick layer. Each bucket covered only a foot or two, and it was a long roof, so McLendon had to make many trips back and forth. The wheel on the front of the barrow was wobbly and it was hard to push the contraption in a straight line, which added to the chore. It was mid-afternoon before Hanrahan pronounced himself satisfied.

"There's a good two feet of protection on there, a considerable improvement," he said.

Billy Tyler, a veteran teamster, asked if maybe there wasn't too much roof dirt now. "The weight of it might split the ridgepole," he said. "That happens, the whole roof could cave in and kill everybody inside."

"Oh, the ridgepole is good, stout cottonwood," Hanrahan said. "It will hold almost infinite weight, so there's no danger of collapse."

McLENDON SPENT the rest of the afternoon helping Billy Dixon with the horses. All of them needed to be curried and have their hooves checked. A few needed to be reshod, and Tom O'Keefe took care of that.

The blacksmith had dozens of shoes ready for use, but had to fit them to the hooves of individual horses. Like humans, their feet varied in size. It was critical for hoof and shoe to size up perfectly; an ill-fitting shoe might soon come loose, or else pebbles or thorns might work in between shoe and hoof, laming the horse. So, with each animal, O'Keefe measured hoof against shoe, then briefly returned the shoe to the fire until it was heated enough to tap into a shape that perfectly matched the hoof of the horse. Shoeing each animal took a half hour or more, which was why O'Keefe charged a dollar per horse's leg. The sound of iron being pounded reverberated all day from his boxy blacksmith shop.

As he and Billy worked and made cordial conversation, McLendon thought that his boss seemed preoccupied. Finally in the late afternoon, when all the Dixon crew horses were ready to go, he asked Billy what was bothering him.

"Oh, I just have this sense," Billy said. His red setter, Fannie, lay on her back beside him, grunting with pleasure as Billy scratched her belly. "The Indian girl last night. I know there are always some squaws out on their own for whatever reason, but those women usually look a lot more badly used than that one did. Her ribs weren't poking out from starvation, and in an odd sort of way she seemed pretty. I know we didn't find any other Indians out there when we went looking, but still." He switched his scratching from Fannie's belly to behind her ears, and she liked that too. "Tonight we better set up a strong guard, just in case. And when we set out in the morning, we should be especially watchful. There was just something odd about a squaw showing up like that."

"None of the other boys seemed to think so."

"Those I've mentioned it to have pronounced me overcautious, but where that woman is concerned, they're still thinking with their dangles. By the by, I heard about you and Shorty scrapping. Bat mentioned it.

You were correct in making things right with Shorty this morning, but you were also right taking him on last night. You're a good fellow, Cash McLendon."

"Thanks," McLendon said, wondering if Billy would still feel that way when he quit the crew in a few more weeks. Of course, he could still choose to stay for the entire summer, but winning back Gabrielle trumped loyalty to Billy Dixon.

JUST BEFORE DUSK, many of the men took their horses out of the picket corral and tethered them just outside of camp where the grass grew thickest. The horses could comfortably graze all night, which meant that in the morning the expedition would not be delayed while the animals were fed oats.

There was less drinking that night. Everybody wanted a clear head in the morning. But there was still some beer consumed. Around midnight, almost everyone went off to sleep. Most chose to curl up outside. It was a fearfully hot night. All the doors of the camp buildings were left wide-open to the slight breeze, but it was still stifling inside. Billy asked a few of the most veteran frontiersmen to stand guard, and in particular to watch the tree line along the creek, where Billy said any Indians were most likely to launch an attack. Bermuda Carlyle, Mike McCabe, and Dutch Henry said they would. Billy said that of course he'd join them, but Carlyle told Billy to try and get a good night's sleep instead.

"You're the leader here," Carlyle said. "We'll need you fresh in the morning to make sure things get off as they should."

With the exception of the guards, the last four up were Billy Dixon, McLendon, and the Scheidler brothers. When Isaac and Shorty said they were off to sleep in their wagon, Billy suggested that they first move it farther into camp, maybe down in front of the saloon.

"In the event of attack, you'd likely be too exposed in your present position," Billy said.

Isaac was inclined to agree, but Shorty argued that it was late, he was tired from loading supplies into the wagon—cases of canned goods, sacks of dried fruit, other food for the morning expedition—and besides, there were lookouts who'd give plenty of warning if any Indians approached. Isaac said that made sense, and the brothers trooped off. Maurice loped between them, apparently preferring rest to another assault on McLendon's leg.

"Fannie and me are going to sleep beside my wagon outside Hanrahan's," Billy said to McLendon. "Join us?"

"I think that I will. My rifle's still inside the saloon, though."

"It'll keep there until morning. Keep your Colt close to hand, just in case. Meanwhile, you go on ahead, I'm going to go get my favorite saddle horse and tether it to the wagon. That way I'll be ready to mount up at very first light."

"I'll go with you," McLendon said, and they made their way to the corral. Fannie trotted alongside. Billy found his mount and led it back toward the wagon.

"Back in Texas, they call this a Comanche Moon," he said, pointing up into the night sky. "Full moon, that's when the Co-manch generally attack. I suspect that's another reason I feel uneasy."

Despite the heat, McLendon shivered.

TWENTY-NINE

Several scouts rode ahead of the war party. Besides the white men that they intended to attack at the meadow camp, there were also scattered smaller groups of white hunters in the area. The plan was to fall on these groups if they encountered them, taking care to see that none escaped to warn the camp in the meadow. But all they saw was a herd of several dozen buffalo that had strayed far from the main herd. Quanah and Gray Beard exchanged glances, and when Quanah nodded, Gray Beard sent Medicine Water and the other dog soldiers off to kill some. It was late afternoon and a good time to stop and eat fresh meat.

Within minutes, the dog soldiers had most of the buffalo dead on the ground before them, all of the beasts taken down with arrows and lances so that the sound of gunfire would not alert any white men in the area to the war party's presence. Usually it was the job of women to skin and gut the buffalo, then cut up and cook the meat. Mochi was the only woman in the band. She helped kill the buffalo and did some of the butchering, too, joined by the other dog soldiers. In time of war, it was not shameful for men to help with such tasks. Some of the People and Kiowa built cooking fires. Since every scrap of edible buffalo flesh was used, including the livers and hearts, there was enough meat for all to eat their fill.

Afterward Quanah, Lone Wolf, Gray Beard, and Medicine Water told their tribesmen to rest. They were not far away from the meadow camp and there was a while to wait before making a dawn attack.

"We don't want to get too close, then ask our young men to wait," Lone Wolf cautioned. "Their blood is up and they'll want to fight as soon as they see the huts of the white hunters."

"We'll stay here until the moon is high," Quanah said. "That way everyone will be rested."

The warriors prepared for battle in different ways. Veterans of many fights carefully inspected their weapons, testing bowstrings for tautness, arrow fletchings for stability, and knife blades for keenness. They counted their bullets to know for certain how many shots they had. Once this was done, they calmly sat and smoked and talked quietly among themselves. Younger men who were mostly still untested in war checked their weapons, too, and then paced nervously or stared hard at the horizon, willing themselves to be brave and bring honor to themselves in the hours ahead. Mostly the People, Kiowa, and Cheyenne stayed with their own—gaps opened between the groups of tribesmen, which was to be expected, since their customs were so different. But Gray Beard motioned for Quanah to walk with him a little, away from the others so that no one would overhear.

"You've done well, Quanah," he said. "You understand what a leader must do, using others."

Quanah's eyes narrowed. He said, "I don't know what you mean."

"I understand it all," Gray Beard said. "You saw that the only chance to make the whites leave us alone was to fight them a different way. Even though the People don't believe any other tribe is their equal, you came to us and the Kiowa anyway because you needed our help. When the Comanche don't need us anymore, you'll fight us or ignore us, whatever you decide. But for now you call us your friends."

"You're wrong."

"No, I'm not. It's all right. We want to chase away the white men too. For now, they're the enemy. We'll worry about everything else later. You were very persuasive. If we didn't know the Comanche so well, we might have believed you. Maybe the Kiowa did. But not the Cheyenne."

Quanah swallowed hard. "Then why are you here?"

"I told you. The whites are the enemy of us all. We can fight among ourselves again after we drive them away. Meanwhile, those of us who know better will pretend just like you that we believe in your fat prophet and all his talk about spirits and magic. Look at him there."

Quanah looked. Isatai was sitting apart even from the warriors of the People. His eyes were closed and he was humming so loudly that Quanah and Lone Wolf could hear him even though they were many paces away.

"You used his foolishness to make everyone do what you wanted," Gray Beard said. "I approve. If this attack fails, he'll be blamed instead of you. Everyone will say it was his magic that was wrong, not Quanah. He'll be killed or driven away and you will still be respected, still be a leader. Very, very good."

"The attack won't fail," Quanah said. "There are too many of us and the white hunters are going to be surprised."

Gray Beard patted the younger man on the shoulder. "I think so too. And, of course, we both know that winning tomorrow won't be enough. We'll kill all of them and take their guns, but that won't scare away the rest of the whites. You think that, after winning this fight, the warriors will be so happy that they'll agree when you say we need to make another attack somewhere else. And if we do that and win again, and then two or three more times after that, maybe the whites really will go away. That's your real idea, the one you haven't told anyone else."

Quanah couldn't help smiling. "Next time, I think maybe we will fight whites near an Army camp. We'll kill the people and the soldiers who come to save them. There's a place to the north. The whites call it Dodge. You understand what I'm doing, Gray Beard, and that you help the Cheyenne when you help me. You're a smart man."

"Leaders must be, and maybe after this everyone will call you a great leader. Now let's go back to the others."

WHEN NIGHT FELL, there were more preparations. Almost everyone had put on paint before leaving the main village, but now they daubed on more. Warriors among the People traditionally coated every inch of exposed skin with black paint, which they believed intimidated their enemies. Isatai didn't put on any paint. He said that the spirits wanted him to do this just before the fight began. The Kiowa and Cheyenne adorned themselves in brighter colors, mostly blues and some red. But Bear Mountain, the hulking Kiowa, shocked everyone by completely covering himself with black paint.

"I do this in honor of our Comanche brothers," he announced. "And I also want to honor our great chief, Satanta, who will be with us in this battle but won't fight himself. Satanta has given me his metal horn to blow into during the fight, the one that he took many years ago from a white soldier. When you hear the noise from this horn, fight even harder." There were whoops of approval.

"The Cheyenne have a gift for our friend Quanah," Gray Beard said. "The honesty in his voice when he told us that the Comanche now think the Cheyenne are their equals has touched our hearts. So we give him this to wear in the fight." Medicine Water and Mochi came forward carrying a long, many-feathered headdress just like the ones worn by Cheyenne chiefs.

"Put it on," Mochi said. Quanah did. He didn't want to fight while wearing such a cumbersome thing, but there was nothing to do but smile and thank Gray Beard for the present.

WHEN THE NIGHT was at its darkest and the full moon was high enough, they rode on again in formation, four abreast, with the Cheyenne leading, then the People, and the Kiowa last. Quanah and Lone Wolf rode in front with the Cheyenne chiefs. There was some whispering in the ranks, but mostly everyone was quiet, thinking of the fight ahead. Almost immediately they entered some low hills and followed the river cutting through them. As they did, there was some rustling in the grass and brush and small nocturnal creatures fled. Some skunks scurried right in front of the riders. Several of the young Cheyenne braves near the front of the procession laughed and loosed arrows. They were very nervous, and shooting at these animals seemed a good way to relieve some of the tension.

Almost immediately, there was a loud howl. Isatai had been riding with the rest of the People, but now he rushed forward.

"What have they done?" he cried. "What have they done?" He dropped clumsily off his horse and bent down in the grass. Quanah, Gray Beard, Medicine Water, and Mochi rushed to see what had disturbed him so.

"*Look!*" Isatai squealed, pulling back tufts of grass. In the light of the full moon, they saw a skunk skewered by two arrows. It was clearly dead. The fat Spirit Messenger shouted, "The spirits said that skunks were holy! Now you fools have killed one, and the spirits will be angry. Whose arrows did this thing?"

No one stepped forward.

"Tell me!" Isatai raged. "Maybe if we kill you in your turn, the spirits will forgive the rest of us. Tell me! Tell me!"

"Do something," Gray Beard hissed to Quanah. All Quanah could think of was to wrap his arms around Isatai and drag him away. Isatai struggled and it was hard for Quanah to get a good grip, but he managed to haul the Spirit Messenger away, whispering that he must be quiet, he was ruining everything.

"We're ruined, but it's not my fault," Isatai moaned. "I told everyone that skunks were sacred, I told them." He began to cry, great heaving sobs. Quanah was appalled.

"Stop this, stop it now," he commanded, but Isatai kept crying. Quanah looked past the fat man and saw that many members of the war party were staring. Mochi's lip curled in disgust. She whispered something to her husband, Medicine Water, who nodded. Quanah knew he had to get Isatai under control.

"Enough," Quanah hissed in the fat man's ear. "We're close to the white camp now. We need to keep going. And after we kill everyone there, it will be clear that your own magic is so strong that it can overcome anything, even this. The spirits love you. They're still with you. Don't you feel it, Isatai? Stop crying and be strong the way that the spirits want."

Isatai sniffed and wiped his eyes. After a moment he said, "Maybe so. But whoever killed the skunk must go."

Quanah consulted with Gray Beard, who beckoned Medicine Water. Medicine Water and his dog soldiers walked briskly into the ranks of the Cheyenne. Moments later, three young braves rode away north.

"They're gone, Isatai," Quanah said. "It's time for us to ride on."

"First I must bury the skunk," said the fat Spirit Messenger, and everyone had to wait while he did, and also while he offered an interminable prayer. Then he said gravely, "I believe that the spirits are satisfied. Buffalo Hump tells me so." By the time they resumed riding, Quanah knew they would have to move fast in order to make their attack just before dawn. He sent scouts ahead. Soon they rode back and reported that they'd gone into the brush along the creek leading to the meadow and observed no guards posted there or anywhere else. Most of the whites seemed to be asleep out on the ground in front of their huts, ready to be surprised and slaughtered.

THIRTY

When the sharp *crack* broke the night stillness, everyone at Adobe Walls was startled awake. The immediate impression was that they were under attack. Stumbling out of their blankets, the men fumbled for guns and looked frantically out into the dark, trying to identify assailants. But beyond the single loud report, there was no noise other than the soft hooting of owls in the trees along the creek.

"Be watchful, boys," Billy Dixon ordered, his voice thick with sleep. "C.M. and I will go out and confer with the guards."

McLendon wasn't pleased. Wakened from his own light doze by the sound, the last thing that he wanted was to go off into the brush where, for all he knew, Indians might be waiting. But he couldn't think of how he might avoid going with Billy without looking like a coward, so he followed him toward the creek.

"Hello the guard," Billy called softly. "What's the situation?"

Mike McCabe stepped out of the trees, startling McLendon. He automatically dropped his hand to his Colt.

"Keep that in its holster," McCabe snapped. "Billy, Dutch Henry, and Bermuda are out circling the meadow. I've followed the river back a ways and didn't find anything. Whatever that noise was, it didn't come from here."

Moments later, Carlyle and Dutch Henry returned. They hadn't seen anything, either.

"Then what the hell—" Billy said, breaking off as they heard shouts from back at the camp. "Let's go see what that commotion's about." Along with McLendon and the three guards, he hurried back.

Everyone was gathered in front of the saloon, where Jim Hanrahan looked sheepish in the light of the lantern he held.

"Well, boys, I'm put in my place," he said. "Billy Tyler is a smarter man than me. He said that too much dirt was put on the roof yesterday, and predicted the ridgepole would crack. Now it has. Everything in my saloon is in danger of imminent burial."

"So that was the noise?" Andy Johnson asked. "We weren't being fired upon?"

Old Man Keeler said, "Cottonwood is of a stout nature, so when it breaks, it makes a noisy job of it. So it's a false alarm. We can all go back to sleep, since it's but two in the morning by my pocket watch."

"Now, hold there," Hanrahan said as the other men began to move away. "There's the matter of saving my saloon."

"No, it's a matter of getting our rest," Charley Armitage said. "This is bad luck for you, Jimmy, and you have my sympathy. But many of us are moving out tomorrow, and need all the shut-eye we can get."

"Charley, I thought you a wiser man than this," Hanrahan said. "Sure, tomorrow some of you go on your way for a while, but then you'll be coming back here with hides, and when you do, you'll be wanting drinks. If this saloon and every bottle in it is deep beneath a mountain of dirt, all you'll find to wet your whistles will be creek water. Are you really wanting that? Take an hour now and help me get this ridgepole propped up. Nobody's asking you to sacrifice an entire night's sleep. It'll be easy work, and I'll stand drinks for every man who joins in. The good stuff, mind, the very best bourbon."

The offer lured a few helpers—Jim McKinley, Frenchy, Bat, Hiram Watson, and Billy Ogg. McLendon was certain that he wouldn't go back to sleep, so he pitched in too. Oscar Shepherd and Mike Welsh worked for Hanrahan in the saloon, so they had no choice. The work wasn't easy. They had to take lanterns out to the cottonwood grove along the creek, cutting and trimming logs by lantern light. Then they had to carry the logs inside the saloon and use them to prop up the ridgepole. That proved difficult, because, no matter how hard they tried, it was impossible to tell the exact spot in the ridgepole where it was cracked. Finally they braced almost every inch of it with new poles anchored in the saloon floor just behind the bar. Shepherd, Hanrahan's bartender, complained that this wouldn't leave enough room for him to move around comfortably as he mixed drinks, but the others shushed him, because they were tired and wanted the free liquor that Hanrahan had promised. Shepherd poured generous drinks, and as he sipped his, McLendon heard Billy Dixon arguing with Dutch Henry just outside the saloon.

"You guards need to get back by the tree line along the river," Billy said. "I told you, that's the way an attack would come."

"It's just turned three-thirty, Billy, and daylight's not so far away. And I told you that after the cracking woke us up, we patrolled the entire area. There are no Indians to be found. We're going to grab an hour's sleep."

Billy shook his head as Dutch Henry wandered off toward the Myers and Leonard's store, apparently planning to sleep just outside it. When McLendon joined him, Billy said, "I'm still uneasy. I wish it were already daylight."

"I guess that I could stand lookout if needed," McLendon offered, hoping that Billy wouldn't take him up on it.

"No, Dutch Henry's probably right. If any Indians with violent intentions were near, they'd probably be in place by now and our scouts would have sniffed them out. What I'll do, in your company if you're willing, is just kind of stay alert right here. I see Hanrahan and Ogg are remaining on their feet too. Let's have a drop of bitters and some conversation with them so as to avoid drowsiness, and then we can begin rousing the others as soon as there's the slightest speck of dawn on the horizon."

Like most of the others, Billy was convinced that bitters were a much more healthful drink than beer or whiskey. McLendon had his doubts. To him, the alcohol content of bitters was every bit as potent as liquor. But he sipped a glassful anyway and listened while Billy, Ogg, and Hanrahan talked about the expedition. They were optimistic in the extreme. There were still plenty of buffalo to the west and north of Adobe Walls, and even after another six weeks or so of hard hunting there should still be enough left to provide for a good season in summer 1875.

"Which means we should keep this camp open through the winter," Hanrahan said. "Charlie Rath will agree. Between us, we should have enough men to defend it if need be. You and your crew ought to winter here, Billy."

"I doubt that they'd be willing. They'll prefer Dodge City and its whores as they pass the cold months."

"We might bring some whores here," Hanrahan said thoughtfully. "Would that keep you content on these premises, McLendon?"

Billy answered for him. "At the end of this season, C.M.'s departing for Arizona Territory and a woman there. We see him again, I suspect it will be as a married man who's too true to dally with whores. He's proven himself to be a good man, one of the decentest I know."

"That so?" Hanrahan asked, his tone making it clear that he wasn't interested in further discussion of McLendon's character. McLendon understood. If he was leaving soon, then he was of no further use to Jim Hanrahan, and so Jim couldn't care less about him. Rich men were all the same. Still, it warmed McLendon's heart to hear himself praised. There had been few such compliments in his all-too-checkered past.

"I believe I see some red sky to the east," Ogg said. "Might it be time to start rousing the boys?"

"Oh, they can sleep a few minutes more," Billy said. "You and me and C.M. can go collect the horses staked out near the creek. We'll bring those in, then sound the wake-up call. It seems likely to be a peaceful morning, the heat notwithstanding."

Billy, Ogg, and McLendon stepped outside. Billy was right: it was already quite warm and there was still no breeze. All along the fronts of the stores and blacksmith shop, men lay snoring. There was just enough light from the full moon to silhouette the high stack of buffalo hides between the blacksmith's shop and the picket corral. Some quarter mile away, one of the tethered horses whickered, and McLendon thought it was a pleasant sound.

"I need to stop at the wagon and collect my Sharps," Billy said. McLendon went with him, and Fannie romped alongside. After they'd fetched the rifle, Ogg was about a hundred yards in front of them as they walked out of camp toward the grazing horses. On the way, they passed the wagon where the Scheidler brothers and their dog were sleeping under a tarp despite the heat. As Billy Dixon had suggested, it was a peaceful morning.

THIRTY-ONE

Since he was most familiar with the route, Quanah led the war party on its final ride along the river to the white hunters' camp. He followed the creek branching off from the river, and guided the others southeast using the trees and brush along its banks as a screen to avoid detection. There was no talking now. Everyone was anticipating the fight. Quanah insisted that Isatai ride beside him, so that he could cut off the fat Spirit Messenger if he lost control again and began sobbing or babbling.

But Isatai was quiet, too, until they reached the edge of the meadow and in the moonlight could just make out the huts of the white hunters. Then he whispered to Quanah, "It is time to make my magic."

"You already have," Quanah said. "You've prayed that all the whites will be asleep when we attack. Even if they aren't, you've also made magic so their bullets will pass through us without doing harm."

"The spirits still require ceremony," Isatai insisted, and, sighing, Quanah directed the warriors to a place where the high bluff was between them and the white camp.

"Isatai will make magic," he announced, and quietly cautioned the fat man, "Nothing else about skunks."

"I leave for a moment to speak to the spirits," Isatai commanded. "Wait for me to return." He rode off into the darkness and out of sight. Quanah quietly fumed. It was almost dawn, and the men, especially the young braves, were ready to fight. Then Isatai rode back and all of the warriors gasped.

The Spirit Messenger had stripped naked and now wore only a hat fashioned from sage stems, which were believed to bring wisdom and good luck. He and his horse were both completely yellow; the moonlight reflected off the fresh paint. Isatai's belly and genitals flopped as he got down off his mount and spread his arms wide. He was an impressive though not at all attractive sight.

"The spirits, especially Buffalo Hump, have brought us here," he said, and Quanah worried that the sound of Isatai's voice might drift down and warn the hunters. "This is a time of great magic. Here is a pot of yellow paint. Everyone come and dip in a finger, then rub the paint over your heart. This will make any bullets from the whites pass right through your body without injury to you. Of course, the white men will probably not fire a single shot, since my magic will make them sleep as you ride up."

While some of the warriors formed a line and took turns dipping fingers into the yellow paint, others didn't do as Isatai had told them until, in response to a gesture from Gray Beard, Medicine Water and the dog soldiers herded the stragglers along to obey. When everyone had marked themselves with an extra dot of yellow, Isatai blessed them in the name of the spirits and told them to fight well.

By prearrangement, some of the youngest, untested warriors from among the People escorted Isatai and Satanta to the top of the bluff, where they would watch the fight as nonparticipants. The youngsters reluctantly agreed to stay and guard them. They wanted to participate in the battle, but Quanah promised that afterward they would be honored as much as the men who actually fought. As he followed them, Isatai called back, "Remember—they will all be asleep, like the spirits promised. All of them."

"Say your final words," Lone Wolf suggested to Quanah, who offered a general battle plan. With three different tribes participating, it was impossible to attempt anything complicated. So everyone would assemble and, at Quanah's signal, charge around the end of the tree line and into the meadow, spreading out to form a long line with the Kiowa on one wing, the Cheyenne on the other, and the People in the center. Quanah would ride just in front—not as any statement of superiority, he was careful to note, but simply to focus the attack. They would kill all the white men sleeping on the ground and then quickly rush in through the open doors of the huts to finish off anyone inside. It would not take long.

"Don't waste bullets," Quanah cautioned. "Kill with arrows and lances and knives if you can. After the fight there will be many new guns and too many bullets to count. But no shooting now."

"Why not?" someone asked. "If we run out of bullets, your Spirit Messenger can belch up some more."

"We should save all the magic that we can," Quanah said hastily. "Anything else?"

"Remember to listen for my horn," Bear Mountain said. "I will make it sing loud."

Mochi stepped up and tapped Quanah on the chest. "You said that I could ride in front with you."

"Yes. Let's go. Everyone remain quiet until I begin the charge." Medicine Water beamed with pride as he watched his warrior wife take her place of honor.

With Quanah and Mochi in the lead, the war party moved to the edge of the trees on the creek bank. The early moments of dawn provided a pinkish tinge in the sky to the east. It was finally time. Quanah raised his arm and shook his lance above his head. He led the way as they splashed across the creek, and the first exultant war cries echoed across the valley.

THIRTY-TWO

As he walked alongside Billy Dixon on the way to where the horses grazed, McLendon lost himself in pleasant daydreams about his impending reunion with Gabrielle. When he'd tracked her to Glorious, she hadn't known he was coming, and her greeting was chilly. This time she was expecting him. He could count on at least a warm hug, maybe even a kiss, and after that kiss—

Billy grabbed McLendon's arm, interrupting the enjoyable fantasy. He pointed toward the tree line to the right. "Look there."

McLendon looked. A line of something emerged from the trees, and at the same time he saw it he felt the ground tremble because there were many things—hooves?—thudding against it. From the corner of his eye McLendon seemed to glimpse Billy Ogg stopping, staring in the same direction, then whirling and running back toward camp. Why?

"Indians!" Ogg shrieked, and Dixon hollered, "We're under attack!" He yanked on McLendon's sleeve. "Run!"

But McLendon hesitated, mesmerized by what was approaching so fast—what looked like an expanding line separating into tightly packed but individual parts, and, yes, those parts were Indians, many, many Indians, all of them painted and feather-bedecked and screaming and waving weapons, rifles of every variety as well as spears. McLendon would not have imagined that spears could look so menacing. He found himself trying to count the Indians—one, two, three, four—and then came the horrifying sense that he might not know a number high enough.

"Run, you fool!" Dixon shouted again. When McLendon still didn't move, Billy yanked his Sharps .44 to his shoulder and snapped a shot at the approaching horde. Then, with a final pleading glance at Mc-Lendon, he turned and ran himself, heading to the buildings behind them. McLendon noticed Billy's dog, Fannie, run off in a different direction into the brush, and realized that he had to run, too, but for some reason his legs were suddenly rubbery and not willing to cooperate. McLendon managed a slight lurch, a minuscule movement toward camp, and Billy Ogg dashed past. He paid no attention to McLendon; his eyes were wide and white-rimmed with panic, and spit flew from his mouth and he wheezed as he ran.

McLendon saw that now the line of Indians was coming closer, perhaps two hundred yards away, and there were so many of them, seemingly from one end of the horizon to another. One end of the line, the left end, seemed to detach itself and flow above camp where the grazing horses were, and also some of the warriors in the center of the line moved that way. McLendon thought, *Good, they're only here to steal the horses,* it was an odd thing how his mind was so nimble and his legs not at all. But only about a third of the Indians went that way. The rest were still bearing down on the camp. There were a few riding in front and these seemed to be racing right at McLendon. It occurred to him that he ought to at least draw his Colt and shoot at them, but his arms were as limp as his legs. In another split second he remembered the horrible torture Indians inflicted on their victims, and that finally gave life to his limbs and he began running, too, harder than ever in his life but not fast enough, hearing the pounding of hooves behind him, the screams of the Indians—how did they shriek so *loud?*—and in front of him he saw the Scheidler brothers' wagon and Isaac and Shorty moving sluggishly under the tarp. They'd claimed to be heavy sleepers and now by God they were proving it. There was a lot of noise all around, the Indians coming up hard, and Billy Dixon and Billy Ogg shouting and the men in their blankets in front of the buildings rousing, scrambling to get inside. McLendon could see them ahead, yet so very far away, he would never get there in time to join them. He reached the side of the Scheidler wagon and Isaac asked an odd question, "Is it really Indians?" McLendon tried to answer but all that emerged from his throat was a strangled croak. It was at that moment he realized that he had run as far as he could for now, because the Indians were right on them. He had to turn around, draw his gun, and fight. It wouldn't do any good but he had to try. In the camps, in the saloons, he'd heard the buffalo hunters and their crews talk about preferring to shoot themselves rather than be taken, he should probably do that instead of shooting at the Indians, but no matter what, he had to turn around and get out his gun. But when he turned, it got even worse.

The Indians were on them, they were right there, and the leaders were coming straight for the Scheidler wagon. In the last moment before they got there, McLendon noticed things about them, one had his face painted black and wore a long headdress of white feathers, what a curious thing to wear in an attack. The Indian directly to Headdress Indian's left was much smaller and had a knife, such a very long-bladed one, the blade seemed almost as long as the tail of the headdress, there were a few others just behind them but what caught McLendon's eye, maybe ten yards farther back, was a huge Indian whose entire body was painted black. This one held a bugle to his lips and was blowing into it. The resulting bray was the loudest thing of all.

McLendon managed to get his Colt from its holster, but before he could decide whether to shoot Indians or himself they were right there and it was all he could do to sag down weakly and roll just under the wagon, not far enough to miss seeing what happened next. Isaac, apparently still foggy with sleep, hopped to the ground. As soon as he did, Headdress Indian jammed his lance into the place under Isaac's chin—how did he manage that angle?—and blood spurted. Isaac made a sort of convulsive hop and dangled there on the end of the lance. Headdress Indian seemed to be pushing his lance up rather than straight, so his victim's toes scratched feebly in the dust. McLendon thought Headdress Indian must be very strong to support Isaac's weight like that. Then the Indian tried to yank his lance free, but it seemed stuck on something inside Isaac's skull.

Then to McLendon's horror, another Indian, one with yellow face paint, bent down and peered under the wagon. He saw McLendon, gave a triumphant howl, and pointed a gun. McLendon tried but couldn't make himself fire his gun first, and he knew he was about to die when something huge and black launched itself from the wagon and onto the Indian, and the Indian was knocked back. Maurice the Newfoundland had his massive jaws locked on the Indian's arm and McLendon wondered if the dog was going to bite right through the bones, but at that moment Shorty Scheidler finally made his way off the wagon and though McLendon knew that he ought to run or fight or kill himself, something, anything, he couldn't look away from what happened next.

Shorty had a Colt in his hand and he aimed it at Headdress Indian, who was still trying to yank his lance out of Isaac's head. But before he could fire, the smaller Indian who'd also been in front jumped on him and buried the long knife in his shoulder. Shorty screamed and dropped the Colt. He fell on the ground close to McLendon, who got a good look at the small Indian. Despite the yellow and blue face paint, it was obvious this one had been in a recent brawl, because his right eye was swollen shut. Enough pure hate and rage radiated from his left eye to make up the difference. Small Indian wore a dangling breastplate. McLendon wondered exactly what that garment was made of, and then as it swung to the side he thought he glimpsed an actual breast, what was this? And then Small Indian and Shorty and McLendon all realized who the other was. Shorty just had time to scream once before the woman he'd brutally raped and beaten began cutting him up, filleting him with swift strokes, white teeth gleaming against tawny lips as she smiled. She sliced so deep and fast that Shorty's guts were spilling out even before he knew it, except he must have known it because his shrieks got louder and more horrified. Sadly for Shorty, he didn't die quite yet. He was still breathing when she yanked down his pants, cut off his pecker, and waved it in his face. His own severed penis was surely the last thing Shorty Scheidler saw before he expired in god-awful pain.

While this was going on, the rest of the Indians swept past, but to McLendon there was nothing now but the Indian woman and her bloody knife. She turned her attention to him, some of Shorty's blood was actually dripping from the knifepoint. McLendon didn't want to die the way that Shorty did so he made himself raise his gun to his head. But she was quicker. Before he could pull the trigger she swung her knife arm at him, he expected the pain of being stabbed, but all she did was knock down his arm, banging her wrist against his. Then, to McLendon's amazement, she gave a barely discernible jerk of her chin in the direction of the camp buildings. He didn't understand. Behind her, something was going on with Maurice and the Indian he'd chomped down on, they were still rolling around, and there was an Indian behind them who saw McLendon and aimed a rifle, but the woman saw him, too, and took a step to the right, she was between them, and she jerked her chin at the buildings again, more adamantly this time, and finally McLendon got it, or thought that he did. She wanted him to run, and he did, though he thought she might be playing with him, drawing out the pleasure until she hacked him up like she did Shorty. He turned and got going, faster with each stride, finally running hard again and damned if she was not right there behind him, practically herding him, he expected the knife in his back any second but it didn't happen. There was plenty of other danger, bullets everywhere, they made curious crackling noises when they whizzed by close, and some of the fire was coming out of the buildings at the Indians. Cash ran through it all, confused as hell, and somehow found himself by the front door of Hanrahan's saloon. He looked behind him and the Indian woman was gone. He pounded on the door and yelled, "It's McLendon, let me in." The door opened briefly and Bat Masterson hauled him inside.

THIRTY-THREE

Things immediately went wrong. As Quanah led the war party around the trees and at the white hunters' camp, what he initially saw was a few of the white men walking out to where their horse herd was grazing. That meant two things: first, that Isatai of course had been wrong when he promised all of them would be asleep, and this was no surprise to Quanah. The second thing, the real problem, was that unless they killed these three quickly, they would raise an alarm and rouse the rest of the camp.

So Quanah turned his galloping pony directly at the three men, but the distance was too great. They saw the war party and began to shout and run, two of them anyway, and so there was nothing to do but sweep down on the camp and kill everyone outside the buildings that they could, then take the time necessary to finish off the others who got inside. As long as the war party remained in one group, it would be possible to storm those places and overwhelm their defenders with sheer numbers.

Then another bad thing happened. The Kiowa on the right side of the line began veering off in the direction of the horse herd, and some of the People in the center did the same. They did this out of habit,

Quanah realized, this was the traditional way when attacking big white camps, stealing the horses first so there would be booty afterward no matter what the outcome of the fight. He thought he had made the battle plan clear in advance, but in the actual moment there were those who reverted to the old ways; he should have expected that. Now there was nothing to be done, and a substantial portion of his fighting force was out of the immediate attack.

But most of the People were still in place, and all of the Cheyenne. Discipline enforced by Medicine Water and his dog soldiers on their tribesmen could be thanked for that. So Quanah led on, and in moments he and Mochi were close to a wagon on the north end of the camp, there were white men stirring in it and also one of the original three who'd been walking toward the horse herd. Quanah momentarily wondered why this one hadn't run. Perhaps he considered himself such a great warrior that he wanted to stand and fight. That might be a grand thing, to begin this battle in hand-to-hand combat with the finest fighter among the white hunters, he could beat him and enhance his own reputation. But then another white man, a tall one, jumped down from the wagon and he was closest, so Quanah instinctively lowered his lance and shoved it under the man's chin, that good soft place, and felt the point push through and up, what a glorious sensation, next he would pull it free and use it to skewer the brave one who wouldn't run. But the spear was caught on something in the first man's head, Quanah tugged and it wouldn't come loose even though the body of the dead white man jiggled up off the ground. Quanah let himself become too absorbed in getting his lance free, and a second smaller white man came off the wagon and pointed a gun at him, he was going to shoot and Quanah would die. Quanah began singing his death song but Mochi was there, she got her knife into the small man, and then for some reason took a while to kill him. At the same time there was motion directly to Quanah's left. He looked and saw a dog, a big black one, savaging his Cheyenne friend Spotted Feather. So Quanah finally let go of his lance—the body of the white man stuck on the end of it crumpled to the ground—and in one swift motion pulled the white tool he used as a war club from his belt and smashed it into the back of the dog's head. The beast yelped. Spotted Feather managed to pull his mangled arm from its jaws. Then he pointed his small gun at the animal and shot it in the head.

Now Quanah could turn his attention to the remaining white man, the brave one, but Mochi already had him, she stood right in front of him with blood dripping from her blade, and Quanah waited for her to plunge it into her second victim, good for her, but Mochi did not. The white man raised his gun and Quanah lifted his Henry rifle, but Mochi didn't need help, her knife arm finally flashed, but instead of stabbing the white man she knocked his gun arm down and why did she do that? Very strange. Co-bay, a warrior of the People, was right there and he raised his rifle to finish off the white man. When Mochi took a step to the side, it was clear to Quanah that she deliberately got in Co-bay's way, and with that the white man finally turned and began running the rest of the way into camp, Mochi on his heels. By now the rest of the war party that held the line had swept down on the camp and were milling around the huts where the remaining whites had taken refuge, so this last fleeing man ran right into that. Anyone could have cut him down but Mochi was right there with him and he was clearly hers, so the other warriors chose different targets. Quanah thought that Mochi must be toying with the man, waiting until the last moment to kill him, but then the door to one of the huts briefly popped open, someone dragged the white man inside, and Mochi turned away, coming back toward the wagon and her horse.

"You let him get away!" Quanah shouted. "Why?"

Mochi unslung her shotgun. "He'll die with the rest of them," she said.

"But you could have killed him right now."

"Are we going to talk or fight white men?" Mochi asked. She leaped on her horse and charged at the biggest hut.

Quanah took a deep breath and assessed the battle so far. Warriors swarmed around three of the four huts. The one they ignored was the small wooden one; looking through the gaps between its wooden walls, the attackers could see that none of the whites were in there. The places where they had taken refuge were the substantial huts made of dirt and earth, frustrating the warriors because they would not burn and were impervious to arrows because of the thickness of their walls. They could be penetrated by bullets, though, and so all of the attackers were shooting, there was no helping it. Quanah wished they would fire less randomly, because until they won and had access to the stores of ammunition inside, their supply of bullets was limited—but of course they were frustrated. They'd been promised sleeping victims, playthings to torment in inventive, entertaining ways, and instead only two white men and a dog were dead for sure. Warriors in pitched battle wanted to kill. They had to. The attackers jammed their guns through window openings and fired inside, or else stood back a few paces and blasted away— it was impossible to tell to what effect. Everyone was shouting, Indians and whites alike, and there was constant gunfire. Bear Mountain never stopped blowing into his metal horn, but it was annoying rather than inspiring. Every once in a while Quanah thought he could hear a woman shrieking inside the hut farthest to the south, it had to be the scrawny old woman he'd seen while scouting the white camp. Perhaps she was wounded. Then Quanah saw that the defenders had begun to fire back effectively; the first members of the war party began to fall, not many, but a few—he recognized Crippled Foot and Wolf Tongue as they both sprawled on the ground. Of course, any Indian too badly wounded to save himself, whether one of the People, a Kiowa, or a Cheyenne, was immediately pulled to safety by someone else. That meant the whites eliminated two Indians for every one they shot—a dilemma when part of a small group, but less of a disadvantage for such a large war band.

Still, the attackers were used to avoiding any unnecessary loss of life. Quanah decided it was time to lead an assault that would end the still-uneven fight. All they had to do was break inside the huts. How hard could that be when they were so many and the defenders so few? Quanah dug his heels into the ribs of his pony and galloped straight at one of the huts. Like the others, it had a wooden door, secured, he knew, from the inside. He wheeled the pony, yanked on its tether, and backed its legs into the door. Panicked, the pony lashed out with its hooves, which battered into the wood. Quanah was sure the wood would splinter, but it didn't. He howled in fury and kicked the pony's ribs again. It fought him, trying to move away from the hut, but he sawed on the hide tether, cutting the pony's mouth. It kicked at the door again and again but the door held. Unlike white men, the People had no obscenities in their vocabulary. Quanah howled again and gave up. He hopped off the pony and clambered onto the dirt roof of the hut. Then he pointed his Henry down and fired through the dirt down into the hut, certain he would hit someone inside. Other warriors followed his example. Within moments, the roofs of all three huts were occupied by Indians firing down, hoping to annihilate the whites inside.

Then a curious thing happened. There was a puff of dirt by Quanah's feet and a bullet clipped feathers from his headdress. It happened several more times before he realized that the whites inside were now shooting up through the roof: he was as vulnerable as they were. On the roof of an adjacent hut, a warrior screamed and fell, rolling off the side and tumbling to the ground. *"Get down, get down from there!"* someone screamed, and Quanah and the others did, scrambling down and flattening themselves against the earthen walls, but that wasn't safe, either, because now the crafty white men poked the barrels of their guns through the walls, making little holes through which they could fire point-blank. They weren't just shooting back through the broken windows anymore. More warriors fell, too many, and though most were picked up and dragged to safety, a few were obviously dead and left in the dust.

How are they still alive in there? Quanah wondered. *We've fired so many shots. How can this be?*

For just a moment, the attack flagged. The war party didn't retreat, but they hesitated. In that moment, sustained fire poured out of the three huts, through the windows and the walls. Serpent Scales, one of the Cheyenne dog soldiers, shouted something incoherent and ran straight into the gunfire, somehow surviving, not even hit once. He took his small gun in his hand and thrust his arm right through one of the window openings, firing until the hammer clicked on an empty cartridge, and that was when a white bullet obliterated his face. But his courage inspired everyone. The rest of the war party rushed the huts again, everyone screaming and shooting, but they could not break down the doors or get through the windows despite their great numbers. The fire from inside the huts was constant and too many warriors fell. There was great confusion. Quanah, caught in the middle of it, was startled when Gray Beard appeared at his side and shouted, "We need to get everyone back, too many are getting hurt!"

"No," Quanah protested. "We can't give up."

"We're not giving up, we just need to think of another way. Now get everyone back," Gray Beard insisted, and when Quanah didn't immediately agree, the Cheyenne chief signaled for the dog soldiers to organize the fallback. Medicine Water, some bright blood on his shoulder from a slight wound, barked orders and gradually all of the attackers withdrew back across the meadow toward the creek, some still firing at the huts, some scattered shots coming back. Angry and frustrated as he felt, Quanah was pleased to see Mochi was apparently uninjured. In the sudden quiet he heard a new sound, a high-edged sort of keening, and he looked to see Isatai high atop the bluff. The fat man was still painted bright yellow. He had his arms spread wide and was chanting. What a fool.

THIRTY-FOUR

After the saloon door banged shut behind him and was secured, McLendon wanted to lie limp on the floor and catch his breath, but he had no opportunity.

"Get your Colt and start shooting, C.M., we got to drive these bastards off!" Bat cried, and when McLendon looked around he understood the immediate peril that they were in. Furious red faces were jammed up against the broken spaces where window glass had been. Bullets penetrated the sod walls in every direction and at every angle. Besides Bat and himself, perhaps nine or ten other men were also inside the saloon—Billy Dixon was among them—and everyone had his handgun out, shooting back through the windows and walls as fast as he could pull the trigger. To stop shooting meant death. Summoning desperation if not courage, McLendon drew his Colt and starting firing, too, not aiming at any Indian in particular, just shooting at all the movement outside the broken windows. Like the other defenders, he tried to pull overturned chairs in front of himself as partial cover. Then he saw a table on its side and huddled behind it. He was certain that any moment one of the bullets tearing into the saloon would hit him but somehow none did. When the hammer of his Colt clicked on a spent cartridge, he reloaded. He had some shells in his pockets. His hand trembled as he tried to insert the fresh ammunition.

A shrill sound rose above the shouts and gunfire, and someone said wonderingly, "Ain't that a bugle? Is the Army here?" but the notes were weird and jangled. "Who's blowing a goddamn bugle?" the same man asked again, and McLendon thought, *It's an Indian painted black,* but didn't say it out loud because he was concentrating so hard on reloading.

McLendon was just ready to resume firing when the first bullets began slamming into the saloon from above. "They're on the goddamn roof!" someone shouted; McLendon looked and it was Bermuda Carlyle, with Carlyle and Billy and Bat at least some of the best fighters were in the saloon with him, thank God. Caught completely by surprise, for a few moments everyone crouched and flinched, and then Billy Dixon said, "Shee-yit," drawing out the cussword, pointed his gun at the roof, and fired right up through it. "They can shoot down, we can shoot up," Billy urged, and they did, all of them at first, but then that left the Indians on the ground unaccounted for and their shooting intensified. Some of the white men in the saloon shot through the walls again.

The saloon fogged with gunsmoke and stank of sweat and fear. The stench was so foul that McLendon wondered if he'd pissed himself. When he reloaded a second time he took a moment to check his pants and felt a brief twinge of pride because they were dry.

After what seemed like an eternity it occurred to McLendon that the Indian assault was slackening. There was no more shooting down through the roof; they'd apparently driven off those attackers with their own gunfire. Billy, Carlyle, Bat, and a few others—Jim McKinley and Frenchy, McLendon saw—began using rifle barrels to poke small portholes through the sod walls. This gave them wider angles of fire, and now they picked out individual targets. Watching them, McLendon felt unabashed admiration. He'd always known they were wise in the ways of the frontier, but he had never realized how brave these hunters and their crewmen were. In this deadliest of situations, they kept their wits about them and found the most effective ways to fight back. McLendon couldn't credit himself with anything similar. He still wielded his Colt, he fired some shots, but he didn't move from his spot behind the table in the middle of the saloon floor. It just seemed safer there.

There came almost a complete lull, just some scattered shots popping on either side of the saloon.

"Wonder what condition the others are in," Bat said. Though the Rath store was to the south of the saloon and the Myers and Leonard store and its corral to the north, because of the window placement it was impossible to look directly at either of the buildings.

"There are some still alive in each; you can tell by the way the Indians have been charging," Jim Hanrahan said. McLendon hadn't previously noticed him, but of course he was in the saloon. So were several of his employees—Oscar Shepherd, Hiram Watson, Mike Welsh. Billy Ogg was there too. "Jesus, look at the damage to my property."

Broken glass from windows and bottles covered the saloon floor. The chairs being used as extra cover were scored by bullets. McLendon looked at the table protecting him and saw several bullet holes. He thought that passing through the sod walls must have cost the bullets some velocity. Otherwise they would have smashed through the table and into his body.

"Anybody wounded?" Billy Dixon asked. "By that I mean disabling hurts, of course, not scratches." Everyone had some cuts from flying glass and splinters, but nothing more. "All right, then," Billy said. "Let's assess remaining ammunition."

"Are the Indians gone?" McLendon asked hopefully.

"Far from it," Jim McKinley said. "In fact, here they come again." With shrieks of fury, the Indians attacked.

The second assault frightened McLendon more than the first, because this time he immediately understood what was happening. A
howling hoard descended on the saloon, and once again the defenders
fired through the window openings and walls and their makeshift portholes. McLendon was more aware of individual moments than an overall
fight. An Indian face covered with bright blue paint appeared momentarily at a window, and McLendon simultaneously fired and wondered,
How do they make that color? He must have missed his shot, because
moments later the same blue visage appeared again. Then the trigger
guard on McLendon's Peacemaker seemed loose, and he wondered if
he had his screwdriver in his pocket but didn't have time to look, let
alone pause and fix it. If the trigger guard fell off his gun, he hoped the
weapon would still fire. For his next few shots he was concerned about
that, but the guard stayed on and then he forgot about it. At one point
Bat Masterson hollered, "Use your rifle, C.M.—more stopping power!"
but when McLendon looked in the corner where he'd left his Winchester
so many hours ago, he saw that the stock had been smashed and the
weapon was useless.

Hiram Watson crouched near one window, shooting his Colt into the
surging mass of copper-colored bodies outside, and just as he emptied
the handgun a long Indian arm poked through the window opening,
and at the end of that arm was a pistol, and the pistol began spraying
shots wildly into the saloon. Frenchy was grazed by one of the shots; he
moaned a little, and McLendon surprised himself by leaping forward
and aiming his Peacemaker just above the invading shoulder where he
knew the Indian's head had to be. He pulled the trigger and besides the
bang of his shot he heard an odd sound like the pop of a child's balloon.
Something wet flew onto his face and as he wiped at it with his sleeve he
was yanked down by Bermuda Carlyle. When he looked at what he'd
wiped off, he was puzzled.

"What's that mixed with the blood?" he asked, and Carlyle told him that some of the savage's brains had splashed on him.

Shortly after that, the shooting stopped again. Billy Dixon, taking a chance and peering out a window opening, said it looked like the Indians were backing off in the direction of the creek.

"They'll just be catching their breaths, is all," Billy said. "There are too many for them to quit. They came to wipe us out, and this early setback won't change their minds."

"We'd best prepare for more," Hanrahan agreed. "I believe I see a canteen that went unpunctured, so let's each take a sip of water." They passed the canteen around. McLendon thought the lukewarm water tasted better than the coldest beer he'd ever had.

They gradually became aware of a constant keening from the Rath store off to their right. "Mrs. Olds, I don't doubt," Hanrahan said. "You know, I worry most about the ones over there. We're decent fighters here in the saloon, and some other good men must be defending over at Myers and Leonard. But the Rath bunch will mostly be shopkeepers with little if any fighting skill. Dixon, can you see anything of the Indians just now?"

Billy cautiously craned his neck by the biggest window opening, which faced east. The Indians had moved back to the northeast. "It's hard to tell, but I think they're gathered and palavering," he said. "I've never seen so many savages together at one time. And a curious thing—there's Co-manch, a bunch of them, but also Cheyenne, and damned if I didn't think I saw some Kioway."

"A united Indian army," Carlyle said. "Any white man's worst nightmare come true, and why in hell did it have to be on us?"

"Keep a sharp eye out for them, Billy," Hanrahan said, and he cracked open the door. "Hello, Rath and Myers!" he shouted. "Can you hear me? What's your condition?"

Almost immediately, there was response from the north. "Ten of us at Myers, all still fit to fight."

"Mike McCabe," Billy Dixon said. "He's a cool man in a fight. Nothing from Rath?"

"Nothing beyond that damn woman screeching, but I'll try again," Hanrahan said. He called, "Rath store, can anyone hear me?"

Jim Langston, his voice reedy with fear, called back, "Just five men and Mrs. Olds. Someone come help us—we can't hold them off again."

"Sounds like they're done for," Frenchy sorrowfully. "Bad for them and for us too. They get overrun, the Indians will turn more of their attention to this saloon."

"I think we should reinforce them," Billy Dixon said. "I'll try to get over there; maybe one more could come with me?"

McLendon couldn't imagine continuing the fight without Billy. "I'll go."

"All right, then, get your gun and we'll— Hellfire, here they come back at us."

This time the Indians altered their assault. Instead of an all-out charge, they came up cautiously, using the corral and stalls of Myers and Leonard's and the towering hide ricks behind the Rath store as cover. Though less immediately terrifying, it caused the white defenders considerable frustration. Hampered by the limited sight angles of the windows and self-made shooting portholes, it was impossible for them to see much until the attackers were almost on them. All they could do was wait nervously until a target presented itself and then try to shoot fast and accurately before the Indian could conceal himself again. McLendon mostly kept himself ducked below a window opening. When he tried cautiously peeping out, he found himself flinching involuntarily, waiting for a bullet to smash between his eyes. This weakness shamed him—none of the others seemed to flinch. Once Bat Masterson glanced over, saw his reluctance to stand steady, and said, "C.M., if a bullet's going to find you, it will. Ain't nothing you can do about that. Get to sending back some shots of your own, make them the ones to feel shaky." McLendon tried. When he saw any Indian movement he fired at it, though he was certain he didn't hit anything besides the ground or corral posts. The shift in Indian tactics brought a different kind of tension to the fight. Because there were stretches of near inactivity with no targets to shoot at, the men in the saloon had more time to think about the dire situation in which they found themselves. Rough, tough Bermuda Carlyle, who'd openly mocked church attenders back in Dodge, blurted, "Lord Jesus, preserve us from the heathens." Several of the others muttered, "Amen."

The discordant bugle blats continued. At one point Mike Welsh said, "Shit, I see the damn bugler, and it's a black man, a big fat one."

"What's a black bugler doing with the Indians?" Billy Ogg asked.

"It must be one of those so-called buffalo soldiers, an Army deserter," Hanrahan said. "I've heard of such. They get sick of the discipline, so they run off and throw in with the Indians. Goddamn traitor is what the man is. Whatever else we do, let's kill that one. At least it'll end that hateful noise he's making."

McLendon thought again about telling them that it wasn't a Negro, just an Indian painted black, but his throat was dry and it didn't seem worth the effort. Thinking of that Indian with his bugle, he next remembered how Isaac and Shorty had died. He felt badly about Isaac.

A few minutes later Frenchy, peering out a front window, said, "I see the black man again; he and some others are at the Scheidler wagon." Billy Dixon moved over to take a look, and so did McLendon. The Indians had turned the wagon on its side so that they could take shelter behind its raised bed. Several of the savages, including the stout one painted black, could be periodically glimpsed behind it, gorging them-

selves on the food supplies that had spilled down—bacon and bread and
dried fruit.

"I do hate to see them in such delight," Frenchy muttered. "But it's,
what, a hundred yards or more and they're mostly under cover. Billy,
what do you think?"

Billy looked toward the other side of the saloon, where Oscar Shepherd, Hanrahan's bartender, was posted at another window. "Oscar, is
that a big Sharps you've got there?" When Shepherd said it was, Billy
asked, "Would you swap it for a lighter weapon? I believe my .44 caliber
would do you fine, and if I had that Big Fifty, I might make use of the
increased range and power."

"You're the best shot among us, Billy," Shepherd agreed, and they
exchanged rifles.

"Ahh, a Big Fifty," Billy cooed, stroking the barrel of the heavy rifle
before lifting it to his shoulder. "Frenchy, C.M., step back a pace. I got
to lean out and get the angle right." Some shots drove Billy back; bits of
displaced sod sprayed through the air. "Damn," Billy said. "Lay down
some cover fire, boys," and Frenchy and McLendon did. As soon as they
paused, Billy popped his head and shoulders out the window, swung the
Big Fifty into shooting position, aimed, and fired. He jerked back inside
and grinned. "There's one less bugler now."

"You got him?" McLendon asked.

"I drove the shot right through that wagon bed. Big Fifties have some
wallop. I doubt we'll hear that bugle again." They didn't.

What they did hear almost immediately afterward were the pitiful
sounds of animals in death throes—higher-pitched from horses and
mules, lower but still agonized from oxen.

"They're killing all the stock in the corral and stalls," McKinley said.
"Why would they do that? I thought Indians liked to steal horses, take
them for their own use."

"It means they're settling in for the long term," Bermuda Carlyle said grimly. "They're making sure none of us can steal away on a mount and ride for help."

"I hope those left in Myers and Leonard can restrain themselves," Billy said. "Some of them have powerful attachment to their animals, I know." The words were hardly out of his mouth when there was shouting from that direction, a volley of heavy fire from the Indians, and a man's loud screams, which ceased almost instantly.

"Someone acted foolishly and got cut down," Billy said. "These Indians are so damn smart. God knows what they're going to try next."

There was another lull, a longer one this time. "I need to piss so bad," Billy Ogg complained, and as soon as he said it, McLendon's bladder throbbed too. Though he was still convinced he was about to die, probably in some way terrible beyond his current imagination, the urge to pee was suddenly paramount.

"I suspect we all need to go," Hanrahan said. "Be sure to take turns, boys, we need to keep lookout. They'll be back on us anytime." He glanced around the wreckage of his saloon, then rummaged behind some bullet-riddled barrels. Hanrahan came up with some mostly empty, unbroken whiskey bottles and said, "Pee in these, and then we can throw 'em out the windows. If you just piss on the floor, it'll stink in here even worse." Everyone cracked nervous jokes about what a terrible thing to do to liquor, but McLendon noticed that nobody drank any of the whiskey dregs before relieving themselves in the bottles. *If hide men don't drink,* he thought, *they must believe themselves in the utmost peril.* When they were done, they tossed the sloshing bottles out the broken windows and settled back to prepare for the next assault.

It came sometime around noon, when war whoops and gunshots announced that the Indians had resumed the fight. This time, clumps of attackers concentrated fire on the saloon and two stores from about a hundred yards away while other groups staying low to the ground wormed their way close. It was an effective tactic. The cacophony of the constant barrage mixed sharp reports from repeater rifles, deep booms of shotguns, and even the belches of ancient muzzle-loaders. The Indian arsenal apparently included every type of gun. "I can't see them!" Jim McKinley shouted. "The bastards are invisible."

"Watch the tops of the bushes and the high grass," Billy Dixon said. "There's breeze coming from the west—if anything waves in another direction, it's because of an Indian for sure." McLendon had lost any sense of direction, so he had no idea of which way west might be. He watched Billy, and when Dixon fired, McLendon shot in the same direction.

Once again some Indians got near enough to the sod buildings to fire through the saloon windows point-blank. The defenders returned fire and perhaps once in twenty shots were rewarded with screams of pain. When they had a chance to glance out, they saw with great satisfaction that more Indian bodies lay strewn about. These fallen attackers lay still and were, apparently, dead. The Indians were still bearing away their wounded. Enough were still on the offensive to pound on the barred wooden door and fire through the sod walls. With bullets whizzing past his head and body and legs, McLendon would have screamed in abject terror if he could have summoned the breath, but he couldn't. Panting with fear, he kept firing his pistol and reloading because there was nothing else he could think of to do. In a terrible moment of clarity, he thought for the first time that the others in the saloon were showing more outward signs of fear, too; even Billy Dixon seemed to fumble with cartridges as he reloaded the Sharps Big Fifty. The attackers were very close to overrunning the saloon.

McLendon had the sickening sense that this was it, the Indians would get them this time. There were too many Indians, and as the hammer clicked down on a spent shell and he crouched to reload, he saw that he had just four cartridges left for his Colt. At almost the same moment, the other men inside the saloon began calling back and forth, asking who had extra shells.

"We're all of us about out," Hanrahan announced. "Nothing for it: we'll need to make a run for one of the stores. They've got boxes and boxes of ammunition there."

"That's suicide," McKinley said. "It's, what, thirty yards in the open whichever one we try, and Indians out there everywhere. We'll never make it."

"Some of us might," Billy Ogg said. "It's worth trying."

"McKinley, you want to stay in here and try fighting them off with dirt clods?" Hanrahan asked. "Or maybe kill yourself and save the savages the trouble?"

"Well, we better use what we got, and then each man can make his own choice as to what he does next," Billy Dixon said, and McLendon decided he would do whatever Billy did. He loaded his final four bullets, peeked out a window, and fired three times. He thought that maybe he should save the final shot for himself if that was the way that Billy chose to go. Then Bat Masterson said, "Wait a moment—are they backing away? Why are they stopping now?" Incredibly, at the very moment when the white defenders in the saloon could no longer resist, the Indians had broken off their assault.

THIRTY-FIVE

Many in the war party were furious with Isatai after the first assault fell short. As the dog soldiers herded the war party away from the white huts, several warriors screamed at Quanah that the fat man had lied.

"He promised all the whites would be asleep on the ground and easy to kill!" a Cheyenne brave shouted. Quanah couldn't blame him, or any of the others. Isatai had unwittingly contributed to the resentment felt toward him. As it fell back, the war party could see Isatai high atop the bluff, standing with his arms spread wide as though bestowing a blessing. It was a hateful contrast to the situation below, where too many of the attackers groaned with pain from wounds. Because so many had believed Isatai's promise that any white bullets would pass through their bodies without doing harm, even the slightest injury seemed not only painful but a repudiation of the Spirit Messenger. Further, eight Indians lay dead in the dirt around the white huts—a small number in terms of the overall size of the war party, but still more battle deaths than the one or two that were traditionally acceptable.

The Kiowa were especially incensed. Several shouted threats to rush up the bluff and kill Isatai. But before Quanah and Gray Beard could intervene, Iseeo the Kiowa demanded that his tribesmen relent.

"If some things he promised have not come to pass, maybe it's not the Spirit Messenger's fault," Iseeo said. "We don't know what the spirits are thinking right now. The Spirit Messenger is still a holy man; let him pray while we go back and fight."

"But he promised," a Kiowa complained.

Gray Beard said quickly, "Yes, and he also promised that there were many good things in those huts for us if only we can kill the white men in there. We know that at least this part of what he said is true. Let's finish this fight. We can worry about the Spirit Messenger later." Before anyone could resume railing against Isatai, Gray Beard began describing a new plan of attack. The white guns were too effective for the war party to launch another all-out charge. Instead, they could use the stacks of buffalo hides and the wooden animal enclosures for cover and get close that way.

"We'll keep fighting until the last white man falls, and then we'll feast on their food and put their bullets in our guns," Gray Beard concluded.

The new tactic was effective, especially in reducing casualties. The Indians were able to get close enough to the three huts to pour fire in through the walls. Almost all of the white men's shots missed. This emboldened a Kiowa to stand and mock the defenders in the hut farthest to the left, and he was instantly cut down for his trouble. It reminded everyone else to be more cautious.

Quanah, leading a contingent of the People against the hut with the big corral, was encouraged. There didn't seem to be quite as much fire coming from that hut as before. Inside the odd wooden rooms the whites built for their livestock, he could hear horses, unnerved by the constant gunfire, kicking against the boards. If all the attackers maintained discipline, victory seemed inevitable. The Cheyenne in particular were fighting well, with the dog soldiers circulating among them and reinforcing Gray Beard's battle plan. To a great extent, the Cheyenne chief had supplanted Quanah as leader of the attack, but that was all right. Quanah was learning a great deal from him. After the whites were chased away, of course, Quanah would use what he learned against the Cheyenne and the Kiowa, too, as the People reestablished their superiority.

Quanah and his fighters were almost up to the side of the hut when more of the Kiowa blundered. Since the early moments of the fight, the wagon where Quanah and Mochi had each killed a white man had stood unguarded, and in its bed rested many tantalizing boxes that undoubtedly contained treats and treasures. Now Bear Mountain, still painted black and blowing the white man's horn, could no longer resist. He and several other Kiowa broke off fighting and ran to the wagon. Putting their shoulders underneath it, they heaved so that the wagon turned on its side, spilling its contents on the ground and providing what appeared to be solid cover from the white men as they fired from the three huts. Bear Mountain and the others broke the boxes open and yipped with joy. They began stuffing things in their mouths. The mutilated bodies of the two white men lay at their feet, but that didn't discourage their appetites. "Get back to fighting!" one of the dog soldiers shouted at them, but they ignored the command. They were Kiowa, not Cheyenne, and so not subordinate to him. Then Quanah detected motion by a window opening in front of the middle hut. A white hunter with a rifle was trying to lean out. Quanah and several others shot at him and he ducked back inside, but a moment later he leaned out again and fired. The bullet tore through the wagon bed and hit Bear Mountain right in the mouth. He sprayed blood and half-chewed bits of dried fruit all around as he fell. The sight disheartened the rest of the war party. Despite the best efforts of the dog soldiers, almost everyone began falling back. Instead of the spirits being with them as Isatai had promised, it seemed that all the magic of the day belonged to the white men. How else could a bullet have penetrated the thick wood of a wagon bed?

There was other commotion in the corral as Medicine Water, Mochi, and a few other dog soldiers systematically killed the animals there, mostly horses and a few oxen. They cut their throats when they could, or fired arrows into them, prudently conserving ammunition. Medicine Water caught Quanah staring and said, "Now none of the whites can ride away," and Quanah nodded. It made sense. The animals raised loud cries of agony, and to everyone's surprise the door of the hut by the corral burst open and two white men came out, firing guns and trying to get to the dying stock. The attackers shot back, and Quanah was certain that a bullet from his Henry caught one of the white men right in the chest, driving him back toward the door. The other white man was apparently unscathed. He and the wounded one collapsed back inside and the door slammed shut.

But the momentum of the latest attack was broken. Again the war party moved back, this time toward the far end of the meadow rather than the creek. Quanah guessed Gray Beard led them in that direction to keep them as far as possible from Isatai at the top of the bluff.

Once more, there was considerable dissension, particularly among the Kiowa. Satanta came down from the bluff to join them. "I've been asked by the Comanche Spirit Messenger to tell you this," he said. Satanta kept his voice calm, but the doubt he felt was clear from his expression. "He says that the spirits are still with us, and the whites are all going to die."

"I never believed the fat one," a Kiowa warrior said. "The white bullets weren't going to hurt us? Look at my arm." There was a deep gouge on his biceps. "I've had enough. I'm going home. Who will come with me?" He began to stalk away, but Iseeo hurried in front of him.

"Don't leave in the middle of the fight," he said. "We will win, and you won't be here to get your share of the good things in those huts."

The other Kiowa dabbed at his bloody arm with a bit of cloth. "Satanta, do you believe in this Spirit Messenger anymore?"

Satanta hesitated before he responded. Quanah thought, *He thinks Isatai is a liar, but he doesn't want to say so and end a fight we still can win.* Finally Satanta said, "I'm not sure. I think everyone should decide for himself."

That was enough for about two dozen Kiowa. They took their horses from the young men holding them, mounted, and rode away. Another sixty or so from among all three tribes also left; these were either wounded men able to travel on their own or else family members of badly hurt warriors who needed help getting back to their respective camps. Counting them and also the eight dead warriors, the ranks of the original war party were reduced by about one-fourth. That still left more than enough attackers to obliterate the whites in the camp if only they could break into the three huts.

Lone Wolf, the Kiowa chief, joined Quanah, Gray Beard, and Medicine Water a short distance away from the rest of the war party. "Bullets," Lone Wolf said. "We'll need more soon, there's been so much shooting."

"There are bullets in those huts, too many to count," Quanah said. "Tell your warriors to go in there and get them."

"Didn't your Spirit Messenger say that he could belch up all the bullets that we needed?" Lone Wolf asked. "Was *that* true, at least? If it was, why don't you bring him down here and let him do it? Or else is this another thing he promised that won't happen?"

"I don't know," Quanah said, even though he did. The only time Isatai had ever seemed to cough up bullets, it had been a trick. "This is something Isatai has to do or not do. I never said that I was part of any magic."

"But you let us believe that you were," Lone Wolf said.

"Enough," Gray Beard said. "Lone Wolf, do your warriors still have a few shots left? Quanah, do the Comanche? Medicine Water says that most of our people may have five or six bullets each. Forget magic. Let those who have bullets stay back and fire on the huts. At the same time, the others will quietly approach them, using the high grass and rocks for cover. When they are close enough, they will all run forward and throw themselves into the openings in the walls. The white men won't be able to stop them."

"Many of those warriors will die, the ones who come in close," Lone Wolf predicted.

"Do the Kiowa fear death so much?" Gray Beard asked, speaking slowly and letting the insult draw out. "Then let the Kiowa be the ones to stand back in safety and do the shooting. Cheyenne and Comanche warriors have all the courage necessary." He looked meaningfully at Quanah, who said quickly, "I'll lead one of the attacks," and Medicine Water said that he would too.

"Then we have our plan," Gray Beard said. As they walked back toward the main group, Quanah reached up to take off the Cheyenne headdress. "Don't do that," Gray Beard said.

"Why not? It's long and could catch on the brush."

"When you wear it, it reminds the Cheyenne that the Comanche are now our brothers. Take it off, and some will wonder."

"All right," Quanah said. "Let's fight again before all of the Kiowa go away."

The war party moved back into place. The Kiowa broke into three groups. Each concentrated fire on one of the white huts. Packs of Comanche and Cheyenne began working their way close, mostly moving on their bellies through the high grass and taking occasional cover behind rocks. Based on the whites' return fire, they appeared to be confused. If they focused on the long-range Indian shooters, the other attackers would squirm up close; but if they leaned out the windows to try and shoot the closer Indians, they'd be easy targets for the Kiowa.

Some Cheyenne reached the outer walls of one of the huts and began firing through the sod. Quanah and his Comanche weren't far away from the hut to the south. It was now a matter of time. Quanah was just considering barking an order to jump up and charge when he heard loud voices behind him. The Kiowa were shouting for everyone to come back. It was a foolish thing when they were just about to rush the white huts. Quanah would have ignored them, but many of the other groups in the front didn't, and instead of rushing forward they turned around and crawled away. That left Quanah no choice but to do the same. He burned with anger and frustration.

"*What?*" he hissed at Lone Wolf when everyone was back at the far end of the meadow. "We were on them, we almost had them. Why did you stop us?"

"The Kiowa have no more bullets," Lone Wolf said.

"None at all? Not one more shot?"

"Maybe a few. But as we watched, we saw that the Comanche and Cheyenne were going to jump in those huts, kill the whites inside, and keep all the good things there for themselves. By the time the poor Kiowa came, there would be nothing left for us."

"Everyone will share," Quanah said. "You know that, I told you that." Lone Wolf's eyes narrowed. "What about the white men's guns?"

"What about them?"

"All of them must belong to the Kiowa. You promised this."

Quanah was uncomfortably aware of Gray Beard standing just behind him. "There will be plenty of guns," he said softly.

"You gave your word," Lone Wolf repeated, and his voice was loud. "All the guns to us, not any to the Comanche or Cheyenne."

"Is this so, Quanah?" Gray Beard asked. "You promised this to the Kiowa?"

"I can't remember," Quanah said helplessly. "Just before battle, a man might say many things."

Gray Beard regarded Quanah for a long moment. "This can wait. We need to kill the white men first. But leaders must always speak carefully, because others will remember what they say."

"Of course," Quanah said, relief washing over him. "Let's finish this fight."

"We still need bullets," Lone Wolf said. "But there is an easy way for that. We'll just summon the Comanche Spirit Messenger and he can make us some."

Panic surged through Quanah. "No time for that; let's resume the attack. We can use arrows, maybe."

"An easy thing," Lone Wolf said again. "This is what we Kiowa were told. It's time now. Summon your Spirit Messenger."

Quanah looked at Gray Beard, who shrugged. "All right," Quanah said reluctantly. He signaled for Timbo and Yellowfish, two of the People's younger braves, and told them to go to the top of the bluff and fetch Isatai.

After posting a few guards to keep watch over the whites in the huts, the main war party once again moved back across the creek. They milled about until the Spirit Messenger arrived. To Quanah's astonishment, the fat man appeared completely unabashed by the failure of his prophecies. If anything, his attitude was haughty.

"You interrupt my prayers," he said. "Why?"

Some of the warriors began spluttering angry retorts, but Gray Beard held up his hand. "We have a request of you."

"Be quick with it. The spirits are waiting." The heat of the day had Isatai sweating, and much of the yellow paint on his face and chest cascaded down his body in grimy rivulets.

"Bullets," Lone Wolf said. "Give us bullets like you promised. Vomit them up."

"Bullets," Isatai said. "I'll go and consult the spirits." He pulled his pony away but Lone Wolf caught his arm.

"We want the bullets now."

For the first time, Isatai seemed uneasy. He darted a pleading look at Quanah, who gently eased his own pony back, away from the fat man.

Iseeo, perhaps the truest believer, said, "Please, Spirit Messenger. We need the bullets."

"I'll pray on this."

"Bullets now," Lone Wolf said, and some of the Kiowa moved closer.

"The spirits speak to me," Isatai mumbled, and then, more forcefully, "They are angry because the skunk was killed."

"Vomit up the bullets," Lone Wolf commanded, but Isatai couldn't. He sat on his pony sweating and muttering about the dead skunk and someone shouted to kill him and there was general agreement. Several Kiowa grabbed the fat man and yanked him off of his horse. As he sprawled on the ground, Lone Wolf held a knife to his throat. Quanah sat on his pony and watched, thinking Isatai had earned this hard fate and hoping that they'd be satisfied with killing Isatai and wouldn't turn on him next. But Gray Beard muttered something to Medicine Water and the dog soldiers pulled Isatai away from the furious Kiowa. Mochi was among them. She had her knife out and even the most outraged Kiowa shrank back from her.

"Let this man go," Gray Beard said, his voice quiet but commanding all the same. "He will have to live with this disgrace; that's a worse thing than dying." He said to Isatai, "Go back to your Comanche camp if they'll have you. Go *now*," and Isatai did, mounting his pony and riding off. He wept; his shoulders shook. Isatai had gone perhaps two or three bowshots when he looked back and screamed, "It was because you killed the skunk!"

Gray Beard ignored him. He said to the others, "We still have to kill these white men." But instead of riding back in the direction of the camp, Lone Wolf and the Kiowa began trotting away to the north.

"We were tricked into this fight," Lone Wolf called. "No one will trust the Comanche again." Quanah started to ride after the Kiowa to argue, but Gray Beard called him back.

"Let them go. If you plead with Lone Wolf, that would show weakness, and leaders can't do that. We'll take everyone left, your people and mine, and go finish the white men. Then we'll talk about what to do next."

WITH THE LOSS of all the Kiowa, the war party was significantly depleted, but the remaining force still totaled nearly three hundred. The sun was midway through the afternoon sky. There was still time to finish this fight before dark, Quanah thought. Kill all the whites, take their ammunition and other supplies, and then maybe give some of the spoils to the Kiowa, win their allegiance back. It stuck in his throat to forgive Lone Wolf for leaving, but that insult could be overlooked for the present. After the whites were driven away, there would be plenty of time for Quanah and the People to deal with the Kiowa. The important thing was that Isatai, not he, had been blamed for everything that went wrong.

The guards reported that some of the whites had moved back and forth between their huts, but nothing more. None of them had tried to flee the meadow. They were all back inside now. Quanah and Gray Beard agreed they'd retain the same strategy that had come so close to working before. Some groups would fire long-range and keep the whites at bay in their huts, while others would use ground cover to move up close and overrun them.

Quanah knew it was critical for him to demonstrate courage and leadership, so he said the Cheyenne should supply the cover fire while he himself led the warriors of the People in on the huts. He told his warriors to hand over their remaining shells to the dog soldiers; when they got inside the white huts, they would kill the enemy with knives and war clubs. "Everything in there will be shared equally," he assured Gray Beard. He refrained this time from promising too much.

Quanah tried again to take off the Cheyenne headdress. Its feathers were tattered now, stained with dirt or torn and hanging loose. But Gray Beard said he should keep it on: signs of brotherhood were more important than ever.

The war party surrounded the camp again. The Cheyenne unleashed a volley at the three huts, and Quanah's men dropped down and began inching forward. There was steady return fire from the whites, but in his gut Quanah felt that it was almost over, that this fight would be won. As he crawled through high grass toward the hut farthest to the south, he hissed back over his shoulder for the others to keep up, keep moving, and someone called back, "Lead us," and he did: it was exhilarating. In fact, he was probably moving too fast—the others might not be right behind. There was a large, jagged rock sticking up just ahead and he decided to pause there and let everyone else make up ground. When they stood up and charged, they needed to be together. The hut was twenty or thirty paces ahead. The whites in it were trying to shoot out the windows, but the gunfire from the Cheyenne kept driving them back.

Just as Quanah reached the stone, the trailing feathers of his headdress caught on something. He reached back and tugged, but it didn't come free. He wanted to take the headdress off, just leave it there in the high grass, but he'd promised Gray Beard to keep wearing it and he didn't want to break his word. So Quanah paused by the stone, yanking at the tail of the headdress and waiting for the other belly-crawling warriors to reach him.

THIRTY-SIX

McLendon thought the increasingly lengthy pauses between attacks might be worse than the fighting itself. In the chaos of battle, at least there was little time to think about dying, about all the terrible ways the Indians might choose to end his life.

"What's keeping them?" he complained after half an hour had passed since the early afternoon assault. "There's so many of them: Why don't they get it over with?"

"Be glad they're taking all this time," Bat said. "Maybe these delays will give the Army time to get here."

Jim McKinley snorted, though feebly. Fear made it hard to catch his breath. "Forget the Army. They got no idea of what's happening here. MacKenzie's got 'em all down in Mexico anyway, protecting foreigners instead of us from the savages."

"I agree we're on our own," Billy Dixon said. "We need to use this quiet to our advantage if we can. What's the situation out there?"

Some of the others gingerly peeked out the window openings. There were some scattered Indians a few hundred yards away, maybe a dozen in all, spread out along the perimeter of the meadow. Of the others, there was no sign. Bermuda Carlyle speculated that they'd gone back beyond the creek to get water and plan new devilment.

"I never seen Indians acting so," he said. "Thirty years on the damn frontier, and this is the first time I've encountered tribes aligned in one big war party. Co-manch, Cheyenne, Kioway, I guess maybe some Arapaho, who knows?"

"It's a puzzler," Billy agreed. "Well, whatever their reasons, we've another respite. A few of us should run for the two stores, and the others need to man the windows and be ready to provide cover fire if needed. I expect I'll go to Rath and stay: they'll need some assistance there. Somebody else come, too, so you can return here with some boxes of shells."

"I'll go, Billy," McLendon said. Bat volunteered to run to Myers and Leonard's. Hanrahan said he'd go to Rath, too, and return to the saloon with food as well as ammunition. They moved toward the door, and at Billy's nod Frenchy swung it open. The men staying behind leaned out the windows and fired at the Indians standing watch. The Indians returned fire but it was just a few shots, and McLendon surprisingly didn't feel in much danger as he darted along after Billy and Hanrahan toward the Rath store. The door there swung open and Jim Langton urged them inside.

McLendon thought the interior of the saloon had been wrecked, but the condition of the Rath store was worse. Like the saloon, all its windows had been shot out, and sunlight leaked in from bullet holes and improvised gun portholes in the sod walls. But the people in the store had evidently tried to shield themselves with bags of flour, dry beans, and grain. Remnants covered the floor; every step kicked up clouds of flour dust and oat flakes. Someone had vomited repeatedly, probably from fear, and the sour smell hung in the warm air. The store's defenders looked awful too. Tom O'Keefe, the blacksmith, had been cut over the eye and dried blood clotted the side of his face. Andy Johnson, Jim Langton, and George Eddy were merchants, not fighters, and there was an odd distance in their stares as they looked out the window openings, shoulders hunched as they anticipated imminent assault. William Olds sat slumped in a corner, coughing. He had a Sharps Big Fifty across his lap and the heavy gun jerked each time that his chest spasmed.

Hannah Olds was across the room from her husband. She stood close to the wall but didn't lean against it, her body stiff and straight. She was apparently screamed out, her throat too raw to continue shrieking, but the sound coming now from her was worse, a low snuffling moan that seemed more dull acceptance than fright.

"Can you see to the lady?" Billy Dixon asked McLendon, who went over and tried to place a comforting hand on her shoulder. But Mrs. Olds shrank back.

"The Indians are coming," she said, her voice quiet and scratchy. "They're coming back and they're getting in here."

"Shhhh," McLendon said, trying to sound soothing. "They're not getting in here. We're protecting you."

The woman's bony body shuddered. "They're coming. They're going to do things to me."

"No, they're not. They won't." McLendon tried patting her again, and this time she let his hand fall briefly on her arm.

"Kill me before they do it," she pleaded, and all McLendon could think of to say was "I will." That seemed to comfort her a little.

"Can you see to your husband?" he suggested. "He seems poorly over there."

Hannah Olds nodded. "I'll help him," she said, but didn't budge. McLendon patted her arm one more time and went back to Billy Dixon.

"She's lost her mind," he said.

"Well, so long as she's quiet," Billy said. "The screaming made us all feel more fretful."

Jim Langton said everyone in the Rath store was exhausted. "There's only five of us, not counting the woman, and Bill Olds, soon as things commenced, he started hacking and couldn't hardly hold up a gun, let alone shoot it. We others just did what we could. There were savages stacked against the windows and up on the roof. Say, what are you doing, Hanrahan?"

Hanrahan had found a cloth sack somewhere. He was stuffing boxes of shells in it, and also containers of crackers and hunks of bacon.

"I'm putting together supplies for the others back in the saloon. We're out of ammunition, and hungry besides."

"Make a record of what you take, so afterward I can charge you properly."

Hanrahan's face reddened. McLendon braced for some sort of violence, but instead Hanrahan said softly, "Tell you what. We survive a thousand goddamn Indians descending on us, we walk away from this goddamn place, and I will pay you every penny you want to put down on a bill. Agreed?"

"Well, now," Langton said, sounding aggrieved. "I'm just trying to keep track, is all."

"You do that," Hanrahan said. He slung the bag over his shoulder. "Billy, still staying here?" Dixon nodded. "You, too, McLendon? Then I'm going back to my saloon. Good luck."

Tom O'Keefe barred the door behind Hanrahan and Andy Johnson asked, "Why don't we all get into one of the buildings, make our stand there? More firepower."

"No," Dixon said. "That would let the Indians concentrate on just one point of attack. It's better to keep them spread out like they are."

George Eddy, staring out a back window, said, "Get ready, looks like they're back and starting up again." Moments later, there were crashes of fire as Indians hundreds of yards away began shooting.

"Look lively, that's cover for others coming forward through the brush," Billy said. "Damn the angles from these windows—I can't see much."

"You might climb the ladder, Billy," O'Keefe suggested. "There's a small window up there with a better angle down below. We tried it a few times but the fire from the savages drove us back."

"All right," Billy said. O'Keefe, Langton, Johnson, and Eddy began firing out. William Olds stayed coughing in his corner, and Hannah Olds shrank to the floor and tugged a half-empty flour sack over herself. McLendon didn't think it would stop a bullet, but maybe it made her feel marginally safer. "Come on, C.M., come up with me," Billy said. "I'll bring my Big Fifty; you get some shells." McLendon fetched the shells and also a Winchester he saw lying beside the store counter. He clambered up the ladder after Billy. They found themselves on a wide shelf meant for storage. There were sacks of food stacked to the side. It was very hot up there. Sweat dripped onto McLendon's split lip and it stung. He'd forgotten about it. The injury from Shorty Scheidler's punches that had been so bothersome not long before seemed insignificant now. The lip would heal if he lived.

"This is a fine angle," Billy said. "I can look a little down now, see the bastards as they try crawling up." He gestured. McLendon looked, and it seemed to him that fifty yards away he could see the tips of the high grass stalks quivering from movement below rather than the breeze.

"Turkey shoot," Billy said. "Let me get this Fifty loaded and sighted in. You give them some what-for, C.M., but aim at the ones standing back. I want these crawling sons of bitches to think they're goddamn invisible to us."

McLendon leaned past Billy, pointed the Winchester out the window, and blasted several shots. He didn't think he hit anything but it was satisfying to try. "There seem to be a lot of them coming, Billy," he said. "Let 'em come," Billy said, and took a look. "Okay, over there's a bunch. See all the grass move? What's that up in front? Feathers? Shit, one of those bastards has him a fancy headdress."

McLendon looked hard. He saw the grass moving but no feathers. "If you say so."

"No, see that rock? The big one? Right in front."

There was a flash of white, a flicker against the yellow-green grass. "Yes, now I see them, the feathers."

"Well, watch this." Billy aimed and fired, but it wasn't his best shot. Instead of hitting the Indian, the heavy Sharps slug ricocheted off the rock with a sharp clacking sound. "Goddamn," Billy swore. He ejected the spent shell so he could load and fire again. The thick grass boiled with movement and it seemed to McLendon that a dozen Indians popped out. He recognized one, who staggered to his feet. Why was that?

"The one there by the rock, the one with the headdress," McLendon said. "I saw him kill Isaac Scheidler—I think he's their leader. Shoot him, Billy, do it fast!"

Billy had the Big Fifty reloaded and swung it back out through the window. "Turkey shoot," he said again, and squeezed the trigger.

THIRTY-SEVEN

When the bullet ricocheted off the big rock, Quanah felt a terrible impact to his back between his neck and right shoulder blade. The pain was awful and he couldn't stifle a scream. His right arm flopped limply at his side. The shock caused him to rise up on his knees, which lifted his head and chest above the high grass and, he instantly realized, made him a conspicuous target to whoever was shooting from inside the earthen hut. He wanted to duck back down—he tried—but he was in agony. His body writhed independently from what his mind commanded it to do.

Quanah's eyes lifted toward a window opening high up on the wall of the hut. It seemed to him that a long gun barrel was being poked back through it and swinging toward him. He couldn't look away. Then, from behind, hands pulled at him, making the injury to his back hurt even more. Warriors were all around him, dragging him away. There were shots from the hut and some of the ones trying to save Quanah went down themselves. He was sure it would soon be his turn to be shot again, he just couldn't move quickly, but there was the drumming of hoofbeats behind him and then he was being hauled up on a horse behind someone and they galloped off, riding away from the hut and its hateful guns.

Quanah made a great effort and twisted to see his rescuer. It was Medicine Water. It occurred to Quanah that not long ago he was plotting to steal away the Cheyenne dog soldier's wife, and now here he was saving Quanah's life.

When Medicine Water thought they were a safe distance away, he brought his pony to a halt, dismounted, and helped Quanah down.

"Let's see your wound," he said, and Quanah sat on the ground. Medicine Water examined his back and said, "Good, there's no open wound. The bullet hit you but did not enter your body. You're not even bleeding. It will hurt you badly but in a few days you'll be able to use your arm again."

That was a relief. "I've seen such wounds," Quanah said. "I'll be all right. Let's get back to the fight."

"What fight?" Medicine Water asked. He gestured back toward the white camp and Quanah saw that the warriors of the People who'd been crawling toward the huts were now on their feet, retreating. Behind them, the Cheyenne no longer provided covering fire. Some of them had their bows out and were arcing arrows toward the huts, but these stuck harmlessly in the outer earthen walls.

"Why have they stopped?"

"We've used our last bullets. Now everyone wants to get away from the white guns."

"But we were so close! We can still fight, we can still kill all the whites."

"Perhaps," Medicine Water said. "Can you get back up on my pony with me? Gray Beard is calling us all together at the end of the meadow."

The remaining members of the war party, numbering perhaps two hundred and fifty, gathered northwest of the white camp at the base of some low hills. They were a dozen bowshots or more away from the huts. Gray Beard summarized the situation. They had no more ammunition.

Because the huts were impervious to arrows and lances, and since the defenders had too many bullets to count, it would be foolish to keep charging. They might be able to overrun the huts with sheer numbers, but in doing so too many attackers would die. But there might be a better way. The fight could still be won.

"These whites have no way of escaping their camp," Gray Beard said. "All of their horses are dead. They could try to walk or run, but there are enough of us to make a circle around this valley and stop anyone who tries. We have our bows, and if they try to get away they have to come out from behind their earthen walls and we can kill them then."

Wild Horse, who came from the same Quahadi camp as Quanah, asked, "What if the whites never come out? They can just stay inside and laugh at us."

"They'll come out," Gray Beard said confidently. "They'll want to get away from here. Look, some of them are coming out now."

Down in the white camp, a few figures emerged from the huts. They talked and one pointed across the meadow to where the war party was gathered below the hills. Some of the Indians couldn't resist screaming insults. In response, the whites raised their rifles.

"They're too far away," someone said, and there were puffs of smoke, and even as the *crack* of the shots reached their ears, two Cheyenne were knocked from their horses and one of the People swayed as a bullet tore through his shoulder.

"Move back!" Medicine Water shouted, and they did, galloping across the creek toward the high bluff. Several of the Cheyenne paused to help their fallen tribesmen, and one of these would-be rescuers was killed by another long, accurate shot.

Quanah still rode behind Medicine Water. When Mochi rode up beside them, Quanah said, "They're hunters, they can shoot very far." Mochi didn't reply. She looked furious.

The war party made its way up the bluff and stopped at the top. They were far enough away from the white camp now that it was impossible for bullets to reach them there. It was close to sunset and shadows cut across the floor of the meadow. Quanah dropped down from Medicine Water's side and slumped on the ground. His back hurt terribly. Some of his friends among the People bent and whispered words of encouragement, but in general everyone seemed discouraged. They'd expected to win easily, then they fought all day, and now they'd been driven up the bluff and the white men walked freely out in front of their huts.

"Stay strong," Gray Beard said. "Tonight the white men will try to gather their courage and tomorrow they'll run. We'll get them then."

The dog soldiers sent out warriors to guard the edges of the valley and report any attempts at a night escape. The rest of the war party camped on the bluff. They ate pemmican. The dried buffalo meat was flavored with honey but no one cared to savor the taste. They drank creek water and those who were hurt nursed their wounds.

Spotted Feather, Quanah's Cheyenne friend, came over to where he was sitting and offered some pemmican.

"You need to eat something," he told Quanah. "You've been injured and you need nourishment."

The pemmican didn't seem worth the trouble of chewing, but Quanah choked down a few bites to be polite. "What's that black thing on your belt?"

Spotted Feather pulled free a hank of dark fur and held it out for Quanah's inspection. "The dog that fought me had great courage. I scalped it to do it honor." In the fading light, Quanah saw that Spotted Feather's arm had been deeply scored by the dog's teeth; he would have many scars.

"It was a brave dog," Quanah agreed, and settled himself as comfortably as he could. He lay awake all night because his back hurt so much.

THIRTY-EIGHT

Warriors pulling their injured comrade away thwarted Billy Dixon's plan to finish off the Indian leader. Billy took down a brave with a quick shot and had hopes of sharpshooting the wounded one in the headdress, but then another Indian on horseback swooped in, hauled the injured man up behind him, and galloped off before Billy could shoot again.

"Goddamn, he got away," Billy said. "I wanted that one bad." But there were other targets out in the grass, and he kept firing. So did McLendon and the others down below them. The barrage drove back the attackers who'd slithered forward in the grass. They stood and ran, and then behind them the other Indians stopped shooting altogether. It seemed to McLendon that they were in full-scale retreat. "What's happening?" he asked Billy. "Why are they running? There're still so many of them."

Billy rested the heavy barrel of the Sharps on the bottom of the window opening. "They may be running short of ammunition, I expect. The Indians seldom have much of a supply, and they've put down a fearsome amount of fire all day."

For the first time, McLendon felt a surge of hope. "Are we home free, then? Are they finished?"

"Oh, I doubt it. They made this fight in a different way, all the tribes combined. They'll not want to leave here defeated. Even lacking bullets, they still have considerable numbers on us. We're not out of this fix yet."

They went down the ladder and rejoined the others on the ground floor of the store. William Olds still coughed in his corner, and Hannah Olds had her fist pressed to her mouth. But everyone else was jubilant.

"They run, damn them!" Andy Johnson exulted. "We fought them off. Tales will long be told in our honor."

"We don't know the end of this tale yet," Billy cautioned. He peered through a window on the north wall and, craning his neck to see around the far corner of the corral adjacent to Myers and Leonard's, pointed to where the war party had gathered at the foot of the hills. "They've reconvened at some distance. I believe it's far enough removed so that we might step just outside this room, should any of you wish to. But be alert. They could turn and be back on us in an eyeblink."

William and Hannah Olds stayed inside. The others followed Billy out the door, blinking like moles in the late afternoon glare. Men emerged from Myers and Leonard's and the saloon, too, looking around cautiously, rifles ready. They edged away from the buildings but not too far, stepping carefully over bodies of dead Indians, poking them with gun barrels, but eliciting no signs of life. McLendon looked at the corpses, at the swarthy skin torn by bullets and smeared with paint, dirt, and blood. Most had their eyes open. He tried to think of them as fellow human beings, but couldn't. They were Indians and they had been trying to kill him.

"I believe they're all properly dead," Mike McCabe said. "The hurt ones were carried off. I hate the damn savages, but they demonstrated courage doing that, not abandoning their wounded."

"Mike, it seemed to me that you at Myers and Leonard might have lost one or two of your own," Billy said. "It was about the time that the Indians killed off the animals in the corral."

"Billy Tyler and Fred Leonard made a foolish dash out. Fred somehow got back unscathed, but Tyler took one through the lungs. He was alive when we pulled him back inside but passed soon afterward. He suffered considerably."

McLendon stared at the Indians near the base of the hills. There were still so many. They weren't that far away. He thought that if they turned and charged together, they would probably cut off at least some of the whites before they could get back inside the sod huts.

"They're not leaving, Billy," he said to Dixon. "What should we do?"

"They've made us jump all day, now it's their turn," Billy said. He told the hunters—Dutch Henry, Bermuda Carlyle, Charley Armitage, and a few others—to lift their Henrys. Together they fired a barrage at the Indians, who were about five hundred yards away. Several fell back off their horses. The white men reloaded and fired again. The Indians began riding away hard; they pounded across the creek and were lost to sight behind the bluff. A few stayed behind, trying to help away wounded braves. Dutch Henry dropped one of the would-be rescuers with a fine shot and yelled exultantly.

"We've drove 'em off, boys!" he proclaimed. But Mike McCabe pointed to the top of the bluff.

"Nope, they've just repositioned," he said. "Up there's a good three-quarters of a mile distant, well beyond our shooting range. They're going to perch awhile, I expect."

"To what purpose?" George Eddy asked.

McCabe jerked a thumb toward Eddy. "There speaks a man who keeps books in an office. Mr. Eddy, those Indians are working out new ways to slaughter us."

"But I heard Billy Dixon say that they've run out of bullets."

McCabe heaved an exaggerated sigh. "Mr. Eddy, maybe they have no more ammunition, but they've still got arrows and lances and knives and the surliest of dispositions. Look at them all up there. Likely there's further fighting to come."

Dutch Henry, Jim Campbell, Old Man Keeler, and Tom O'Keefe made their way to the Scheidlers' overturned wagon. They called Billy Dixon over and McLendon went too. Isaac and Shorty Scheidler's corpses had been butchered like cattle, cut into chunks that were strewn for yards in the dust. Both had been scalped, pubic hair as well as head. The Indians had even ripped off the growth in their armpits. O'Keefe turned away and puked.

"We can't leave 'em like this," Campbell said. Bat Masterson fetched two shovels from Myers and Leonard's and he and Campbell hastily dug a wide grave. Then, using the shovels, they picked up Scheidler body parts and deposited them in the hole. Mostly there was no way to tell one brother's bits from the other's, except Isaac's legs were longer and of course their heads looked different. Then they took Billy Tyler's body from the Myers and Leonard store and placed it in the same hole.

"When all this is finished, we'll dig those boys a proper grave," Billy Dixon said. "Let's fill this one in for now and get back inside. We can take turns on guard tonight, and everybody can get some supper and sleep. We'll need to be fresh for whatever happens in the morning."

McLendon had tried not to look at the Scheidlers or Billy Tyler. Instead he found himself gazing at the body of Maurice, the black Newfoundland. There was a pink patch on its head where some fur between its ears was missing, and McLendon wondered what happened to it. When Billy Dixon called for him to come on, McLendon reflexively leaned down and patted the dead dog's side. As he did, he noticed that there was still something on the sleeve of his shirt, stiffened matter that he knew was dried blood and brains from the Indian whose head he'd burst during the battle. Before, the sight, even the thought, would have repulsed him. Now he simply tried brushing the gore off with his fingers. He felt that something in him was changed forever. If he lived, he'd try to think about what it might be.

After the guard was posted—Ed Trevor, Billy Ogg, Jim Langton, and Frenchy stood first watch—the others gathered in the Myers and Leonard store, since it was the biggest space. Old Man Keeler fixed a good supper of buffalo steaks and coffee. Mrs. Olds was supposed to help him but didn't. She and her husband stayed away from everyone else. He coughed and she cried. McLendon and Masterson tried to comfort her but couldn't. After a while they gave up, got plates of food, and ate. McLendon was surprised to feel so hungry. Bat told him that it was natural after a long, hard fight.

"Don't pretend you've ever experienced anything else like this," McLendon said.

"I haven't, it's true, but neither has just about any other fellow living. We're making history here, C.M. Books will be written about it."

"Will you be the one to write them?"

"I might. But right now, I'm thinking that in the morning we can maybe run off that bunch on the bluff and then make our way back to Dodge City. I expect to entertain the whores there for hours with thrilling tales of my exploits in the Battle of Adobe Walls."

"All that's happened, and you're thinking of whores."

"I don't have a lady friend like yours to run to, that one out in Arizona Territory."

McLendon realized that he hadn't thought of Gabrielle once during the entire day. He made up for it the rest of the night, working out how he'd tell her about fighting the Indians, how he'd felt, what he'd done—

not exaggerating his actions, of course, but if she wanted to think that he was the bravest man in the West, well, that was her right. Although, since Gabrielle understood him so well, she'd undoubtedly know better. He'd be with her soon, thank God.

Exhaustion set in. The terrors of the day had caught up with them. Billy Dixon urged everyone not to slip over to the saloon for a quick drink. The Indians were still out there; the defenders would need all their faculties tomorrow. They changed the guard—Mike McCabe, Andy Johnson, Jim McKinley, and Charley Armitage took the next turn— and everyone else slept as best they could. Hannah Olds cried all night, but her soft sobs actually seemed soothing after a while.

McLENDON MISSED GUARD DUTY. He suspected Billy passed him over because he was so inexperienced, but he didn't mind. Just as the sun sent its first morning rays over the hills to the east, he went outside. He hoped the Indians were gone from the top of the bluff but they were still there, mounted and watching. Most of the morning the whites braced themselves for another attack, but the Indians didn't move.

"They want us to run," Bat said. "They know we've got no mounts; we'd have to go on foot. We do that, they'll overtake us on their horses and cut us down. They're out of our rifle range up there. We seem safe if we stay where we are."

"So what happens?"

"I got no damn idea."

Everyone in camp stayed close to the buildings. They couldn't relax in case the Indians charged from the bluff. It was another hot day, and the bodies of the dead Indians and animals began to bloat and stink. They needed to be buried, but that would attract too much attention from the war party on the bluff.

By late morning the stench and the tension had everyone on edge. Dutch Henry and Bermuda Carlyle almost came to blows over a twist of tobacco. Old Man Keeler told Hannah Olds to please shut the hell up with the sobbing. William Olds, still hacking, perked up at that and told Keeler to apologize to his wife or fight him. Keeler apologized and Mr. Olds took his Sharps Big Fifty and made a show of standing guard by the Rath store front door, though he had to set down the heavy gun after a few seconds when he was wracked with a particularly heavy coughing spell.

Billy Dixon and Jim Hanrahan talked about what to do. Hanrahan thought the only choice was to stay where they were.

"We've got food, we've got water," he said. "We just have to show more patience than the savages."

Billy disagreed. "They've got water, too, and there's plenty of game in the area for them. Besides, there's lots of small white hunting parties scattered around the area. Some of them are bound to come this way, planning on selling hides in this camp, and they'll be picked off as they do. We got to get those Indians down from that bluff, drive them off."

"You figure out a way, be sure and let me know," Hanrahan said. "Less than thirty of us, probably still more than a thousand of them. Bastards are having a fine time, sitting up there and watching us sweat."

Shortly after noontime the wind picked up, blowing across the camp from west to east. Peering up at the Indians, McLendon thought he could see some of the feathers in their war bonnets being pushed back by the breeze.

"Feels good to have some air, Billy," he said to Dixon, who looked thoughtful. Billy wet his finger with some spit and held it up.

"Maybe," he muttered to himself. "Nothing lost if not." He picked up his Big Fifty and walked to where a wagon stood near the front of the saloon. He pointed the rifle at the Indians high on the bluff, resting the barrel on the rim of the wagon bed.

"Oh, don't waste a bullet, Dixon," Bermuda Carlyle said. "Three-quarter mile, you won't come within twenty yards."

"Maybe not," Billy replied, squinting as he sighted. "But I'm using a charge I packed myself, extra powder grains for more carry. And the wind will help."

Everyone gathered behind Billy. It seemed to McLendon that the Indians up on the bluff weren't concerned. They didn't pull back from the edge or try to take cover.

"Now," Billy said, and he fired. The Big Fifty gave a concussive thump. It seemed like a very long time and then up on the bluff an Indian screamed and fell back.

"Goddamn," Carlyle blurted. "Ever'body with a big Sharps, fire away." They did. Puffs of dust partway up the bluff indicated that their shots were falling well short, but the gunfire was noisy and the way the Indians milled about indicated that they were panicking, Billy's shot had been that spectacular. As the whites in camp watched, the Indians gradually moved back from the edge of the bluff and out of sight. The last one left wore a long headdress, and one of his arms dangled at his side. By now McLendon knew him well; he would appear in his nightmares for years to come. Headdress Indian stared down at the camp for several moments before turning away.

"Get ready to duck inside, they may be massing for a charge," Billy warned, and everyone moved toward the buildings. They waited almost an hour, but no Indians came. Some of the men wanted to go out toward the creek, see what the war party might be up to, but Billy said they needed to wait some more just in case. It was mid-afternoon before he said it might be all right to take a look, though it would be very dangerous if the Indians still lingered back behind the bluff where they couldn't be seen from camp. Bat Masterson, Mike McCabe, and Billy Ogg volunteered. They went out cautiously, looking behind every tree and rock, and eventually disappeared into the brush by the creek. They were away for a long time, and when they returned they said that there was no sign of Indians anywhere, even down past the bluff. The war party was gone.

THIRTY-NINE

In the morning, the mood of many in the war party atop the bluff approached mutinous. All night, warriors gathered in small groups and complained, about false prophets and poor preparation and the unfair advantages of the white men down below—their earthen huts, their endless supplies of ammunition, their near-magical rifles that fired so far and so accurately. There was rampant grief, too—almost everyone among the attackers had lost a father, son, brother, cousin, or at least a close friend. The remaining hope for victory was that the whites would try to escape the valley on foot, but they stayed where they were. Inaction gave the warriors even more time to brood.

"We should wait through the day and go in at them after dark, maybe," Quanah suggested. He and some of the Cheyenne leaders were huddled, discussing possible strategy. "We might take them by surprise."

"They put guards out last night, and tonight they will again," Stone Calf said. "They know we're still here, we can't surprise them anymore."

"Let's pretend to leave," Quanah said. "We'll let them see us ride away. Then tonight we can circle back."

Stone Calf shook his head. "No. If my people leave, we'll keep going.

Most of my warriors want to go back to the agency. Then, when the white army hears about this fight and looks for someone to punish, we can say we were never here."

Quanah thought that was cowardly and started to say so, but Gray Beard intervened. They might as well stay up on the bluff a while longer and watch the white camp, he said. Perhaps the men down there would still try to escape on foot. If they didn't, then at the end of the day the war party could disperse. At that point, everyone could make his own choice: to return to a village or the agency, or to stay out and find other white victims who might be easier to kill.

"I know what I'll choose," Quanah said angrily as Gray Beard led him away from the others.

"You won't be able to fight for a while, until your arm is healed," Gray Beard said. "Anyway, this fight is over. You know that. Those whites down there are too smart to let us attack them out in the open. We'll stay up here a little more so they'll know we're leaving because we choose to, not because they chased us away. Stone Calf is right: when they hear what's happened the white soldiers will come. We'll need all of our warriors to be willing to fight then, so it will be good to get away from this place and its bad memories. There are going to be more battles—many of them. Be wise: Know when to give up in one fight so you can lead in others."

"We should have won here."

"But we didn't. Learn from this and win next time."

MOST OF THE INDIANS gathered on the front edge of the bluff and looked down at the white camp. The stink of putrefying human bodies and animal carcasses wafted up. It galled the warriors to see their dead comrades bloating in the heat. The war party's continued presence was for show now. There had been no formal declaration of this from the leaders, but everyone knew it. Some of the People gratified Quanah by telling him that they knew none of this was his fault, it was all because of fat, lying Isatai. Though the self-proclaimed Spirit Messenger had escaped death at the hands of the Kiowa, Quanah wondered if he might not end up dying at the hands of his own tribesmen. Some of the Quahadi muttered things about slitting his throat if he dared to show his face back in their village. Quanah didn't care whether Isatai died or not. At least he himself had escaped blame. He would lead war parties again, just as soon as his arm was better. He felt compelled to kill more white people very soon, to wipe away the shame of failing to annihilate everyone in the hunting camp. There was no chance of any future tribal coalitions, he knew. It would be back to the old ways of individual camps and smaller raiding parties. Because the spirits and magic had failed them, the People would return to tradition for some measure of comfort. But at least there would still be fighting.

The sun was midway through the sky and Quanah was sprawled on a blanket, looking up at the clouds, when Spotted Feather called him over to the precipice facing the white camp. "Something strange is happening," he said. "You'll want to see this." Quanah wondered what could possibly be so unusual but obligingly got up, cradling his right arm as he did.

Down in the white camp, one of the men stood behind a wagon and aimed his rifle up at the bluff. He was so far away that he was really just a tiny dot. The Indians laughed and hooted at him. Spotted Feather, standing at Quanah's side, could scarcely control his mirth.

"He'd have a better chance throwing his bullet at us," he said. Then some smoke puffed from the end of the white man's rifle. It took time for the sound of the shot to reach the war party, and at that same moment there was a meaty *thunk* and Spotted Feather yowled and staggered back. Quanah thought at first he had fainted and wondered why, and then he looked at Spotted Feather where he lay and saw a bloody hole in his abdomen. His friend had been shot right through the black dog fur scalp that he so proudly wore on his belt.

All around, warriors cried out in surprise and horror, and down in the camp the rest of the white men started firing furiously. No one else atop the bluff was hit but that didn't matter, because they knew now that they were vulnerable. The white men could kill them even up there. Some of the Indians clambered down the back of the bluff to where their horses were tethered and rode away fast, going north and west back to villages or agencies. These desertions came steadily. Before Spotted Feather's blood was dry in the dirt, more than half of the war party was gone.

Medicine Water had some of the dog soldiers wrap Spotted Feather's body in blankets and tie it to a horse. "We'll take him back to his family in our village," he told Gray Beard. "Are you coming?"

"I am," the Cheyenne chief said. "Quanah, you need to take your people home too. This is over."

Quanah saw Mochi standing by her husband. Her right eye was still puffy but a small slit had opened between the lids and he thought she could probably see a little out of it. "Are you going home too?" he asked.

"For a little while. Then I'll go out and kill more white people." She meant it, he knew. For Mochi, the fight would end only with her own death.

When the Cheyenne were gone, only men of the People remained, obviously waiting for Quanah. For all the disappointments of the past few days, he was still the leader until they returned home.

Quanah walked back to the edge of the bluff to take a last, lingering look at the white camp. He knew it was dangerous—that they might shoot him—but he didn't care: maybe dying that way would be best. He wondered how he'd be treated when he got back to his village. Would they honor him there for what he had tried to do? Down below, the whites stared back at him. Quanah thought about making some grand final gesture, screaming in defiance, perhaps, but his dangling arm hurt and he simply sighed and turned away. At the bottom of the bluff someone helped him mount his pony, and he rode off without looking back.

FORTY

It was mid-afternoon before everyone felt sure that the Indians were gone—"At least for the present," Billy Dixon cautioned. "We must remain alert." But there was no more immediate danger, and that was liberating. People laughed for no reason. Some couldn't seem to stop smiling. McLendon's mood was thoughtful. He had trouble believing he'd survived such a pitched battle. He hadn't been a hero, but he'd done his best. Now he wanted to get far away from Adobe Walls. Billy and some of the others seemed to think it might be at least a few more days. There were no horses and they didn't want to risk walking out, so they'd have to wait until help arrived, probably from other white hunting parties.

The smell was the big problem. They had to get rid of all the dead animals, and the Indians too. They stitched together some buffalo hides, inserted ropes through holes cut along the edges, and rolled individual horses or oxen on top of the hides. It was messy work. If they didn't roll them just right, their hands ripped through the skins and into the putrefying, jellied insides. Then, using the ropes, they dragged the hides away from the camp and out into the meadow. They dumped the dead beast there and went back for the next. This took nearly until dark, because there were almost sixty dead animals. Everyone pitched in except Mrs. Olds. When she saw that her pet foal was among the slaughtered horses, she cried anew. Bat asked McLendon, "How much water can that woman have in her?" But she was the only nonparticipant. Even her husband tugged on a rope.

When the stock was disposed of, they turned to the Indians. First, many of the hunters and crewmen stripped the corpses of souvenirs— beaded belts, scalping knives, anything that caught their eyes. Even Billy Dixon took a fancy silver-medallioned bridle off a dead Indian pony. McLendon didn't want such grisly mementos, and turned down a war club that Bat Masterson offered him.

"You ought to come away with at least one keepsake, C.M.," Bat argued, but McLendon said that the memories of the battle would be plenty for him.

Dutch Henry Borne, Bermuda Carlyle, and Frenchy lingered by the body of the Indian who'd painted himself black. They pushed at the corpse with the toes of their boots and lamented that they couldn't find the bugle. One of the Indians must have picked it up and carried it off during the fight. To McLendon's dismay, Borne and Carlyle argued over which of them had killed "the buffalo soldier deserter."

"You shot him, Billy," he said to Dixon. "And it's obvious he's not a black man, he's an Indian covered in black paint. Anybody can see that. They're standing right over him and lying."

Billy chuckled. "Ah, people see what they want to. It's a rule in life. They want that dead'un to be a bugle-blowing buffalo soldier deserter, so he is. You wait until they get back to Dodge and hear the stories they'll tell then."

"But they're taking credit for something you did."

"So what? Those boys know what happened here will be the stuff of legend, and they want their prominent places in it. For the rest of their lives, they'll speak of shooting down the black bugler, and there'll always be somebody to buy them a beer for the privilege of listening. I don't mind. I know what really happened, and that's enough."

The state of the Scheidler brothers' bodies evoked considerable comment. Jim McKinley said the mutilations proved that the Indians were nothing but animals—"Sick, crazy ones at that."

"Anyone who desecrates a man beyond killing him should burn in a special place in hell," Bermuda Carlyle declared. "I always hated Indians, but now I hate them more."

Before they allowed the dead Indians to be hauled off on the makeshift hide travois, Carlyle and McKinley took axes and hacked off the corpses' heads. Then they stuck the heads on poles along the corral fence.

As darkness fell and buzzards swooped in to pick at animal and Indian carcasses, everyone ate dinner, bacon and biscuits, plus all the coffee they could hold, and talked about the fight. Nobody was sure how many Indians had attacked. Estimates ranged into the several thousands, and never less than eight or nine hundred. When asked his opinion, McLendon said truthfully, "I don't know, just more than I thought I could count," and everybody laughed and clapped him on the back. He volunteered to stand guard that night, and didn't see or hear anything suspicious. It really was over.

THE NEXT DAY, a party of a dozen hunters and crew members rode in from the north with a load of buffalo hides they intended to sell at one of the camp stores. They hadn't seen any signs of Indians at all, and were astonished to hear about the battle. Two volunteered to ride to Dodge for help, and several others rode back out to find and warn other hunting parties in the area that hostiles were on the warpath. By nightfall, three dozen more white men had arrived and there was almost a party atmosphere in camp. Jim Hanrahan found some cases of unbroken beer bottles and reopened his saloon. The merchants cleaned up the two stores and found that some stock remained to sell. Prices doubled. Jim Langton said he no longer felt the need to return to Dodge immediately because it was apparently going to be business as usual, except with additional profit.

"Aren't you worried that the Indians might again return in force?" McLendon asked.

"Ah, we whipped 'em once, and will again if they didn't learn their lesson the first time."

"I don't know that it was a whipping," McLendon said, but Langton was busy selling canned tomatoes to one of the latest arrivals.

Some of the battle survivors, Carlyle and Dutch Henry and Bat Masterson in particular, reveled in telling wide-eyed camp newcomers all about the fight. Even William Olds did a little bragging. He said he'd used his Sharps Big Fifty to "lethal effect." The sickly man was so energized that, on the third night after the battle, he said he'd stand guard duty. He struggled up the ladder to the loft in the Rath store where he'd left his rifle, retrieved it, and then tumbled off the ladder on his way down. The stock of the rifle hit the floor and apparently he'd foolishly had the weapon cocked. The rifle fired and blew his head off. Hannah Olds proved that she hadn't yet screamed herself out. It took a long time to sop up all the blood. The dead man's wife cried less for him than her foal. After so many tears, Bat speculated, she was finally running dry. They buried Mr. Olds by the Scheidlers and Billy Tyler, and promised Mrs. Olds that they'd soon have her back in Dodge. From there she could make her way to family in the East.

Five days after the fight, they organized a traveling party to Kansas. There were plenty of wagons in camp now, and the newly arrived hunting crews all had extra horses. None of the merchants wanted to go. They struck deals with some of the teamsters to return from Dodge with wagonloads of supplies for the stores and saloon. But all of the original hunters and their men were ready to go, some sick of Adobe Walls and its bloody memories, others anxious to return to civilization and enjoy the celebrity they felt certain they'd enjoy there. McLendon couldn't wait to leave. All he wanted now was to get to the Dodge City train depot and begin the long, circuitous route from there to Arizona Territory— a train east to Kansas City, another west to Denver, and from there the stage to Tucson and Florence and finally Mountain View, where Gabrielle was waiting. He sat on a wagon bench beside a teamster who quizzed him about the battle. McLendon offered vague responses and wished the Dodge-bound procession would move faster.

They were almost six hours out of Adobe Walls before McLendon realized that he'd left his few possessions behind in the camp—spare clothes and his copy of *The Last of the Mohicans*, that cherished gift from Gabrielle. For a moment he mourned, then shrugged. These were just *things*, even the book. He was escaping Adobe Walls with his life, and on his way to the woman he loved. He didn't think much about St. Louis, his young wife who had died there, his vengeful father-in-law, or the hulking killer he'd set on McLendon's trail. That was all in the past. He was moving on.

The trip took six days. It should have only taken five, but on the afternoon of the second day they came upon a sickening scene. A small party of buffalo hunters had been caught out by some roving war party. Seven corpses, mutilated almost beyond imagination, attested to the fury of the Indians. The bodies were solemnly buried, and prayers were said. That took some time. McLendon remembered the horrific demise of Mirkle Jones, the amiable Creole, and had to wipe his eyes.

.   .   .

WORD OF THE ADOBE WALLS fight reached Dodge well before the caravan arrived. People lined the streets and greeted them with cheers. The fight survivors were practically pulled down from horses and wagons and hauled directly into Tom Sherman's dance hall and saloon, where their admirers stood them to endless drinks. The worshipful throng wasn't just made up of town working class—McLendon saw business leaders Herman Fringer and Fred Zimmermann at the forefront of the crowd. Some of the Adobe Walls survivors vied for attention. Bermuda Carlyle and Dutch Henry Borne both claimed to have killed a buffalo soldier bugler, and to McLendon's dismay Bat Masterson also insisted it was his shot that brought the "black fella" down. Sherman, awed by the tales, offered "my whores—no, I mean, my *dancers*" to Carlyle and Henry and Bat "on the house in honor of your achievement, whichever one of you it was." They trooped off with the women on their arms. The others sat and drank and talked some more. A lieutenant from Fort Dodge appeared and asked if the gentlemen from Adobe Walls might come talk to the commanding officer. They informed him that they were still too tuckered from the battle to go just then, but would as soon as they recovered, maybe in a day or two. The lieutenant said that the commander was excited. This attack was just what was needed to convince the brass back in Washington, D.C., that the Comanche, Kiowa, and Cheyenne hostiles had to be exterminated once and for all.

"Full war on them's coming, wait and see," the lieutenant predicted. Someone handed him a beer and he toasted the men of the hour before reporting back to the fort.

Billy Dixon got caught up in all the worship and described his shot that took down the Indian high up on the bluff. The distance was a mile at least, Billy estimated, maybe a mile and a quarter or even a mile and a half. He'd aimed at an Indian who'd been especially active in the previous day's fighting, and hit him square. That elicited gasps of wonder, and Dixon beamed. McLendon tried not to feel too disappointed. Billy was human, after all.

McLendon himself lingered for about an hour of backslapping. He drank one beer and took some polite sips of a second, but then slipped away. He had a chit for two hundred dollars signed by Fred Leonard to be redeemed at the Pioneer Store. After that, he wanted a bath, a bed for the night, and a morning departure on the train. It would have been nice to say good-bye to Billy and Bat, but they were busy and he knew they wouldn't notice that he was gone. Maybe he'd see them in the morning if they were up early enough, though he doubted it.

McLendon remembered the boardinghouse run by the Burgesses, where he'd planned to live before he decided to go along on the Adobe Walls expedition. They were nice people. Surely they'd be able to give him a hot bath and a room for the night at a reasonable rate. He didn't have all the money he'd wanted before making the journey to Mountain View. After cashing his chit and accepting praise from the Pioneer Store staff as well as the money, he had enough for train and stage fare to Arizona Territory with some money left over, but not sufficient to get himself and Gabrielle, plus her father if she wanted, the rest of the way to California. Well, they'd figure it out. That Gabrielle would choose him over Joe Saint he had no doubt. He'd lived through the battle for a reason. McLendon stopped on his way to the boardinghouse to send a telegram to Gabrielle. It said simply, "I'M COMING ARRIVE MAYBE TWO WEEKS LOVE YOU CASH McLENDON." He wanted to say more, but it was a dollar for ten words.

He was almost to the boardinghouse when he remembered he still had on the same shirt that he'd worn during the fight. Rust-colored bloodstains remained on one sleeve, and there were numerous tears from bits of flying glass and other debris. It wouldn't do to wear that shirt for a romantic reunion. In fact, he needed a complete new change of clothes. Well, there went another ten or twenty dollars.

There was a dry goods store near the Burgess boardinghouse and he stopped in there. The clerk, a stout young man, lit up as McLendon entered.

"You're one of them!" he exclaimed. "I came out and saw y'all arrive on the wagons. I wanted to come to the saloon, but couldn't leave the shop unattended. Sir, you're a hero and it's an honor to be in your presence."

McLendon reminded himself to be gracious. "You're very kind. As you might have noticed, my clothes are worse for wear and I need to replace them."

"Look at that split lip on you—those hostiles busted you up some," the clerk said. He added hopefully, "Hand-to-hand fighting?"

McLendon's lip was somewhat healed but still swollen. He saw no point in telling the truth: that punches from another white man did the damage. "There was a lot going on. All of us got marked a little. Now, about some clothes?"

The youngster hustled to set out shirts and trousers, drawers, and socks. McLendon made his choices based on price and practicality: denim rather than gabardine pants, because they were cheaper and more durable. The shirt he selected was light brown; he thought the dust inevitably kicked up by stagecoach teams would show less on it.

"Can I put these fresh things on if I promise to pay for them?" he asked, and the clerk nodded enthusiastically. So McLendon went into the back of the store, shucked off his old garments, and put on the new ones. The clean clothes felt wonderful. He wished he could have bathed first, but he'd attend to that next at the boardinghouse. He tucked his old shirt, pants, and drawers under his arm, went to the counter, and handed over twelve dollars.

"No charge for a hero," he was informed. "My boss would agree, and, if not, I'll pay this myself."

McLendon thanked him. "Would you dispose of these for me?" he asked the clerk, indicating the old clothes.

The boy reached out and took them. He spread them on the counter and touched the bloodstained shirt reverently with a fingertip.

"Could I keep this, sir?"

"What for?"

"Oh, you know," the young clerk said, suddenly sounding very shy. "This shirt is special. Why, it was at the battle of Adobe Walls. It's part of history now, just like you."

McLendon considered that. "Yes," he finally said. "I suppose it is."

NOTES

Buffalo Trail is history-based fiction. With the exception of Cash Mc-Lendon, all the main characters really did exist. In general, the battle happened (mostly) as described, though I've conflated some events for storytelling purposes. For those who want more of the real history, I have three books to recommend: *Billy Dixon & Adobe Walls: Life and Adventures of "Billy" Dixon* by Billy Dixon (Leonaur Press); S. C. Gwynne's justly acclaimed *Empire of the Summer Moon: Quanah Parker and the Rise and Fall of the Comanches, the Most Powerful Indian Tribe in American History* (Scribner); and, above all, the comprehensive and masterful *Adobe Walls: The History and Archeology of the 1874 Trading Post* by T. Lindsay Baker and Billy R. Harrison (Texas A&M University Press). If more fiction is what you crave, you must read Jan Reid's *Comanche Sundown* (TCU Press), a brilliant novel based on much of Quanah Parker's life.

You can visit the Adobe Walls battle site if you're willing to endure some rough-and-tumble driving. Take Texas Highway 207 north of Borger and Stinnett, then turn east at the appropriate highway marker.

After following narrow blacktop and dirt roads for another fifteen or sixteen dusty miles, you'll be there. I promise, it's worth the effort. On the way home, stop off in the town of Canyon to visit the amazing Panhandle-Plains Historical Museum, which has a display of Adobe Walls memorabilia, including Quanah's eagle feather war bonnet.

ACKNOWLEDGMENTS

Above all, thanks to the wonderful staff at the Panhandle-Plains Historical Museum, who patiently answered all of my questions and offered additional information that proved invaluable—for instance, about Mochi's probable presence at the battle. My imagination took it from there.

Anne Collier provided last-minute research assistance. My agent, Jim Donovan, was always supportive, and Christine Pepe, Michael Barson, Kelly Welsh Rudolph, and Ivan Held at Putnam were there when I needed them.

As I wrote, my usual team of readers followed along, providing constructive criticism. James Ward Lee, Carlton Stowers, and Mike Blackman always make my books better.

Cash McLendon will be back soon.

Everything I write is always for Nora, Adam, Grant, and Harrison.

TURN THE PAGE FOR AN EXCERPT

Cash McLendon faces stone-cold enforcer Killer Boots in an Old West showdown. After Killer Boots kidnaps Cash's old flame, Cash hits the trail in hot pursuit, hoping to make a trade before it's too late.

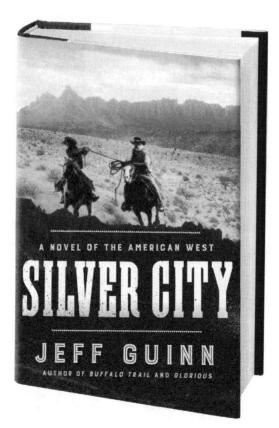

 Penguin Random House

ST. LOUIS, AUGUST 1874

The fat man brought two armed guards with him to the midnight meeting along the Mississippi River docks in St. Louis. The bodyguards were rough-looking men who obviously relished a fight. There was a full moon, and its light revealed that both had pistols tucked into the waistbands of their trousers, with the handles angled for easy extraction. They stood close together behind their boss, shoulders almost touching. But Patrick Brautigan, unarmed and alone, was pleased rather than intimidated. He liked it when the opposition had guns. The weapons made them overconfident.

"Mr. Foley, my boss has raised his offer for your warehouse property another three hundred dollars," Brautigan said. His voice was low and void of inflection. At such a late hour, nothing else stirred along this stretch of docks. "You're getting somewhat above fair market value, enough to move on and start over somewhere else. This is the final offer. Take it."

Foley glanced over his shoulder at his thugs, then smiled. "And if I don't?"

Brautigan looked impassively at Foley and the bodyguards, and said nothing.

"I know Rupert Douglass needs my warehouse lot for that foundry he wants to build," Foley said. "If I don't sell, he can't build in the best location. So I want more than just somewhat above fair market value. I want double. Go back and tell him that. Double, and we have a deal. Otherwise, no."

Brautigan shifted his feet. The moonlight reflected off the steel-tipped toes of his boots. He was massive, and even this slight movement caused the two gunmen to reflexively twitch their hands toward their pistol butts. "You have the boss's offer," Brautigan said. "He's fair, but never foolish. Take it."

"I worked hard to build my business," Foley said. "It might not seem like much to a rich bastard like Douglass, but I'm a proud man and if he won't meet my price, then to hell with him."

Brautigan asked, "Is that your final word?" His tone remained calm, but Foley still instinctively stepped back behind his bodyguards.

"I know your reputation," the fat man said. "When Douglass's money won't get him what he wants, he sends you along to see what muscle can do. Killer Boots, they call you. This time it won't work." He nodded to the gunmen. "Show him, boys."

The two men reached for their pistols. They were very fast, and Brautigan seemed to move in slow motion. But somehow before they could pull the guns from their belts he grasped each of their wrists in one of his huge hands and twisted. There was the sound of bones breaking, and screams of pain. These were short-lived. Brautigan yanked one gunman toward him with his left hand and delivered a crunching head butt that rendered the man unconscious. Then he shifted his right-hand grip from the wrist to the throat of the remaining bodyguard. With little effort he raised his writhing victim high in the air, then slammed him down hard against a wooden crate. The crate smashed; splinters flew. The second gunman lay still.

A few feet away, Foley stood paralyzed with fear. He opened his mouth to scream for help, but no sound emerged beyond a strangled croak.

"Now you," Brautigan said.

Foley tried to run, but the giant was already on him. He hammered a punch into the fat man's belly, driving the wind out of him. As Foley collapsed, struggling for breath, he twisted his face toward the sky. The last two things he saw were the bright moon and its reflection on the steel toe of Brautigan's right boot just before it caved in his skull.

Brautigan leaned down, grasped Foley's shirt collar, and dragged the fat man's corpse back to where the two bodyguards lay. Both were raggedly breathing, but unconscious. Brautigan put an end to that with several more well-placed kicks.

The warehouse Rupert Douglass wanted to buy from Foley stood about fifty yards away. One at a time, Brautigan threw the corpses over his shoulder and carried them to its padlocked front door. He tossed them down and placed their arms at their sides. When all three bodies were properly positioned, he kicked them in the face repeatedly until their features were completely pulped. The only sounds were the sloshing of the river and the increasingly soggy thuds of metal toes against skulls and skin. Brautigan spent a quarter hour at this chore. When he was done, he used Foley's jacket to wipe his steel toe tips clean. Then he straightened his own clothes and walked away, whistling tunelessly and appearing for all the world like a man returning home from a relaxing late-night stroll.

AT PRECISELY TEN THE NEXT morning, Brautigan presented himself to Rupert Douglass in the upstairs study of his employer's mansion in central St. Louis. It was a grand house, filled with the finest furniture and rare antiques. Brautigan usually had time to study the exotic clocks, vases, and other items because his boss invariably kept him waiting. But on this occasion, a butler ushered him directly in.

As the door closed behind him, Brautigan sensed something else. Rupert Douglass, usually cool, was trying to keep his emotions under control.

"Last night's business was concluded satisfactorily?" Douglass rubbed a forefinger along his bristly moustache. "Foley is no longer an impediment?"

"I suspect it will be in the afternoon papers," Brautigan said. "Three bodies discovered outside Foley's warehouse on the dock."

"Three?"

"Foley brought along two gunmen. They shared his fate."

"And no connection here?"

It was unlike Douglass to question the quality of Brautigan's work. The giant took pride in making clean kills that in no way implicated his employer. "None."

Douglas nodded. "Then tomorrow I'll call on the widow Foley, ease her bereavement with some comforting words and ready cash from a property sale. All right, so the warehouse will be mine. We'll have it razed within a week, get that foundry built. Later on today I'll go over and visit with Chief Welsh, make sure his officers don't look too hard at last night's events. Never hurts to remind Welsh of his obligations."

Making payoffs to the St. Louis chief of police was one of Brautigan's responsibilities. "You don't want me doing that?"

"No, you'll be otherwise engaged." Douglass dropped into a high-backed, overstuffed chair and gestured for Brautigan to sit on a wide couch that offered sufficient space and support for his bulk. "How long have you worked for me?"

Brautigan sat. He was puzzled but didn't let it show on his face. "Four years, just about."

Douglass rubbed his moustache again, a telltale sign that he was agitated. "Four years. I brought you in from Boston when I faced those strike threats in some of my factories. And you handled them for me, handled them well, the strikes and other things."

Brautigan nodded. "Other things" meant bringing Douglass's property negotiations to successful conclusions when prospective sellers wouldn't accept what his boss considered fair offers. Usually, people quailed before Patrick Brautigan, and agreed to take Douglass's money. On the rare occasions when they didn't, Brautigan did what was necessary, and afterward Rupert Douglass negotiated, always successfully, with their survivors. The St. Louis mayor, police chief, and reporters from every significant city newspaper and magazine were in Douglass's pocket. These killings were never attributed to Douglass or even Brautigan himself, though kicked-in faces, the Killer Boots trademark, sent a clear message to anyone doing business with Douglass in the future. Counting the three last night, the kill total over four years was eleven—Brautigan remembered, and did not in the slightest regret, each one. He did what he was paid to do, acting without remorse.

"Four years," Douglass said, "and in that time you've only failed me once."

Brautigan nodded again. Two and a half years earlier, Ellen, Rupert Douglass's only child, had been murdered in this very mansion by her husband, Cash McLendon, Douglass's trusted second-in-command. Actually, only Douglass believed his daughter was murdered. Everyone else at all familiar with the Douglass family knew that Ellen was crazy, her self-destructive violent tendencies held in check only by regular doses of laudanum. While Douglass and his wife were away, McLendon accidentally left a glass jar handy and a manic Ellen used its sharp shards to cut her wrists. McLendon fled to Arizona Territory, and Douglass sent Brautigan to fetch his son-in-law back and kill him before Douglass's own eyes. To Brautigan, it made no difference whether Ellen's death was self-inflicted or not. His boss had given an order, and he would carry it out. But in the small town of Glorious in Arizona, McLendon slipped away from him with the help of some raggedy frontier dwellers. After that, his quarry seemingly vanished. Brautigan stalked the major towns in California, where he and his boss suspected McLendon would eventually turn up, but didn't. Finally, after six fruitless months, Douglass summoned him back to St. Louis, where Brautigan resumed his enforcer role. But he never forgot McLendon, whose escape was the single blight on Brautigan's strong-arm history.

Now Brautigan said, "Do you mention this because there's word of McLendon? Has he finally shown somewhere?"

Douglass poured himself a cup of coffee from a steaming urn on a table beside his chair. He didn't offer any to Brautigan. "I've kept my lines out. I imagined myself inside McLendon's head, tried to understand what he'd be thinking. And it all came down to that Italian girl, the one he was with before my Ellen. After he murdered my girl he ran off to that Eyetie out in Arizona, in that dirty little town. That's where you nabbed him, then let him get away."

"Yes." Brautigan didn't add that McLendon escaped only because of Douglass's ironclad rule that none of his employees should ever publicly break the law. A backwoods sheriff interceded for McLendon, leaving Brautigan no choice other than to let him go.

Douglass sipped his coffee. Agitation caused his hand to tremble as he raised the cup to his lips. "It took a while, but I figured it out. The Eyetie. Wherever she ended up, sooner or later that's where McLendon would be, too. Gabrielle Tirrito. Unusual name, easy for people to notice and remember. I learned that she went to work in a hotel in some other godforsaken town out in Arizona Territory. So I paid somebody there to keep a lookout for McLendon. Paid and waited. It's been hard. I want my girl avenged. And now, finally. Finally." He set down his coffee cup and pointed at Brautigan. "Pack a bag and get moving today, this morning. Take the train as far west as you can, then I suppose a stage from there. You'll have all the money you need. I'd prefer McLendon brought back alive. I want to watch you work on him. But this time if you can't get away with him clean, finish him there. One way or the other, I want him dead so my Ellen can rest in peace."

Brautigan said, "You've not told me where he is."

Douglass pulled a crumpled bit of paper from his pocket. It was a telegraph cable. "This came an hour ago, from my watcher out west. I'll give you that name, but make contact only if necessary. As much as possible, I want McLendon snatched discreetly."

He handed the paper to Brautigan, who smoothed it and read the simple message: "*MOUNTAIN VIEW, ARIZ TERR. HE'S HERE.*"

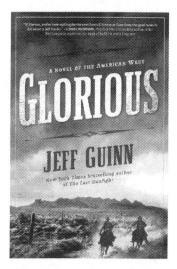
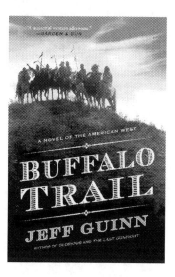
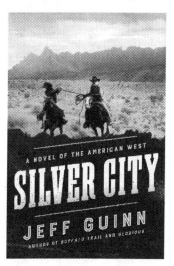

Printed in the United States
by Baker & Taylor Publisher Services